# SANDYMANCER

ALSO BY

# DAVID EDISON

*The Waking Engine*

# SANDYMANCER

DAVID EDISON

TOR

TOR PUBLISHING GROUP

NEW YORK

This is a work of fiction. All of the characters, organizations, and events portrayed in this novel are either products of the author's imagination or are used fictitiously.

SANDYMANCER



Map by Rhys Davies

A Tor Book
Published by Tom Doherty Associates / Tor Publishing Group
120 Broadway
New York, NY 10271

www.tor-forge.com

Tor® is a registered trademark of Macmillan Publishing Group, LLC.

The Library of Congress Cataloging-in-Publication Data is available upon request.

ISBN 978-0-7653-7960-3 (hardcover)
ISBN 978-1-4668-6921-9 (ebook)

Our books may be purchased in bulk for promotional, educational, or business use. Please contact your local bookseller or the Macmillan Corporate and Premium Sales Department at 1-800-221-7945, extension 5442, or by email at MacmillanSpecialMarkets@macmillan.com.

First Edition: 2023

Printed in the United States of America

0 9 8 7 6 5 4 3 2 1

*For George, who is missed.*

# SANDYMANCER

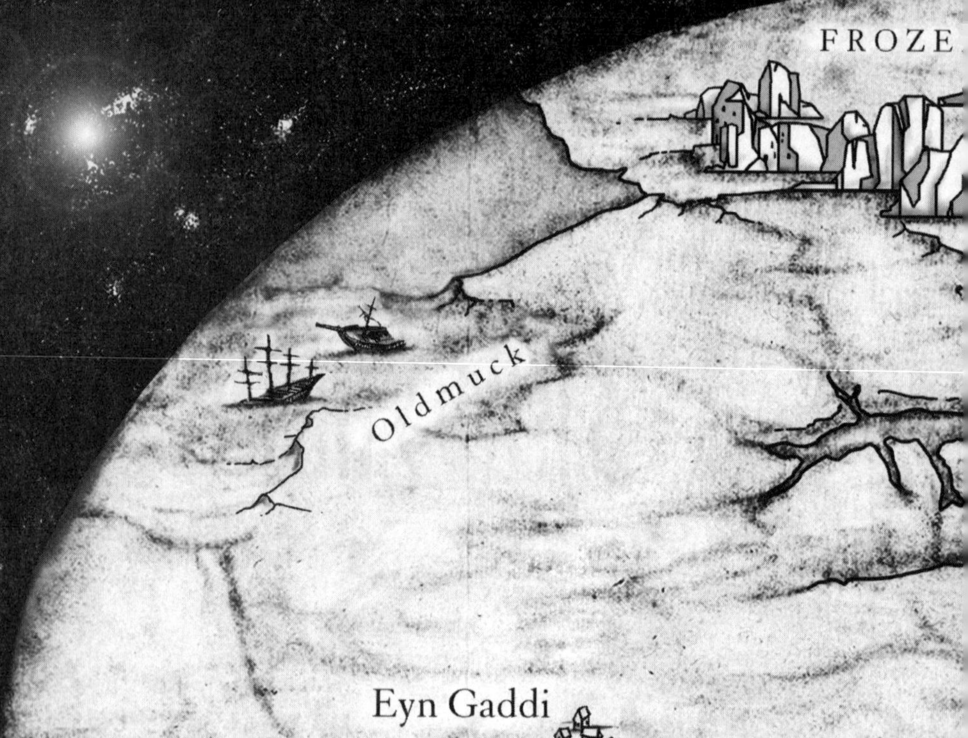
FROZE
Oldmuck
Eyn Gaddi

THE WASTELAND
Nameless Run
BARRIE

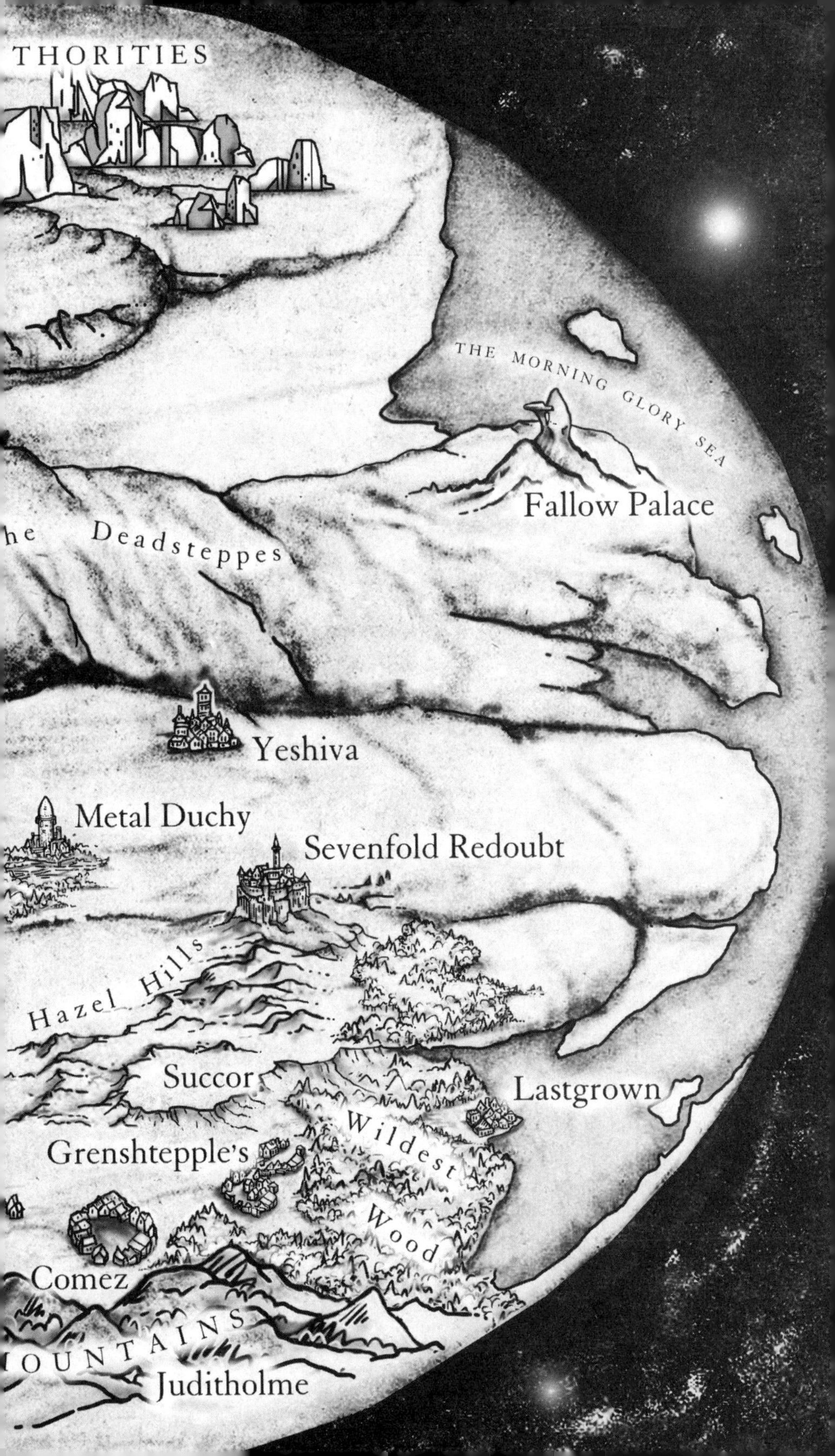

THORITIES

THE MORNING GLORY SEA

Fallow Palace

he Deadsteppes

Yeshiva

Metal Duchy

Sevenfold Redoubt

Hazel Hills

Succor

Lastgrown

Wildest Wood

Grenshtepple's

Comez

OUNTAINS

Juditholme

# 1

The day the monster stole Caralee's future started out as dull and shiny as any other—with children and young folk scattered around the sandy circle that served as a gathering place for the families of the nameless village. In this half-ruined amphitheater, they took their lessons from a woman dressed in undyed linen, her head, neck, and chin wrapped about with a threadbare gorget. Later, most would return to the cable fields with their elders, or stay within the village for piecework and other chores.

Caralee sat cross-legged on her favorite schooling seat, smiling at the crack in the sky. An age ago, her seat was a column; now only the plinth remained, scoured smooth by centuries of sandstorms into a seat-shaped groove that cradled Caralee's bottom just so. The stone fit her far better than her burlap shmata ever would.

Marm-marm pointed at the fractured sky. The morning sun rose above the horizon, gold and brilliant, but the sky, she'd taught them, was far too dark. Once, it had been a much lighter blue, which was a color Caralee found difficult to imagine so far above and in such quantity. Wouldn't that be awfully bright? She'd learned that when the sky had been light blue, the stars had been invisible during the day. That, too, she struggled to imagine.

The crack in the sky looked like frozen lightning, jagged and forking. At noon, when the sun passed behind it, you could see that the crack was four or five times longer than the sun.

Other students lazed or whispered, but Caralee leaned forward, elbows on her knees, eager to answer Marm-marm's questions and ask her own.

"Who can tell me about the sky?" Marm-marm shielded her eyes from the sun with one hand while pointing with the other, tracing the lines over her head. "Is it broken? Why is it broken? *How* is it broken? How can we *tell* that it's broken?" Marm-marm always asked too many questions at once, which was

Caralee's favorite thing about the woman. Caralee never said that to her face. That would clam up Marm-marm's curious mouth, which was the last thing Caralee wanted on any day.

"Mphh!" Fanny Sweatvasser grunted through a mouthful of her own hair, then wicked her wet curls out from between her teeth so she could offer up one of her habitually bizarre answers. "A mightily infestatation of metallicky creatures"—Fanny pronounced the word *cree-aht-choors,* which gave Caralee a headache— "crawled from their nests—their nests are the stars—and are a-spinning their bea-ut-iful cobbyweb across the sky." Fanny hunched her shoulders and gazed at the sky with delighted horror. "They want to catch the sun and steal away its light until it's as wee as a star. Then they'll hatch more cre-a-tures from that star and lay eggs in our brainpans with their rustipated penises." Fanny spread her lips in what would have been a smile if it hadn't been as flat and haunted as the wasteland horizon. "That, Marm-marm, is my answer."

"Oh, Fanny." Marm-marm looked like she'd swallowed some vomit. "Can anyone offer a less, hmm—a *different* answer?"

"Hey, Fanny," sassed Diddit Flowm, bouncing his knee. "If your stupid star-critters are gonna hatch from the sun, then why're they gonna put eggs in our heads? That makes no sense."

His friends smirked, and Caralee laughed to herself. For Diddit, that was a truly massive amount of insight.

"I asked for an answer, Diddit Flowm." Marm-marm scolded the boy without much enthusiasm. "A little help, Caralee?"

Caralee wanted to point out that, as usual, Fanny had taken a tiny grain of truth—*tiny,* mind you—and ran away with it, returning with something so ridiculous that the truth could no longer be found. But Marm-marm had asked her for answers, and Caralee loved answers.

"Well, Mag says that the crack in the sky used to be a little thing." Caralee didn't have facts, so she began with observations. Caralee had been raised by Mag, alongside her grandson, Joe Dunes, and was the wisest person Caralee knew, even if she didn't have as much book learning as Marm-marm. "Mag also says that the sky was lighter during the day, although I don't see how that would work. I mean, how would we—"

"Yes, Caralee, thank you." Marm-marm always called on Caralee, but never let her finish. "When Old Mag Dunes was wee, that-uppa-there crack was wee, too, and the day sky shined bright blue."

The other students oohed at the thought of such a pretty, bygone sky, but

Caralee liked the crack below the sun. It was *interesting,* a commodity in short supply, here at the fringes of the wasteland. She loved the sky, with its stars peeking through their darkly colored veils.

"*And,*" Marm-marm pressed her advantage. "We couldn't see the stars whenever the sun came out. Back then, the sky only darkened to shades of indigo near dawn and dusk."

"What's a findigo?" asked a boy with wild hair and one eye that was always staring at his nostrils.

"Anyone?" Marm-marm asked the seated students, propped up on stone blocks and other remainders of the Land of the Vine. "What, asks Marmot Kleyn, is *findigo*?" She scanned the faces of her students, most of whom were still sleepy, and cared little for learning. Caralee waved her hand high, but Marm-marm gave the rest of the class a few seconds to catch up, if any were so inclined. They were not. "Yes, Caralee?" She braced her hands on her hips and stretched her weary back. "You can put your arm down, girl. You know full well that you'vc no competition here."

*Don't call me "girl"* is what Caralee almost said, but thought better of it. She grabbed her arm like a separate thing and dragged it into her lap as if it had a mind to shoot up and start waving again.

"Yes, Marm. For starters, 'findigo' ent anything, but *indigo,* was a plant—and it's a color, too. It sits right between violet and blue, on the rainybow wheel." *Which we learned last year and there are only seven scatting colors to remember,* she thought but also did not say.

"That's right. Now, can anyone tell me why a crack in the sky and a darkening sky might be connected?"

"Well," Fanny began, and Caralee suspected that she was *not* about to answer Marm-marm's question. "First of all, the rainybow wheel was invented by the droods to hide the fact that they keep all the green in one super-secreted underground well, excepted for water, it's got green. *All* the greens."

"No, Fanny, just no." Marm-marm pressed her hands to the sides of her head, fidgeting with the wrapped burlap gorget that hid her neck and cheeks. "If there are still droods in the world, they may not be singing fruit from treebones anymore, but they have most certainly not stolen all the *green* and hidden it in an *underground well.*"

Fanny narrowed her eyes, now convinced that Marm-marm was part of the plot.

"And the rainybow wheel is real," Caralee added. "Marm-marm has a picture of it in her learning-book. You've *seen* it, Fanny."

"But *have I*?"

"You have!" Caralee was aware that she was shouting. "You've seen it! You've seen the rainybow wheel, and green and indigo are both scatting *on it*!" Fanny was a fool, but Caralee wasn't cruel enough to say so out loud.

"*You're* on the rainybow wheel, chucklehead." A sandy-haired older youth—not one of the students—entered the open space and strolled up to Marm-marm as if she were a girl at a dance. Caralee wilted.

"Hullo, Marm," he said, angling for charm and not quite succeeding.

"Good day to you, Joe Dunes." Marm-marm forgave him with a twitching smile, and Caralee wondered what it would feel like to have Joe Dunes aim his charm at her and fail. Sands, he could even win! Caralee wouldn't mind.

Not that she'd ever say *that* aloud, either.

Joe Dunes rubbed the hay-bright fuzz that had covered his big square jaw for almost two years now. Caralee knew exactly how many days it'd been since she'd noticed he'd begun to beard.

Joe crossed his thick arms and smirked his square-jawed smirk. He winked at Caralee, who blushed, though she tried her best to keep the blood from rushing to her face.

*Dunderhead,* she thought. Joe'd never had the luxury of sitting and learning, busy as he'd been helping Mag do the work of towing the processed cable plant products for trade.

Joe kicked a rock and hopped when he crunched his big toe. Was there ever an opportunity to stub a toe, that her Joe passed up? He lacked any trace of physical grace, but his heart was as big and warm as his hands. Caralee shook her head and hid a smile.

"You're here for—" Marm-marm started to say.

"Caralee, get your—"

"Of course you are—"

"—bottom off that rock and follow me." Joe stuck out his tongue at her. Joe's tongue wasn't exactly charm, but it'd do. "Come on. We better be in the cart before the burden-critters get hungry."

Which was ridiculous. The burden-critters were the sweetest things ever, and Caralee would let them kiss her hand for whole minutes at a time. Their soft proboscises would suckle her fists or slobber-up her face with kisses. Joe Dunes was the chucklehead, and Caralee said so.

Marm-marm cleared her throat.

"Those sweet critters eat scat all day, Joe Dunes, and if they *did* get hungry, they'd go after *you*," Caralee sassed him right back. She tried to make a habit of sassing Joe back—at least when people were around. "You don't scare me."

"Aww, don't you ever snack, Caralee?" Joe kicked the dirt and stubbed his other big toe. "Ouch. They *love* to crunch on a head so full of chuckle," he said, and mimed cracking open her head and sucking out her brains with a slurp. "Better not tempt fate, huh?"

"Atu would never!" Caralee protested, despite the sheer idiocy of the thought of the gentle burden-critters—with their furry antennae and meek nature—snacking on anything more than a juicy pile of shit. "And Oti's too shy."

"Please continue this dance outside my classroom." Marm-marm ushered them out of the disintegrating amphitheater, which was *already* outside, but Caralee upheld her policy of not sassing Marm-marm. "As it disturbs anyone unfortunate to be trapped anywhere near the two of you." Marm-marm massaged her temples, then rolled her eyes with the hint of a smile. "Caralee, you are excused for work duty."

The teacher turned her gorget-wrapped head to the student body and began picking on one of the sleepier boys, wrestling with their ignorance until someone cried out:

"*Dust trail!*"

Caralee whipped her head behind her, looking toward the entrance to the unnamed village. A banner of dust flew from the deep wasteland that lay to the northwest, and it stopped just before the crusty remains of the village walls.

"What's that?" Joe asked out loud, though how was *she* to know?

Caralee tasted the air. Something smelled different than usual. Prettier.

"You smell that, Joe?"

"Wossit?" He sniffed, nose twitching like a dust hare. "That smoke?"

"Naw, Joe, that's incense." Joe wasn't keen enough to argue the difference. "You know what that means!"

"Patchfolk? But they ent due for another month."

The class erupted in excitement, and after a few useless flaps of her arms, Marm-marm surrendered. The students scattered—racing one another the extremely short distance to the sad cairns that served as the gates of the village.

"It's Patchfolk, for sure." Caralee smiled.

Twice a year, the nomad caravans emerged from the deep wasteland, where icy dust storms and hungry quicksand ruled. They came to trade and to maintain the relationships upon which both groups relied. The wasteland was more dangerous than anyplace in the whole world, and both the travelers and the settled folk benefited from trading information about what hardships they'd faced, and where—what routes were safe, and which were dangerous. Who'd disappeared and where.

The Patchfolk and the villagers were like estranged cousins, a family born not from any common culture but out of need. Folk elsewhere rightly feared the ever-spreading wasteland that would one day consume every corner of the world, but the villagers and the Patchfolk, they *knew* the wasteland. They survived on its feeble offerings and lived in its clouded, shifting glare.

"What if they got a sandymancer with 'em?" Caralee heard the whine in her voice, but didn't care.

Often the Patchfolk traveled with a sandymancer or two—wizards from the far northeast, who commanded the elements and told stories of the old world, when the wet green Vine snaked across the land, instead of the mummified fingers of cable plant that had to be hacked apart with machetes and milled three times before it approached edible. The sandymancers told one particular story over and over again, as if on a mission, and although Caralee had heard it a dozen times, she never lost interest—largely because the candle-backed wizards never finished the tale.

"Yeah, yeah, what if . . ." Joe knew how this conversation would go. "Mag's waiting on us, Caralee."

"*Patchfolk,* Joe!" She tugged on his sleeve. "Mag can wait. She'll understand. You know she will." She very likely would not, but Mag could sit on it.

Joe rolled his eyes. "You skitter off to watch those sandymancers whine about how Ol' Sonnyvine wrecked the world every time one rolls into town. Do they ever tell you anything new?"

"Not yet." Caralee climbed back onto her comfortable plinth and crossed her arms behind her head. "But this time, I'm *gonna* learn the end of the story."

Joe and Marm-marm both sighed. The three of them were alone in the amphitheater, which was quiet now, but would soon be busier than before.

"All-a-right, chucklehead, but when Gran starts spittin', the blame's on you. Deal?"

"Deal!" Mag would most definitely start spitting, but Caralee didn't mind taking the blame—not if it got her what she wanted. If she couldn't *see* the world, Caralee would learn about it, spit or no spit. "Now sit down, dunderhead, and grab a good seat before the class comes back and brings the whole village with them."

Through the shattered pillars of the classroom, they saw the Patchfolk lurch into the village, hitching their train of wagons just outside the walls. The colors they wore were all browns and beiges, and they'd be buying rolls of cable burlap from Daddy Flowm, whose ridiculously handsome sons spent most of their time at the loom, when they weren't giving wrong answers in class.

Beside burlap for their namesake robes, the Patchfolk bartered for powdered cable flour for gruel, cable wicker and rattan for their wagons, and filled their water casks from the village's last working well. In exchange, the villagers got weapons and tools they couldn't make themselves, as well as other goods the rovers scavenged from the wastes or collected on trade visits to farther, unknown markets. Some said the Patchfolk knew of oases hidden deep in the wasteland, where they built camps that were lived in year-round, but Caralee didn't think that even the Patchfolk would risk a visit from Ol' Sonnyvine—if he was even real. That was why they kept moving.

Alderwoman Jackie stood at the gates, chatting with the Patchfolk matriarch while the nomads entered the village to set up shop, opening the doors of their fully covered wagons, which served as home and storefront alike.

Marm-marm had cleared the little stage where she gave her lessons, brushing it to something akin to clean with the world's oldest broom. The amphitheater filled quickly, as families with their children trickled in from every direction. That meant the caravan *did* have a sandymancer. Caralee smirked, and Marm-marm—whose eyes caught every little thing—sighed again.

A wagon had opened up, and a figure dressed all in black had emerged, unfolding himself to stand taller than the wagons, though he didn't stand straight—his spine and arms and every other bit were bent, gnarled, and twisted. His face was painted white, and a tiny candle topped each of his flared epaulets. Their wicks each burned with a teardrop of yellow fire. Beneath oily black feathers sewn into the collar of his dark robe, his fingers worked back and forth, preening at the tapers on his wide shoulder pads. When he walked, his gait looked painful. Tall as treebones and twice as crooked, the sandymancer lurched the few dozen meters to the stage and took to it, wincing, without introduction.

A sandymancer needed none.

The candles at his shoulders were a measure of his rank, and their fire never so much as guttered—the yellow licks of their flame kept flush with the line of his neck no matter how he craned it, or how he stooped, and they cast his white-painted face in a jaundiced glow.

All sandymancers looked more or less alike, with those tapers burning above their black-padded shoulders, thick white paint on their faces, and feet swollen round. Their crow-feather collars all shimmered with dark rainbows of purples and greens. This particular sandymancer broke the usual mold with his knotted bones and skeletal fingers. He looked like he'd been cobbled together from old cable wicker and brought to life with magick.

If you ever asked a sandymancer about their appearance, they would tell you that the wind itself painted their faces white and that their ballooned feet were armored with water that they summoned up from the bottom of the world. At least, that's what they'd told Caralee whenever *she'd* asked.

To Caralee's eye, though, paint looked like paint, and a limp looked like a limp.

If the old wizard's body was crooked, his hands were a maze—each finger looked like it had been broken several times over. He waved his insect arms, and silence settled over the crowd; he opened his black-painted eyes ghastly wide, and the villagers bristled with anticipation.

Caralee felt the tingle of what she called her "sandysense," and her whole body tensed, waiting for the sandymancer to work his craft.

Looking down his nose at his audience, the sandymancer twitched and hooked his fingers, breath loud but not ragged, engaged in some internal process—and the sand below him began to rise up to the stage as if gravity had been flipped wrongside round. A mound of sand and dust and dirt lifted itself up, bulky below the wizard's hands but sliding from the ground until a wave of sand had spread across the entire stage.

Some folk gasped in delight, while children squealed and were shushed. Marm-marm looked at the broom still in her hand and popped her tongue. The sandymancer ignored them all, face ghost-white beneath his caked makeup, his lank hair pasted with sweat to the sides of his head. He cast his wide-eyed gaze over the crowd and crossed his wrists, waiting for silence to settle. When he spoke, his voice thrummed out loud and deep.

"The world!" The corny wizard stretched his arms as wide as his joints would allow. "The world never changes. Is that what you think?" He cupped a hand to his ear, but it was only pantomime.

"*You* change, don't you?" He pointed at a babby in its mother's lap. "*I* change, don't I?" He pointed to the jagged line in the sky. "The sky above you changes, doesn't it? We know of changes that are predictable, and we know changes that are anything but. So, too: the world."

He bowed his head for a beat before continuing. Caralee heard his neck creak in objection.

"I, Eusebius Gibberosus Kampouris, Sandymancer of the Sevenfold Redoubt and wizard at large, shall tell you a tale of change and terror:

"This land was once green beyond green, wet beyond wet, and warm as a womb. The Land of the Vine! In the Vintage age, great green tendrils crossed the whole of the world, a magickal plant that sustained life everywhere it grew, and we were never hungry, nor lost, nor doomed."

The painted sandymancer paused to let his audience imagine that paradise and the treebones and dust and cable plant that remained.

"The Land of the Vine died." He nodded and pulled a sorrowful face as if to cry. "But you know this. We *all* know this."

The crowd agreed.

"Yes, see. Still the grans and gramps at their cable-mills tell of it, how the wasteland came to be, and the death of the Land of the Vine, what we now call *the world.* Grizzled old Patchfolk guides tell it, too, squatting over firepits beside their caravanserais, chewing brown leaves and spitting into the dirt while regaling children with the story of the birth of the desert and the slow death of the world. You tell the tale yourselves, don't you?"

He jabbed an arthritic finger at the crowd. A fair number of them nodded. It was an old tale, older than the world they knew, but for the people of the village, it was a tale that had happened in their backyard—more than a tale, a warning.

Except that nobody ever finished the tale. No one knew quite how it ended, or why it began. Of the story of the death of the world, they knew only the dun, dry middle, which stretched for centuries and kilometers.

The sandymancer nodded, his painted face a mask of feigned worry. "They scratch their flour-dusted or dust-caked faces and say: *It came like sunset, the death of our land.*"

He twitched an inflamed knuckle, and the sand at his feet birthed a disk of dust that floated as it passed over the miniature dune from left to right. It touched the opposite side of the stage and fell apart in a patter of grit.

*A little sun!* Caralee thrilled at the sight before she caught herself. Everyone else oohed, but she forced herself to remain distant, critical. Fancy feathers and magick candles or not, this man was her peer, not her better.

In her gut, Caralee knew that she could sandymance the socks off this actor.

Caralee was the village sandymancer, whether or not the villagers cared or knew or laughed at her. This git was an intruder, but that didn't mean that he had nothing to teach her. Lessons are everywhere, if you care to find them. Marm-marm had taught her that.

It wasn't a secret that Caralee Vinnet could conjure up little balls of dust—the village treated it no differently than Ezel Grunion's missing nose, or the fact that Burr Bits couldn't make eye contact but wove the loveliest baskets. The villagers tolerated Caralee's difference; so long as she did her share to keep them all from starving, nothing else mattered.

What the villagers didn't know was Caralee's ambition. Her rigorous practice. Her determination to *be more.* She made sure that folk only ever saw her weak-looking dust balls, as she pushed herself to gain more and more control over the sand, whenever she had a moment to herself.

*Dead or not, there's a world out there.* She bit her cheek. *Imma see it. I am.*

The sandymancer kept on: "From west to east it passed, and in a sunset wave their gardens fell and their rivers baked into runs of white clay. An oven breath of eastward wind brought more sand, and more, until the Land of the Vine lay smothered beneath it. *That* was how their lives ended, the people of the Vine, whose wondrous plant once coaxed the whole world to blossom. Only a single member of the people of the City of the Vine survived, if you can call his wretched existence life, and it would be eight hundred years before *some say* he walked out of the desert—simply walked out, one day, and disappeared into the land he'd broken. Still others claim that *you-know-who* is dead and gone, and we need not fear his frightful power." The sandymancer paused for effect. "They are all wrong."

One of the children turned to her mother. "He's talking about Ol' Sonnyvine!" she cooed before being quieted.

"Is he dead or isn't he?" Diddit Flowm asked his brother, a fine-looking man without a thought in his head.

"Shh," hissed a woman. For his trouble, Diddit earned a slap upside the head from one of his too-handsome brothers. One day soon, with his family resemblance, Diddit would be trouble himself. Also, he'd made another good point. Two sensible arguments in one day from Diddit Flowm—surely the world would end any minute.

The wizard pointed at the exchange and exulted. "All should heed the tale of the demon some call Ol' Sonnyvine, whose ghost has been bound in stone, lo these eight hundred years, by the terrible and awesome powers of the sandymancers of old! Were it not for the very powers which I possess, were it not for the forebears of the Sevenfold Redoubt, where all sandymancers are trained in the ancient Vintage mysteries, that selfsame world-killer would be *free.* Free to wander the wasteland in search of bodies to steal, that he might strike the world with a final killing blow.

"But *once—*" Here the wizard lifted his arms up and outward in what Caralee supposed was supposed to be a grand gesture, and the dune of sand beneath him sprouted buds that grew into waving tentacles, reaching to the edge of the stage and tickling the sandymancer's outstretched palms. "Once the monster was a man, a royal man, who was set to inherit a world of plenty, where green plants grew thick at this very spot—right here!—and food hung ripe and juicy on living trees."

He let silence settle with an actor's timing, tempting his audience with a vision of prosperity that they could hardly be expected to imagine.

"His father was god-king of the Land of the Vine, whose title was the Son of the Vine—until his villain child cut him down and took the title for himself. His siblings were many, and each of them a rival for the throne, so he killed them all by turns. Lovers, friends, subjects, all died by the Son of the Vine's evil hand."

The sandymancer paused, as if what came next offended him personally. "Though the Son of the Vine was—is—the most powerful sandymancer this world has ever seen"—the wizard exhaled, offended at the very thought—"his reign of terror was ended by the good wizards of the court of the Vine, who killed his body and trapped his spirit in a stone monument that the ancients called a *matzeva*."

Now, the wizard hung his head, looking up from his shadowed face at the crowd, a sly smile on his white lips.

"We owe our lives and our thanks to those brave sandymancers, whose tradition my brothers and sisters and I maintain, so that the world might be ever safe from the Son of the Vine. Yes, they smote him. They caught his ghost and imprisoned it, but not before the Son, with his wicked power, destroyed the Vine. In an instant, he killed the world-plant at its green heart. In a trice, the Son of the Vine buried his city beneath the sand and doomed the world to die in this slow apocalypse of famine and drought."

One of the babes began to cry.

"Yes, cry! Cry, for the world is dead!" The sandymancer clawed at his black-feathered throat. "The Son of the Vine offered us no mercy—in fact, he cursed his own mother, the tale says, for turning him over to those brave adepts, heroes one and all, who sealed him away forever, that we might live a little longer."

Two babes crying now. The sandymancer grinned, yellow-toothed and rich with anticipation.

"Picture the world as it was! The great steles that stagger our wasteland bore the weight of the Vine as it stretched its stems to the ends of the world and gave us all succor. The treebones that jut from our dead ground like the ribs of some long-dead beast, they grew green and thick as the forest at Lastgrown, all the way across the world."

Longing sighs from the crowd.

"Yes, before the Son's betrayal, our desert was a breadbasket. Minarets and domes dripped with green, and wherever the vine touched the land, we built fountains, canals, and deep wells bubbled up through black soil: the Land of the Vine had plenty of plenty, and when it quenched its thirst, it drank *deep*."

The tendrils of the conjured sand-Vine at the sandymancer's feet slowed their waving and re-formed into the splendid shape of a many-spired palace.

"Some say the Land of the Vine drank *too* deeply and that the legend of the Son is but a folktale invented to explain away the drying of the world. We who *know*, you and me, we blame that monster, the Son of the Vine. Hearken to this true sandymancer, a wizard alive and trained in the ancient mysteries! My colleagues from the Sevenfold Redoubt—we command the seven elements. We sing down the wind and drum up water from the deep where it sleeps, cold and dark. We call out to fire, and, as you can see, we summon the sand as easily as we breathe."

The tableau of moving sand erased itself, swirling into a wild eddy, a spinning funnel of sand that waved back and forth between the sandymancer's knees. Nearly everyone aahed.

"Those of my order know much that has been lost to the world, yet even we sandymancers can only imagine life in the Land of the Vine. Ah, the Vintage! We know the Vine grew like rolling hills, sprouting from the capital in the heart of what is now the wasteland, and wreathed the world—those hundred-foot steles and the menhir-holes through which its filaments grew, they gape, one-eyed and empty, half-buried in the dust. We do not remember how to read their markings or work the wonders of their builders."

The funnel of sand became a tower of stone with a hole set into its upmost section—the very picture of the massive standing stones that littered the wasteland and the world beyond.

"There is no one left alive to describe that garden realm, nor the madman who crowned himself the Son of the Vine, nor the trail of bodies he shall steal should he ever escape, nor how far or near his prison sits from these very hovels. No one will tell you more of these things than I have, and I have told you all I will." The sandymancer looked beyond the crowd, glaring at the horizon. The stele he'd summoned collapsed to the stage, where it lay still. The tingle of sandysense winked out, and Caralee felt a kind of stillness.

"If you would know more, then you must ask the wasteland and hope that it answers."

The sandymancer folded his arms to his sides and said no more.

The crowd murmured. They knew all of the wasteland's dangers. They lived on the edge of nowhere, where if one villager worked, then another kept a keen lookout for the shapes of danger: the telltale lumps of an alpha dunderbeast; the almost-flat profile of a sandfisher lying in wait for its dinner; ball-shaped chucklers with their too-wide smiles and bloody teeth; and also—though the villagers might not admit it—a lone human shambling in a body beyond repair. *Him.* Ol' Sonnyvine.

The sandymancers' tales were full of their own glory, but glory didn't keep you alive—not in the wasteland. There were plenty present who were all too afraid that Ol' Sonnyvine had indeed escaped, that the desert was littered with his abandoned bodies, and that one day he would come for them.

*"Ask the wasteland and hope that it answers." What kinda shatterscat is that?* Every time, the show ended the same way, exhilarating for the audience, except for Caralee, who knew that "hope it answers" was only the beginning of the end of the story. She needed that ending. She thirsted for its beginning.

The easily pleased villagers picked themselves up and began filing out of the amphitheater, nodding gratefully to the sandymancer, unmoving on his stage. Caralee decided this was her moment. She squared her shoulders and walked to the side of the stage, craning her neck to stare at the wizard.

"Oy, Eusebius!" Caralee heckled him, and the sandymancer turned his head and shoulders to arch over her, candlelit and imposing. "*I* ask the desert all the time, and it never says scat."

Caralee took a breath and did her thing. She summoned her sandysense, which felt like a mixture of sight and touch and something else she didn't have words for. When she extended it to see, or whatever, she could sense the world around her—the grains of sand and grit and dust beneath her feet.

With her sandymancer's strength, Caralee pulled the dust up from the ground, calling it to her hands. She shaped it—a roundness here, a twitching nose of sand, two ears waving in the air, made of shifting grit. With the sand, she conjured the shape she liked most—a little dust hare, with thick hind legs, a lozenge of a torso, a round head with a tiny twitching nose, and ears of sand that were twice again as tall as its body. Privately, Caralee had named the mannikin Dustbutt.

The sandymancer's eyebrows rose comically high, and he frilled his broken fingers with mock delight.

"What have we here?" he cooed as if to a child. "A sandymancer of your *very own*, grown right here in the wasteland, where naught but hardship and cable plant find purchase. What a wee rustic delight!" His face looked cheery, but Caralee didn't feel any cheer from him, only scorn.

"Right. That's me, Caralee Vinnet. I'm the village sandymancer, and this here's Dustbutt." She shifted her feet, wondering what she'd say next. She'd dreamed of showing her talent to a true sandymancer, but she'd never thought about what came after that.

"Yes, and . . . ?" The sandymancer gave her nothing.

"And, um," she stammered, then found her gumption. "You say there ent nobody alive who can tell me more about Ol' Sonnyvine, but *you* don't know everyone alive, do you? And we already *know* allawhat *you* said, don't we?"

She made Dustbutt jump at him, and the conjuration cleared the stage easily—she'd used only a handful of sand in its construction, so that it would be as light and nimble as a real dust hare.

"What a bright *young* mind! What *adorable* wee talent!" The sandymancer angled at the waist to catch the attention of the lingering villagers. "What a shame it is, girl, that your life will be far too full of work, cable plant farming, and babby-whelping to ever visit the Redoubt for instruction. It is *possible* you might have some insignificant mite of talent, but most likely you'd be turned away. You and your little Dustbutt, too."

Everyone laughed at that.

Caralee felt the sandymancer call upon his own sandysense, and with a twinge of apprehension, she tightened her grip over Dustbutt. Sure enough, the wizard pursed his lips and summoned a whorl of sand into the air, punching it hard into Dustbutt's darling face.

Caralee felt the impact of magick on magick, but managed to hold Dustbutt together. She'd done it! She'd stood up to a trained sandymancer, and he hadn't dashed her work to bits. Caralee puffed out her chest while the dust hare twitched its nose. She felt extra proud of the flourish.

She saw the sandymancer's white-caked eyebrows twitch, and he faked a knowing chuckle.

"Here, I shall play with your dolly!" His smile to the remaining audience was a nervous one. "It is the least I can do for such a weak and small child, who will never see the Redoubt, let alone learn *true* sandymancy."

The villagers laughed again. Scat and shatterscat, Marm-marm was right—Caralee was too clever for her own good. She could summon the Son of the Vine himself, and nobody would give her any credit.

He called balls of sand to each hand and wove his arms theatrically. Caralee didn't doubt that she could maintain Dustbutt beneath the wizard's sandballs—one had been easy enough, after all, but she'd already lost the duel. She could command the sand better than this fraud, she just couldn't make anyone see it.

"Shall we play dress-up next, little girl?" asked the sandymancer nastily.

More laughs. Caralee let go of her sandysense and let Dustbutt return to the earth. She thought she saw Eusebius the sandymancer relax a little and shift his weight from one bloated foot to the other.

"Oy, forget that! You answer my question!" Caralee stomped her foot. "And don't call me '*girl*'!"

Another voice shouted from the far edges of the crowd. It was Mag. "*Joe Dunes!* What do I say about lallygagging?"

Caralee couldn't make out Joe's reply, but she was certain he'd hold true to his word and lay all the blame on her.

The sandymancer wiggled his fingers, and one of his sandballs blew into Caralee's face. She rubbed the grime from her eyes and sneezed.

Everyone laughed again. Caralee blushed and hated herself for it.

Mag didn't care about crowds, or Patchfolk—and she certainly didn't care about any black-robed goon with a painted face. Mag cared for chores, and for Joe, and for Caralee—though it didn't always *feel* like she cared. Mag had taken Caralee in when her parents died, first her mother and then her father, so Caralee minded Mag like she was Caralee's own gran. It was all the family that Caralee would get; the fringe of the wasteland was not a warm place.

"Joe Dunes, you grab that girl and hurry up. We're late, and if I get swallowed up by a dunderbeast, it'll be on your head. Yours and *that girl's*."

Joe's big hand took Caralee by the scruff of her shmata and hauled her off before she got a second chance to duel that mean, ugly sandymancer.

"I *said* don't call me '*girl*,'" she muttered, but she must have done so too loudly, because the crowd laughed once more.

Caralee fumed as she and Joe scrambled over the innermost ring of village walls, where folk lived in the ruins of ancient houses, thatching the roofs such as they could, patching walls with stones and cable waste to keep out the cold wasteland winds. Branching gray pillars of treebones ringed the boundary of what was once the village vegetable garden, a hundred years ago or more.

The memory of the crowd's laughter followed her all the way out of the village and into the beige fields, where bony spirals of cable plant whorled across the ground from thick central stalks.

Caralee didn't understand why her curiosity exhausted everyone.

*Suppose that's what you get, living in a place with no name, in a world that's dying.*

"Joe?" she asked. "If Ol' Sonnyvine killed the world eight hundred years ago, then what's the deal with the sky?"

"Huh?" He fiddled with that old jacket he always wore. Joe kept to long sleeves and light colors to keep the sun at bay. Caralee wore a shmata made from a cable plant sack with holes for her arms and legs—her skin was darker than poor Joe's and didn't blister in the sun like his did.

"I mean, Marm-marm said that fifty years ago the crack was only half as big, and everybody knows we could still grow some green plants a hundred years ago, before the wasteland crept up on us." She chewed on that thought and added, "Even the cable was green. Well, greenish."

Cable plant, the only crop that grew these days that was worth selling, provided gruel and hay, straw for weaving, and wicker for making baskets and furniture and doors and roofs and everything else. Rattan, too. Mag and Joe were in charge of hauling the harvest from the outer fields to the village, and from the village to nearby settlements for sale.

"Yap yap." Joe nodded, clearly not paying her much attention. "That's the right of it, Caralee."

"Hey, listen!"

"So?" Joe tossed a rock in his hand, but failed to catch it. He bent down to grab the rock and try again. Joe often used the sides of his fingers to move things. His hands were like blocks—he wasn't clumsy so much as fingerdaft. So long as he used his hands like mittens, he could manage small objects. Give him something heavy to move from one place to another, on the other hand, and Joe was your man.

"So," Caralee began. "If the Son of the Vine killed the world eight hundred years ago, and everybody knows it's been a hundred and fifty years or so since the sky cracked—"

"*Who* knows that?" Joe Dunes looked around, as if to find someone who knew that. Caralee growled.

They came to the ruined walls that guarded the dead pastures where, two hundred years ago, things called "lambs" would eat green plants that grew all over the ground. The only things that could eat the brown scrub that grew here now were the burden-critters, though they preferred a sloppy pile of scat from the shatterscat ditches, which got their names from the spray of human filth that never seemed to be contained to the ditch itself. It was also Caralee's favorite curse word.

"Well, Mag is seventy, and she said *her* gran saw the Metal Duchy fall from the sky."

"That's just jazz, Caralee." Joe rolled his eyes. "Nobody drops a duke from the sky."

"Yeah, well, folk who stay in the village all day say that Sonnyvine's just jazz, too, but we still follow the rules so we don't get eat up by him, don't we?" Mag was a stickler for those rules, and Caralee trusted no one better than Mag.

*Touch no body. Accept no gifts. Let no stranger come closer than fifty paces. Kill any stranger who won't respect those rules, lest they scoop your body up and kick your ghost out into the desert to wander forever.* Those were the rules, and Mag rode Joe and Caralee hard if they didn't follow them to a letter.

"Sonnyvine's not jazz, Caralee—he's out there, and he'll getcha!" Joe reached out a hand to poke her. Some distance ahead, Mag waited in the cart.

"Shaddup." Caralee brushed him off with half an effort, though if she was being honest with herself, she didn't really want to push his hand away. "Fine, forget the metal folk who *cracked the sky.*" She couldn't believe that a shattered sky wasn't cause for more concern. "If Ol' Sonnyvine got trapped in his *matzeva,* how'd he get out and when? What happened for six hundred years and more? And if he killed the world, why're we still farming? If we're dead, why ent we *dead*?"

Joe shrugged. She'd asked too many questions, when one was too many. Stubborn as an overfed burden-critter, Caralee stopped in her tracks and refused to take another step.

"Come on, chucklehead." Joe squinted against the sunlight and waved her on.

Caralee turned to the northwest, where, far, far away, the center of the wasteland sat, ancient and secret. She put her hands on her hips and shouted as loudly as she could manage.

"*All right, you great big wasteland, with your death and your terror, you tell me* more!" She howled to the wind. "The sandymancers—I mean the sandymancers-that-ent-me—they all say you've got the rest of the story, you vasty nasty desert, and I *need* it."

Joe's blond eyebrows pulled together like two fuzzy worms trying to kiss, and he looked at her as if she'd grown a second nose.

Caralee called upon her sandysense, pulling from deep within her with a strength and a rage that she'd never done before, and she blasted it out as far as she could in all directions. The world burst into an overlay of new colors and vibrations; the shock wave of her sandysense felt like a second horizon, spreading as fast as all of her unleashed frustrations—one that only she could see. She pulled up sand and grit from all around her and spun it up into the sky, a cloud twice as tall as the Patchfolk's dust trail. She reached deep into the ground and she *raged*. The cloud shook when she shouted, taking her voice and repeating it as loud as thunder. The ground trembled, and her suddenly thunderous voice echoed off distant bluffs.

"*Tell me, you fucker! Tell me about the Son of the Vine!*" her voice boomed. Caralee almost startled herself out of her sandysense—she'd never done this before, nothing even close.

"Caralee, stop it." He sounded alarmed.

"No!" She reached for more of the power, stretching her sandysense across miles of dead wasteland. She shouted, and the earth drummed her message across the stupid, voiceless wasteland. The shaking ground rumbled harder, sending pebbles skittering across the fields.

"*Give me something, you critterfucker!*"

"Caralee, cut it out!" Joe grabbed her by both arms. "You're scaring me!"

She dropped her sandysense, and the shaking ground grew still. She felt ashamed for giving Joe a fright, but more than that, she still felt rage at her own helpless ignorance.

"Sands, you caused a tremor, Caralee. What are you thinking?"

"Joe, I need to know. I need to know *more*. About *everything*."

"Don't I know it." He rolled his eyes. "That's no reason to tear down the world, you chucklehead."

"I mean it, Joe!" She punched him in his big chest. She might as well have punched a stone man, for all the effect it had.

"Aww, Caralee." Joe looked at her with sympathy. "You're too smart for your own good. When folk say stuff like 'Sonnyvine killed the world,' they're just telling tales. Truth is, the world changed for the worse eight hundred years ago, and since then, it's been changing for the worse in other ways. To scared folk just trying to get by, that feels a lot like murder."

"You think you know how the world works, Joe Dunes?" Caralee spat, although she knew Joe was right. Close to it, anyway.

"Caralee Vinnet," Joe said in his most grown-up voice, "it don't matter how the world works—just do what Mag says and you won't be gobbled up or get yer body took. Sands, the thought of Ol' Sonnyvine and you together, *that's* a thought to give anybody nightmares."

"Shaddup, and it does too matter!" She kicked a stone and almost stubbed her toe like Joe. "Sonnyvine's the monster of the wasteland, and he'll steal your body and use it till it's dead! Sonnyvine was born *eight hundred years ago.* If he's been skipping bodies ever since, why ent he left the wasteland? What if he only escaped more recent-like, and now he's coming for the rest of the world? What if he ent escaped at all? What if, what if, what the fuck *if*?"

"I ent finished! Sands, you can talk." Joe forgave her with a wink and a smile. "Now, maybe Ol' Sonnyvine killed his family, or maybe he even killed his whole kingdom! But the world's right here, and *we*'re right here, and so nobody murdered the world, okay? It'll keep on changing, and hey, maybe one day it'll change for the better, and folk'll *still* tell tales about who done it and why it got done that way. Don't mean they know a git."

"*I* know a git . . ." Caralee cracked wise.

Joe tickled her armpit, and Caralee locked her jaw to deny him a giggle, and together they marched through the empty fields. The stubborn wasteland wind howled but refused to speak.

# 2

Mag didn't look so old up close, once you saw beneath her weathered locs—and Wet Sam was older—but for some reason that Caralee hadn't yet worked out, people called her "Old Mag" all the same. Now, Mag *did* order everybody about worse than Wet Sam, who tended the shatterscat pit and had nobody to yap at. Joe told Caralee that the nickname "Old Mag" was a sign of respect, but Caralee didn't think that told the whole story. Alderwoman Jackie did more ordering-about than anyone, but her hair hadn't gone gray, and wasn't *she* respected? Mag also knew a fair bit more than most folk in the village, but Caralee didn't think that explained it, either. Nobody called Marm-marm *old*, and she knew more than anyone for miles.

*What a life aheadda me.*

Caralee couldn't understand why folk expected a young woman like herself would stick around in a place with no name—especially if all she had to look forward to was being called *old* just for being capable, and when would people start to notice that, anyway? She was still sore that nobody'd noticed how she'd totally won her first wizards' duel.

Mag's hair was locked into tight twists, that hung thick over her shoulder, and was blasted by sun and sand into a sort of gray-white-brown speckle. Her dark face had lines, sure, and her swollen knuckles looked like they hurt, but she'd hopped into the cart almost as spryly as Caralee. Caralee wondered if Mag had ever wanted to see the world and whether or not she had done so.

Joe sat up front with Mag on the cart's proper seat, while Caralee rode in the back with a dozen bags of cable plant, six sacks of cable flour, two bushels of cable wicker, a bundle of cable rattan, and another half dozen bushels of cable hay. That was a full shipment, all bound for market. Caralee bounced around like a sandfisher's bait ear, but whenever the ride became too rocky, she'd whistle a certain up-and-down critter-call, and Oti and Atu would steady their pace. Mag held the reins, but the burden-critters always listened to Caralee—she let the docile insects show her their love, sloppy as it was, and she fed them her own scat in secret. There wasn't a better way under the sun to befriend a critter than a fresh handful of your own shit.

The critters, Atu and Oti, were a life pair—hatched from the same egg, they were sterile workers, but mates all the same. The way they frittered over each other, tendered each other when one was injured, and screeched whenever parted—it was a bond as tight as any marriage, if sexless. Then again, it seemed to Caralee that once folk made a babe or six, things turned away from lust toward partnership.

The wisdom of bugs.

Their gleaming bronze-and-green antennae rose above the cart, almost as high as Joe's head, frilled with long, soft bristles that looked like fur or feathers. Their heads and thoraxes reflected the sky through bronze mirrors, and their mottled pink-and-black proboscises were soft as toothless gums. They loved to kiss and suckle Caralee, and she liked it, too, even when her cheek came away scatty.

Beyond the two pairs of antennae, Caralee saw the wasteland open to a mostly flat platter of wind and sand interrupted by craggy outcroppings and wrinkled with long fingers of what had once been riverbeds. Above the wasteland, the noonday sky was almost purple, and the brightest stars twinkled even now. Caralee knew that the sky had once been brighter during the daytime, but when she imagined it—wouldn't the world be hard to see, with all that light up above? Wouldn't it be blinding?

The wind's howl calmed into a thready fluting, and Caralee scanned the horizon. Would the wasteland ever answer her questions? Could she conjure up a sandy mannikin to tell her the truth? Caralee thought she'd sacrifice anything to *know* more, to *go* places, to *be* someone.

The halfway point of their trip to market rose in the distance at its awkward, leaning angle. A towering block of beige stone with a circle cut out toward the top, these steles had supported massive tendrils of the Vine as they crept across the land to touch the corners of the world. The Vine had wormed through the earth, slid across the soil, and coiled overhead. Once, the Vine had been everywhere—but now, only giant tombstones remained. Tombstones and cable plant.

So tall was the stele that as they approached, the monument seemed to rise higher than anything should—and they were still a good hour away. Soon they'd be able to see the worn carvings the stele bore. It thrilled Caralee to run her fingers over the sandworn inscriptions, written in a language that hadn't been spoken in hundreds of years.

"Hoo boy, Caralee." Joe lumbered right through her train of thought. "You ent never been to Grenshtepple's before. The way you moon over them standing stones, I reckon you'll just *eat up* all that Grenshtepple's has to show."

"Joe, leave the girl alone. She's got thoughts enough in her head," Mag scolded Joe without looking, also watching the horizon. Always scanning for danger, Mag kept her brood close and safe. She'd taught Caralee and Joe the same, although only Caralee seemed to listen.

"I have too been to Grenshtepple's!" Caralee argued, anyway. "So leave me alone. . . . I need more room for my thoughts."

Mag hissed a laugh and looked over her shoulder toward Caralee with a wink.

*Joe.* In more than a few of those thoughts in her head, Joe did *not* leave her alone, but that was a whole other thing.

As the cart rumbled on, Caralee pictured how the land might have looked all those centuries ago. Vines as tall as the mountains sprouting from the northwest and never far from sight all the world over. A wicked prince, captured by all the king's soldiers and sentenced to a death that kept him alive forever as a spirit trapped inside a stone.

She imagined that the prison—the *matzeva,* Eusebius had called it—looked like a giant tombstone ten times as tall as any stele, only instead of carving his name into the stone, they carved *him,* trapped. Sandymancers full of the old power, who could stop the man but not the ghost—who could save the day but not the world. *Real* sandymancers, not that candle-capped treebone who'd embarrassed her in front of *everyone.*

Just as Caralee had put Joe out of her thoughts, he stumbled into them again.

"Naw," Joe said, still teasing Caralee about their destination and the sights she wouldn't have time to see there, "you been to Grenshtepple's, but did you get farther than the outsiders' market? Did you listen to the singing stones? See the upside-down garden?" Joe shook his head. "Nawp. Don't think you did." He began humming a merry little tune. She hadn't heard that tune before. Where'd Joe go and learn a new song? Grenshtepple's? Stones don't sing.

Unless they *did.*

"Late. We're late." Mag clocked the sun and huffed. They were late already? "Now the girl will be calling up that mannikin of hers in the middle of some woesome ruins, and her sandymancy will shout out to all the dust wights and chucklers and shadoweyes and spinecrunchers and wobbledygrouks, and she'll get us all killed because of your teasing."

Mag made up half of those names, but she made them up scary. Caralee pressed her lips into a line as Mag complained.

"That's what I get for raising an orphan girl alongside my pup Joe. Shoulda kept to my own litter's litter and left the wee wizard here to the mercy of the sands. Shoulda—but didn't—and that's more than half the wisdom I've learned in sixty years living in this wretched, broken, roustabout world." Mag didn't mean a word she said, and they all knew it.

"Mag?" Caralee asked. "Ent you seventy?"

"That's what I said, girl." Mag spat and pretended to wipe at a spot on the side of the cart that didn't exist.

"Naw, you said sixty." Then, "And don't call me 'girl.'"

"Naw, I said seventy. I shoulda said seventy-four, anyway, so we can all agree that I misspoke." Mag looked at the horizon again. "We'll make the bunkadown well before sunset at Caralee's favorite place *ever* and reach Comez tomorrow afternoon. We'll lodge there and get to Grenshtepple's in three days' time total." Mag grunted. "Which is a day longer than usual, thanks to you two and that goon of a wizard. . . . Buncha shatterscat, anyhow, that sandymancing."

"*Three days?*" Caralee whined. She heard the girl in her voice and pinched herself for it. She was basically sixteen now and far from a girl, and she should talk like it.

"Aww." Joe kicked the front of the cart and winced. "Three days is forever."

*That's another thing we can agree on.*

"Yes boy, three days." Mag looked behind her to flash Caralee that look—it had more power than any sandymancy. "I know you're hot in the pants to go exploring, but you keep calm about it. We bunk for the night, each and every time. You hear?"

Caralee hung her head. "I hear, Mag."

"You, too, Joe Dunderhead." She poked Joe's big, round shoulder. "Either of you feel like reminding me why we don't ride at night?"

Caralee answered first on her schoolgirl's instinct. "Because we ent Patchfolk who know the secret ways, and we ent burden-critters who can skitter away from a dunderbeast's maw, and we ent got guards to keep away the chuckleheads, scavengers, and dust wights. And because we ent stupid, is we, Caralee?" Caralee wagged her own finger in her face. "No, Caralee, we ent stupid. We're smart and go to sleep in safe places so we don't get eaten up in the dark."

Mag sucked her teeth and scratched her forehead with a gray loc. "You got a smart mouth, girl, but that's the sum of it, with no remainder."

Caralee thought to add that you didn't *get* remainders when doing sums, but kept her peace. That might count as smart-mouthed talk, even though it *was* smart, and Mag was smart, too, so what was her problem? Caralee long ago decided that if she had a family of her own, she'd let all her daughters talk as smart as they wanted, even if they did tend toward sass from time to time.

After some lip-biting on Caralee's part and a measure of silence from Mag, the cart wobbled down into the dry riverbed that cradled this section of the road. From here to the stele, they followed the dead river that eventually became more canyon than riverbed. Caralee felt relief at escaping, for a while, the flat world that she saw every day, with its endless and endlessly tempting horizon. On either side, the riverbanks ran unevenly, like teeth in a maw, striped in shades of golds and reds and oranges.

They rode on, merrily enough if silent, until the critters crawled to a stop and would not be budged. It took a moment for the humans to hear what had startled Oti and Atu into stubbornness. It was a groan, a groan loud enough to be heard over the clackety wheels of the cart and the sixteen skittering legs of the critters.

Mag's ears pricked up and her face went dark. She held her arm out to protect or stop Joe from moving, as if either were possible with Joe Dunes.

"Don't. You. Move," Mag growled through clenched teeth. Mag was always fiddling with something—the reins, a stray loc, boxing Joe's ear for some completely understandable reason. You knew things were dire if Mag froze up, and just then, she was still as a fallen rock. The woman had a nose like none other, and hearing sharper than Caralee's own.

The groan sounded again, from behind two toothy outcroppings separated by a narrow crevice.

Mag's breath came fair to stopping; she looked afraid to exhale.

The noise grew closer, louder from the gap, joined by scraping, shuffling sounds. The crevice looked narrow, but not narrow enough to hinder many of the dangers Mag had taught Caralee and Joe to fear.

A woman stumbled through. She was caked in blood, her eyes white with sun-blindness, feeling her way with her hands. Crusted black blood covered most of her skin, and one of her legs was badly broken, with shattered yellow bone jutting out above her knee. Somehow she walked, anyway—hopping on her good leg, but still she put some weight on her broken leg, which sagged sideways with each limp-hop-step, pushing the broken bone farther out of her torn thigh. Ragged holes ruined her face, peeling away in patches. A dead woman, or near enough, moving about when she should be rattling her last breath.

The wounded woman groaned again, and it sounded like something rotten had snapped in her throat.

"Hhh-ello . . ." The stranger's head rolled around a neck too weak to support its weight.

Aside from the horror of a walking corpse, Caralee saw something odd at once—felt, more like. Sandymancy? Beyond the woman's nigh-impossible injuries, something strange shimmered around her body—like a mirage down a long flat road. The stranger, she . . . she *changed.*

Her short hair was brown. His long hair was black.

He laughed. She whimpered.

The woman shook. Her broken face was whole, then broken again. His perfect jaw was lined with dark stubble, then hers was smooth and shattered again. She was short, then tall, then short again. Full-bosomed, then muscle-chested. It was as if two people warred for the same body.

The stranger collapsed to one side, clawing with an arm at the dirt.

"She's hurt!" Joe cried and jumped out of the cart, pushing past Mag's outstretched arm.

Mag and Caralee both reached out to stop him, but he'd already slipped past their reach, and besides, Joe was beastly strong. Apparently, he was also suicidal. Mag's rules weren't for nothing, and Caralee knew it. Joe knew it, too.

*He's too kind,* a part of her fawned.

"Joe Dunes, don't you dare!" Mag shouted, and the burden-critters screeched, but Joe paid no heed. "The rules, Joe—don't you *dare*!"

Caralee scrabbled out of the cart to give chase, and Mag shouted at her, too.

The shifting, wounded stranger pulled herself across the ground. "Who was my guide?" she said in a voice that was not a woman's voice. "Where is my good wizard, who shook the earth to lead me *out*?"

The horror drooled onto the riverbed, eyes rolling back into their sockets, and coughed up a blood clot the size of Caralee's fist.

Joe squatted low and reached out with his big hands to help her. He slipped one arm underneath her armpit, and with the other, he took her hand in his, ready to heave her up. She moaned when he moved her, in her womanly voice.

"You're okay. You're gonna be fine." Idiot Joe lied to the dying, flickering wanderer. "I'm gonna get you up, all right?" His concern was obvious, as was his distress. For all his size and strength, Joe wasn't made for tending to the injured. It shook him to see that kind of pain up and close.

"*Joe Dunes, don't you dare!*" Mag screamed. Caralee had never heard Mag so wild.

"Come on now, one big lift and that's it. I'll be real gentle. It'll all be fine."

Only Joe stopped still. Instead of lifting the woman to her feet, Joe froze in place—not a wary stillness like Mag but an awful, unnatural paralysis. Mid-squat, mid-lift, arms and legs flexed—there was no way that anyone, even someone as strong as Joe, could stop in that position and stay there, so terrifyingly still.

Mag screamed over and over, chiseling the air with pure panic.

Caralee rushed to Joe, but stopped short and pulled away when she saw the look in his eyes. Joe's eyes were light brown—at least they should have been. Instead, Caralee saw eyes much darker, almost black. If eyes could smile, these were laughing.

*No, it can't be.* But those flashing dark eyes were real. They were real, and they looked out from Joe's face. *No. NoNo. Nononononono.*

Owing to her head so full of stories, so pesky and bothersome, Caralee knew just what that stillness meant. Caralee knew exactly who'd walked in that dying woman's body and who, now, would walk in Joe's.

She'd never hoped to be wrong so badly in all her life.

Caralee's heart dropped and her gut clenched. Blood rushed to her head so fiercely she felt the pounding.

Then Joe unfroze and let the woman drop to the ground, lifeless.

Joe straightened his back and turned to Mag in the cart.

"I'm so sorry, Mag," he said in his own voice. "Ent it funny, I never listened?"

He took two steps toward them, but they were odd steps. Like he was walking through knee-deep sand. Two steps, and then he fell.

It all happened so fast.

Joe flopped on the ground, fighting with his own body. He flipped onto his back and cried out. Caralee fell back onto her bottom while Mag screamed and the critters went wild. They bucked the cart, throwing Mag to the riverbed, where she held her hip and raged.

Joe went slack, rigid, and slack again. When he spoke, it wasn't with his own voice. The voice that came out of Joe's pink lips sounded cold, weirdly accented, and cruel.

"Don't call them! I am *so* close. No!" It sounded like a bad dream. *Another man's* bad dream.

Joe twitched and seized, flopping on the ground, arching and relaxing his back over and over, with such might that Caralee feared she'd see him snap his spine in two. His mouth frothed, his jaw clenched, and his eyes rolled back in their sockets.

He began to make such a noise as Caralee would never forget, somewhere between a scream and a whisper. She heard Mag whipping the reins at the critters, who'd managed to turn the cart around.

"Mag, *get out of here*!" Caralee screamed. The look on Mag's face cut Caralee to the bone. Caralee never knew a face could hold so many emotions at once—heartbreak and fury and fear and regret and hate and love and resignation and, somehow, *encouragement*.

Mag sobbed, nodded, and scrambled backward. And then she was gone.

"Caralee!" The word came out of Joe's mouth with that same awful twinning of two people, only two men instead of a woman and a man. His eyes snapped back to normal for just a heartbeat, and he looked at her, and Caralee saw a terrible concern—a concern for her. "Run, Caralee. You *run*. It's *him* inside. He's *real*."

All the fight drained from Joe's body in one exhausted breath, and he lay on the ground unmoving, except for his lips, and his eyes, which darted this way and that, even though he faced only the cracked indigo sky.

"I know, Joe. I know!" Caralee screamed again.

It felt like a nightmare. Caralee never thought she'd rue all her lessons, but she knew exactly what had happened—she'd known it *as* it happened, and there was nothing she could do. Knowing it was agony.

"Joe! Joe, look at me, Joe. Joe!"

*It's already too late. That's* him *in there now. The monster.*

Joe's eyes turned from sandy brown to dark brown and back again. In a voice that wasn't Joe's, he said, "Apologies. I get my words confused when I first slip on a new mask."

In a single fluid movement, he sat up and leapt to his feet. Joe could never manage grace like that.

The thing cocked Joe's head, taking a long look at Caralee. His gaze was lightning—Caralee had never been subjected to that kind of searing focus. It burned through the fear that paralyzed her.

"It was you who quaked the earth, wasn't it?" he asked in that odd accent. "Wasn't it you, who called to me with your seventh sense? Yes. You led me out of the blinding dust storms. *You* brought me to this nice, strong, young body. *You* called me to freedom—and I had no idea how close I'd come, at last, to the edges of my wasteland. What a funny little worm you are, to have saved me."

Caralee's jaw dropped.

"You asked me a question. You asked me for my story. For the rest of it?" Not-Joe shook Joe's head. "Rather a stupid boon to ask for, the end of my story, but you're the worm, not me. In exchange for my freedom, I'll allow you to know the end of my story. In the future, if you have a future, I wonder if you'll be more careful with what you ask."

Caralee tried to say "*What?*" but all that came out was a quaver and a line of drool.

"The desert grew, you see. And bodies are hard to come by in the wasteland. It's been centuries, I think? With every stolen step, my desert outpaced me. That's how the end of my story begins."

Somehow, Caralee found herself.

Her blood still pounded in her ears. She couldn't believe what she was seeing, let alone what she was hearing, but a rage surged through her such as she'd never known before. It felt like a kind of lust, but for violence. She would tear this ghost from Joe's body with her bare hands, if it came to that.

*This is all my fault.*

With a leap forward, Caralee launched herself at the thief who had been Joe. He stopped her with an outstretched hand, Joe's big fingers warm against her chest bone. She screamed and clawed and kicked, but Joe's strong arm held her at bay. Her reach came pitifully short; not even her kicks connected.

Then Joe's hand slipped from her chest up to her throat. Joe's fingers squeezed. He lifted Caralee till her feet left the ground, and the blood that had rushed to her head was now trapped there. Pain ballooned beneath the skin of her face and behind her eyes.

"I do not know who you are, girl." The monster's voice was flat, infinitely threatening. It came out of Joe's throat but sounded nothing like Joe. "Let me establish one thing before I decide whether or not to squeeze the life from you: *fear me.*"

Caralee's rage trapped her better sense. He might as well have said nothing at all. Though she saw stars, she didn't stop kicking, or punching, or spitting. Her spittle landed, if nothing else, across the legend's cheek.

He regarded her with wonder. It was still Joe's face, for now, but the eyes—

those dark eyes—they belonged to the sand divvil, whose name needed no guesses.

"You're a brave girl, aren't you. Even braver for a worm." That was not a question: he'd assessed her and cataloged her with one glance. "But of course, you don't know me."

"I know you, Sonnyvine," Caralee growled despite the grip around her throat, the blood pooling in her head.

"If you know me—which is a questionable claim—then you must know that this body is *mine.*" He looked pleased, but his words cut through her heart. "What's mine is mine, and those who don't respect that law tend to die."

Caralee's growl died in her throat and her vision darkened, and she thought the bastard would snap her neck then and there. To her surprise, he dropped her to the ground where she curled up, sucking in air, head spinning.

"Get. Outta. Joe." Caralee forced air into her lungs and out again, fighting for each word.

"Joe? Joe is my mask now. It's not a body, it's a mask, and soon the face you see will be my face. A strong body, but it will look like me, and smell like me, and taste like me. *Me.*" The monster stroked his chin, and Joe's square, blond-stubbled jaw took on a slimmer, darker shape. "Have you ever slipped away from a masquerade with a pack of lovers? Discarded your costumes and tossed aside your masks to fuck in the hot blue waters of a mineral fountain?" He scanned her face. "No, I suppose you haven't. I did desiccate the world, after all."

Caralee squinted at the fiend in Joe's body. If he could know her in a glance, she could at least study him back.

"You really are him, aren't you?" Caralee asked, her sense of wonder betraying her rage. "Real and true in the flesh? In *my Joe's flesh?*"

The abomination sneered. "This flesh is a mask for my soul; I own it, I will change it to suit me, and when I decide to throw it away, this body will die."

She couldn't hear that. She couldn't think that. She had to think something else, anything else.

"You talk weird." Caralee said. He did.

"I am old." He considered that.

"Old and like from someplace else."

*Not someplace—somewhen. Did they talk like that in Vintage times, all tish-bosh-parrump?* Caralee found it hard to imagine filling her mouth with so many fancy words.

"Well, language does change, but . . . has it been so long?" He put a hand to his head. Joe's short yellow hair went black and long, of a sudden, then back again.

Looking skyward, he found the crack far overhead, and his eyes widened. "To see that . . . that *vandalism* unobscured by dust or sand-blinded eyes . . ." His expression held murder, and that wicked gaze slid down from the sky to glare at Caralee. "I am not from someplace else. I am, in fact, the least foreign person in this entire world. *My* world."

Caralee pleaded with her better sense, begging for an explanation of what was happening, to make it something different from this killing loss.

"All things belong to me." Joe's body bent and grabbed a handful of grit from the ground. "I told them. I warned them. Instead, they chose *this*." He sneered. "And now someone has desecrated my sky? What witch . . ." His thoughts seemed to swivel. "How long has it been?" the owner of the world asked the cable hauler. It wasn't a question so much as a command with a rise at the end.

"Eight hundred years, give or take, say the stories," Caralee answered on instinct, *again*. "How do you not know that?"

The monster blinked at the question and began to try to explain, turning to gesture toward the wasteland above, but Caralee seized the moment and leapt upon the world-killer's back. She wrapped her arm around his windpipe and pulled his throat toward her as hard as she could.

*Choke me, will you?* Caralee took a deep breath. *Guess what? I can choke you right back.*

She wrestled him down as he sucked in a rasp of breath—that shadow of a fancy man, he swung his shoulders as if to toss her off like some cape, but Caralee held fast to his neck, twisting herself against him, and managed to wrench him off balance. She rode him all the way down to the ground.

One arm still wrapped around the monster's head, palm to his temple, she put her free hand on the other side of Joe's head and reached out with her sandysense. Sure, she'd shamed a traveling sandymancer—or tried to—but faced with this terror, all of Caralee's confidence evaporated like a rare morning's dew. She might as well have spent her life playing in the dirt.

*Please, please.*

Caralee extended her sandysense. With it, she reached into Joe's head with every bit of her raw power, and she *pulled*. Self-trained, guessing at the ways of the art she'd been born with, Caralee sought out the mineral in Joe's head and pulled with all her strength.

It had to work. It *had* to.

*I'll rip him out of Joe's body with his own sandymancy.*

Joe screamed. The god-king screamed. Pinpricks of blood appeared on his face, beneath her fingers. Bits of stuff began to pop out of them, mud from a man. They dropped upward onto her palms.

How he howled. How his face contorted with agony. Caralee all but cheered when she saw that agony and heard that howl. The taste of *power* blasted away her doubt as his blood dripped up onto her hands. Her strength swelled out into the world, where it worked *her* will. At that moment, Caralee thought she could do anything. She could become an avenging monster herself. She could become as evil as this divvil beneath her, feeling blood and sweat spilling upward out of Joe's head.

The power and its illusion of freedom flooded her thoughts to distraction.

A divvil knows no distraction.

He got his hands up from beneath her and threw her off him with incredible force. Caralee flew backward and hit the wall of the canyon, falling to the ground with the breath knocked out of her chest.

She watched the monster stand and storm toward her. Already, he moved Joe's body like it was his own—he walked with a different gait and didn't swing his arms in clumsy circles. A shadow of long, dark hair flipped in and out of existence—less of a flicker now and more of a moment. He was taking root.

"Did you," Joe's thief began, breathing hard from exertion and whatever Caralee had done to him, "just try to *pull me out*?" He closed the distance between them and loomed over her, then slammed one of Joe's boots into her chest with force just shy of rib-crushing, pinning Caralee to the ground. "Am I looking at a girl who threw herself at her *god-king* and tried to suck the *earth* out of his new *skull*?" His eyes were wide, no trace of Joe's face on those slender brows, chin narrower and more sparsely stubbled. "Do you *want* to die screaming?"

*Are you giving me a choice?* Caralee wondered as she tried to escape the big boot that trapped her. *Fucker!* Horror filled her, and a little exhilaration. She expected to be pulped into the ground at any second.

"Easy off, now." Caralee talked while she still could. She tried to think what someone brave would say, only she couldn't imagine anyone brave enough to confront an evil out of legend. Except, Caralee *had* to face him. "You need me, monster!"

Laughter had never been so mean.

"Who could possibly need *you*?" The boot twisted; the monster sneered. "I wouldn't so much as wipe these boots with you, worm."

Caralee's mind raced, thanking her instinct for answering without thinking. "Been eight hundred years, but you don't know it?" she asked, trying at snotty and, presumably, failing. Doubt threatened to undo her entirely. "Sky's been cracked over a century, and you don't know who did it?" *Fuck doubt,* she thought. "Way you talk, seems like you only just stumbled out of the wasteland you made. Been shrouded in sand and dust storms since whenever you escaped your slab, ent it, body thief?"

The monster's sneer slid into a smile. "Continue, girl." The pressure of the boot on her chest lightened a touch.

"You asked who was your guide. Who rumbled the ground to lead you out. Fuck me for it, but that was me. You needed a guide out of your mess, but you ent out of it *yet.* The whole world's your mess, but you don't know scat about it. I'm your guide." Right. That could be true, couldn't it?

He removed the boot crushing her ribs and sucked air through his teeth.

"That's . . ." He laughed again, this time at himself. "That's almost *correct.* What a wonder." He put a finger to his lips. *Joe's lips,* Caralee reminded herself, though they didn't look like Joe's lips anymore. Not big and pink, but sharp and beautiful. Awful, but beautiful.

"There's one flaw in your reasoning. You've just assaulted me. With magick. Historically, that has gone poorly for my assailants, and I am not as generous with my trust as once I may have been."

*Scat.* That was a good point. Only what threat could Caralee possibly pose to the owner of the world, its king and its god? She said so.

"All I did was make you sweat a little blood . . ." She tried to make it sound harmless.

The world-killer wrinkled his lips and arched an eyebrow, telling Caralee how badly her attempt had failed. Then he reached out with one snake-muscled arm and yanked Caralee to her feet. Standing on watery legs, she brushed herself off as best she could. Blood from her attack still beaded across the monster's face.

"*Sweat a little blood . . .*" Caralee felt pathetic and struggled to find herself again. She was desperate to stay alive long enough to save Joe. "And don't you ever call me 'girl,' got it?"

The monster's lips twisted into a sneer of a smile, but he nodded. "A fair request from a worm and—apparently—my guide. You've led me into the world again. It's astounding, what a shit-covered young woman can do."

*What?*

They stood there, facing each other, without a thing to say.

The moment stretched on.

"I'm gonna get my Joe back," Caralee declared, deciding it was only fair to say so.

The monster snorted and started giggling. Of all the things, he got the *giggles.*

"Shaddup! I mean it." How dare he!

Caralee started to snort herself. *Oh no.*

She caught the giggles, too, and soon they were both doubled over with the most absurdly inappropriate laughter, and neither could stop.

"I might kill you at any moment!" the monster howled through his laughter, perfect white teeth sharper and longer than Joe's.

"I know!" Caralee howled back, stomach cramping up from laughter.

"What in the Vine were you thinking?" The monster smiled, laughter settling.

"I have no idea," Caralee admitted, breathing hard but recovering. Then, dead serious, "I gotta get back my Joe. I'm *gonna* get back my Joe."

"I don't believe you." He winked. "Young worm."

The creature pulled back his hand as if to strike her, but kept it still, frozen behind his shoulder. Caralee felt the tingle of sandymancy just before the air itself slapped her fiercely across the cheek, wrenching her neck. He used his awful sandymancy and slapped her again, and a third time, until she lay on the ground, unmoving but determined to endure.

Not once had he touched her.

The monster scrubbed his head and face with his fingers. The pinpricks of blood that Caralee had pulled from his head mixed with sweat into a slippery red veil. "Eight centuries and I've never met anyone so bravely stupid, or so ingeniously inept. You look like nothing. You—obviously—come from nothing. You surely know nothing. What manner of shit-covered worm *are* you?"

Gasping and tasting her own blood, Caralee pushed herself up from the riverbed on all fours.

"Answer me, little worm." Joe's boot nudged her arms out from under her, and Caralee fell face-first into the dirt.

"What am *I*?" She pulled herself up yet again, spitting silt. "You stole my Joe's body and still got the nerve to ask *me* what *I* am?" She threw up her arms in defeat. "You're the monster, entya? Look at me. What else am I gonna do? Cuz I'm not stupid or inept."

"Oh, dear me." He put a hand to his chest, seeming—of all things—charmed.

"I'm *smart,* and better than that, I don't ever, ever, ever give up. You hear me? You gonna kill me, you shoulda stomped me into the ground, because I'm coming at you with everything this world you broke gave me. I'm chasing you to the edge of it, you hear me? I'm gonna kill you till you're dead, and I'm gonna get back my Joe, and that's scatting *that.*"

"You idiot hero, thinking that something as insignificant as a girl could . . ." He waved away the notion.

Caralee jabbed her chin in the air, squirming with all she felt—rage, humiliation, terror. She was a worm in hot ashes.

"I told you not to call me 'girl,' monster." She balled her fists.

"Pfft. You'd only kill Joe. And you won't kill Joe. A girl—a *young woman*—who never ever, ever gives up wouldn't go and do that, would she?" He pointed a finger at her chest. "What's to stop me from leaving Joe's body right this minute—leaving it dead—and taking *you* instead?"

"Because I'm not fit to be your boot-wipe. Because I'm a shit-covered worm, and that's not a *mask* you'd want to wear," she spat.

"Fair argument. You *are* repugnant," said the thief. "You'll never win, you know."

Caralee spat again. "Sounds like loser talk to me."

*What am I* doing?

"What do you call yourself, young woman, shit-covered wizard-worm?"

"My name is Caralee Vinnet." She squared her stance and faced him down. "I'm no wizard, but I'm gonna end you, anyway, Sonnyvine."

He held out his hand, palm thrust forward, holding it perpendicular to the ground. Caralee braced herself for some sorcery to slay her, there and then.

"If I can't get rid of you, Caralee Vinnet, you might as well dispose of that ridiculous sobriquet." Still he held out his hand, steady as a blade. "My names are mysteries into which you are not inducted, but you may address me by my title." He bent at the waist, just a little. "I present myself, the Lord of a Thousand Names, Child of the World-Tree, Beyond-Whisperer, Druid Extreme, Archmage Royal, Admiral-General of War, Cognoscent Prime, First Functionary of Time and Deception, High Cryptobotanist, Keeper of Machine Secrets, and God-King of All the World: Amauntilpisharai, the last Son of the Vine."

The truth, when she heard it confirmed out loud from the divvil's own mouth, drained the blood from Caralee's face.

"It's a pleasure to meet you." He moved his extended palm forward, just a bit.

She recoiled. It wasn't an invisible blade or a spell in his hands—it was, of all things, the offer of a handshake.

Caralee's stomach convulsed, and her vomit sprayed his hand and his feet.

Caralee followed the Son of the Vine back to the cart, wiping puke from her chin. The cart stood intact, with no sign of Mag. Oti and Atu comforted each other with their moist mouthparts and stroked their feathered antennae together, still shaking with fright. Caralee saw Mag's footprints leading back home and remembered that all-at-once look on Mag's face when Caralee had told the older woman to run. Mag was no fool, but if her main concern had been self-survival, she'd have used the wide-bristled broom they kept tucked under the cart to brush away her tracks as she ran back to the village. Instead, she'd left a trail for Caralee to see.

Mag had given Caralee a choice. Bless Mag's heart for knowing that if Caralee somehow survived, she wouldn't let go of Joe so easily, no matter the danger. On the slim chance that Caralee chose to run home, however, she could follow Mag's path and catch up.

*Which way?* She faced a choice between two whiches—but which which was good, and which which bad?

Mag had hit the ground hard when she'd been thrown from the cart, but her footprints led west—back home. They were staggered, perhaps from a limp, but didn't look so uneven as to suggest that she had broken a bone. Mag would be safe, or safe enough. She wouldn't make it all the way home on foot, but she'd get close enough to draw the attention of one of the outlying sentinel patrols before they fell back to the village for the night.

The trail leading back home was as clear as daylight; one last lesson, one last opportunity to save herself—an opportunity that Caralee didn't even consider taking.

*I gotta get my Joe back.*

"What good fortune! Wise woman, your grandmother, to save herself." The Son approached the cart. "She's left us transportation, which, as you might imagine, provides a welcome change for me. You know, once I traveled upon a palanquin." He thought a moment, then glanced at Caralee's sandaled feet and her toes caked with sand and talc. "That's a fancy cart with servants instead of wheels."

"Mag ent my gran, she's your—*Joe's* gran. Raised me, though." Then, "You made your servants *roll like wheels*?"

"Roll?" The Son stretched his neck and arched his back, reaching up to the sky with delicate fingers. "No, you little idiot. They carried me upon their backs and sang with joy at the privilege."

"Sounds like a scat job."

"No. To be part of my honor posse was, well, an honor."

The Son climbed into the cart, testing its sturdiness by shaking it by the sides. Oti and Atu calmed themselves at his approach. Must be they smelled Joe.

"I always did have a fondness for bronzebacks, though they were smaller in my day." The Son clicked and cooed, and Atu looked behind her as best she could, her eight eyes black and curious. "My grandfather, the Most Holy Son of the Vine, used to boast that mating a spider to a beetle was one of our ancestors' least appreciated accomplishments."

The Son looked to the east. "Grandfather had a talent for seeing the greater prize hidden inside feats of quiet genius."

Caralee couldn't imagine this Son having a gramp, let alone a gramp who was a god-king that liked critters.

"Hello, insects." The Son reached out to brush Atu's thorax. "My, how you've grown. You're doing most of the work now. That tells us something, doesn't it?" He looked bummed out. "Grandfather was right yet again. I half wish Father were here, so I could see him pout over being *so fucking wrong*."

"Was your daddy Sonnyvine, too, after your gramps?"

"Not for long." The Son made figure eights with his hands, combing his fingers through the air like a storyteller around a campfire. "He didn't need a long reign to imperil the world. My father was not a strong man, although he held strong opinions and feigned strength by clinging to those opinions despite any and all evidence that he was wrong. And he was so very, very wrong."

"Yeah? About what?"

"Tell me, Caralee Vinnet, do you *really* think that one person can doom an entire world? Absent any myth concerning my misdeeds, would you believe that a single soul could destroy a world that took the ancients centuries to construct?"

Caralee craned her neck to look at the horizon, but the rocky walls of the ravine blocked her view. She knew from memory that the southern barrier mountains, like always, looked like they were trying to climb the sky, gray and lifeless. In every other direction, above the ravine, the horizon lay flat and brown, and the only things that she could have seen moving were drifts of dust and the slow slither of sand ripples shifting under the wind. You didn't see the monsters until it was too late.

"I grew up here," Caralee said, "so I can believe a lot of things."

"Fair." The Son rolled his eyes and gave up his hand-waving to scratch Oti's hairy thorax. "Might you consider the notion that—after eight hundred years—what details remain of my story might, just possibly, fail to tell the entire story?"

Of course Caralee knew that. She'd gone to the wasteland and asked it for the rest of the story, just like the old wizard had said. Look what she'd gotten for it. Now that the wasteland had answered her and taken its price in flesh, Caralee didn't know which was worse: what she'd done, or the curiosity that buzzed inside her head in spite of Joe's fate.

"If you're the only one left to tell your story, how's that change anything? What was it that your daddy was so wrong about?"

"Mmm . . . no." The Son shrugged off Caralee's question. "You're right. Why should anyone believe *me*? More to the point, why should I care? I am god and king."

Oti hissed blissfully as the Son dug his fingers into the critter's hairy exoskeleton.

Caralee stood before the cart, watching the familiar stranger sit in Joe's seat. Was that by accident, how he knew just where the critters liked to be stroked? Or was Joe in there and the Son knew what Joe knew? Did the Son really know how bronzeback critters had been bred from other insects? Wonders and lies were hard to separate when they came from the mouth of a legend.

*Only way to find out is to keep going.*

With care, Caralee climbed into Mag's seat and took up the reins. She realized she had no idea what came next, and said so.

"Where were you headed, Caralee Vinnet, my young worm?" the Son asked.

"Well, uh . . . Grenshtepple's . . . by way of Comez, camping overnight at that big monument." She pointed to the stele, its top just visible over the neck-high walls of the ravine. "Where were *you* headed?"

"I promised you the end to my story, not my itinerary. . . . Why don't you ride at night?" He stroked the lovely planes of his chin. "What is it you hide from when the sun sets?"

"Let's see." Caralee listed them on her fingers. "Cold; dunderbeasts; chucklers; sandfishers; bandits; scavenger critters too hungry to wait for us to die; and *you*." She bared her teeth. "Most of all, it's you."

"Rightly so. I am the original danger. That's the story, anyway. There is wisdom in fear, no?" He cocked his head. "How the world has changed. I don't recognize either of those place-names, Comez and Grenshtepple's. Villages?"

Caralee nodded.

"No large towns? A city, if possible?"

Caralee shrugged.

"A guide who knows nothing. . . . Well. Why were you headed to these two villages?"

Caralee's face screwed at the question, and she cocked her head behind her. "Cart fulla goods, ent it? We had a mind to sell or barter our goods, see, till *you* happened."

*Had a mind to do a lotta things, till you happened.*

"Coin, then," the Son mused. "Coin is good."

"No scat." Caralee resigned herself to her circumstances. This was happening. "We need to pick up our pace."

The Son agreed. "That stele's quite a ways a way, I should think, and the daylight fades." He looked up to the dark, cracked sky. "It does, doesn't it? The sun tells me the hour as it ever did, but why is the sky so dark?" He stared at the daytime stars and frowned at the crack in the sky, its spiderweb lines gold beneath the sun.

*He can seem so unthreatening,* Caralee thought, watching the Son measure angles in the sky with his thumb and forefingers. Squinting like Marm-marm at her shapes on the chalk-rock, the Son looked nearly as harmless as the schoolmistress. Caralee reminded herself that he was not. Her bloodied lip and sore neck proved it so.

"Marm-marm says it's air leaking out, or nighttime leaking in—but I think nighttime leaking in is a stupid idea."

"It *is* a stupid idea. The void beyond is a vacuum—an absence. It's our air that's precious." The Son's expression couldn't be read.

"What's the void?"

"You weren't surprised," the Son mused, "when I mentioned the building of the world. But you don't know what's on the other side?"

Caralee raised a finger. "How would *I* know what's above the sky?"

The Son whistled, but Caralee couldn't tell whether he was impressed or mocking her. "In that case, tell me what you know about the breaking of my sky."

Caralee didn't know much, but she supposed she knew more than anyone who'd been stuck in the heart of the wasteland for however long.

"They call themselves the Metal Duchy, and people say that they're made of, you know, metal." That sounded like a tall tale to Caralee, but she didn't say so. "I've never seen one. The Metal Duchy punched a hole through the sky more than a century ago, but nobody saw any of their people till a few decades back."

The Son took a breath and nodded as though Caralee's tall tales made any kind of sense at all.

"A ship, then?" He bared his teeth. "It's too much to hope that the impact object would be a simple extrasolar asteroid—our ancestors wouldn't have built a sky vulnerable to any mundane celestial knockabout, and they swept the system of anything larger than your head. A ship's engine, on the other hand . . ."

"You took that well." Caralee didn't want to test the Son's good humor. "I wonder how they did it. And how'd they move through the void if it's nothing, and if it's nothing, then where'd they come from?"

"Took it well? You need to learn to distrust your senses. Just because I am not stomping my feet and sucking blood out of the nearest face doesn't mean that I am not angry." The Son didn't seem bothered, but as he'd just said, seeming didn't mean being. Caralee didn't trust herself as much as he thought she did. "I don't like trespassers, nor vandals, nor interruptions, and these aliens are all three."

"Are we gonna see the Metal Duchy?" Caralee's heart quickened at the thought, and at all the thoughts that followed. "Are you gonna kill them all?"

"Stay alive and see for yourself, new worm!" His laughter was a shallow kind of cruelty. "You have my word, you will learn the end of my story—but it's up to you not to die before then."

Caralee grunted, snapped the reins before slackening them, kept her eyes fixed forward as the cart rolled on, and kept her mouth shut for a long time. The Son returned the favor. A few hours of shared silence let Caralee think and adapt to the idea of riding in a critter cart beside the Son of the Vine himself.

Getting Joe back would require more than just sitting next to the monster. For now, Caralee clenched her jaw to keep her lips from quavering and kept her eyes fixed ahead and wide open so that the wind would dry her tears. Try as she might, Caralee couldn't shrug off the memory of her angry demand from the wasteland. A life of grubbing in the dirt for cable plant, never going farther than the stalls outside Grenshtepple's, never learning, no chance to be *anyone*. She'd felt so angry at her lot and so dismissed by that hack of a sandymancer.

"*Ask the wasteland and hope that it answers . . .*" If it hadn't been for that knot-boned wizard, Caralee would never have thrown her tantrum, never hammered the wasteland with sandymancy in some stupid hope that a desert could give her answers.

It was easier to hate Eusebius than herself, and Caralee knew that. Eusebius hadn't summoned the Son of the Vine by ringing the ground like a big, loud dinner bell and serving up Joe Dunes on a platter.

*I led him straight to Joe, and he ate Joe right up.*

For better or for worse, Caralee discovered that no matter how she blamed the old wizard, she couldn't manage to hate herself any less. This . . . problem? . . . was too awful to be real. The horrible warnings taught in stories were jazzed up so that they made their point—the nightmare wasn't supposed to be *real.* The Son was supposed to be trapped in his *matzeva,* held forever by the awesome power of long-dead sandymancers.

She wished this was just a story. Stories get told, and then everyone eats dinner. Caralee would have to live with this for the rest of her life. Even if—when—she put things aright and got back Joe, she'd always be the curious girl who handed her friend over to the boogeyman. She'd be a real-life monster for the rest of her days.

Churning on such dark thoughts, Caralee had mentally exhausted herself by the time the little cart rolled beneath the shadow of the stele. Her body ached, as tired as her head, and she pulled the critters to a stop just as the sun surrendered to the horizon.

Frequent travelers had tamped down the ground around the stele, and a rock-ringed firepit waited to roast a dust hare or brew some gruel. Thanks to the Son's attack and the upset of the cart, they hadn't water to spare for gruel, so Caralee made what camp she could while the Son inspected the stele. Caralee wondered if he thought the monument as impressive as she did, and decided that he definitely wouldn't.

*I should be doing the exploring.* Was it petty that she resented the Son for the idle time she'd otherwise have to adventure, while Mag would be ordering Joe about the campsite?

Her mission to save Joe would involve adventure enough, Caralee accepted, and she couldn't deny that a part of her thrilled at the notion of seeing the world. Still testing the waters of her adversary and companion, she said so.

"If you're as good as your word to follow me, I suspect you'll learn that *adventure* means something more, something less, and something entirely different from what you expect," the Son answered simply. He cocked his head at the tower behind him, its top and middle vanished by night. "But 'monument'?" He mocked her with a mild sneer. "You do realize that this structure is nothing more than the remains of a support system for the *actual* marvel? Your monument is nothing more than abandoned scaffolding for what was, in essence, a tremendously capable aqueduct."

The Son grabbed a sack of cable flour and tossed it to one side of the cart, sour-faced at his cramped sleeping space. He cocked his head toward the cargo to tell Caralee where she would be sleeping.

*Why is he doing this? Why am I alive? Ent because he needs me.* They both knew that. The Son had spared Caralee because of . . . what? Her smart mouth and sassback? She was essential to no one—the Son had the right of that—so why keep her with him?

*Is there Joe in there? Does he feel what Joe feels?* She didn't dare to hope so, nor did she think it likely. The Son was not the sort of person who could be influenced—certainly not by as innocent a soul as Joe. Joe hadn't the tooth for it.

"Why do you bother playing it nice-like?" Caralee didn't know how to approach an evil god-king, so she stuck to the directness that had kept her alive so far. She took a flour bag for herself, padding down two bushels of wicker to sleep upon. Her eyes never left the Son. "Is it because you think that you're invincible? Or is it so you can strike first? Do you even *have* a reason?" She ground her teeth. They were toothy questions. "And what's an ackyduck?"

"I strike first to strike last." No hesitation before his answer. "An aqueduct is an elevated road that carries water far away. The Vine carried much more than water, but the principle of its design was similar."

The Son settled into the cart, forced to lie with his knees bent, head on his flour pillow.

"Should I? Run far away?" Caralee did the same on her makeshift wicker bed, but propped up on one elbow to face the Son. She had no intention of running—of course she didn't.

"From home? Only if you want to see the world. From me? Absolutely yes. We've established that more than once. For what it's worth, 'more than once' is a personal record. Congratulations, you didn't die. That's twice today." The Son rolled away from her, such as he could, exposing his back. "I don't 'play nice-like'—say *benign* next time, it will make you sound like less of a fool. In any case, just because a thing is malignant doesn't mean its malignancy is always apparent, or that it is *only* malign."

Settling into his awkward sleeping arrangement, the Son added, "Your worthless cargo makes for an awful pillow."

Quiet followed and lingered till it became the silence of sleep; tonight, Caralee faced that silence as a vigil. She leaned back, arms crossed behind her head, staring at the stars. She loved the way they seemed to swirl in thick clouds of magenta and blue, bleeding into green. The stars seemed to pour from the glowing clouds, as if spawned, and some instinct inside Caralee knew that the stars *were* born inside those impossible clouds beyond the clouds.

*How does truth just come to a person like that?* Caralee wondered. Something clicked. She *knew* she would get her Joe back. Sure as starbirth, she knew it for truth.

On the subject of truths, Caralee considered the wide broom that Mag tucked under the cart. The one she'd left behind for Caralee, to show those limping footprints. Maybe Mag had given Caralee more than one choice? Maybe Mag knew Caralee better than anyone. A broom with a real wood shaft cut from one of the rare treebones that was still sturdy and not a bleached husk. The shaft was almost as hard as stone. A shaft that even short Caralee could swing with some force, if she kept herself steady and struck first—to strike last.

The ride *would* be easier if Caralee were the only one conscious. Easier still if the other were tied up tight as the critter-bond.

From the foot of the cart eased the Son's voice—alert but soft, not cutting through the sleepy silence. "Break off the crossbar with the bristles first." He hadn't moved, still facing away in that pose of, Caralee realized, false vulnerability. "The shaft alone will make for a decent quarterstaff, but you'll hit yourself in the face with the broomy part and deny your opponent the fun of cracking your skull open." He sounded almost concerned for Caralee.

"A quarterstaff is a good weapon for a beginner," he continued as if the subject were academic. "You'd stab your eye out with a knife, and a sword would be a terrible idea. Do you have guns? Bows? Don't ever touch a bow; you haven't the focus."

Caralee had no response at all, other than to wonder if a gun was like a bow. Nobody ever let her touch a bow. Could the Son read her mind, or was he so smart that he'd thought her thoughts faster than she could think them herself? It made her head spin, and she couldn't follow her own thoughts, let alone find any further truth in them.

"Oh," she said through the spin. "Just to be clear . . . this is about me not attacking you while you sleep?"

"Is it? The thought hasn't even crossed my mind." He took a deep breath, the liar. "What a violent young woman you are. It's a shame you're as worthless as spittle in the dirt."

Caralee kept her sassback to herself. She curled up and willed herself to sleep with fancies of beating the pompous god-king to bloody death with a broom handle.

# I

Listen to me, voiceless winds of my wasteland. I am the Son of the Vine, and I am imprisoned in my stone monument, forever. Our Earthborn ancestors called such a stone a *matzeva,* but I call it hell. Listen to me, please. I am begging you. Please:

When I claimed the Grown Crown——for no one would crown me——I grew its seven tines myself. In my pursuit of the crown, I followed our occasional tradition of slaughter. Bloodshed is no great crime in the City of the Vine, and in ordinary times, when a natural death did not prompt succession, a simple patricide would have sufficed. In ordinary times, the seven superlatives, paragons of the seven magickal disciplines, would have each used their respective arts to grow a tine from my skull. Antler, iron, blackthorn, oak, ivory, dogwood, and aloe vera.

Mine were not ordinary times.

My beautiful world, once named the Glass Gardens by its long-dead builders, was rotting. The Vine rotted, root-bound and molding in the depths where none could see, save those few caretakers who could stomach the notion that our immortal world was, in fact, not.

My grandfather, the Most Holy Son of the Vine, had such a stomach——and a mind for staving off apocalypses, a spleen to bring will to action, and the care of the world held foremost in his heart.

My father, the Most Holy Son of the Vine, had none of these organs.

He stomached nothing but watered wine and challah bread; his mind dwelled only on his own weaknesses; he saved his spleen, such as it was, for rebuking the good sense of Grandfather's science; and his heart——well, I confess——I never knew Father's heart until I held it in my right hand.

Death creates a king. Grandfather lived into my teens and kept me close. Ours is another tale, but he died suddenly, and of natural causes. Father's coronation was rushed and dull, like the man himself. Mother looked radiant becoming the Bride of Plenty, and Father managed to be both jealous and dismissive of his queen.

Within weeks, Father had undone Grandfather's work to study the Vine's sickness and any investigations into its rejuvenation. To question the eternal perdurance of the Vine was blasphemy. He rolled back edicts and censored scholars and druids. He called me treasonous when I appealed to his better sense, for he had none.

Life——am I alive, as a ghost in my stone?——has a sick sense of humor. I became the world-killer because I lost a family spat. I attacked my family because I had seen one god-king squabble over the warnings of another, and the world had run out of time for dynastic bullshit.

If the Child of the Vine was both king and god, then the Glass Gardens needed a ruler who acted both godly and kingly. Else it would die, and I would be king and god of dust.

Well. Just look at us now.

I loved some of my siblings, hated others, was indifferent to most——but I did not want to kill them. I did not want to slay their children.

I had to end any and every claim to the Grown Crown. My mother's mother taught me that. Grandmother Athinne was kind to me, but that particular lesson was a cruel one. Crueler than cruel.

I had seen how one god-king can unmake another. I would rule until the work was done and the Vine restored. I estimated that the work would take two centuries, maybe longer. Although it was never my purpose, I had plans to ensure my longevity.

I still do.

My siblings should have lived. Their families, too. Athinne had ordered me to secure my rule——but that should not have required their deaths. I had a choice. Every one of us has a choice. I chose slaughter, and it shattered my heart.

As a child, I always worried that I would break something precious. I feared to touch my newborn siblings lest I kill them with a thumb to the head or trip over my feet while holding them close. I watched them from a safe distance, wanting to hug them but afraid of myself. I watched my siblings grow and change, and in their ever-changing variety, I was reminded of my favorite fairy tales, which were tales of the ancient seasons, far away on the world where our kind evolved.

The only season I had ever known was the season of plenty, and I lived in its cradle.

The megaflora that sustained our world began at the City of the Vine, which was built around the fruiting body of the Vine——a mountain of green-and-white succulent plantflesh, not unlike the simple aloe vera that sits in a pot by so many kitchen windows, waiting to soothe a burn. Our city sat at its foothills and wreathed around its lowest stalks, while our palaces and temples draped across the higher stems. From this holy mount, the Vine reached across the entire world. Its farthest shoots crawled up the glass walls that ring the world, green fingers that curled higher than most mountains.

Centuries ago, when the world thrived and I was young, a child's abilities——if any——with the seven magicks were measured at the age of ten, and if any were found to be present, then appropriate instruction was arranged. Some children expressed aptitude earlier, and as one might surmise, they received an accelerated education. Nearly half of my siblings were such prodigies, and they were celebrated for the occasion.

To show such a talent was to become an adult, no matter the age. Children without talent became adults at thirteen, a tradition that endured from Earth itself.

At six, my sister Raclette mastered the martial enchantment when she poisoned our music tutor with a rock and a toy sling. Tilcept-Arri, whose command of the elements nearly rivaled my own, had lit Mother's *pre-world* vintage shawl on fire when tugging on it failed to earn her attention. Zincy, our eldest, showed their talent for the cantrips of bureaucratic magick at the age of seven, when they trapped a server in the illusion of a procedural time loop at breakfast and ate sweet corn masitas until they threw up all over the table.

My siblings' accidental transitions into adulthoods, being much celebrated, made it difficult for me to understand Father's violent reaction to my own . . . manifestation.

On my sixth birthday, my tutors threw me a party. Mother stopped by for a cocktail and showed me what kindness my father allowed, for he was jealous of her love. My younger siblings attended, and brutish Esk-Ettu, who was older but always my champion.

We sat on stools at short tables, eating cake while Mistress Carol inflated long ball-johns with mighty breaths and then twisted them into the shapes of animals. Though the floor of the playroom was laid with black and gold tiles, and four of its seven walls built from sandstone and walnut, the three remaining walls were carved into the Vine itself——as one often saw in the palaces above the City of the Vine——and chlorophyll-filtered sunlight colored my white smock green.

The room glowed. I was happy. Everyone wore a smile except Mistress Besset, who fended off my older brother. All of nine, Esk-Ettu would not leave Besset's weighty breasts alone, but kept grappling with her big nipples that no amount of fabric seemed to be able to conceal. She looked miserable, but Esk-Ettu laughed like a lion roaring. He was my hero.

Squeals soon broke out as Mister Fastness produced finger paint, a last resort in the arsenal of children's entertainment. We began to play, each defacing a canvas of Vine or walnut or sandstone with our fancies. Esk drew a dick and laughed like an idiot.

For my own drawing, I picked black paint, which I thought would most resemble charcoal, pencil, or ink. I dipped the nail of my little finger into the jar, careful not to get any on my skin. Finger painting was meant for the younger children, and I'd been learning to work with proper media.

I brushed my nail across a luminous green wall, tracing a thin black line. The skin of the Vine felt as warm as my own. Where my finger touched the Vine, I was surprised to see that sparkles of gold whorled beneath the Vine's membrane. Bright light pinwheeled and orbited my fingertip wherever I moved it.

I must have made some noise of joy. It was always my joys that proved most dangerous.

Someone gasped. Then another. I remember ignoring them. On the wall of Vine, beneath my fingers, a purple symbol pulsed into view, circling around my index finger. Giggling with delight, I spidered my fingers across the wall, drawing arcs of gold as the purple sign grew larger. It throbbed in place now, squiggles and blobs constrained within a square shape. I knew that the purple sigil had some meaning, and turned to ask Mistress Carol what it meant.

Then a hand grabbed my arm, twisting it until it hurt, and I was lifted up and carried away. It was Father, come to my party at last. I felt something pop in my shoulder and screamed.

"Do you understand what you've done, you little shit?" he shouted, dragging me from my party by my wrist.

"What damage you could have done to our world, you unworthy ejaculate! Our *world*, Amaunti. You nearly shunted the northwestern aggregate. An eighth of the world would have been without potable water." He frowned, then pulled me into a close hug. His smooth hand felt hot cradling the back of my head. I smelled his fear.

"What did you do?" He rocked me as if I'd begun to cry, though I hadn't. "This is not another prank, Amaunti. You almost summoned the Beast of——" He cut off. What had I almost done? How desperately I wanted to know. "This time, my son, you have made yourself a true monster."

One remembers the first time one is called a monster. Father pressed his liver-colored lips into a single line, and his perfume stung my eyes. Just one carefree moment had branded me a monster. The word would haunt me——it haunts me now.

After Father left, I lay still as the dead on my bed, my thoughts raging against my father's abuse. I had only painted on the wall, like everyone else! I had done nothing monstrous at all, yet I wanted to sob into my pillow as I had done any number of times before. Holding back my rage and humiliation, I kept my little face still and dry, and my bed felt very small.

I fell asleep dreaming of hands that cradled the world, of monsters without names and beasts without faces.

I spent the next four years locked away in a tower of stone, where every effort was made to teach me to control myself, the monster.

By the time I was grown, I had seen that my father's weakness was the actual monstrosity, and I took steps to preserve our world from his failures. My grandfather and I had seen eye to eye, and we had both disagreed with my father. When the seven superlatives sang the Grown Crown from my father's skull and made him the Son of the Vine, Grandfather's era of cautious, vigilant respect for the Vine came to an end. The truth about the Vine's mortality was buried, all work and research stopped and destroyed——if the world was to survive, that work, that research, would have to begin anew, and all the while, the Vine's unseen rot spread, making its resurrection less and less possible.

Father took no steps to ensure our survival, for the idea that our survival required any action at all terrified him——and so I followed the long, long path to restore the Vine. I slaughtered my family to cement my sovereignty. I did it.

One by one, they died for me. Some with tears in their eyes, others with bald hatred. Esk-Ettu, curse his loving heart, went willingly. I told him this path was one I must walk alone, and I told him why.

"You will always be my brother." Answers came so easily to Esk. He thought and spoke with his heart. "And I will never abandon you."

We held the knife together as it slipped between his ribs.

I tore the heart from Father's chest, and then I crowned myself. A prodigy, I had mastered all seven forms of magick. I needed no superlatives from the seven disciplines to sing the Grown Crown from my skull. I sang myself to godhood and the monarchy. How I must have terrified those who survived my apotheosis.

The remaining members of my court reached an illegal consensus. They came for me while I napped beneath a sung-wood pergola, in a garden nook all but buried beneath a thundercloud of rhododendron and crawling peony. Sunlight filtered through leaves, and palm-sized purple flowers dappled my sleeping body. A minor tendril of the Vine coiled overhead, shading the grass with loops and curls.

There, a sixfold shock cracked my bones and smothered my breath. I woke to agony and paralysis.

Spells from six of the seven magicks bound me in place as I raged. The seventh, the antimagick, came later. Seven viziers chanted wards of law and time, using the magick claimed by the bureaucracy to delay my magickal retaliation. Seven bishops recited unholy chants, to cast my soul into the stone. Seven druids broke the Grown Crown from my skull——the tine of antler, then the tine of oak, the tine of dogwood, the tine of ivory, the tine of aloe vera, the tine of blackthorn, and finally the tine of iron——the last of which cracked my skull and exposed my brain. Seven generals crossed their blades to form a star, each sword shining with the greensleeve, the poisonous battle enchantment that paralyzed my body.

Seven elemancers stilled my blood.

Seven cognoscents stole the agency from my thoughts, as if I were asleep, in thrall to a dream.

Where was the seventh magick? I felt it hold me, more tightly than any of the others——I could not work any magick of my own, so she could not be far. Mother was not a contender for the crown, so I had let her live, fool that I am. She was a joy, and as I have said, my joys tend to become brutal mistakes.

I heard some of the betrayers laugh to see the Son of the Vine helpless at last. If I'd felt this powerless at the hands of a lover, I might have thrilled at such sudden weakness. So foreign a sensation. Such unchosen submission.

This was not love, nor war——not even politics. This was the end of the world.

I thought of the path I had chosen to walk and why I had chosen it. I thought of my family and the choices I had made, and knew that my fratricides had been for nothing.

The world-dooming blasphemers lifted me, and they passed my body toward the shadowy green of the palace interior. Inside, I saw vaulted Vine ceilings ribbed with dark wood, plain ceilings made from beams of wood of a dozen shades and grains, sandstone and limestone and marble ceilings, frescoes and mosaics inspired by the sacred geometry our ancestors had once used to construct the world.

The army filled the hallways of the palace, passing me hand over hand toward the mountain-tall cathedral carved from a sunlit green stem of the Vine called Holystalk. At last, I heard the sound of the seventh magick, the antimagick, which is family. Love. Had my mother joined the coup willingly——had she *helped*?——or had this junta forced her to lend them her strength?

Seven magicks now bound me, the worst of them called family.

I heard Mother screaming, and I could not decide if she screamed *at* me or *for* me. By then, I was all that remained of her family. It could have been either. It was probably both.

The procession of sevens followed behind, holding fast their sevenfold binding.

One slip of focus, and the spells that held me would unravel, and everyone present knew that I needed but a heartbeat of freedom to obliterate them all.

The last view of anything at all that I saw with my trueborn eyes was the infinite greens of Holystalk, its distant ceilings carved so close to the rind of the Vine that great swaths glowed like stained glass, irregularities and veins marbling the skin of the Vine with whorls and logarithmic branching. The Vine needed no artists, no tiled mosaics or painted plaster to reproduce a perfect illustration of the ancients' holy mathematics.

There, on a burl of sung-wood, my slab——my *matzeva*——had been laid. I felt it cool on my legs and back; the stone prickled my skin with magick. The prickle spread and became sharp like a bed of daggers. I sobbed when I realized that the *matzeva* must have been prepared in advance, a process that took many days.

I sagged with despair. My execution had been arranged weeks ago. The fact enraged me, and rage brought me a cruel, false clarity: everything that I had done, I did for my world . . . but my world did not deserve me. It did not——these people who thought me the danger, they did not deserve to be saved.

I would correct them. Did they think me a monster? I would show them monstrosity.

Careful runes had been chiseled by viziers and blessed by priests. Druids had brushed alchemic plants and oils across the runes. The generals struck the stone with their glowing swords, chipping greensleeve poison into the *matzeva,* which began to shine. The elemancers led their adepts in a braided dance of the seven elements, and the granite shone ever brighter, colors pulsing beneath me. I could no longer see, but I could hear the cognoscents whispering observations and ruminations to keep my mind distracted, weak.

Mother wept, the antimagick of family binding me more tightly than any of the others.

I was the Son of the Vine, and the Vine itself trembled at my pain, rippling my cry across the palace, across the city, and out across the world to the barriers that walled in the sky. The ground shook, and I heard gasps and other small noises of fear.

I could not breathe. My eyes bulged, and I realized my lungs had begun to dry. They popped and hissed as I failed to exhale. The greensleeve paralyzed the larger muscles of my arms, but my hands clawed at the stone of my *matzeva* as my fingers shriveled. My gut swelled and then shrank, organs withering. My skin dried to leather; my eyes collapsed, emptied of fluid that ran down my face. My bones crumbled to dust beneath my muscles, and my muscles dissolved beneath my leathering hide. My brain blackened, rendered into fat that oiled the marble.

I died. Had I not been the Son of the Vine, death would have been enough to stop me.

The Child of the Vine is more than a position or a title. It is an actuality, a *relationship*. When I became the Son of the Vine, the Vine became my third parent. It screamed for me. It felt for me.

Now, it would die for me.

My ghost fell into the marble *matzeva,* to be bound there forever, and I reveled in a dismal glory. If I could have torn down the sky itself, I surely would have.

As my killers smote me, I begged a favor from the Vine. The Vine, a doting parent, complied without a moment's hesitation. In that stolen moment, I reached out to my divine parent and stretched myself for miles and miles and miles and, together, we detonated.

By deposing me, the usurpers had sentenced the Vine and the world to death. Nothing remained but quick mercy and a measure of revenge. I would not permit the slow execution to which a rotting Vine would condemn the world. If my world would die, then the Son of the Vine would see it die in a single stroke.

A quick death. Isn't that rich?

The explosion erupted from within the Mountain of the Vine like a volcano, a firestorm that immediately consumed the heart of the towering world-plant. The blast radius set fire to the air for miles, boiling away the rolling hills and verdant terraces that spread closest to the City of the Vine. As towers blew to dust in an instant and the heat baked soil to sand, the wailing of my grief rang out through the cables of the Vine as they shook, as they died, even to the edges of the world.

When the furnace-winds died, my slab of now-unbreakable marble lay where it had landed, at the edge of the smoking crater where the Holystalk had once grown. My *matzeva* stood nearly as erect as its architects intended, though not where or how. The charred remainder of the body of the Vine collapsed sideways onto the ruins of the city, its hundred tendrils severed. Trapped in my memorial prison, the ghost of the last Son of the Vine could do nothing but witness the death of his land.

My rage cooled, and my madness ebbed, but the monsters had taught me a new joy. There is a dark grace when mercy turns rancid. This wicked euthanasia.

But my mercy failed us, didn't it? At every step, I have served only to condemn the world to worse suffering than that which I'd sought to prevent. My spirit will survive here forever, voiceless, driven mad by an eternity of my own thoughts, as I watch the world I tried to save die, painfully, from my own wretched deeds.

I saved the world, almost. I broke the world, willingly. Now I'll watch it die.

A second calamity followed the fireball. Massive, world-spanning cables of the

Vine took months to shrivel away, and the rush of heat and poison wind killed all but a few of the survivors of the City of the Vine.

Where the Mountain of the Vine had collapsed, it had protected small pockets of the city. Here and there my enemies struggled to die, and from my prison, I could sense, could see, and I relished their torture.

The viziers who barred the doors of the remains of a garrison——they drank the last of a tainted vintage and died shrieking, gnawing on each other's tendons. The last laundress hung herself from the balustrade of a broken stairway, a noose of bedsheets around her neck. Everything died, agonized by my hidden hand.

My heartache transformed into something that I could endure without going mad. I was, after all, cursed to endure——so I embraced the horror, and I fell in love with it. While the world burned, I became the monster that my father had named me years earlier, and I delighted in the carnage. It was the time of my life: a hundred days of beaten gold gleaming in the desert sun.

It was the last of my lusts, a final sip before I would be doomed to spend forever alone——or so I believed.

The priests died last. Their cache of ciders and brandies held them out weeks beyond the others, and narcotic pomanders numbed their minds to the final ache.

Trust a priest to slip the taxman.

# 3

Caralee awoke alive, which she thought was a nice surprise. She said so, and the Son ignored her.

He climbed out of the cart to relieve himself, and Caralee did the same on the opposite side of the road. She returned to the cart to rub a handful of cable flour under her armpits, and the Son, glistening naked, appeared to be stretching, of all things. He dropped to the ground and began doing push-ups.

"This body is *strong*," he bragged as he pushed, not a bit out of breath. "Do you know how many broken, half-dead starvelings I've worn? I can't remember the last time I wore a healthy body. It's becoming *me* so easily."

Again she wondered if the Son's easy attitude toward her was genuine. Who was she to him? Nobody, surely. Whom might she connive to become, who might interest him? Confidante? Reformed rube? Enemy? *Apprentice?* Roadkill, most likely.

"So young, so ready, so full of hormones." He winked, bringing his morning exercises to a close, sweat trickling down his neck, skin the color of wet sand. He bowed to the risen sun and leapt into the cart with one hand braced on its rickety side. "I imagine it's capable of all manner of buggery. Was he a talented lover, this Joe of yours?"

Caralee blushed and turned away, faking a coughing fit. The Son took the opportunity to seize the reins and tugged till the critters roused from their rest, eight legs curled underneath them as if they were dead.

Not only did the question humiliate her, but any answer would betray her feelings—to Joe if he was still inside his own body, and to the Son as well. She sulked, icy-bottomed from scatting in a ditch. That wasn't Joe's body anymore—there was no more flickering between the two men, not even a mirage of Joe's straw-colored stubble. So the Son took Joe's strength, too? He used Joe's muscles, although he *looked* like the Son of the Vine. What he said about

Joe's . . . hormones? Would what's in his trousers belong to the Son, or to Joe? Caralee turned her head away and willed herself to disappear.

The Son puzzled at Caralee's shame. "I don't know why it should mortify you that I know your business. I've the nose of a monster. Besides, your sexual development is nauseatingly generic. You need not fear the various carnal deeds, nor their nuances. For instance—" He made a circle with his hand and moved it up and down toward his mouth, poking one cheek with his tongue. He mocked her with a gagging noise she didn't quite recognize, until she did. "Blech-ech-ugh-blurlge-gup. Like that."

*Monster.*

"Fuck you," Caralee muttered, climbing into the cart beside him.

"Oh, I've *been* fucked, Caralee Vinnet," he reminisced, poking at her pique. "*So* hard, though I like gentle fucking better. Soft but ruthless is best. Soft, ruthless, and relentless." He exaggerated his sigh, broadcasting his fucking wisdom to taunt Caralee with the depth and breadth of his erotic experience. The Son seemed happiest when talking about himself, though she supposed that wasn't such a surprise. He may have been women, but he began as a man.

"Enough of you." Caralee sulked while the Son mocked her and whipped the critters to a skitter. The sun no longer hid below the horizon, and the spangled night sky continued its slow lightening. The starbirth clouds faded away, and soon only the daylight stars remained.

That morning, when they'd woken, Caralee had looked to the Son for some vestige of Joe, but saw none. Her heart ached to see a glimpse of Joe's wide shoulders as the Son stretched, but Joe was gone, replaced by a pretty, wicked stranger.

The Son's body was more beautiful than any body Caralee had ever seen, even though it wasn't the kind of beauty that tickled Caralee's fancy. She liked a big and strong man with a heart of jelly. The Son's body was dagger-perfect and attractive as a matter of simple fact—she didn't deny he had the looks of a legend—but she liked *more* to her man and a kindness the Son could never have.

Kindness lives in the body. Caralee could see it in the turn of a head and the slouch of a shoulder away from an unkind word, in the quickness to leap up and help another, in the way big hands can touch you soft as a kiss. Caralee didn't know what it was, exactly, that she saw when the Son moved, but it wasn't kindness. He hid himself too well.

"Oh, I nearly forgot." The Son, who forgot nothing, looked to Caralee with mischief. "I have a present for you. Consider it a reward for not embarrassing yourself with a *broom*." He shook his head. "Good-*ish* behavior should be rewarded, and here's hoping you've learned that lesson, little assassin. If not, I can always beat you again."

From beneath Joe's jacket, which sat between the Son's booted feet, he pulled a bundle of decaying leather and handed it to her. Did he have a stash underneath that jacket?

"Nicked it from my last body. She had no more use for it, and I don't need one."

Caralee turned the thing over and over. It was rectangular and real leather. Real skin, anyway. A clasp held it closed, fashioned from a wooden peg and a loop of wicker. She tugged it open, unwrapping the leather that folded around the whole thing twice. Inside, she found a bound sheath of rectangular leaves, yellowed and thin, each the same size as the others. It was . . .

*A book.*

Beneath the leather wrapping, the book's pages were as naked as the Son, if paler. Caralee ran her fingers over the grain of the page. Fine as sanded wood—not at all like the stalky pulp she'd seen in Mag's ledgers, or the decomposing lesson-book that Marm-marm taught from.

"What's this?" she asked, and then, when he opened his mouth: "I *know* it's a book. But it's blank."

"You're the smart girl—sorry, smart young woman. What do you think a blank book means?" he sassed her, which was different from mean—more like how Joe would act, which confused Caralee. "It means it's *your* book, to fill with whatever you like."

"What do I fill it with?" Caralee couldn't imagine. Her heart was broken, but her mind was free—an impossible situation for anyone and a special flavor of torture for her.

The Son turned his head and looked at her, sizing her up for something. He let a moment pass before he spoke, although he did not answer her question. Not straightaway, at least.

"I'll share something with you of my past." He ruffled his dark hair with one hand, the other holding the reins. His expression went just a bit distant, as if he stood in a doorway looking at the room beyond.

"My past. Sharing it with an excremental dollop such as yourself is a gift rarer by miles and magnitudes than any book, so listen as closely as your runty brain stem will allow, and don't interrupt unless you want your skull smashed against your monument to scaffolding." He turned his head to point his chin at the towering stele growing smaller behind them, golden in the morning sun. He chuckled, and it was mean.

Caralee nodded in agreement. A tale from the Land of the Vine?

*Of course I'll listen.*

The Son waved a palm out to one side and began his story:

"At my sixth birthday party, I touched a wall of the Vine—in addition to walnut and sandstone, our playroom had walls made of the rind of the Vine itself. Most of the architecture in the City of the Vine incorporated such pastiche, out of both piety and necessity—the Mountain of the Vine was plant, not stone, but the City of the Vine was a mountain town all the same—our boulevards and palaces were garlanded about and within its green-skinned bulk, and bored through the white flesh in its colossal middle.

"Mind you, we weren't forbidden from touching the Vine, which would have been near impossible to avoid, anyway—on the contrary, a brush of the hand against the Vine was considered an act of reverence.

"However, for a Child of the Vine and their immediate family, the Vine responded to touch much the way Oti and Atu here answer when you flick their reins. A touch from the god-monarch or their kin would call up an interface—which is a kind of complicated set of reins, that we used by tracing their fingers along the skin of the Vine, rather than whipping a rope back and forth. With this power, we could administrate almost any function relative to the Vine: track the distribution of resources worldwide; initiate repairs or shutdowns; manipulate local or worldwide weather; manipulate local or worldwide plant and animal life; and even summon mighty helpers called the Beasts of Care, who could accomplish tasks that human and Vine could not."

*Beasts of Care.* That was a part of history that Caralee had never heard of before. She wondered if there was anyone living who had.

"When I was very young—too young—I brushed the dark, lime-green skin of the vine in the playroom. Its rind was rough and porous. When I stroked the Vine, my finger left a trail of gold light. This had never happened before, and I was too young then to have seen my grandfather, the Most Holy Son of the Vine, using the interface—nor any of his functionaries.

"Naturally, golden finger-light would delight any six-year-old, and I painted wild lines across the wall that glowed before fading. My siblings, our friends, and our caretakers were all enraptured by the display. None of them knew the first thing about bioengineering or cryptobotanical programming, let alone the intricacies of the *metaflora mundus*, the World-Tree, our Vine."

"Not so my father, the Lord of a Thousand Names, heir to the Grown Crown. He was late for his appearance at my party—an appearance was more than his usual effort—but of course he walked in just as all smiles had turned to me, and just as I had lost myself in the happy wonder of this new treat.

"I had focused on making tight spirals of golden light, and at their centers, a purple or violet shape had begun to appear. It was a sigil—which is a square squiggle that represents a word or concept—and my father entered the playroom just in time to see it.

"He was a jealous man, at times petty, but fiercely responsible in his way. Often wrong, but not that day.

"The next thing I knew, Father was dragging me out of the playroom and down the hallway. He was shouting, and I was crying. He had broken bones in my hand and dislocated my shoulder. Later, I learned that I had almost awakened one of the Beasts of Care, those mighty creations I mentioned, which for the most part sleep deep beneath the ground—for the world is much, much deeper than it is wide, and although we live at its very top, most of what lies beneath us is made of metal and fire and materials the nature of which were forgotten generations before I was born.

"The nature of the Beasts is benign—they were designed to maintain the world—but in the hands of a six-year-old at play? Any number of disasters could have occurred. Father was right to be furious, and terrified, and jealous—no potential heir had ever displayed such an ability at such a young age. It was the first sign of my power, which to our knowledge the world had never before seen.

"I spent the next four years locked up in a pretty tower receiving an education according to an emergency curriculum. I was allowed seventeen stories of lovely libraries and work spaces and barred windows and not so much as a fern to water. Father killed my cat—still not sure why. My family was allowed visits, but my instructors were locked up with me, poor souls.

"The experience was brutal and necessary, and it is one of the few acts for which I do not blame or hate my father."

The Son stopped talking, finally, and Caralee realized her jaw had been hanging open for who knows how long. The Land of the Vine sounded . . . she didn't have words.

*Bet I'd have words if I'd been locked in that tower.* It sounded like the best thing ever, being *forced* to learn all about everything.

The Son looked at her blankly. He blinked.

"Wow," Caralee said, picturing a mountain of greens, from pale to dark, that sprouted stalks thick enough to fit through the hole in the stele under which they'd spent the night—a plant big enough that a whole city wrapped around it, with palaces at the top.

"But what does that have to do with this?" She held up her journal with both hands, careful not to ruffle the pages.

The Son closed his eyes and took a patient breath before explaining.

"In the Land of the Vine, the first signs of adulthood were taken at face value. If your furrow bled, or if your cock-a-vine shot white, if you killed a rival or grew a garden or broke a horse, if you raised your siblings after your parents died, if you left your family behind to start your own life—then you were *adult*. I found my adulthood at my sixth birthday party and spent four years learning my own nature."

He smiled at her—a direct smile with that piercing, uncomfortable eye contact—and it was a dazzler for its charm.

"Now, you've found your adulthood. You left home behind; you made a bargain with a god-king; you swore an oath; you fought a battle; you picked a fight you will *never* win." The Son looked her up and down, squinting at her head and grimacing at her filthy feet. "Never mind your uneven tits or your skinny legs, your fat wrists and ugly face—forget your whining and your crying and your adorably suicidal notions concerning my unmaking. Forget that thing you do with your lip! You, Caralee Vinnet, are a grown-up—a shitty and worthless adult, as are the majority—but if she has the means, then an adult should keep a journal, or at least have a journal to feel remorseful for not keeping regularly."

Caralee turned the pages of her book. Each one was as perfect and empty as the next. The Son had given her a gift beyond price; he saw straight through to the heart of her. At the same time, he offered insults that missed her heart by miles. And a beating that hadn't missed a mark, though he'd never touched her, not once.

"I don't understand. I tried to kill you? A buncha times. You stole my only friend."

"And now I've given you a journal." The Son looked at her to see what she would make of that odd list.

He handed her something smaller. "Now, here is something just as rare as paper: a real pencil. That's graphite in the center—it's made from charcoal and wrapped around with fine-grade wicker and some variety of insect silk. Keep it sharp, and it'll last you awhile."

"Wossit do?" Caralee looked at the thing. Straight, yellowish, with a tip as dark as cable char.

"You write and draw with it." He took a moment. "Oh. You're not illiterate, are you? Words? Can you read and write them? Look at you—you must be illiterate. Just draw, then. . . . Drawing means—"

"Marm-marm taught us letters, even if I was the only one who paid any mind."

The Son took a breath and let it out slowly—he seemed relieved and a little astonished. "Surprises abound. Then you write your feelings, your doings, your plans and fears and hopes. Draw the same, or follow the line as your hand sees fit. You'll keep a record of your thoughts and sights, preserved in the pages of your journal."

"Ha!" Caralee laughed in his stupid, flawless face. "You killed everyone you knew. You murdered the world. You live forever, stealing the body of whoever's convenient. When did you last give anyone a gift?" She bit her lip. "Let alone *three* gifts?" She would write down the Son's coming-of-age story at the very first chance she got.

"Corrections, in order." The Son of the Vine cleared his throat. "I only killed those who chose to die, or crossed me, or stood in my way; the world was broken long before I was born; no one lives forever; and it's *whomever.*"

"Got it." Caralee nodded once, just like he had, which earned her a smile. He liked it when she mimicked him. "You really gonna be my schoolmarm now?"

"I think I am, worm." He grinned. "For the moment."

She kept her face lowered, but she bared her teeth in a smile as the critters pulled the cart down the road, eastward. It wasn't a happy smile, more like she was pulling back her lips to sharpen her teeth. Even as she did so, Caralee worked over all the angles of her situation. Looking for a weak spot in her logic, or in his; looking desperately for signs of Joe in the Son's face, and looking even more desperately for herself, the sudden adult. She'd said she wasn't a girl, but that didn't mean she knew what or who she'd become instead, did it?

Caralee Vinnet, *journalist*. She hadn't expected that. What surprises waited beyond the only road she'd ever known?

Then came a darker question: What mattered more—who Caralee loved, or what she could learn?

*Isn't it convenient, teaching me to write down my thoughts where he can read them. Or is it really just his way of marming?* The grit or the gruel, as folk said back home whenever two choices were equally scatty.

"No one's ever really *talked* to me before," Caralee said. "No one's ever given me anything before, not even when I made the sand itself dance better than any goon-eyed sandymancer ever could. I'm as good as ten of those candle-backed buttfuckers!"

"Hey, now," eased the Son of the Vine, reaching out as if to stop her. He barked once with laughter at some hidden thought. "The world all but runs on buttfucking. Where are you going with this?"

"Why would a legendary prince, a monster out of telling-tales, wag his stolen tongue at Caralee Vinnet, let alone give her gifts? Only real book I've seen is Marm-marm's schoolbook. Mag's ledger is more a mess of dried, flattened, bleached scat."

She turned the virgin pages one at a time; marveling.

When the Son spoke, it was gently. "Marm-marm didn't tackle the boogeyman. Marm-marm didn't try to scour him away with fucking *dirt*. Marm-marm didn't swear an oath to hound the aforementioned boogeyman to the edges of the broken world and win back her friend or doom all three of us in the attempt."

Caralee aimed to learn from the Son. She'd be stupid not to. Well, less stupid—a smart woman would run.

"Where *are* you going, anyway?" Caralee changed the subject, unable to face the idea of being heroic when she knew that wasn't it—she was just more reckless than she was scared.

"Going?" The Son breathed deeply, and Caralee realized that she'd been waiting to hear Joe's loud and grumbly sigh, and it stung her to hear the Son's restrained exhalation instead. "I need to know where I *am*, first. Then, what kind of world I made." He picked at a loose string on the shoulder of Joe's sun-bleached jacket. "No plans possible before basic orientation."

The Son frowned at his dark and broken sky.

"Welp." She cocked her head behind them, northwestward. "Your home is back thataway."

"*You* have a home. I own the world." The Son wasn't talking down to her, not this time, just telling the truth. It would be easy to believe him. "That's something more and something less than having a home, truth be told."

Mischief rippled across the Son's expression, and he cut eyes at Caralee. Then he leaned forward and half stood, crouching with a staggered stance. He stretched out his arms, and something inside Caralee's chest began to hum. His arm span was wider than the cart itself, and Caralee was forced to lean back a little when he raised his hand. The reins were on the floor, and she had to scoot her foot around them so that she could grab ahold.

The Son held each hand outside the toothy-planked sides of the cart, palms facing down. Atu and Oti skittered on.

The humming inside Caralee's rib cage grew into a drumbeat. She felt its rhythm separate and different from her heartbeat, and though it was a strange sensation, it did not frighten her. It was sandymancy—but Caralee had never guessed that it could feel this . . . big.

She held her breath, eyes wide to see just what the monster could do.

"Caralee, I am the child of all bounty. When I sing, every mote of this world responds in harmony."

Easy as breathing, two pillars of sand rose from the road to touch the Son's outflung hands. His power kept them shaped like two straight columns, perfectly still as if the cart had pulled to a stop midway through two stone posts. Within the borders of their shapes, the pillars were two storms of whirling dust, moving exactly as quickly along the road as the cart itself. Caralee admitted to herself that she couldn't have conjured anything nearly as tidy.

The Son stood to his full height with his arms stretched wide, and the columns rose accordingly, all the while keeping steady pace beneath his hands as the burden-critters pulled the cart forward at a clip.

*Show-off.*

Oti and Atu paid the sandymancy no mind. It never did seem to bother them.

Caralee splayed her fingers over her lap, imagining how to tune and tighten her control over the sand. Her sandysense seemed something like sight and something like touch, but was neither, and with it, she not-saw and not-felt how the Son kept those pillars so perfectly level. Caralee would have had them dragging behind her like two loose ropes, but the Son's power pulsed slowest just beneath his palms while beating faster farther down, spinning tighter control where he wanted it.

That was the *opposite* of what Caralee'd been doing. When she summoned Dustbutt, Caralee imagined that her hands were dying of thirst and the sand was water, sucking him up quick from the ground and controlling tightly below her fingers. But if instead she formed the mannikin by lifting the ground from beneath, rather than pulling it toward her hands from above, Dustbutt could have stolen the sandymancer's show from the start.

Caralee hadn't ever given much thought to *how* her magick worked. Marmmarm's book listed nothing on the subject, and there was no one in the village who knew anything about it. Tabbin Talc the sandpainter might have been of some help, but he'd passed away when Caralee was wee. Fanny Sweatvasser would have "some thoughts" and then Caralee would get in trouble for kicking her in the shins.

Watching the Son brandish his power, Caralee rubbed her hands together and wondered why she'd never put one and one together before: the sandy-mancy didn't come from her fingers, so why pretend that it did?

Then, mind rolling on before she could catch up to her thoughts: *Could I* lift *the Son outta Joe's head, insteadda suck?* If she did that, Caralee might end up with eyeballs on her shmata, and it was no good if Joe didn't have a face.

Joe was definitely gonna need a face.

The Son roared into the wind until his cheeks reddened and the tendons in his neck bulged like a bundle of cable fibers. There were no words, just a howl of freedom and fury centuries in the building. The silence after his voice died was its own kind of thunder.

Caralee pulled her elbows in close to herself, trying to stay small. After a moment, the Son dropped his hands, and the pillars of sand flew away like veils on the wind. He sat. "This world is mine, till the day I die and return to the soil beneath our feet."

"You're gonna die? *You?* You're gonna go in to the dirt?"

"One cannot forever enjoy all this fucking and killing and ruling. Even a god-king will fade." He paused. "I told you—no one lives forever."

Caralee thought about that. Fucking and killing and ruling.

"Oh? Are we a curious cat?" the Son asked, whatever a cat was. "What desultory questions are hiding behind your lips, darling wizard?"

Caralee didn't want to ask, but there *was* something. Since the Son seemed to know her thoughts, she wasn't surprised when he pressed her on the matter of rutting.

"Well . . ." Caralee found herself shy again, struggling to find the right words without sounding like a chuckleheaded girl. Almost, it was like she had Joe back again, along with that sweet and hopeless *want.*

"Oh. Oh!" The Son looked at Caralee blushing and smiled with his whole face. "Oh, curious virgin, I do like you." He laughed, and that beastly thunder rolled again. "Spit it out, Caralee Vinnet."

"Shaddup. It's just that . . . I mean you carry on about the fucking more than the killing or the ruling, and I wondered . . ." She struggled to finish the question and squeezed her nails into her palms, angry at her bashfulness.

"You wondered if so legendary a slut as myself might impart a few words of wisdom to his unpenetrated guide?"

*Sands, he talks filthier than the shatterscat ditch.* Which was pretty filthy, being the village toilet *and* the critters' feeding trough.

"Naw that ent it well maybe a little but mostly I was thinking—"

"If my life before and after eight hundred years of body-thieving has afforded me certain insights into the pleasures of the flesh?" He liked to taunt her, which reminded her of Joe, which was altogether too close to the subject of conversation for Caralee's liking.

"Look, I'm just saying—if I were a prince, right?" She flexed and preened, sucking fake kisses. "And I was all charming and talented at turning folk to my purposes? And, even if my perfect muscular body wasn't what my sweetheart were chomping at, I could slip into another body as easy as my shmata?" She tugged at her shapeless sack.

"Caralee, you are more dangerous than I had hoped!" The Son of the Vine clapped his hands and leaned back into the morning sunshine, while the burden-critters followed the smell of scat that marked the road.

"Well?"

The Son said nothing, kept his gaze steady, his abdominal muscles tense and taut beneath Joe's open shirt. Caralee held out hope that Joe fought against his invader, and if she tried, she could picture Joe's body where the Son's now sat. Blond chest hair thick as a beard. Pale and and hairless skin on a form smaller but more densely muscled. One born there, one *insisting* on being there. One she wanted, one she had. One safe, one dangerous—but full of everything that Caralee had ever wanted. Except Joe.

Her thoughts couldn't chase each other in circles like this; she'd get nothing done.

"Tell me something I couldn't learn from a living . . . from anyone else."

"Well asked. In fairness to the living, I couldn't steal flesh until after they'd killed me, and as you might imagine, the wasteland isn't exactly a closet full of lovely bodies from which to pick and choose. . . . Although there was a Patchfolk caravan guard who did the most amazing things with cold pebbles." The Son of the Vine sat up straight and squared his shoulders toward Caralee. Pinned by his gaze, her awareness shrank until it seemed that nothing existed but the two of them. The attention of the Son of the Vine could shear away the world.

*That's my first lesson from this question.* How many beauties had wetted or swollen before that solar gaze? It was easier, now, to believe that he'd once been worshipped as a living god, born from a plant that filled up the world. The Son of the Vine was well named.

"Let's start with the simple things, which you *could* learn from another living soul, but most likely wouldn't. I mean, just look at you. Besides, taking your time to learn the simple things is what makes for a fabulous fucker." He chewed his plump lower lip. "The terrible lays are the ones who try to dazzle you with too many clever tricks. Unless you're lucky, and the pebbles are smooth, and the guard's fingers aren't . . ."

"*Please.*" Caralee was almost sorry she'd asked.

"Here's your daily allowance of my fucking wisdom." He pulled Joe's shirt open all the way. Caralee half expected Joe's big pink nipples surrounded by whorls of sandy hair—but instead she saw the Son's smaller, browner nipples and his darker, nearly hairless skin.

"These?" He pointed to his nipples. "Are the key to *some* folk's wildest pleasure. Touch, lick, suck, flick, bite these, and you might bring them to climax with little else." He held up two fingers in warning. "However, some feel nothing at all in their nipples, except perhaps annoyance and discomfort. If you keep at it, you'll bore them, which is death to lust. So *ask* first, as you begin, but not too keenly. Keep your question soft, insistent, and above all, *eager.*"

"Oh, all right." *Ask about nipples.* "Is that all?"

"*Is that all?* I teach you a cornerstone of capturing and keeping a lover, and you want more? That's enough for now." He clapped, as casual as a real person.

*Is he a real person?*

Time and road rolled on, smelling of dried scat, in silence. Eventually, Caralee asked another question.

"Is my Joe in there, at all?"

The Son shook his head. His jaw was set.

"Liar. I saw him fighting against you. And . . . and for a little bit, I could still see his face underneath yours. Know what I think? He was in there enough to struggle, when you stole him. I don't think he's done fighting, and you're a lying monster, so I don't know why I'd even bother."

"Why would I lie? Why would I need to? You're nothing—and now, so is Joe." The Son seemed genuinely baffled by the question. "For what it's worth, he felt no pain."

"Don't." Caralee let tenderness into her voice, though it cost half her pride, and she scraped her nails across the skin of her forearms.

"It was as peaceful as dying in your sleep. I swear it on my own heart. Does that help?"

*How could that ever help?*

"Sorta," Caralee lied. "So he can't hear me?"

"No. He'll never hear anything again." The Son brushed his long black hair from his face—the dust of the road had settled and dulled its midnight gloss. "He went to sleep, and now he's gone."

In the distance, the blue roofs of Comez appeared as a dot of color below the beige horizon.

"You need to hear this." The Son touched Caralee's hand. "It's unhealthy for you to maintain an attachment to this body. It's mine now." He paused, like a sandfisher before the kill. "What's mine is mine, forever."

*Liar.*

"Keep fighting, Joe. You keep fighting him, y'hear?" She wondered if this was the time to play coy and decided it wasn't. "I love you, dunderhead, and I'm not letting you go. You hear me, Joe Dunes?" Her eyes got wet.

"Enough of that." The Son's voice took on an edge. "Stop talking to my wardrobe; you're embarrassing yourself."

*They both know that I'll never give up, and I know a lie when I hear one.* Caralee huffed.

"Attaboy, Joe. He ent nothing but another fella, and a fella's just as strong as his heart." She met the Son's gaze and didn't shrink. "Joe, you got more heart than this jazzed-up ghost. More heart than ten of him."

"I said *enough.*" He did not like this subject.

Caralee sulked in silence for the next hour, wondering, plotting, and fearing. They closed the distance to Comez.

"What's that?" The Son of the Vine pointed to what looked like any other broken-branched treebone, only this one was black and no taller than a man . . . and waving.

*Naw.*

Caralee squinted, then groaned. Black robes, crooked spine: she'd bet ten shekels that the waving black treebone wore candles on its shoulders and had a bad attitude.

*Shatterscat. That mean old man lost his caravan already?*

"If you asked him, he'd tell you that he was a wizard. Ask me, he ent anything but a fraud," she said. "You can kill him any way you wanna, and I won't tell."

"You *know* it?" the Son asked. "That's . . . a person?"

"Ayup. Oh, he thinks he knows all about you, that one does."

Caralee's nightmare mentor smiled and didn't stop until they reached the black treebone.

Eusebius Gibberosus Kampouris stood in the middle of the path with his arms crossed, the thin candles waxed onto his black-feathered shoulder pads burning feebly under daylight. Mag's cart rolled to a stop and spat forward a puff of dust, which parted for the sandymancer despite drifting around and above him. That was a trick of sandymancy that was unfamiliar to Caralee, and his cloth-a-bare robes remained spotless. His black feathered collar caught the sunlight and shimmered with purples and greens.

The gnarly figure craned his neck up to meet their faces and pursed his lips. When he did, the cloud of dust that had parted around him collapsed to the ground at once, as if each speck became as heavy as a stone—another trick of sandymancy that Caralee didn't yet know, but would work out for herself now that she'd seen it.

The Son sucked his teeth. Caralee felt his muscles tense. Eusebius blinked his black-painted eyelids at them—the know-it-all sandymancer stood before the villain of his favorite, unfinished tale, and he hadn't a clue. Caralee liked that. She liked that very much.

*What will the Son think of our wizard?* Not much, Caralee predicted. Eusebius looked like one of the mannikins folk set up in the cable fields to frighten away scavenger beasties.

How could this old critter think himself a better wizard than she? Even if she'd only had her first *real* lesson in sandymancy today, watching the Son raise his twin sand pillars, Caralee knew that between herself and Eusebius, she was the better sandymancer. She had some learning to do, sure, but she was *better.* That was another fact that she knew for truth in her bones.

The sandymancer took a few steps forward on his bloated feet, his joints popping, and turned his head southeast, toward the bright blue clay roofs of Comez—but Eusebius wasn't the only oddity the Caralee and the Son had found along the road. Some distance beyond the wretch in black robes, on the side of the road, stood—of all things—a metal *door.*

Just a metal door, plain as daylight, built on the side of the road, standing there without a building for it to be door-like and do door things for, though it was set over three steps of freshly cut wood. The door looked harmless but weird because, well, it was a door and the road was a road, and Caralee didn't think roads needed doors?

The freestanding door was made of dull gray metal, set in a doorframe of the same material, and its surface was flat and plain. Caralee had seen metal tools and metal jewelry, but she'd never seen this *much* metal, certainly not in one single piece. The three steps leading up to the door from the road made it that much weirder, like someone had begun building a house the wrong way.

*Where'd they get the wood?* Nice, brown wood like that didn't come from anywhere nearby. Who'd go to all the trouble to build three steps out of wood that must have come from kilometers and kilometers to the east?

Caralee hopped out of the cart to take a better look at the door, ignoring Eusebius—which was what he deserved—and the Son followed her, stepping over the side of the cart with his long legs and only a hand to brace himself.

The sandymancer cleared his throat in polite confusion as they walked past him without so much as a nod.

No walls had been built on either side of the out-of-place door, but Caralee could peer around the doorframe easily, which seemed to defeat the purpose of a doorway. *Something* lay on the ground behind the door—what seemed like a pathway, or the floor of a hallway or, maybe, some fallen ladder? Whatever it was, the ladder-on-the-floor thing looked like it was made out of a shinier metal than the doorway and, like a ladder, was made of straight rods and crosswise rungs, beneath which the ground showed gray and gritty as everywhere else.

Walking around the seemingly useless door, Caralee saw that the ladder-hallway-thing was more like a narrow road, and it ran off to the north in a straight line. Much farther away, it began to curve toward the northeast, lit by the sun to become a shining arc near the horizon. On the back side of the door, there were no steps down, so the front steps and the whole getup made even less sense. Did you open the door and then jump down onto the ladder-road, and wouldn't you risk breaking an ankle on the road-ladder's metal rungs?

If it was a road, it looked like no road Caralee had seen before. What did a road need a door for, and what good was a door without walls? Even the dead gardens back home had walls. Granted, the garden walls didn't do much these days, but they had been built to serve an obvious function, even though the gardens themselves were long gone. Nothing about this strange door and its stranger road seemed obvious.

"What is this thing?" the Son asked her.

Behind them, Eusebius cleared his throat.

"It's metal," she said. "A lot of metal. Is it sandymancy or something, do you think?" Maybe if you opened the door, it took you somewhere else? That would be *terrific,* and Caralee resisted the temptation to imagine the places that a magick door might lead.

*Anywhere but here.*

"What is a door doing on the side of my road?" the Son asked Caralee.

"Well," Caralee began, "it wasn't here last time we hauled the cable harvest this way." And she'd surely have heard of a weird metal door if Joe had seen it without her. "Weird door. Weird metal."

"It's not a door," said the Son, "and it's not weird metal. It's tin."

"How're you gonna say that door ent a door? It's a door! It's *one* door, not ten."

"Tin, not ten. Please use those massive platters you call ears; they protrude for a reason." The Son frowned at the metal door. "Tin," he mused. "It's a tin ramp."

He chewed his lip, and Caralee saw his gaze tracing the metal road that curved off to the northeast.

"Who built this so recently, then?" The Son looked down at Caralee, then over toward Eusebius, and then southeast to Comez. "None of *you* built this."

*Nope. We didn't,* Caralee agreed, looking up at the cracked sky.

"Bet it was them metal folk."

"The metal folk who fractured my firmament?"

"No, the *other* ones," she sassed, snorting back laughter and wondering what firmament was.

*Dunderhead.*

Eusebius chose that moment to greet them, stepping forward, though he bit back a wince at each step. If sandymancers really did summon water into their feet to show off their control of the elements, Caralee thought this was a stupid way to do it. She wiggled her sandaled toes and grimaced at the notion.

They turned as one to sneer at the sandymancer, and the Son raised a hand to guard Caralee. Without bothering to whisper, he said to her, "Please behave out of character for a moment, and let me speak. This could be something . . . I don't know *what* this is."

"I know what it is," Caralee grumbled. "It's a git, is what it is."

"Not the git, the tin ramp," the Son corrected her. "Memorize its details, then sketch it later in your journal."

"Fair day, fair strangers!" Eusebius cawed, sounding every bit like Caralee thought a crow-bird-man should sound. The sandymancer pulled his body as straight as he could, then sagged back into the shape of a charred treebone—its trunk kinked, its branches knotted, with big ugly burls for feet. Beside him sat a deep wheelbarrow, with a cracked handle for pushing. It seemed to be filled with odds and ends—satchels and hardtack and one rolled-up carpet that sagged over the handle.

The Son shot Caralee a warning glance, reminding her of his order to she shut up and let him take the lead. That, she decided, was not going to happen.

"Oy! Eusebius!" Caralee called out in greeting. "You lost? Comez is only an hour thataway. Blue roofs, can't miss 'em. See?" She pointed to the blue roofs in the distance.

The sandymancer squinted and shielded his face from the sun with an arthritic hand. "Who knows my name?"

"I do, and you know mine, or can't you remember?" Caralee strode up to him and held out her hand. "Didn't think you'd see *me* again?" She blinked her eyes the way innocent girls did, but with a nasty twist. "I'm that *rustic delight* with *adorable wee talent.*"

Eusebius looked down at her. Despite his body's odd angles, he was still a head or more taller than she.

"Pardon me, young miss?" His painted face looked a touch affronted. "I don't believe I have had the pleasure of making your acquaintance." To the Son, he nodded with the shadow of a bow. "Most kind sir, hello."

"Cute." Caralee glanced at the Son, who wore a dangerously blank expression. "The git's pretending he doesn't recognize me."

"What. Is. This. Person." The Son did not conceal his disdain for the wizard.

"He's the only other sandymancer I've ever met. Well, besides . . ." She cocked her head toward the errant god-king.

Eusebius inspected Caralee closer, and the cart as well. "A burlap shmata, a cart filled with cable goods—are you by chance from the Nameless Run?"

*The Nameless Run* was what most folk called the land just west of Comez. Caralee's village was the first of a string of settlements that were either too desperate to bother naming or so old that their names had been forgotten.

Caralee grabbed the Son by Joe's wrist and pulled him into the conversation. "I kinda ruined his show at the village, my village, I mean. Where I live. In the Nameless Run, yeah. That's what they call it," she explained. "My village may not have a name, but it's my home, thank you very much."

"Utter nonsense, girl! You ruined nothing, I assure you. You could not possibly manage ruination, not with your little filthrat." The sandymancer hooted, still craning his neck toward nothing, but rolling his eyes toward the Son.

"Hecklers are omnipresent. All the more so when you're entertaining shit-farmers."

Caralee balled her fists and checked a genuine impulse to kick the greasy-headed bastard in the shins until his legs snapped off.

"Filthrat? His *name,*" she growled, "is Dustbutt. He's a dust hare. Fucker."

Eusebius had twisted his neck so far to one side that the taper burning on one shoulder threatened to singe his chin. Relaxing out of necessity, the wizard bowed to the Son again, more deeply this time. Caralee, he ignored.

"If I may present myself, most kind sir, I am Eusebius Gibberosus Kampouris, a Seeker of the second tier, inducted at the Sevenfold Redoubt into the mysteries of the Seven Corners by the late High Caller Loretta Barter Birdsong herself, may her spirit fly free from our slow damnation. It is a pleasure to make the acquaintance of a gentleman traveler such as your fine self."

The Son did not respond, letting silence linger. His mood had shifted during Eusebius's introduction. From the way the Son's brow knitted together, Caralee all but smelled storms in the air. He aimed his attention at Eusebius—Caralee knew that focus, that slice of sunlight laying bare every bit of you, erasing the rest of the world. She hoped it sliced the wizard to his jazzed-up bones.

"*Sandymancer?*" The Son turned to Caralee. "Sandy? Tell me that this creature is not a wizard, Caralee Vinnet." He pressed his palms together in a gesture Caralee didn't recognize. "I pray, I pray that I have misheard you all along, and your *sandymancer* is some sort of jester, his 'magick' mere mummery."

Knowing the answer the Son wanted was not the one he'd get, Caralee found a sudden interest in her toes. They really *were* filthy.

Eusebius answered serenely, "I assure you, sir, I am most authentic. The mysteries of the seven elements have been *fully* revealed to me, my education *long* ago completed, and my powers tested lo these *many* decades against the depredations of our *calamitous* world." The wizard did have his own brand of odd flair.

"So you're a clown." Dead in the eyes, dead in the voice. "This is no elemancer. There is no wizard in all the world so absurd as this . . . thing. I am certain. I must be. I am, always."

"Sir?" Eusebius's off-kilter bones sagged further. "I assure you that I am quite the genuine article. Surely you recognize the trappings of the famed sandymancers?"

As if to demonstrate his adequacy, Eusebius smiled with black-painted lips—and the flame from the taper on his left shoulder stretched high and higher, till it arced over his balding head and his long, stringy black hair. A line of fire slid down to touch the taper on the opposite shoulder. He steepled his palms the best he could and bowed slightly.

*Fire!* So he could do more than keep his tapers lit. *How much more?*

While Caralee gawped at the sight of new sandymancy, the Son looked like he was restraining disdain's bigger, meaner daddy.

"How disgustingly in-ter-est-ing." The Son bit the words and blinked at each syllable. "Seven magicks? These 'sandymancers' command a fraction of a single magickal discipline and have named themselves as a toddler might. *Sandymancy.* Pathetic. Once elemancy was the greatest of the seven arts, and now it's . . . this." He looked ready to vomit. "Fuck me. I might as well have stayed in my *matzeva.*"

*Seven magicks?* Caralee wondered what that jazz was about. What else was there, aside from sandymancy? *What if there are six other types of . . . magick stuff . . . that aren't anything like sandymancy at all?* She'd have to think on that, sketch it up in her journal, as to what other kinds of magick there could possibly be, beyond sandymancy.

"If I may, most kind sir," Eusebius begged of the Son of the Vine. "From whence do you hail, that you've not heard of the sandymancers of the Sevenfold Redoubt? Or perhaps you jest. Surely, most kind sir, you jest." Black-smeared eyelids widened in a comedy of hope.

Both men thought the other a joke.

*This ent gonna end well,* Caralee thought.

She all but felt the thunderclouds gather within the Son. She wouldn't be surprised if his eyes could shoot lightning. Tempting as that notion was, she stepped between the two men and held her hands up.

"Look, Son, if anyone's gonna cut this creep, it's me."

That pleased him.

Caralee wagged a finger at the white-painted wizard. "Think about what we got in common, you and me. What you said to us in your performance for, what'd you call us? *Shitfarmers?* That tale you told?" Eusebius frowned. He seemed less . . . *there* . . . than he had in the village. "Well, I went and asked the desert if there was more to the story, just like how you told us to do. Guess what." She stood shoulder to shoulder beside the Son and straightened her back. "The desert answered."

*It did, and I hate myself so much.* She tried to turn her self-loathing toward the sandymancer.

"It answered *me.* Did it ever answer *you*? Did you ever bother asking, or is that just a cute way to hide all the stuff you don't know from us nameless shitfarmers?" Caralee's anger all but boiled. Her face was hot. Everywhere she looked, she found someone to rage against: the fraud; the god; herself.

The flaming arch above the wizard's head flickered out. His tapers guttered and just barely remained lit. "So the wasteland answered your questions?" Eusebius raised a scandalous eyebrow, examining the Son's perfect, pretty face, his veil of black hair, and his tight body. "Ah, so. It most certainly *did.*"

The wizard winked at Caralee.

*What?*

"A most fetching answer, isn't he? Maybe not the answer you had sought, but a winsome gentleman is far more practical than the ending of a story that, in my learned opinion, shall never be written. The world-killer lies entombed in stone, where my predecessors left him."

Blushing and frustrated, Caralee understood the wizard's mistake. He thought she'd found a lover, not the Son of the Vine. She could hardly blame him, despite having hoped to scare the scat out of his scathole. Eusebius didn't believe her—who would?

"Well, *this* wasn't what I meant with my closing soliloquy, but then again the performance is intended to be evocative, not instructional. Antiquity aside, if I've learned one thing in my many travels, far and wide, it is that young hearts will find a way. Take care with your first love, my, eh . . . *sweet*?" Eusebius tried his best to treat Caralee as something other than a crust of filth. He wagged a yellow-nailed finger too close to her face. "What appears beautiful today may hide something rueful inside."

*How can a git be so wrong and so right?*

"Begging your pardon, most kind sir." Eusebius bowed again to the Son. Caralee was growing sick of that. "I am sure your intentions are faultless, but a young lady ought to hear *some* advice about the world, when she has never—"

"Hey, let's change the subject." Caralee pointed to the tin ramp and the shiny ladder. "What's that ten rump and the metal-bits road?"

The Son, also eager to pivot away from the insulting notion of himself and Caralee as lovers, pointed there as well, his arm parallel to hers and his head cocked at the same angle. They each cleared their throats.

"Yes, please—enlighten us, you . . . I want to say, broke-boned hedge-witch? What is this tin contraption, and what is it doing on my road?"

Eusebius faced their combined curiosity, focus, and displeasure, and a facial tic appeared beside his eye, where the makeup cracked at his crow's-feet. The wizard looked as if someone had bopped him on the head.

"I asked you a question, gelding."

The word *gelding* seemed to jar Eusebius back to his better sense. Caralee would have to remember to add that word to the list of words she didn't know and write them into her journal.

"I . . . I am not entirely certain, most kind sir." Eusebius ran a finger along the seam of the metal. "These . . . contrivances have appeared but recently. Given the timing and the materials, I think it's fair to attribute them to—"

"Yeah, yeah, the metal folk. It's *metal.* I got eyes. So what is it already?" Caralee stuck her hands to her hips.

"Not a door, though it does look like one. See the hinges, here, along the bottom." The feeble sandymancer sounded like Marm-marm. "A door or gate would have hinges on the side. I believe it's a ramp, young miss."

"We know how doors and ramps work, too. A ramp for what, though, and why here?"

"Look there, at that metal road." Eusebius pointed. "It has metal strips that could guide the wheels of some manner of wagon."

"Who wants a wagon they can't steer?" she asked.

"Someone hauling many goods a great distance," the Son answered. "Or many soldiers."

"Eh?" Eusebius bent sideways to reinsert himself into the conversation. "If I might? Perhaps in the wasteland you have not heard of the Metal Duchy."

"Only recently," the Son answered, a questing edge to his voice.

"The Metal Duchy, yes, of course he knows about it." Caralee covered for the Son. "Showed up a buncha years ago. Nobody knows where they came from, but they started coming to the markets when I was a babby. Now it's not so strange to see their trinkets mixed in with Patchfolk small goods. He knows *all* about them."

"Trinkets?" the Son asked quietly. "Just trinkets?"

"Sure, trinkets." Caralee kicked the dirt. "Jewelry and the like. Little bits of shiny stuff—they make good wire, too."

Eusebius smacked his chapped white lips. "There is *much* more to the Metal Duchy than that, which I am only too happy to share. Yes, it is true that the metal folk have only emerged from their palace within the last few decades, but the ducal palace itself fell from the void beyond the sky over a century ago." He pointed to the crack in the firmament. "My colleagues at the Redoubt have agreed upon the connection between the Duchy and that phenomenon since well before I was born, although the exact nature remains a matter of some discussion . . ."

The Son growled and crossed his arms. Both Caralee and Eusebius took a step back.

"So it's true, then, that they are not of this world?" He did not look like he wanted to trust Eusebius, but now the Son had two matching accounts of the metal folk and how they fell through the sky.

Danger lurked in his voice. Concern. Hope. The Son was desperate for *something*, but what?

Eusebius mused. "The evidence does indeed suggest that the Metal Duchy descended from the heavens. Some members of my order have posited that their arrival somehow *scarred* the sky. Others believe that particulate debris, eh, remains, ah, in the upper—"

"We get it," Caralee said, not sure that she did.

"Interestinger and interestinger." The Son looked more murderous than interested. Then with a blink and a breath, he dismissed the subject. "Farewell, hedge-witch. We move on." He returned to the cart.

"Oh, right." Caralee climbed in beside him. "We gotta make it fast to Comez, for, um, where we're sleeping."

"Ah? I'll not keep you. I've just left Comez," Eusebius dithered, anxious.

*Now he's anxious?*

"And you went back west?" Caralee questioned. That wouldn't make any sense. Eusebius seemed to have parted with his Patchfolk caravan after passing eastward out of the Nameless Run. He should be heading anywhere *but* west.

The question fazed Eusebius. He held a hand to his head and seemed to shrink. When he spoke, it was in the same freshly met tone of voice he'd used to greet them.

"Oho! Fair day, friends! Such comfort, to see other travelers upon this desolate road. Might I inquire as to your destination?"

*What the scat?*

"You already asked us that." Caralee tried not to sound mean. "Remember?"

He looked lost. Eusebius did *not* remember, she could see that. Whose memory could possibly be that bad? He blinked rapidly, then smiled a big, fake smile.

"Ah, I—yes." The wizard positively squirmed. "I seem to have gotten turned around!" He laughed so weakly that Caralee thought he might cry. "Oh, how you've rescued me from a day's travel, wasted! I shan't see you in Comez, sadly. I must hurry on!" Eusebius took his wheelbarrow by the handle. "On to, eh . . ."

"Please do so immediately," said the Son dryly as he whipped the critters into a crawl, then to a skitter, leaving the addled wizard behind, in their dust. Caralee turned to wave goodbye with a sneer that faltered when she saw the wizard following them step by wincing step, leaning on the handle of his wheelbarrow and falling farther and farther behind. Her grudge faltered. The wizard looked older than he was and weathered his poor health without complaint although his suffering was plain to see. On top of that, his confusion made Caralee . . . worried for him, of all the stupid surprises.

*Guess I'm a chucklehead, after all.*

The Son sat in silence a long while.

"Does that person strike you," the Son asked Caralee, "as the sort who would run west, when his destination lies eastward, while his edema pains him with every step?"

"I mean, the sun only rises in one place, and it only sets in one other. You think he's right in the brainpan?" She whipped the reins and brought the critters to a canter. "I wish *I* could play with fire."

"Oh, you will."

The Son glanced over his shoulder at the tin ramp and the metal road beyond it.

"I might even let you melt these metal persons right into the ground."

Caralee wasn't at all put off at that prospect. She'd melt a bunch of rampy-roady sky creatures, sure—especially if it meant learning fire sandymancy.

Sky creatures? That was another question about the Metal Duchy. Were they actual people, or were they just called "metal folk" because what else do you call a bunch of things-who-have-a-duke-and-build-stuff-outta-metal? Did they look like her? Were they made of metal, or did they just use it? Where'd they get all that metal? Did they fall from the sky on purpose or by accident? Most people don't fall on purpose, Caralee reckoned, but then again, most people weren't metally or have dukes. There were dukes and barons way up north past the sandymancers' redoubt, and a witch-queen all the way out west, across the world on the other edge of the wasteland, but none of them had anything to do with metal, or coming from someplace that wasn't the world.

And if they didn't come from the world, where could they come from? The stars and the starbirth clouds didn't look very homey, and they looked awfully small. Maybe that was why they fell?

"Wossa metal folk even doing here." It wasn't a question. Caralee wasn't asking the Son—that was one thing that he couldn't know. She just had to say it aloud, to see how the thought sounded. The thought sounded complicated.

"Metal." The Son said the word the way Caralee would say *fuck you.* "And a *duke.*"

She'd heard murder in a man's voice before, but never slaughter.

# 4

After an hour of simmering silence, the road forked. One path led south to Comez, but where the other led, Caralee had no clear idea. She'd reached the border of the world she knew. They took the road south to town, the cart rolling along the dust trail until Caralee could see the gray stone walls surrounding Comez, below the twinkle of blue roofs cozied within. Folk said the roofs of Comez were the color of the old sky, but the tiles seemed awfully bright.

Outside of the old triple gates that led into the town stood a market specializing in traveling gear and necessities, as well as a stone shed with a thatched roof so far past its prime that from within you could see the stars. Inside was space for bedrolls, and for a small fee, travelers could bunk down there to spend a night in safety before moving on.

Joe would always tease her about the comforts of Comez, partly because they were always in such a hurry to reach Grenshtepple's, and Mag would never spend the shekels for a proper room at the local inn. Joe, though, seemed to know *all about* the inn and didn't shy away from sharing every single detail with Caralee: soft pillows; roast dust hare; boiled beet stones; and *herbs* taken from out east near Lastgrown where green things still grew, and kept alive right here, in little pots.

Caralee had always thought that Joe's stories were made up to torture her with sights she'd likely never get to see. Now she wasn't so sure.

Scat, nobody even knew if Lastgrown was real, only that the land was greener the farther east you traveled and that the green grew denser and denser in one spot such that it became impossible for most folk to travel through. Those who claimed to have found their way through it told tales of wonders that were harder to accept than Joe's tales of pillows stuffed with featherdown. Living treebones taller than the steles of the Vine, plants with all the colors of the rainybow wheel, and leaves that ate your face. Crazy stuff.

Or it had been. Now Caralee knew that some crazy tales were dead true.

*Bet Joe never thought he'd be stole-up by Ol' Sonnyvine, neither.*

Joe was gone, and in his place was an ancient, evil wight. That wight was king of the world, and he listened to Caralee, and he taught her and gave her priceless gifts, and he recognized her as an adult. That wight found virtue in her strange interests, and he nurtured her wanderlust. Of course, he was also meaner than scat and probably going to kill her. Joe might have teased her, but he'd protected Caralee like nobody else, not even Mag.

Caralee had thought allegiance was an easy thing. There were people whom she loved, and there was everybody else. There was *us* and *them*. She didn't imagine that a person could be more *them* than the Son of the Vine. Yet here he was, not teasing Caralee outside the walls, but riding beside her through the gates of Comez.

The burden-critters pulled the cart past the wall of stone and through the gates of Comez, built in a three-key design, with three staggered half walls so that comers and goers had to snake their way into and out of the town. Each key could be manned and maybe had been long ago, when there was anything worth fighting over and enough people to spare for a fight.

Blood was too precious now to spill—and folk too few to station at each turn of the gates. Maybe the people of the Metal Duchy—or whatever they were—would change all that? Caralee didn't like that idea at all.

Atu and Oti took the turns through the stone keys with care and pulled the cart around the last curve of the gate. Comez had been built within a bowl of bedrock, and its streets crisscrossed that bowl in a square grid so that entering Comez from the gates at the top of the bowl meant seeing nearly all of the town at once, and Caralee's heart pounded at the sight. She all but threw herself out of the cart, her eyes as big and dark as a critter's.

They'd entered a world of colors, impossible to imagine a monochrome moment ago. Up close, the clay roofs were a brilliant blue, far more . . . colory. The streets were square-bricked and painted in stripes of red and yellow. Most of the houses were the same gray brown as the walls and gates, but some of the older buildings were built from red stone rectangles with whitish lines in between. The windows and their slatted shutters were painted a yellow ocher. Below them, Caralee saw *green* sprouting from little boxes hanging below some of the windows. Scrubby, struggling green plants, but green all the same—some even grew tiny little sunbursts of purple or white.

*Flowers!*

Coins spilled from a careless merchant's purse, the shekels ringing as they landed on neatly cobbled stones. One man played the guitar while another man sang. *Sang,* out in the open, just to nicen-up the day. People bustled here and there, but none glared at the strangers who entered through the gates—the Comezze were both too busy to care and too safe behind their stone walls to fear for their lives, day-to-day. Some of them even looked happy.

The Son sensed the excitement bubbling up inside Caralee and—perhaps for his own relief—redirected her giddiness toward something useful.

"Now we face our first true test, Caralee Vinnet," the Son counseled as the critters ambled downhill onto the main street. "Our first public appearance as a pair of travelers come to market. You will use your own name, but will address me as *sir.* You are my ward; I am your tutor. I am an eccentric; you are a *quiet* young lady."

Caralee walked alongside the cart and tried to imagine what a quiet Caralee would be like.

"Tell me," the Son asked, "is Auld Vintage still spoken?"

"Old what?"

"Do they still speak my language. *Layngooage.*" The Son drew out the word as if it were another new addition to Caralee's vocabulary. "Auld Vintage, the royal tongue?" He rolled his eyes as if he'd said something foolish. "Even then, it was only taught to scholars and students of privilege, or kept alive in the demimonde for the privacy of guttersnipes. . . . Quite a lot of overlap between those groups." He closed his eyes. "Why am I still talking."

It was during those moments when Caralee understood the Son the least that she could most fully enter the long-lost world he conjured with his vivid words and cool-blooded earnestness. She imagined sketchy trade down vine-shaded alleys, a secret language, and knives behind silk behind knives.

"Auld Vintage is the oldest language from this world. Not the oldest language of them all, of course, just the oldest one that's from our world. My world."

*Languages older than the world.*

"Our ancestors, the builders—of the *world*—spoke many different languages, and some of their words are still in use. *Shekels,* for instance, and in my day, *matzeva,* which was the name for the kind of stone monument in which I was imprisoned for oh-so-many centuries, *mezcal*—I would kill for a bottle—and *aloe vera,* which once grew from my skull, right here." The Son tapped the left edge of his forehead, just past the hairline. "Auld Vintage was the language spoken by the earliest descendants of the builders, according to one version that was taught to me. That was thousands of years before my birth, you understand—by my time it had long been replaced by this language, which I speak and you mangle."

Builders of the world. Shekels, *matzevas,* and mezcal. Something that grew from the skull of the Son of the Vine. Of those conjured pieces of the past, Caralee was most moved by one thought: that the world had been built by people so different from one another that they didn't even speak the same language.

Caralee had always known that one day she'd learn that her world wasn't what it seemed. That didn't take a gift for prophecy so much as keen eyes and imagination. So Caralee wasn't surprised to learn that her world was small, no; what shocked Caralee was the realization that people's worlds might have always been small. Yet what they'd built was so big.

*Could we still build wonders if we all worked together?*

"Are you listening to me?" The Son jabbed her in the ribs with a finger. "I'd like to know if I've killed a language or not." The way the Son said it, Caralee wasn't sure whether he'd like that, or hate it. "I mention language because it's an easy thing to teach, and, if it's not widely spoken, then it's an excellent scrim for all manner of deceit. As we are tutor and ward, and as we pass through this Comez, I will instruct you in Auld Vintage." He stared at her. "And you will pay attention."

"How do you say *bastard*?" she sassed.

"*Nasso-gag zith-zu,*" he answered. "Repeat."

"*Nasso-gag zith-zu.*" Caralee wrestled the words out of her mouth. She didn't say it anywhere near as fluidly and fancily as the Son, but she mimicked each sound.

"That's . . . right." The Son looked at her as if she'd done a backflip. "*Nasso* means 'bad' or 'wrong'; *gag*—'won' or 'earned'; and *zith-zu*—'son.' Put them together and you have a word meaning 'wrongly-earned son.' Say it again." The cart joined the traffic on the central street, but Caralee kept her eyes and ears focused on the Son as best she could. Colors dazzled the edges of her attention, Marm-marm's rainybow wheel sprung to life.

"*Nasso-gag zith-zu*. Bad-won son." Impressed with herself, Caralee smiled. "That's you, all right."

"If the bastard is female," the Son continued without reaction, "then the phrase becomes *nasso-gag sef-sey.*"

"So *sef-sey* means 'daughter,' right?"

Caralee gawked as a lanky man covered in sores approached them, his teeth stained red, and gawping a loony expression. He carried a basket filled with folded paper packets from which dribbled stains of a red powder. His posture pegged him as a street peddler—but peddling what? The Son stiffened at the sight of the man, then stared straight ahead.

As they passed, the Son punched his fist so quickly that the peddler went flying and the basket flew overhead, spilling its contents across the cobbled road. Desperate and gasping, the lunatic began scrabbling across the street, howling in despair. The man gathered his scattered envelopes as best he could. Red powder painted his skin.

"No no no no no no . . ." he said to himself. His arms were covered in sores, too. Red powder clumped there, caked with pus.

"What the scat?" Caralee squawked at the Son, startled by the violence. People stared, but she saw approving looks flashed the Son's way and nasty glares toward the crawling wretch. "He was only trying to earn a few shekels."

"That man sells a drug that eats your mind and rots your bones." For all the Son's composure, brutality was never far away.

Caralee knew about drugs, but not about red powder. Some of the cable threshers, who spent all day hacking through tough cable growth, smoked something called lambsbreads, which eased boredom and made them giggle at unfunny things—but that was harmless fun. Their bones didn't rot, that was for sure. She'd seen Joe get all giggly on the smoke—away from Mag's eyes, of course. And almost everybody got drunk on cableshine, even Mag, from time to time.

The Son frowned. "Fun changes like everything else. Sometimes it changes into something awful. Indulge yourself wisely." And then, "*Vellat,* 'wisdom.' *Vellaeke,* 'wise.' *Vellaeke seyim,* 'wise women.' Become one of them. Become a wise woman, a *vellaeke seyfa.*" And then, "Like my grandmother."

"You hadda gran?" Caralee grinned, then burped. She was hungry. "I mean, I know you didn't step outta the Vine whole and nekkid and mean as scat. It's just hard to imagine you as a babby on your gran's knee, is all. You know, pooping."

"Understandably so." The Son nodded. "Yet once, I was a celebrated pooper whose grandmother was glorious. She was brave and wicked and almost always right, and she was exiled for contradicting my father, when he was still the Lord of a Thousand Names, which is what we called the heir to the crown. Alternatively, 'Lady,' or 'Lir,' depending upon one's identity."

"She must have been a big deal." The Son sounded fond of his gran—and Caralee didn't know how to handle that.

"Grandmother Athinne would have enjoyed you. Nobody knew more about the secret wonders of the world than she did. Between the two of you, you'd talk yourselves dry. She polished my languages with legends from the building of the world."

"I wouldn't mind hearing a legend from the building of the world," Caralee dared, still struggling to understand that her world had been *built*.

"I walked into that one. Look, is this the city center? This is all?"

"What do you want, nekkid dancers and tamed chucklers?"

The Son shrugged one shoulder, as if that wouldn't be the worst idea.

The main thoroughfare led directly to the center of Comez, which contained a two-tiered circular arena. At the bottom of the depression sat a funny-looking sculpture: a basin of white stone with a projection rising up from its middle. There were stains in rings along the inside of the basin and in streaks down the weird lump in the middle, which had a hole at its top.

One side of the town center was kept for public use, with benches and steps carved into the tiers of rock. Here and there people sat as they ate or chatted with one another, and Caralee thought this might be the spot for speeches or lessons or performances like Eusebius gave.

The other side of the tiers was packed with merchant stalls where Caralee saw shiny things, unrecognizable goods scavenged from the wastes, and real fruit—dried-up little berries in blue *and* red. This wasn't travelers' fare like the maggoty gruel sold outside the town gates—this was a real market.

Caralee couldn't believe such sights and smells had been so close to home all along, if only she'd ignored the rules and *looked*.

Close as it was to the wasteland, Comez already welcomed a steady supply of cable goods—which is why Mag passed it by to squeeze more coin from Grenshtepple's, where supply was lower and demand higher. Anyway, they'd never had the shekels to buy much in Comez.

Except, apparently, for Joe. Caralee didn't want to think about what Joe had done to get his hands on inn money.

The Son evaluated the market with a look of sad recognition. "If one ignored the paucity of the goods and the wretchedness of the merchants, one could almost mistake this for a market." He pointed to the sky. "*Nepe* means 'air,' and *penta* means 'market' or 'finance.' Here we see the *nepenthe*, literally 'air-sold.' A common sight, once upon my time."

"*Nepe*. Air. *Penta*. Market." Caralee liked this game, and as she juggled the words in her head, she found that she liked putting them in the right order and sounding out the words just right.

"Now, where is the inn?" the Son asked. "*Balang,* 'temporary,' and *ket,* 'house.' Where is the *balangket*?"

"Um." Caralee tried to remember the specifics of Joe's taunting. Mercifully, Joe had a limited number of taunts and repeated them often. "I think the *balangket* is on the other side of the market, and . . . make a right, maybe? Up the first road. Has a sign that looks like a bunch of little balls." Joe especially liked that part, because it ticked off Mag whenever he talked about balls.

"*Fanto.* 'I now thank you.'"

"You're . . ."

"*Tingo.* 'I now appreciate you'—or 'You're welcome.'"

"*Tingo.*"

"*Bona rambabil.* 'I now see goodness in your previous speech'—or 'Well said.'"

The critters grew shy around so many people, so Caralee led them by hand, smacking her mouth and hissing to keep them happy while the Son held the reins. She guided the cart in a wide half circle around the market and rode uphill toward the far side of town. Exiting the town center, Caralee expected the Son to make a right at the first cross street, toward the *balangket*—the inn. Instead, he turned the cart to the left. Caralee wondered why, until she heard wailing and shouting up ahead.

The streets were built at right angles, but Comez's bowl shape made them rise as they led toward the edges of the town. Caralee walked beside the cart, stroking Oti's thorax to calm him while Atu chirruped. They climbed up in a straight line until they came to a small, well-kept plaza where two streets crossed. At a far corner of the square, a crowd of miserable-looking townsfolk were gathered outside of a house with a door painted a happy yellow. The Comezze buzzed about the doorway and craned their necks to look through the windows set on either side. There were perhaps a few dozen onlookers, and their numbers fanned out into the middle of the plaza, where stone benches ringed a raised box built from the same red clay bricks that made up the few Comezze houses that weren't built from the local gray stone.

Caralee secured the cart to a row of poles beneath an empty lean-to roof where sometimes merchants must have hawked their wares, but there was no market today. She tied Oti and Atu to a market pole and secured their cargo.

In the redbrick box at the center of the square lay a sand painting in red and blue, which reminded Caralee of home, although the colors they had to work from at home were far duller. Today's design looked like drops of water, painted with bold blue sand, falling both up and down against a crimson field.

Turning away from the box of sand, Caralee studied the crowd and the house that concerned them so. She saw tear-streaked faces, angry faces, and fearful faces, all focused on the two-story gray stone house. Its windows were cleaner than those of its neighbors, with freshly painted yellow shutters and yellow window trim that matched the door. Rather than the scrubby greenish plants struggling in their boxes, the window boxes of this house, also painted a cheery yellow, sprouted fat green spears as thick as Caralee's finger.

She slid through the edges of the crowd to inspect the plants that grew beneath the windows. The boxes were bolted to the windowsills and reached just as high as her elbows, so Caralee could look down and see from above just how they grew. Each spiky plant grew in a tight spiral, and each arm of the spiral looked the same, with long triangular stalks that grew in a regularly changing pattern from a central whorl. Each stalk was the same shape as the others, but they grew larger the farther they were from the center—they weren't the same, but different in a way that seemed predictable. Where one circle of stalks ended, two or three smaller circles had sprung up, which preserved the arrangement of ever-larger coils of pointed stalks, but were smaller than the larger plant in the same way that their inner stalks grew smaller than the outer spears.

Caralee thought about cable plant, which pushed up from the dirt in a ropier, uglier version of this exact same pattern. That was where the similarity between the two ended, but Caralee wondered if the sameness meant anything. Did other plants grow in that particular type of spiral shape, stalks growing at the same increasing rate, separated by the same increasing distance—with smaller versions of themselves sprouting nearby?

Whether a cable field lived or died depended mainly on the health of its primary plant, but if the taproot was damaged by some idiot with a backhoe, or by a clearing fire that burned too hot, or some other mishap, there were plenty of times when one of its satellite plants would grow larger and fill up the empty space. Could this plant do that?

The Son skirted the crowd to meet Caralee beside the window box, smiling with all of his teeth. Turning his shoulder to the crowd to hide his hands, the Son snapped off a stalk from one of the smaller plants and sniffed the severed end, which glistened with clear goo.

"This is quite a prize in this dust bowl world." He shook the green stalk in Caralee's direction and cocked his head toward the people behind him. "I wonder if they even know how useful it can be."

"It ent a drug, is it?" Caralee hoped the pretty spiraled stalk wasn't bad.

The Son shook his head. "This is true medicine—although one can be the other, depending on the amount. This particular plant is not only harmless but handy for us in particular. Tens of thousands of years before humankind even dreamed of building worlds such as ours, this tiny wonder was one of the first medicines."

"Whoa. And it's just out here in the open? Won't anybody notice that you've gone and stole it?"

"Unlikely." The Son craned his neck behind him, toward the window boxes. "I took a stalk from a chick, not the hen. Those are the smaller plants growing around the bigger version."

*Chicks and hens.* Caralee thought those were funny words and wondered where they came from. For that matter, where did anything come from? *Tens of thousands of years before the world was built,* Caralee frowned. Maybe there were sandymancers in the Land of the Vine who told shatterscat stories, too.

Above the heads of the gathered Comezze, red smoke poured from a gray chimney. Caralee knew that was a bad sign—red smoke was used to banish ill spirits after a murder or an untimely death. Caralee's village couldn't afford such luxuries, and death came quick and often in the wasteland. Also, back home, everything but the dirt would catch fire in an instant. Marm-marm had given a lesson on it once.

The tense crowd made more sense now that the smoke'd gone up. Caralee's heart beat faster at the ideas conjured by the smoke.

"A house-in-mourning," the Son whispered to himself. "Does red smoke still mean . . . Have you ever seen red smoke before?"

"Murder!" Caralee breathed, nodding.

"So some things haven't changed. We called this practice *bleeding the sky.* Common sight." The Son pointed to the afternoon sky beyond the red smoke, beneath that ominous crack, and said, "*Akeyeneph. Akeye*—'sea or water,' and as you've learned, *nepe* means 'air.' Sea-in-air or as we modern people say: sky."

"*Akeyeneph.* Sea-in-air. Sky."

The Son's gaze drifted back to the crack in the *akeyeneph* overhead, white and jagged as fingers of frozen lightning. "Although, however often we may have bled the sky, we never managed to scar it. Caralee, do you think that that crack, etching—whatever it may be—is truly the work of this . . . Metal Duchy?" His lips pressed into a line and his nostrils flared.

"I dunno. Everyone says so."

His expression frightened her, and anyway, the crowd was growing larger and louder—so Caralee turned her focus to the people.

A young woman with a basket of garlic trumpets tied with pale blue ribbons meandered around the distressed Comezze, holding up her stinky white mushrooms with a half-hearted smile. No one was in the mood to buy food, even though garlic trumpets made Caralee's mouth water. The Son stayed locked in silent thought. She wondered what he was chewing over, inside his head.

Then he turned to her with a half smirk—and produced one pale blue ribbon, which he'd clearly nicked from the unfortunate mushroom girl. That scandalized Caralee. Stealing was not something that good folk did.

"I am not limited to stealing bodies." The Son saw through her disapproval and dismissed it with a reminder of his larger crimes. "Besides, you are absolutely shapeless in that shitbag farm sack."

Biting a corner of his lower lip, the Son reached down toward her middle with both hands, the ribbon held lightly between his fingertips. His unribboned hand reached around her waist, and he placed his palm on the small of her back, pulling her a little closer to him. He jerked on her burlap shmata, pulling it taut against her chest and waist, then gathered the slack at the base of her spine.

The Son pulled her shmata tight at the waist and took up the ribbon with his other hand. Somehow he managed to keep the rough burlap bunched behind her while pulling the ribbon round the other side of her belly. The ribbon was long enough—and Caralee's waist scrawny enough—that plenty of slack remained on the ribbon's ends after he'd cinched it tight. She stood a little straighter, took a breath, and tensed her belly muscles.

Keeping his head down and his eyes on his work, the Son nodded in approval.

"Yes, that's how a person stands. It's called *self-possession,* and it shows pride, confidence, and all manner of other attractive things . . . if you've got attractive things to show."

"Huh?" Caralee felt silly just standing there. "Attractive things like what?"

"By truth and shade, we are about to find out."

*Truth and shade.* The Son did this now and then, she'd noticed: cursing and blessing himself the way the Vintage folk must have once done. Caralee paid attention to these little bits of information and reminded herself to write them down in her journal. Was truth a good thing? Was the sun strong enough then that you needed shade to escape it? Poor Joe woulda burned up to a crisp.

The Son tied the ribbon in a pretty bow, off to one side and just above the curve of her hip. He pulled the makeshift garment down again, through the ribbon belt, straightening it till the shapeless collar snapped over the middle of her bosom and fit her as tightly at her shoulders as he could manage. With deft fingers, the Son knotted the hem of the shmata—-on the opposite side of the ribbon, which lifted it to her dark and knobby knee.

He leaned back to evaluate his work and nodded, evidently pleased with himself.

"Hmm. The bad news is that now I can actually see your body, but still—this is a drastic improvement. Sleeves to cover those arms would be nice, and your hair, which could be gorgeous if it had ever been groomed . . ." He looked her up and down. "Hmm. The look has a curious kind of style, not flattering but not wholly repellant. Maybe you'll grow out of it? Or into? I've no idea. Even a god-king has limits."

He stepped away and gestured to Caralee, urging her to do . . . what?

"Go ahead. How does it feel to be pretty?"

Some instinct took over. Caralee ran her hands down her ribs and over her hips to her thighs, and for a flickering few heartbeats, she felt like a real grown woman—and not an overgrown girl demanding what she'd only just begun to deserve. She took a peek down at the sudden appearance of her cleavage and couldn't stop a blush. Caralee didn't care that there wasn't much to look at there—she had a *there* to look at, and the Son had brought it out for no reason at all.

*He doesn't do anything for no reason at all,* Caralee corrected herself, but wondered what purpose the Son could have for prettying up her ugly shmata. Maybe to better fit the role of his student? That might be it.

Then the crowd stirred, and that interrupted her thoughts. The yellow door opened, and a man in a heavy greatcoat emerged, followed by two guards with the blue circle of Comez embroidered on their coats. The fellow in the great-coat would be the alderman. A bald brick of a man with stubble so thick that it looked like a full beard, he held a handkerchief to his nose with one hand and waved away clouds of red smoke with the other.

A wide woman waddled out of the house-in-mourning, also holding a rag to her nose—Caralee wondered if it was a dishrag. Folk in Comez had dishes, and they'd more than a single well for drawing water and enough clothing for leftover rags to wash those dishes. Dressed in the swaddling of a matron, tears streaked the woman's cheeks, and she shook her head over and over, as if unable to rid herself of some terrible thought.

The Son ducked his head and whispered to Caralee, "*Nihnepsolom. Nih,* 'sad.' *Nepe* you know, means 'air.' *Solomone* means 'home' or 'household.' Note the difference between a home and a house, which you now know is *angket* in Auld Vintage. One is a concept, the other merely a building. Literally, *nihnepsolom* means 'sad-air home.' A home-in-mourning."

Caralee watched the scene and listened to her tutor. The words seemed to slot into a place in her mind that had been waiting for them. They didn't quite match up with normal words, and they didn't fit together like normal words, but still they *meant* the same things, and the way they fit together had a different, but similar, manner of sense.

The matron wailed. "My sister! My own sweet sister! By her very son, murdered! In her bed, was she stabbed!" she howled with more than a touch of the drama. "By her very own son!" she repeated before the gathered villagers. "My wicked, rickety nephew, sands take him! Oh, woe!"

"Sorrow is a kind of madness." The Son spoke in a soft voice so that only Caralee could hear. "Like the other madnesses—rage and lust and joy and greed and so on—sorrow can drive people away from their better selves if it isn't held in check. Most feelings must be held in check, but not denied. Deny your feelings and you'll suffer the worst madness of all. From such perversions of one's own nature, all manner of monsters are born."

The mourning-maddened woman didn't much look like a monster to Caralee, but then, the Son looked young and beautiful, and could be kind and generous. That didn't make him anyone other than the Son of the Vine.

They watched the alderman put an arm around the grieving woman. The tails of his stiff-collared coat brushed the ground. "Now, now, Bilmer. You don't know that. Let our watchfolk do their work." The alderman tried his best at comfort, but Caralee could sense his frustration with the overwrought woman.

"You had best find that wretch, Willum Amos!" Bilmer raged in sorrow and shook her finger.

Stern Willum looked like he'd been carved from some quarry, with a manner just as stony. His daily stubble was gray and as thick as scrub brush. The grieving woman turned and beseeched him and, in a half crouch of distress, tore at her blouse elaborately—though the garment remained intact. Her head, wrapped chin to brow in its plain gorget, still shuddered with grief.

"I find this crying person particularly annoying," the Son complained.

Caralee nodded in agreement.

"Oy! Him, it were. In my soul, I do know!" The deranged sister grabbed the alderman by his huge lapels as if to drag him down toward her, though he was a foot taller and twice as thick as Joe.

"This madwoman knows something in her soul, she says. *Aetheneph,* 'soul.' From *aethey,* 'spirit,' and *nepe,* which means what?"

Caralee took apart the word to understand its components. The Son wasn't kidding about vocabulary lessons, but Caralee managed to absorb most of it. It seemed natural to decide to say something in one set of words, rather than another set of words. It was easier than learning fancy words in her own language, anyway. Like whatever a cat was.

*So* aethey *means "spirit," and* nepe *means "air."*

"Air. Spirit-in-air?" She chewed her lip. "The little words change depending on where they show up in the big words. Huh."

The Son patted Caralee on the back.

"My young student," the Son announced for anyone to hear, "you look quite so very fetching. Let's get you a look at yourself in one of these nice, clean windows and leave the poor Comezze to their grief. Privacy is a generosity, as you'll remember from our lessons concerning manners."

Caralee rolled her eyes. For such a subtle creature, the Son could ham it up worse than Eusebius when he had a mind to do so.

He edged them around the corner of the house and onto the side street. This side of the house-in-mourning—the *nihnepsolom*—stood as tidy and clean as the front. The windows were just as clean, though without window boxes.

The Son pouted. "If only I could slaughter the lot of them."

"Can't you?" The question hardly needed asking.

"You know what they say about 'wants' and 'needs.'" He sighed.

"I really don't."

The Son was studying the first window on this side of the house, which, unlike the others, was pushed open on its hinges, split down the middle. Caralee caught a glimpse of her reflection in a frame of glass and was shocked to see that she *did* look more like a woman than some sack-girl. Her waist looked trim, her shoulders wide enough—too wide for her tits, but still—and her legs didn't seem half as scrawny as when her shins had poked out from under the unknotted hem.

Her tutor opened the window wider while examining its casing. He slid a finger along the yellow windowsill. It came away smeared with something white.

"What's that?" Caralee asked.

"We'll find out." He sniffed his finger, then touched his tongue to it and made a face.

The Son turned on his heel and held his finger in front of Caralee's face. "What do you see here?"

"White stuff."

"What kind of white stuff?" He nodded toward the open window. Caralee inspected it—sure enough, one side of the window casing was spotted with the white stuff, and more of it was smeared on the windowsill itself.

"Um." She thought. "Greasy white stuff. Birdscat?" Birds grew more common out east—so as guesses went, birdscat was plausible.

"Smell my finger."

"No thank you?"

The Son stuck out his tongue, teasing her. He pressed his finger onto his temple and smeared it down those brand-new, antique cheekbones. "Does this remind you of anything?"

Caralee thought about it.

"Or of anyone?"

*Naw. Couldn't be.* It was.

"That shatterscat fucktwit!" Caralee punched the air.

"Narrow that down for me. It's been a fucktwitty millennium," the Son said.

"Eusebius, you dunderhead!" She'd slipped, forgetting she wasn't talking to Joe, even though he didn't look at all like Joe anymore. His clothes still smelled like Joe's sweat, but how long would that last?

The Son clapped her on the back again, harder this time—and she staggered a little. "Well done, Caralee Vinnet! Aren't you a proper inspector? Grease paint, made with lead. Utterly poisonous. It eats away the skin, taints the brain, and wrecks the kidneys—that's why his feet look like gourds."

"Pfft," Caralee spat. "I *knew* that wasn't sandymancy." She would have to remember to ask what lead was. More words for her journal.

"Perhaps we should put your skills to the test." With that, the Son pulled himself up by the edges of the window and jumped through, pulling his knees to his chest and clearing the white-stained windowsill. He spun about and held out both hands for her to take.

"Are you sure that's okay?"

"Do you know someone else who owns the world? We'll have a look around and be out the same way we came in." He coughed—the smoke inside wasn't thick, but noxious all the same.

He reached down, grabbed Caralee's forearms, and lifted her up with an ease that embarrassed her, swinging her out and then pulling her through the window, setting her down on her feet. Her eyes watered from the smoke at once.

A single great room occupied most of the ground floor. A washbasin with pots and pans lined the counter on the far side of the room, beside another window, while they'd climbed into a gap between the open window and a long dining table. The space on the other side of the table, in the middle of the room, was empty except for the rectangular outline of a missing carpet that could be seen where the floor was less worn. To its right, opposite the yellow door, a stone hearth burned with something foul, the source of the red smoke that flowed up through the chimney.

Even with the flue open, enough smoke escaped to fill the room with a red haze. The Son plucked two linen rags from a neatly folded stack still sitting on the table; he dashed across the room in two strides, dunked the napkins in the basin, and tossed one to Caralee.

Holding the wet rag to her nose lessened the sting of the smoke, although her eyes still watered like they did when the wasteland wind blew grit into her face.

Safety measures thus taken, the Son scanned the room. He pointed to a butcher's block full of knives. Caralee tiptoed over—there were six slots for knives, and six knives in their slots. Taking the rag from his face and holding his breath, the Son used his napkin to slide each knife from its sheath—all were spotless, and the water in the basin was clean, not at all bloodied by any attempt to clean them. Nor was it clouded by any washing at all. It must have been filled the night before and not used since.

*Sister said the dead lady got stabbed. Huh.*

To the right of the washing area, a set of narrow, steep stairs led to the upper floor of the two-story house. Caralee followed the Son up—he paused halfway and pointed to a handprint of white grease paint staining the banister. Another on the wall. One set faced upstairs, and another—the messier of the two—was smeared and facing downstairs.

*If he walked up, he sure did run down.*

The second floor was clearer of smoke, so Caralee took her napkin away from her nose.

They found themselves in a bedroom the same size as the room below. In a small bed, beneath a bloodstained yellow quilt, lay the victim. Her eyes were open, and her jaw hung agape, awfully so.

The two approached the near side of the bed, and Caralee studied the corpse—aged, pretty with a hawkish nose, her head rested on long, black-gone-silver hair. She wore an undyed sleeping shmata that, upon inspection, was woven from *silk*. Real silk. Caralee had seen bolts of silk once or twice in the carts of wealthier merchants, but to touch it—she reached out her hand to smooth the collar of the murdered woman's pajamas, but the Son grabbed her forearm and shook his head. His grip felt stronger than Joe's—or anyone's, for that matter—and Caralee knew that he used only a fraction of his strength. The strength that she'd have to defeat one day.

"You touched the napkins *and* the knives," she complained.

He flashed her a fragment of that solar gaze, and Caralee relented.

They walked around to the far side of the bed to examine the woman's wounds—there were three of them—and not a one looked like a knife wound. Maybe the sister's grief really was a form of madness: the three injuries weren't slices or stabs but great gouging wounds as wide across as Caralee's hands, and they gaped from the dead woman's chest and abdomen, exposing white ribs and the yellow fat that coddled a person's organs. Whatever had torn her open had scraped across the mattress as well, shredding it and dragging the woman's guts toward the window in blue-white ropes, split open and stinking of scat.

"Musta been some big knives." Caralee would have to draw this scene in her journal. "Knives, really?"

"These are claw wounds." The Son nodded toward the window beside the bed. It, too, was open. That was one reason there was less smoke up here.

"Could a sandymancer conjure up anything that would do this?" Caralee asked, knowing and hoping that a sandymancer like Eusebius couldn't manage anything half so powerful, but wondering if she could. That'd be useful against a certain someone with a monster's grip.

"Pfft," the Son dismissed the suggestion. "I could contrive this scene with a thought. You and I, we can arrange the elements however we desire. Whether your, ugh, *sandymancer* could do so is academic, but doubtful. That half man is not half so vicious, nor cunning, nor motivated."

"He wouldn't do this even if he could." Caralee examined the open window. "The claw marks dragged *this* way." She nodded at the windowsill. "I don't see any white face paint here, but look at these."

Claw-shaped scratches marked the windowsill. Not as big or as deep as those that had slain the woman behind them, but deep and sharp. They'd torn away the yellow paint, but Caralee saw only a few splinters on the floor.

"Well done." The Son sounded sincere. He looked down at their feet. "The claw marks on the floor pierce and drag away from and toward the window, but are heaviest coming in." He pointed toward the bed. "Whatever made them clawed its way in, but had an easier time climbing out. Maybe *climbing* isn't the right word."

After he said that, the Son kept still. Caralee wondered where his thoughts had flown.

*Flown!* It flew, which only brought up more questions, because that was impossible.

"However this happened," she said, "there just *isn't* anything that could do this, Son. Honest. We got animals that'll suck your spine out your eye sockets if you stray, but nothing *smart* like this. Nothing that would come to town, scratch its way inside a lady's bedroom, and cut her to ribbons on purpose."

"Purpose," the Son repeated, and he clasped his hands over his heart, looking waspish in Joe's jacket. He searched the sky in the distance before turning away from the window. His face was flushed. "*Purpose.* Shit."

Outside, Caralee hurried down the side street away from the house and its thinning crowd. The Son whistled low, and she slowed her pace. When he caught up with her and they walked abreast, he explained, "Hurrying draws attention. Keep the steady pace of someone with no worries and nothing to hide. Talk not at a whisper, but in a casual manner, as two people strolling might. People will strain to listen in on whispering, but nobody cares about daily drudgery. Do you understand?"

"I do." Caralee matched his tone, feeling mischievous and a little dangerous herself. "So what killed her?"

The Son straightened his back as they turned another corner, putting more distance between themselves and the *nihnepsolom*.

"Your hedge-witch friend can barely walk. The simplest answer is that a Beast . . . a creature killed the old woman. A creature that entered through the upper-story window and left no claw marks anywhere but the windowsill."

"A creature that *flies,*" Caralee announced, testing her guess. This was fun.

"Well done, and I'm afraid so, yes," the Son asked, strolling along as if flying murder beasts were normal afternoon conversation. Maybe for him, they were. "Do you know of any such creature? I could name two dozen, but I doubt any survived."

"*Do I know any flying creatures?* Are you serious with that scat?" Caralee shook her head. "Ever heard of birds? I dunno of any flying beasties, not outside of scary stories told round the campfire."

"Until recently, wasn't *I* merely a scary story told round the campfire?"

"Naw." Caralee shook her head. "Well, kinda."

"Humor me with your scary stories of flying beasts."

"Sure." She shrugged. "Draygons make for a good story; wyverns, too; aperols can fly in some stories, but if a stone bird can fly, then I'm your mother; harpies . . ." She wondered. They *were* real, unlike the rest of her list. The way Caralee heard it, though, they were rarely spotted, let alone encountered. "Harpies don't grow big enough to catch anything heavier than a toddler. But. Could it be a harpy?"

The Son jerked his head at the mention of harpies. "The harpy? So she . . . The harpy is still hatching? Are you certain?" A haunted expression passed across his face.

"I've spent my life in a village with no name?"

The Son conceded the point.

They passed a little café with rattan and wicker chairs around small round tables, inside and out. The smell of fresh *something* wafted from within. Caralee gave the Son a pleading look.

"We haven't a single shekel, Caralee," the Son reminded her. "And you want brunch?"

"You *broke* the *world.* Pull up your britches or I'm going to die of hunger, and then who'll you treat like scat?" Caralee fixed him with her own look of intense focus, and the Son pressed his lips together in a smile.

Ten minutes later, after a few words from the Son of the Vine, they'd settled at an outside table while the traumatized proprietor prepared a serving of dumplings, which he stammered were "on the house"—whatever that meant. The Son sipped something called wodke. Caralee tried a sip, and it burned as she swallowed, but not as bad as cableshine—the stuff they made back home, out of cable gruel ferment and wastewater.

"So," the Son said in an easy voice. Walk easy, talk easy—he was worried about something. "The harpy."

Caralee nodded. "Fly around out east, I hear. They'll kill small game for food, but I've never heard of them killing folk, or attacking towns. And we're too far west. Besides, that would be one *big* harpy."

The Son frowned and nodded absentmindedly, instantly processing all of Caralee's limited understanding about the winged pests. The proprietor scurried out of the café with a bowl of dumplings, then ran back inside twice as fast. If the Son said anything, Caralee didn't hear it. The smell of steam and dough and fillings became her world.

She'd never seen a dumpling before, and here were six, still steaming in a round straw bowl with a flat bottom. They looked like huge fat grubs, grayish white, wrinkled and pinched all along the top where a seam ran from end to end. Juice dribbled from their wimpled tops down to the bottom of the bowl.

The Son picked one up with his fingers and sniffed it. He didn't grimace, which Caralee took to be a good sign. If dumplings smelled good enough for the god and king of the world, she could only imagine what would happen when they touched her tongue.

Caralee waited for the Son to take a bite. That was a bit of wasteland hospitality that even her empty stomach and watering mouth wouldn't override. Gray-brown juice trickled down his chin, and his eyes rolled back into their sockets as he chewed. She wondered if it had been eight hundred years since he'd eaten, or if he'd survived off looted hardtack from his looted bodies, or if that guard with the cold pebbles had fed him roast vulture, too.

The Son set down his half-eaten dumpling. Caralee saw that the inside was filled with a mince of brown and gray stuff, meat and fat and spices—*spices!*—with tiny rings of bright green that must have been some finely sliced plant. She saw and smelled little white squares of chopped garlic trumpet mushrooms and had to sit on her hands to keep from breaking the rule against eating before her host had finished swallowing their first bite.

The Son nodded, understanding the custom—that was another minor clue and connection between his time and hers—and waved his hand to her.

Her mouth had filled up with drool, and Caralee had to swallow as she reached for a dumpling of her own.

*Dumplings.*

# II

Grandmother's earrings were as big as my fists, her short curls so white they rivaled the clouds, and my favorite brooch dazzled emerald and silver on her lapel. Her cane was blackthorn wood capped with a knob of solid gold.

"See this cane, Amaunti?" Grandmother Athinne shook her golden cane in my face. I was ten, and my mother's mother had smuggled me out of my tower. She'd appeared in my doorway after my bedtime——I was already a few centimeters taller——and filled my bedroom with her perfume. She leaned on her cane, in a gray herringbone suit, a matching hat, sensible shoes——and, always, a cushioned neck brace disguised with a pristine scarf.

Grandmother's spine had shrunk faster than the rest of her, Mother used to say. Athinne never complained, and the difference between good days and bad days was nothing more than a distracted humming and knuckles that clenched——never fidgeted——around the knob of her cane.

Grandmother Athinne had ordered me dressed and marched me out through the main gate. The guards must have been on break, I'd said aloud, and she winked.

"Do you see this cane?" Grandmother asked again. "I've used a cane for years. I was old before you were born, and I'll be old the rest of my days. But you, Amaunti, have always been young. Do you see the dents on the gold, here and here?"

I nodded, afraid that the sound of my voice would summon the guards or, worse, my father, who was then still merely the Lord of a Thousand Names, for Grandfather Moysha had not yet died. The knob of the cane was smooth and nearly perfect, marred only by overlapping lines of dimples.

"Those are your teeth marks, Amaunti. Gold is soft, and your teeth are strong, and while I own a dozen canes, I only use this one."

"That's nice, Grandmother," I said. I was ten.

"You were almost never born, you know." Grandmother's expression was never far from a frown. I followed her down witchlit hallways and grand stairways that we descended at her slow but unstoppable pace. Ordinarily, inching along at Athinne's glacial schlepp would have driven me crazy, but Grandmother had done the impossible and sprung me from my prison. There would be a reason, and I slavered to know it.

"I loved your grandfather, once upon a very distant time."

*Well, of course you did,* I thought, misunderstanding.

"Not my husband, the baron, whom I also loved and love still, may his bone-meal feed the soil. No, I mean our Moysha, the Most Holy Son of the Vine. He wasn't even heir at the time, that's how long ago this was and how young we were. If we had married, then you and your siblings wouldn't be here. Neither would my daughter, your mother. Or your father, I suppose." She laughed and sneered at once——no love lost there.

I felt scandalized.

"No Father . . ."

"I know, it's a vision." Grandmother hummed to herself——that was a telltale sign. She must have been in considerable physical pain even then, though it would be another two years before her heart gave out. "Every silver lining has some hidden tarnish, but oh, the silver! My daughters, my grandbabies——for you, I'd suffer a dozen sons-in-law like your father."

I steadied her with my little hand on her arm, above her wrist, and I rubbed my thumb across the cloth-covered buttons along the cuff of her wool suit. Grandmother leaned on the cane in her opposite hand and pulled me to her side, purring. It wasn't all bad, tiptoeing forward slower than one of Birrat's tortured mice. We didn't have to stop to hug.

"My affair with Moysha," Grandmother Athinne continued, not one to be distracted by sentimentality, "was less an entanglement of the heart and more of an academic romance. No one knows more about the Vine's cryptobiology than your grandfather, and no one knows more about the machines of the world-beneath than myself. Together, we sought to understand the Beasts of Care." She sighed and opened a door hidden within the oak walls of a certain parlor. "But we did love one another, the god-king and I."

Some loves can bring forth life, and some loves can prevent life. Of course, this is a tale of both. Sometimes love can create a monster, and sometimes love can be a beast. Beasts and monsters. The two are not at all the same, and again, this is a tale of both.

We rode three elevators. The first was ordinary, paneled with walnut and brass, and took us beneath the palace, into the white flesh of the Mountain of the Vine. We took apple-cored hallways to the second elevator, which was nonmechanical. A gourd-like lozenge, distantly cousined from a melon, lowered us through a series of sphincters down some repurposed phloem sieve tube or other vascular structure.

"You have studied the world-beneath."

I nodded and pointed at her brooch, which was a miniature of the world: a cabochon emerald atop a silver rod. It looked like a fancy screw. The emerald was our home——the land and seas and sky——while the rod was the world-beneath. The rod was ten times as long as the emerald was wide. The world so big, our part of it so small.

Much as I had teethed on her cane, Grandmother had taught me the shape of the world when I was still in napkins. Such is the way with curious children of enormous privilege——we will at young ages sponge up knowledge from the elites whom we orbit.

"Is that where we're going?" The world-beneath was inaccessible across most of the world. There were depots and access points, but here at the City of the Vine we lived above what was by far the largest occupation of the world-beneath, an underground hive that rivaled the city for size. Below the city, the Vine's taproot stretched down into the dirt and past it, into the deep engines of the world, where it was cradled and pierced by instruments we could not see, let alone understand.

"It is." Grandmother nodded once, both hands clasped over the gold head of her cane. "You have learned so much already, Amaunti. You have mastered your studies and show promise in not one, not three, but all seven magicks. You have been given everything that we know. It is time for you to share the burden of what we have lost."

The third elevator was not itself memorable, but the cube's scuffed black glass and weathered steel said something of its age. It plunged us into the world's vast machine sleeve at a speed I felt in my stomach. Grandmother's humming took on a brief new urgency, but when I looked at her, her red-painted lips smiled, her grooved face serene. When we dropped into the taproom cavern, the darkness of the shaft disappeared, and our elevator fell through an underground cave so hugely massive that I could not see the walls in the distance.

In the center of the cavern I saw the taproot, lit by powerful spotlights that were, from this distance, swallowed by the colossal size of the cavern. Ghost white and bloated like the finger of some netherworld god, the Vine's taproot grew straight and smooth from an excavated hole in the ceiling and reentered the ground a kilometer below, ringed by a crust of platforms and louvered instruments. The entirety of the cavern seemed to be aimed at the Vine's anchor.

The flattened ground of the cavern shimmered and lapped like the ocean. That was an effect of lighting and scale, for on the floor grew a field of dark bracts, ringing the taproot in a pattern of Fibonacci spirals, like the spirals I'd seen in the black middles of sunflowers. Triangular and fluted, the bracts spiraled in an array of sensors and emitters perhaps two kilometers in diameter, and it was only distance and altitude that gave the impression of waves, and the shifting light that set the waves to lapping.

When we reached the bottom of the known world, Grandmother Athinne leaned on her cane and took tiny steps out onto a stone palisade that had been hewn from the bedrock. Four women waited for us beside a sleek black sedan chair, fastened with the dark green livery of my grandmother the baroness's household.

Athinne held out her arms like the wings of a tiny bird, and two of her guards plucked her off the ground and settled her into the sedan's big bucket seats. I climbed up after her, and we cozied into the cushions and warmed our feet beneath thick fur blankets. The four guards took their places and lifted the sedan onto their backs——thick metal bidents settling across their shoulders.

We began a march toward the taproot, that ghost-white ligament connecting the floor of the cavern to the ceiling, far above. I could only gauge the distance to the taproot by my sense of the size of the world above, but Grandmother commanded my attention immediately. Her small black eyes bored through me, as if she could see all of me. I loved her, but I did not care for the feeling of being opened up and seen.

"These underground domains extend for hundreds of thousands of kilometers, far longer than the world is wide. This unfathomable labyrinth comprises ninety percent of the world's volume, and seventy-five percent of its mass. Most of it is lost to us, and I will tell you how.

"While we know its dimensions and some scant other details, we can only access a tiny fraction of the depth of the world-beneath. As you see here, just below the surface of the living world extends a network of tunnels, maintenance cores, and dynamic machine centers that form a worldwide command-and-control network, which is centered here in the taproot cavern. In many ways, this metal and plastic maze is a mirror of the Vine, physically and functionally: it spans the world; it sustains us; it sustains itself; our ancestors built it; and we remember far, far too little of its workings."

Here in the underworld, my paternal grandfather and my maternal grandmother pursued their separate passions for the ancient realm and its secrets. They met, and each became ignited by the other's mind and imagination. Imagination and mind are far more fertile than a cock or a womb can ever be.

"Together, your grandfather and I studied the machine components of the world's administrative subsystems and how they interacted with both the Vine and the Beasts of Care. We were obsessed with the Beasts, the both of us."

"Why?" I asked. The events of my tragic sixth birthday party were never far from my mind——they never are——and the mention of the Beasts of Care had enkindled both curiosity and shame, and each burned.

"Your grandfather Moysha had a future god-king's expert education in the intricacies of the Vine and all things cryptobotanical, and I am one of the only living engineers who can repair certain mechanical systems. I had deciphered some fragment of the builders' machine code, which is how my notoriety began." She coughed a humorless laugh, no doubt chewing some gristle of old arguments with my father, the Lord of the Thousand Names. "Between the two of us, Moysha and I held the bulk of the world's knowledge, and yet each of us suffered from the damning awareness that what we knew, respectively, was so diminished from the knowledge of the builders that we might as well be primitives."

"Why do we know so little?" I asked. "It's *our* world."

"Patience, my peach." She favored me with another smile. "When I was your age, my uncle taught me the basics of wood carving. I carved three wooden toys so that my brother could teach me to juggle. Now my brothers lie dead, and I can juggle. I've forgotten how to whittle wood and I could teach you to juggle, but you wouldn't know that it took a knife and a tree to make a juggling toy. Your daughters might find my wooden juggling toys and never know why they were made, nor who made them." Grandmother straightened the black-and-white scarf covering her neck brace, and I saw her jaw tighten with pain. "Do you see?"

I nodded and looked up from the roofless sedan at the shadowy cavern, bristling with instruments, dominated by the taproot, and I realized for the first time that while my family might rule the world, that did not mean we knew it. How could we protect a world we did not fully understand? I saw the danger at once.

"Good." Grandmother slipped me a caramel candy. "Now, can you name the three pillars of the world?"

"The Vine, of course." You could see it everywhere, even here. "The world-beneath." I pictured the black kilometers of its hull beneath us, the rivers of ancient gel pumping through its tubes. "And the Beasts of Care." Unlike the world-beneath, which was largely unseen but provably *there,* the Beasts of Care were more of a myth. Those that operated autonomously were rarely seen by people, and those that could be summoned were done so only at times of great need, which history told us had been rare.

The Beasts of Care formed the third piece of our world's construction. The Vine above, to nourish the land; the unseen gears and pipes below, to hold the whole together; and the Beasts to move between all the parts, performing what minor and major tasks the first two systems could not.

I cracked my candy between my molars.

When we reached the hole in the world, we exited the sedan.

Two hundred meters across and immeasurably deep, puckered around its perimeter like a pore fit for the cheek of a god. The taproot dropped straight into the bore, but the spotlights that lit it failed to breach the depth of this abyss. Hairy roots sprouted at right angles from the taproot's length, and some of the roots higher up grew long enough to droop down across the enormous abyss, where they were secured to the floor and allowed to pass beneath it. In this way, they indeed mirrored the stalks of the Vine above, which wrapped around the land.

We were yet twenty meters from the slope of the edge when I balked and refused to move any closer. My fear of heights had not yet been burned out of me, and the sheer scale of the gaping nothingness turned my gut with brain stem terror. Leaning on her cane, Grandmother climbed the slope and waved me forward. Unable to refuse, I followed her.

At the top of the lip, my stomach dropped——there was no defined edge to the pit, the slope of the lip continued down on an increasingly steep incline until . . . I felt the tug of something more insidious than gravity. I could not banish the picture of my body falling and falling, forever into the black. Self-destruction is never far away.

"You'll be fine, my peach." Grandmother held her cane out in front of me. This reassured me, which says something of what we meant to each other.

An offshoot of the taproot had pierced the wall of the pit below, and a slender white coil curved up through a coil of pipe to sprout from the floor beside us. Nearly waist-high, the tip of the root fanned out like a palm, webbed with a membrane of hairs finer than silk.

"Touch it." Grandmother nodded toward the pale stalk. "Activate the terminal."

"What?"

"You've done it before."

"But I——"

"——won't get into any trouble. Now summon the Beast of Anticipation."

"What is the Beast of——"

"Trust me, Amaunti." With me, Grandmother was the soul of patience. I'd heard her shred my father and berate his toadies, and I knew that I was an exception, not the rule.

So I brushed my thumb across the furred web of the root coil. The white hairs turned to gold, bright and tiny.

"How?"

"In time, you will learn to feel the Beasts as you do the elements. For now, since you cannot picture the Beast, or know its vibration, simply meditate upon its name. The Beast of Anticipation lairs not far below. It was the subject of much of your grandfather's and my work, and he saw the wisdom in my suggestion to order it to stay close at hand."

It felt stupid, but I held my thumb to the root and whispered the name of the Beast.

I repeated myself, afraid to fail my grandmother. I had no doubt that I was beloved, but also that I was expected not only to succeed but to excel. Nothing happened, and nothing happened, and then the bright gold hairs of the root flickered to indigo, and the white flesh of the root showed an indigo sigil.

"Keep at it," Grandmother whispered. I heard the pride in her voice and narrowed my eyes.

Something big stirred the ground beneath us, and a grating sound echoed from beyond the lip of the great shaft.

A shadowed length arced up from below the wall of the abyssal pit with a waving motion, like the trunk of an elaphent or the neck of a giarappe. Skin mottled violet and gray, the rising tentacle rose and turned its tip upward, raising a mass at its end that looked like an oversized, featureless head.

I startled, but felt Grandmother's hand on my shoulders and knew I must not quit. The neck of the Beast of Anticipation swung its head toward me, too close by far, but I bit my lip and stood my ground, little feet shaking.

The round, knobby head that I had thought featureless opened as if a fist unclenching, and six smaller, stubby tentacles uncurled in my direction. At the end of each tentacle was a humanlike face, violet and gray, with sealed skin where nostrils ought to be and no eyes at all, just skin stretched over hollow orbits. In the center of the Beast's head, like an eye in a palm, a seventh eyeless face stretched thick lips over black and toothless gums.

The neck-stalk waved back and forth in the dank cavern air, and seven mouths aimed at me opened at once.

"Hello, Administrator," the seven faces said to me, their heptafold breath blowing not warm but cool across my face. I blinked.

"Hello," I said, daring myself not to be afraid and wondering what the creature meant.

"No, no, Anticipation!" Grandmother stepped to my side, waving her cane at the Beast. She leaned on me for support, and I clasped her hand across my shoulder, squeezing it tightly. She squeezed back. "This is my grandchild, who is not yet an heir. The god-king does not stand before you."

"Little Athy." The Beast of Anticipation's seven mouths called Grandmother by her nickname, which would have been scandalous had it not been an immortal Beast-thing. Its eyeless gazes never left me. "As full of feints and gambits now as when you were young." Seven mouths sighed. Were they——was it——bored? "You bring me the future, and you play dumb. I am Anticipation, girl, and you could not be dumb if you tried. Indeed, it will be your downfall."

"Feh!" Grandmother stomped her cane on the polymer floor. She sounded angry, but I heard the notes of pride and proof in her voice. "I am too old to fall, and my grandson is here to meet his first Beast, nothing more."

"Yet I see you, Athy. I see the radiant god-king you have brought me. My models and simulations have proved wrong before but not, I measure, today."

Grandmother harrumphed and again pounded her cane upon the ground. The sound echoed like a gong.

One wavering tentacle arched toward me, its face centimeters from my own. Its breath smelled like sweaty feet, of all things. I knew brave people; I tried to act like one of them, clenching my jaw till it hurt and ignoring my trembling lips. The dappled face was huge, twice the size of an adult's.

It smacked dry gray lips over tarry gums.

"You will do," said the Beast.

I shivered.

"I'm not afraid of you," I lied. I don't know why I said that——I must have thought the bluster part of the act of bravery.

"Peach . . ." Grandmother sounded far away. Did her voice tremble?

"Hmmm." Anticipation's tentacle snaked back and forth through the air, hypnotic. "Not yet. It must be awful, not to be born knowing your purpose. Having to find it. Perhaps failing to do so." I could not look away, but I heard another of Anticipation's faces ask, "Shall I cure the Administrator's ignorance?"

"No. No!" Grandmother's voice was no longer kind. It hacked at the Beast like the axe of some story-tale warrior. "That is *my* purpose, and you will not deny me that. Your nature will not allow it. You will not test the child."

"Hmmm." The face so terrifyingly close to my own withdrew toward the pit, just a little. Without meaning to, I took a step forward. The lip of the yawning pit dipped down, but my footing held. "Not much more than a baby. It is good if you are unafraid, Administrator."

"Amaunti, do not move," Grandmother commanded. "Beast, beware me. No one knows your nature as I know your nature. Beware me." Somewhere behind me, the tiny wrinkled woman in the herringbone suit erupted with a torrent of elemantic energy. My seventh sense discerned her in the dissonant way of elemancy, not quite seeing her defiant chin, her wig of pure white curls. How wildly she loved me!

"Are you afraid of heights, Administrator?" The Beast of Anticipation ignored my grandmother.

"I'm not afraid!" I shouted, angry at the Beast for upsetting Grandmother Athinne and for teasing me. My foot slipped on the downslope, and I felt myself begin to fall. My stomach leapt into my throat and whatever mesmerism held me in thrall snapped. If this was a test, I had failed.

I pinwheeled my arms in the air and cried out, but grips like iron vises seized my bones: Grandmother's elemancy reached through my skin and muscles to grapple my humerus bones beneath my armpits, my femurs midway to my knees, and the back of my pelvic bone. Deep beneath the soft tissue, her power wrenched me backward with a fivefold wallop.

My head snapped forward and my hands flew out at right angles, and I sailed through air until I hit Grandmother in the chest——her cane cracked across my spine as she tried to deflect me at the last second, but we both fell to the ground, hard.

I heard Athinne moan. Her guards were beside us in an instant, heedless of the tentacular riddle chuckling overhead. They rolled me away, bruised and shocked, and my face hit the cool polymer scales of the cavern floor. I lay there, too stunned to move, and watched as the green-liveried guards tended to the baroness, urging her to lie still. Her wig was askew, and wisps of damp white hair clung to her exposed scalp. Past the line of her makeup, the skin was as mottled with gray as the skin of the Beast above. Her neck brace had come unfastened, and with the gentlest of touches, a guard cradled Grandmother's skull while another resecured the padding. Stripped of its scarf, the brace was a dingy beige.

Like a mother bear, Grandmother had overreacted and misjudged her own strength. In retrospect, this should have been a lesson for me, but in the moment, I was too distraught for lessons.

Tellingly, Grandmother let her guards attend her without protest. One flared elemancy of her own and steadied Athinne's spine as the others lifted her into the air. The sedan was not far behind, and I scrambled to all fours——long bones aching and the small of my back popping in protest. I pulled myself to my feet and saw Grandmother adjust her wig and wave at me as if to say that the fuss from her attendants was more a matter of concerned loyalty than any real emergency.

That was a lesson. Tell the lie of bravery to those who fear for you, not those you fear. Bravado can be stupid; bravery can be kindness.

"Too old to fall, are you, little Athy?" I spun around to see the Beast of Anticipation rear its head high into the air and fold its tentacle-faces inward till they kissed the central face. "Nothing is too old to fall, nor too robust." The knuckled palm angled its faces toward the ceiling of the cavern, where the taproot entered from above. "Not any thing. Not even our Vine."

Held in midair by the strong arms and steady elemancy of her guards, Grandmother mustered enough energy for a hale hiss.

"Teach the little one his purpose, Athy," Anticipation said. Its voices were softer now. "For unlike myself, you cannot be reborn, and so much depends upon this lesson." It curled further in upon itself. "As you well know."

"Go away!" I screamed at the cephalopod-of-faces. I had never felt such fury. I embraced my own elemancy and held it like a clutch of knives, ready to sever the Beast at its root. "How fucking dare you!" I snatched Grandmother's cane from the ground and lifted it up like some magickal scepter. Its dimpled gold head seemed to shine, reflecting the glare from the distant spotlights that illuminated the soaring taproot.

To my surprise, the Beast coiled its primary neck in what looked like a nod of deference.

"Get out of my sight," I snapped, chest still heaving. "Go away go away go away."

The Beast of Anticipation did not speak, but it did reply. As it receded into the darkness of the chasm, I understood that it would obey me. I still cannot explain it, except to say that "Administrator" is how the Beasts of Care address the Child of the Vine. I was no god-king then, but the Beasts are named plainly. What else had that Beast anticipated? I would like to ask it.

I found Grandmother in the sedan. She'd been stabilized and laid across the wide bucket seats. I knelt beside her and hovered my hands over her, afraid to touch her, afraid to speak.

Her heart raced. The green veins on the backs of her hands throbbed.

I noticed too late that Grandmother was watching me closely.

"Anticipation was always cheeky, but it would never have let you come to any harm. You must learn to control yourself, Amaunti," said the woman who'd just catapulted her grandson into herself. "Now that you have deliberately summoned a Beast of Care, you will move past the events of four years ago. I am not saying that you will forget them——forget nothing, Amaunti. Nothing."

I didn't understand.

"When I look into your eyes, peach, I see so much . . . well, *potential* is the wrong word. All children contain multitudes, all the possible selves that they may become. All *people* contain multitudes, for we are always becoming ourselves. Your multitudes, Amauntilpisharai, are frightening. All of them. There is no future where you do not . . ." Grandmother stopped herself.

"You will *love* and you will *hate,* a force of nature. At six, your father was correct to fear you. At ten, you summon the Beasts of Care with greater ease than many god-monarchs have done after years of practice. What will you do at twelve, Amaunti? At sixteen? Eighteen?"

I blinked back tears. Was I so wrong? I asked her.

"Never! Never say those words again. I forbid it." Grandmother looked me in the eyes. She looked so small. Everything would change soon.

"What you are is mine, and you are the Son of the Vine's. Despite the odds, and indirectly, your grandfather Moysha and I managed to engender offspring. It took an extra generation but *I have you,* my peach. I have Tilcept-Arri and Zincy, who have proven themselves capable. I have Stimenne the artist and Raclette the fierce and Esk-Ettu, whose generous spirit may yet save us all."

"They are mine, and they are Moysha's, and they are splendid——but they lack purpose."

"Purpose?" She and the Beast had both spoken of purpose, and it confused me.

"You remember the tale of the Roc and the Phoenix?" She hummed. Of course she was in pain. Guilt stabbed at me. "The monster and the beast?"

Of course I did. In the picture book, the Roc was a terrible monster, a huge bird that terrorized the countryside and ate cows and sheep by the dozens. The Roc ate and ate and was never satisfied. "Monster!" the people cried when its shadow passed overhead.

Its cousin the Phoenix was also a terrible, huge bird that ravaged herds and pastures. Unlike the Roc, it ate and ate and ate until it grew so powerful that it roared into the sky like a rocket, where it burned to a crisp and was reborn as a fledgling. The ashes of the Phoenix fell across the land and enriched the soil, and crops grew that fed every mouth. The surviving animals ate enriched grass, and their meat and milk made up for those fed to the Phoenix.

But not to the Roc. The soldiers rose up and slew the Roc, and the people cheered, "Monster!" and the soldiers became heroes. The heroes set their sights on the Phoenix and buried its corpse in the mud, where it would never burn. No one cheered. The heroes were shunned. The soil became poor, and the animals grew scrawny, and the fallen heroes realized that the Phoenix was not a monster like its cousin. The Roc served no purpose——it existed only to satisfy its monstrous urges. The Phoenix, which satisfied those same urges, also served a purpose:

The animals we eat and milk are beasts of the field. The oxen and horses are beasts of burden. So, too, was the Phoenix a beast and not a monster.

"You must be a Phoenix, peach. Never a Roc."

"But I'm not a Beast." I didn't understand, not then.

Grandmother's humming intensified. I realized it wasn't only from physical pain. Her voice was flat:

"The Vine is dying." She focused her small black eyes on mine, and I felt her clockwork-critical mind and scalpel-focus lay me bare. "The Vine is dying. As it dies, so dies the world."

My lungs stopped working.

"A solution exists, but neither your grandfather nor I will live long enough to see it through." She coughed, then cleared her throat. "The Child of the Vine suffers a terrible burden, and the world itself knows it. When you are the Son of the Vine, Amaunti, the sky will weep for you every time it rains."

I turned to stone. I couldn't move, nor speak.

"The Vine. Thousands of years old. Our divinity. Our ancestor's greatest feat of bioengineering. A plant to sustain an entire world." Grandmother shook the gold knob of her cane at the taproot, towering and white. She resented it, I could tell. "It's also rotten in the roots, moldy, infected, and degrading. It will die slowly over a century, and by the time symptoms appear aboveground, you will not have enough time left to live to correct the error."

I exhaled. I blinked. I moved my lips.

"Let this be your purpose, my peach." Red and white lights in the distant roof of the cavern gave the impressions of the ridges of the soft palate. A giant mouth. "Harness your extraordinary love and your awesome hate. They will show themselves soon, and you must not fear yourself. Serve your purpose. Serve the world that will belong to you."

"Oh." I would understand later. I thought she must be dazed. "But I won't be god-king, Grandmother."

"The Child of the Vine must have purpose, Amaunti."

And my siblings don't.

"But we contain multitudes. Zincy will find their purpose. I will help!"

"No one's multitudes contain yours, Amaunti." I wished that I didn't know what that meant. "Inheritance is a fluid thing. Obstacles exist to be removed. Heirs die all the time, peach."

I stuttered something senseless.

"Do you understand what I am saying, my heart?"

"Grandmother." I was crying. "I want to go home. I just want to go home."

She sighed and took my hand in hers, and we left the underground world and the knowledge that the world might die if I did not become my correct self. We didn't return via the same route, and we used seven freight elevators so that Grandmother Athinne did not have to be moved from the sedan, and after four years locked up in a tower, I smelled Mother's gardens and broke into a run.

# 5

Dumplings, Caralee decided, were her favorite thing ever. A puddle of savory grease surrounded the last dumpling in the bowl, frothing at its pinched lips with rich juice. If she had to guess, it was a mixture of hard-rendered critterfat mixed with diced green tubes of some kind, which were delicious and stinky all at once. Critterfat turned bitter when hard-rendered—if Caralee was right, the bug lard had been tempered with a mix of critterfat, pan-crisped critter eyes, and a fresh hemolymph—the grayish jelly that insects used instead of the two fluids that Caralee's body used, blood and lymph.

When all your meals were made from only three or four foods—not including the rare dust hare or sandviper egg—you learned how to conjure up flavor however you could.

Like everyone else back home, Caralee dreamed of eating her own chunk of meat and green vegetables and gravy over fresh bread, but here in Comez, she'd found her first delicacy, and the marvel of it was that these dumplings had been made out of the same bland ingredients she'd eaten all of her life. Somehow, the cook had taken what little the land yielded up and, through an ordinary craft, produced something marvelous.

*Forget sandymancy, I wanna learn how to make dumplings.*

Caralee wondered what other miracles waited for her. Not all of the discoveries she sought needed to be *totally* new things—some would be new combinations of familiar things, or even familiar combinations of new things, like the words of Auld Vintage she'd been learning. The world might be filled with hidden wonders of flavor or music or laughter, and not all magick was magick.

The bullied proprietor hustled out from within his café, holding another wodke and a second mug. Caralee held her breath—after the dumplings, her imagination soared. The Son took the wodke without acknowledging the proprietor's presence, but when the café owner handed Caralee the mug, she saw it held a yellowish, cloudy liquid. She took it with both hands, taming her excitement so they wouldn't shake.

"What is it?" she asked the man, balding and sweet-faced, if a touch terrified.

He leaned close to answer, as if sharing a secret. "I'm certain you will enjoy it."

"Is there any of *that* in it?" She pointed at the Son's glass of wodke and the empty one beside it.

"Sands, no!" The shaking man removed the empty glass. "It's just well water, some sugar beetle, and the juice of lemons—which come all the way from hidden Lastgrown, if you can believe the vegetable merchant." The proprietor did not sound like he believed the merchant's tall tales, but he held up a brilliant yellow jewel and handed it to Caralee. "For you, a gift to take when you leave." He skittered away with a nasty look in the Son's direction.

In Caralee's hands, the lemon wasn't a jewel at all but a tough little ball, rough with pores as big as Wet Sam's nose—but not red or ugly or stinky.

"The skin of the Vine could grow like that," the Son said, casually dropping a gem of history into her brain. "When it wasn't as smooth as aloe vera." He patted the pocket where he'd slipped the stolen spear of the medicine plant.

Caralee lifted the lemon to her nose.

"Scratch at the rind with your fingernail, then smell the oils." The Son smiled with one side of his mouth.

Caralee's sniffed her nail with wide eyes. She sniffed the rind of the lemon where she scratched it. Her smile grew so big that she felt like the top half of her head might fall off.

"This *definitely* doesn't smell like Wet Sam."

The Son didn't bother looking puzzled. "Give it here," he said. "I'm the one with the pockets. Maybe we can sell it."

"We can say it came from Lastgrown, which is shatterscat, because the place doesn't even exist." Caralee didn't mind selling off a jewel. What were jewels, anyway, with no Joe.

Caralee tasted her drink. It was tart, sharp on her tongue, but sweet enough not to be gross. Sugar beetle legs swirled around the bottom of the mug. She tried to sip, but the cup was empty before she knew it. She licked up and crunched the sweet beetle bits. The Son tossed back the last of his wodke and stood up.

"Well?" He looked up and down the side street. "To the inn?"

Caralee felt a bald oddness at just walking away from their table without paying, but she'd asked for it and resigned herself to the fact that it hadn't been a nice thing to ask. She followed the Son down the simple layout of Comez's streets, which made it easy to find their way back to the small plaza with the house that reeked of blood and vapors.

Willum the alderman sat alone on one of the stone benches set around the square. He buried his double-chinned face in his hands. The cart remained tied to its post, and Oti and Atu were cleaning each other with soft wet kisses. They gurgled happily at the sight of Caralee, pawing the air with their forelegs. The crowd had dispersed, and the grieving sister as well. The exhausted alderman looked up at their approach and frowned.

"Who are you two?" He looked from one to the other, closely. "If you've come to whinge about the murder, you can fuck right off."

The Son shook his head. "We are sorry for your loss."

The alderman groaned and dropped his face back into his hands. "That smoke's given me a pounding headache," he said through his fingers.

"It wasn't a person that did it." Caralee blurted out the truth before she could stop herself.

The alderman raised his head from his hands, slowly, with a look of weary surprise.

"And who the fuck are you?"

The Son cleared his throat the way people did when they wanted to punch someone but didn't want to get punched back. The alderman waved his hands the way people did when they didn't want to apologize or punch anyone.

"We've come from the west." The Son sounded prim and eager. Caralee almost laughed. "I am a traveling scholar, and this is my ward and apprentice, Caralee Vinnet."

She tried to imagine the face of an apprentice and ward, traveling with her eager and prim tutor.

"Oh, a schoolteacher." Willum's voice was hollow. "Just exactly what I need, more advice—from a fucking marmer. Hang me, please?" the beleaguered alderman begged.

"Forgive Miss Vinnet's outburst." The Son's mask stuck firm. "We're bound for Grenshtepple's to sell a small portion of her family's harvest—to teach the young woman the fundaments of commerce, you see—and on our travels, I've been tutoring the young lady here on the basics of critical thinking . . ."

"Well, isn't that just fucking lovely." The alderman chewed his lip, thinking. "You say it wasn't a man that killed our Dinnal?" He looked at Caralee for the answer.

"Well . . ." Caralee dithered. At least, she hoped she dithered. She didn't have much practice dithering. "If you look up at the window—"

"You know what?" The alderman slapped his hands on his knees and stretched his back. "Why don't you *show* me."

"Sure!" Caralee would be happy to show off. Help—she'd be happy to *help.*

The Son growled, annoyed but trapped by his own pretense. "What a wonderful opportunity to learn from a professional alderman!" He clapped, smiled, and ground his teeth. "Aren't we fortunate."

Willum stood, stroking his square beard. "Before we enter, let me describe what I found, should it sound too gory for the young miss." He sucked his teeth.

"Yes, please, Mr. Alderman, sir!" Caralee thought she possessed little natural charm, but she imagined putting on a mask, like the Son. This wasn't her. This was some pretend Caralee, who was batty and girlish and danced with everyone at the dance, and Caralee could throw away the mask as soon as she wished. "Don't leave out a single detail, I beg you!"

*Maybe a touch too batty.*

"Fine. The front door was locked from within. White grease paint stained the wall of the stairs leading up to the bedroom. Upstairs, Dinnal lay in her bed, eyes open, half her guts scraped across her mattress." He threw up his hands. "That's what I know."

"You say," the Son began, "that the front door was barred from within. Did you notice any open windows?"

"I, uh . . ." the alderman stuttered. "No, I did not. See here, I'm a thorough fellow, but that Bilmer, Dinnal's sister and my idiot brother's wife"—he paused to look aggrieved—"made herself a bit of a distraction."

Caralee recalled the wailing woman from earlier and pegged the alderman guilty of understatement.

"We saw one open window," Caralee said, holding a finger to the corner of her lips like Fanny Sweatvasser would do when about to say something addlepated. "The crowd frightened me, so we walked down that street there." She pointed to the side street in question. "The first-floor window was open, and I noticed white stuff there, too." She pulled a grimace. "Grease paint, you say? Whomever should want to make paint out of grease, I wonder?" Caralee giggled. It hurt her soul to giggle.

The alderman nodded. "Sands, I'd hoped that was just Bilmer's imagination. How could I have not noticed?" He stood with the creaking groan of a strong, tired person—Willum towered over Caralee and was taller than the Son by a handspan. "Dinnal's son is a sandymancer, you see, recently returned from the west himself. I don't suppose either of you have seen a sandymancer in your travels?"

"A what now? Oh, my, no—I would have loved to see him!" Caralee lied.

"Absolutely not," the Son lied better. "However, I have cataloged the known abilities of lesser sandymancers and some few other powers besides."

Caralee noticed that the Son's lies tended to tell as much truth as they could. Like critterfat in the dumplings, as the ordinary could become extraordinary—so the truth could be the most powerful ingredient in a lie. She'd write that down, too.

"Good, then, you can tell me if a sandymancer can do . . . You'll see." Willum took a deep breath. "I don't believe that Eusebius killed his mother. Not only does he adore her—he's always been broke-boned, and I daresay that his mother was the only one who treated him like a real person. His childhood was before my time, but I'm given to understand that it was dreadful, save for his mother. So he's weak of body, and he's no great sandymancer, or he wouldn't have been assigned to the shitfarms in the Nameless Run." Willum threw up his arms. "It makes no sense."

Caralee bared her teeth at that remark, before remembering that pretend-Caralee probably wasn't the kind of person to bare her teeth at much beside her own reflection. Fanny would say something about, like, a vault of stolen names, or sing a nursery rhyme about spontaneously exploding matrons.

"Are you sure that this is the right sort of lesson for your young miss?" With narrowed eyes the alderman examined the Son, who nodded once. The alderman raised his eyebrows and shrugged with his whole body. "Well. I'll say it again—this is a grisly sight, if you're still of a mind to see it. Prepare yourselves."

"Never you fear, sir," the Son reassured Willum. "We are wastelanders. Grisly is our normal. Why, we passed a dead woman on the road here, and this one"—he jerked his head toward Caralee and laughed out loud—"stopped to play with the corpse."

*Motherfucker.*

"In we go, I suppose." Willum stepped through the yellow-painted door, his hand pushing it aside. Caralee saw that the door hung half off its hinges.

"Bilmer insisted we bust open the door," Amos said, "when Dinnal was late for lunch and Bilmer found the door barred. Comezze don't bar their doors—we're safe inside our walls." The alderman bit his cheek.

The interior of the house remained as Caralee and the Son had last seen it, though the red smoke had cleared.

"Her carpet's missing—see the outline on the floor?" The alderman indicated the cleaner rectangle of flooring that Caralee had noticed earlier.

"Comezze really don't bar their doors at night?" the Son asked.

Willum snorted. "Most of these sods don't even bother to use the hitching post for their critters, as you have. Only outsiders are cautious. I've never knocked on a barred door once, in all the years since I came to Comez."

"Really?" Caralee asked, with pitch-perfect innocence. "Then why would this—Eusebius, was it?—bar the door and climb out the window?" She waited for the alderman to think it through. Almost waited. "Why go to all that trouble? He'd not look guilty leaving his mother's house through the front door. I say, he must have been in a frightful hurry!"

Willum shook his head, salt-and-pepper stubble bristling along his close-shaved temples. "Who knows what motivates a sandymancer? That's what confounds me. Besides which, the poor man was born with brittle bones that only worsened with time. I can't honestly picture him creeping about like a shadow-thief."

They headed up the stairs, and Willum pointed out the white handprints up and down the walls. When they entered the bedroom, Caralee pretended to wince at the sight of the murdered woman. "Sands!" she exclaimed, making a show of girding her stomach with her hands.

"I warned you."

The trio walked around the bed, and Willum pointed at the three great wounds that had gouged the body and the mattress, and the entrails dangling off the side of the mattress like a torn blanket.

At the same time, Caralee pointed to the scratches on the floor leading to and from the window, and the deeper scratches on the sill.

The alderman stammered, re-embarrassed at being so unobservant earlier. Bilmer certainly seemed like a handful, though, and Willum was clearly out of his depth—but so was Caralee, so she couldn't blame the man for not seeing the impossible.

Willum studied the floor, and then the window, and then crossed his arms and glared at the body. "I think we can all agree that this is no ordinary murder. I'm curious to hear if these wounds and scratches match up with any gruesome sandymancy."

"Can sandymancers transform into beasts?" Caralee asked, curious herself. She put a hand to her cheek. It was certainly a Fanny Sweatvasser question.

"A sandymancer?" The Son bit out the word with a sneer. "Absolutely not. That is, ugh, *sandymancy* is a discipline of controlling the elements only—it isn't a font of limitless wonders."

That had the ring of truth to it, Caralee decided. Which was the Son's favorite way to lie. A sandymancer like Eusebius might not be able to claw a woman to death, but Caralee had felt the Son's lashes beat her with nothing but the air itself.

"I knew it weren't him." Willum grumbled. "His ma were too dear to him and his body too frail." The alderman sighed again, till Caralee thought he'd faint from lack of air. "Poor Eusebius. He's odd and unpleasant and hard to look at, but the man's a coward through and through."

That also had the ring of truth to it, and Caralee wondered if she'd been too hard on the wizard.

Willum knelt by the bed, examining the wounds and scratches on the floor. "Dinnal here might have been the only person who'd ever loved him, and we all knew her for a sweet, kind lady. No one had any motive to kill Dinnal—absolutely no one, and her boy didn't do it." The big man scratched his chin through his beard. "I believed as much, but I let Bilmer have her say—not that she gave me any choice in the matter. Cursed woman distracted me. Sands, these scratches *are* claw marks, and they go both ways, from the window and back again."

"Whatever does that mean, Mr. Alderman, sir?" Caralee asked, starting to get fed up with her act. She batted her eyes at Willum. She would have to imagine new masks to wear.

*Is that how it starts? Who would she have to become?*

"What it means is that unless he's got a monster for a companion, Eusebius is likely guilty of no more than cowardice. He saw his mother's corpse and fled. He probably barred the door and escaped through the window into the alleyway. Poor lad."

"Indeed," said the Son.

"Oh my." Caralee shook her head.

"But what *manner* of monster could do such a thing?" the Son pressed. That question was the reason for this entire play-pretend. Caralee wondered if the alderman believed in monsters.

Willum shrugged and bent over, stretching his spine. "You're the scholar. I'm just a glorified guard who lets himself be worked half to death. The only monsters I know are bandits and the occasional chuckler nest. The nasty little fuzzballs have been burrowing right under the walls, but we exterminate them before they grow large enough to eat anything bigger than a cat or a house-critter. Besides, chucklers don't have claws, and they can't climb . . . or fly." Willum had just realized that the monster had *flown*, and his craggy face grew even stonier. "Scat. Shatterscat. Scatass shatterscat fucktwit. What kind of beast flies? Just the *mention* of a flying beast will terrify the townsfolk and create another headache for me." Then, "Or, sands, more bloodshed. Fuck me with a mandible."

"All the birds we've studied are scavengers, most kind sir," Caralee fibbed, turning to the Son. "*I've* certainly never heard of a creature that could make marks like this. Have you, sir?"

The Son closed his eyes in what looked like a long blink. It was as if he didn't trust himself to answer.

"I have not." Willum answered first. "Maybe those metal folk have," he mused, and the Son's eyes went wide. "I owe them a grilling since they built their whatever-it-is on our road."

"The, eh, *metal* folk?" The Son poured his energy into the pinched voice of his tutorly mask. "You have met with them?"

"You didn't see their queer metal road?" Willum shrugged. "It appeared overnight, then two people in metal jerkins and metal greaves showed up with the gumption to ask me to establish a trade route." He hacked up a gob of spit. "As if I know scat about the to-and-fro of commerce. Told them they might've asked before they built a fucking metal road. Told them they were welcome to buy whatever they could at market and to sell whatever folk would buy. Was the least I could do. Ent much around here that calls for a brand-new road, I told em, unless you want dirt and stone—and they can get those for free."

"Oh!" Caralee buzzed with curiosity, but tried not to hop up and down. "So they . . . they were real people?"

"Yes, yes." Willum Amos nodded as if he'd answered the question more than a few times. "Flesh and blood, same as you and me. All dressed in metal, sure, but folk all the same. They brought no metal monsters, leastwise not that I saw. You can be sure as scat that I'll ask when they show up again, though. Been quarrying stone, too, and I'm not sure how I feel about that."

The alderman shook his head back and forth, and led them downstairs and out into the plaza without another word, head still shaking.

Outside, he thanked them for their help and pressed some coins into the Son's hand when he shook it. "Fantastic creatures aside, your cart should be safe here overnight. I'll order some guardsfolk to watch the square through the night, anyway, and they'll appreciate having critters nearby—if any monster approaches, might be the critters'll sense it before my dunderheads."

Willum groaned and ran his hands across his bald scalp. "I suggest a nice bed for the both of you, up that way." He pointed toward the inn. "You'll find the Last of the Wine more comfortable than most."

Willum paused, then confessed, "I'd say you've earned half my day's pay, even if the news is mixed. Of course, *I* never suspected him." The alderman rolled his eyes. "If this is the work of some rare creature, we've precautions to take. It'll be barred doors and locked windows for us all. . . . And they say Comezze never change."

After kissing Atu and Oti goodbye, Caralee and the Son left the alderman to his burdens for the comforts of the inn. When they were safely out of earshot, Caralee and the Son turned to each other with matching expressions.

"What the scat?" Caralee said first. "What jazz was that? So what *actually* killed that lady, and *the metal people have been here*?" She remembered the Son's question about harpies and his surprise. "You worried a harpy did it?"

"I never worry, I feel concern—and I'm not at all sure." The Son kept his voice calm but didn't hide his excitement entirely. "And of course the metal people have been here—they built a road. If they really did build it overnight, that bespeaks a certain level of advancement that might concern me. Also, they're gracious enough to inquire about trade, which bespeaks a certain attitude toward diplomacy—but they didn't ask permission to quarry stone. If it's true that they're armored humans who can construct fast-travel overland routes after 'falling' through my sky, then they're some of our—"

The Son broke off.

"Some of our what?" Caralee hated when people stopped talking at the most interesting part of the sentence. Then again, maybe it wouldn't be the most interesting part of the sentence if they'd kept on talking.

"Some of our cousins from among the stars, Caralee," the Son said on a deep exhale.

"I don't get it. We have an aunt and uncle in the stars? How's that work?"

"Never mind." The Son chewed his lip. "I mean to say, whoever they are and wherever they're from, they've the capacity to do what they want, take what they want, *kill* whomever they want—and yet from what the village idiot had to say, they've been both polite and presumptuous."

"So?"

"So what?"

"So what are we going to do about them?"

"We?" The Son blinked rapidly, but considered Caralee's question. "We're going to find out more about them, of course. I don't think that will happen here."

"But you called the alderman an—"

"Idiot, yes. But he's the best Comez has to offer, and he keeps his ear to the ground, and more importantly, the metal folk came to him. We could spend days here, ferreting out anyone with a drop more information, or we could move on to—what did you call it?"

"Grenshtepple's."

"Grenshtepple's, then. The closer we get to the Duchy, the more likely we are to learn about them."

Caralee supposed that was a good enough answer, even if she hated waiting more than just about anything.

"Wait." With a sudden halt and an outstretched arm, the Son stopped at an intersection where an even narrower alley crossed through. He looked down the alley with interest, eyes wide. "What in the name of the sacred sap . . ." Caralee couldn't see anything but felt the buzz of sandymancy from the Son. "What is it?"

"You did very well back there, Caralee." He congratulated her without answering her question. "So well, in fact, that you deserve a reward."

"I really did," Caralee agreed. "What's my prize?"

"Oh, just some *ancient ruins,*" the Son said with mock boredom, flicking his hair away from his face. "If you have any interest in *ancient ruins,* that is. If *ancient ruins* from the Land of the Vine don't sound boring to you."

"Ancient ruins?" Caralee hauled off and punched him in the thigh, not caring for the moment that he was the monster he was. "Show me these scatting ruins *right the scat now.*"

The Son chortled. "Our day is done. If you can wait till tomorrow, I'll show you a wonder."

*Aw, tomorrow's forever.*

"To the inn, Caralee."

Given that she'd never been to an inn before, Caralee knew better than to act impatiently—staying somewhere with food and bed might not be news for the Son, but as far as Caralee felt, it was a second reward. She was wise enough to control herself—just barely.

*Vellaeke,* "wise." From *vellat,* "wisdom." Caralee wanted—needed—to become a *vellaeke seyfa,* a "wise woman." Like the Son's grandmother. That's what he had called her.

*So he loved his gran, or at least he thought she was wise.* How could Caralee use that against him?

She'd get there, one step at a time, till she was wise enough to save Joe.

Caralee knew when they'd found the Last of the Wine, because over its doorway hung a blacksmith's whimsy depicting a clump of balls. *These* were the balls Joe had teased her with? She almost giggled.

*I don't giggle.* When you wore a mask, did the mask wear you, just a little?

"What's funny?" asked the Son.

"That sign-thing up there." She pointed. "Joe always said it was a bunch of balls, but I never believed him. Do you think those are, like, men's balls?" She blushed. It was a blush-worthy concept.

"I wish!" The Son laughed with his whole body, bending back and forth like a sidewinder snake. "No, no, dear Caralee, that right there is what's called *a bunch of grapes.* Do you have any idea what a grape is?"

She shook her head. "I know what an onion is. Is it like an onion?"

"I desperately hope you do not make wine from onions. Grapes are a fruit. Fruits grow on plants—like your lemon. From grapes, wine is made. *Was* made." He indicated the iron grapes. "Thus, I suspect, the name of the inn. May we enter, please? This talk of wine has me wistful, and whatever swill served here will have to do—but quickly."

The Son pushed open the door, and Caralee breathed in warm air that smelled of roast meat, fresh bread, and cableshine. They entered a firelit common room set with chairs and tables, stairs leading up to their right, and a bar at the far end, with a kitchen behind, from which wafted sensations flooding her palate. The tables were almost all full and occupied by what looked like a mix of locals and travelers. The locals looked clean, and their clothes were more brightly colored, while the travelers, who sat in groups apart, seemed as beige and dusty as the world.

The Son strode up to the bartender as if the inn belonged to him and tossed two shekels onto the bar. The wood must have been old to be so big and long and brown. Someone took care of it—the polish of the grain caught the candlelight. "A room, two of your strongest drinks, and two of your best, uh . . . platters?"

*He just paid four times over.* Caralee would have laughed, if her own fortune didn't depend on their lack of one.

The smiling lump of a man behind the bar nodded wordlessly and gestured toward an empty table. Caralee sat while the Son waited for their drinks, and noticed that more than a few heads turned her way. Feeling the gaze of strangers, unasked for, prickled her skin, and Caralee realized that the Son had transformed her and made her, of all things, *shapely.* She felt out of place with this ribbon-cinched waist and knotted hem, and the looks she was getting managed to make her feel glad and uncomfortable at the same time. She was glad to see the Son return with two mugs of cableshine, which was stronger than wodke, and much, much cheaper. The stuff tasted unspeakably disgusting, but only until it dissolved your taste buds.

The Son would be better off drinking onion beer, which she hadn't the courage to tell him was, in fact, a real thing. The Son set one mug before Caralee and sat while sniffing his own. His look of revulsion told Caralee she'd been right about the cableshine.

She sipped hers and kept her face still. Belly, too. Cableshine smelled like feet, tasted like armpit sweat, and burned twice as strong as wodke. They locked eyes, a secret challenge. He took a great swallow and smacked his mouth in delight. Of *course* the Son of the Vine had an iron stomach, on account of all the bloodshed and wickedness and legendary monstrosity.

Caralee sipped the nasty spirit again, but then pushed it away—she already felt her head buzzing and knew to stop. The medicine had done its work, lessening the overwhelming feeling of being watched so closely by a room full of strangers.

"It's disgusting, isn't it?" the Son asked, smiling with his teeth. "You people are devolved, blasphemously primitive, yet still able to create one of the wonders of humankind. This swill could taste like my own shit and I'd drink it dry. Oh, how I've missed strong drink."

He took a great swallow, and then a queer expression rippled across his face. He took a smaller sip and rolled it around in his mouth.

"For all the filth, there's a note in your cableshine . . . that doesn't taste entirely unlike brandyvine." He closed his eyes again. "Oh, for a bottle of the Vine's best ferment."

"Well, it's just cable mash, and cable plant sure ent the Vine."

Caralee noticed that there were still quite a few faces turned their way, and so did her companion. The Son put an elbow on the table and, slurring his words just a little, advised her:

"Ancient wisdom: either dress to impress, or dress to correct." He looked her over and took a swallow of cableshine. "So if you're sick of being called a girl, stop dressing like one. You've been a girl; you know what's expected from a girl. Learn what it's like to be a woman; learn what's expected from a woman. Then you'll begin to understand how to use those expectations. Manipulate, invert, shatter, destroy, murder, rage, destroy—did I say *destroy*? Destroy." He wagged a finger. The man—the monster—was only a little high after a pint of the strongest drink in the world. He should be blackout drunk.

"Right now, you have the choice. In a year, perhaps months, you'll have a woman's body forever—a state with its benefits, but not without significant and multiple dangers. Were I you, I'd experiment with womanhood and girlhood while you can. Study for the battle ahead."

"Alll riiight." Her tongue struggled, after just one sip—maybe two. Counting became hard after a sip of cableshine. " I will . . . and when I pull that off, I'll be *two* people at *once* just like *you*." She burped in his face.

# 6

That night, while the Son slept in a stuffed bed and rested his head upon vulture-down pillows, Caralee sat on the floor beside two candles, holding her journal in her hands. She unhooked the clasp of the extra fold of leather that protected the prize within. Opening the weathered bundle, she ran her fingertips over the first page, still blank. Nothing in Caralee's world had ever looked that clean—not even the sky. She could only spoil it—and how not to spoil it? What would she write or draw? What went in the book, and what should she leave out?

With the pencil in her hand, Caralee defaced the journal. On that first page, in large letters, she wrote: *My Thoughts, I Think.* Beneath that she wrote her name in slightly smaller letters, Caralee L. Vinnet.

She straightened her back and looked at what she'd done. Her letters could be neater, but she'd marked the page with her name. The journal wasn't blank anymore; it belonged to her.

*Mine.*

She turned the page with a smile and found two more empty pages waiting. The thrill of possibilities energized her, and, hunched over her book, Caralee began to pour herself onto the page. Words and pictures, thoughts and imaginings, theories and diagrams—she'd never seen the contents of her head, and breathed hard with the joy and effort of it.

All the words of Auld Vintage she'd learned, and the way they fit together, their "roots," as the Son had called them—they went onto one page, leaving many more blank for the words she hoped would follow. She drew the lemon and the aloe vera and the shape of a plant that grew in tight spirals but stretched across the world the way a cable plant stretched across its acre of field. She sketched the crack in the sky as it was today and as it might have been when Mag was wee and earlier. The tin ramp and the metal road. What she imagined ancient ruins might look like, a dozen ways. Mag's frown and her heavy locs. The Son's hair over his eyes as he slept. Joe's jaw, his neck, his shoulders. Joe's face, over and over.

For a person who'd never drawn more than a pair of tits in the dirt with her toe, Caralee was pleased that her hand seemed to follow her mind's eye—though it was harder for her hand to follow her actual eye, when she sketched the Son's face, looking for a sign of Joe but finding none.

When the night neared morning and the predawn glow crept through the window, Caralee was still scribbling. She worked so intently that she failed to notice the Son roll over in bed to watch her. He didn't speak till some time later.

"At it all night?" he said to the dead silence. "I've created a beast."

Caralee sat up with a shock, and the book slipped from her lap to the floor, landing faceup to one of her drawings. She snatched up the journal, tucked in the pencil, and wrapped the book tight in its leather, fastening the clasp with her lips pursed. The Son pantomimed scandal.

"What ho! Is that *my* face etched upon thy precious page? Pray tell, what other confessions lie within thine precious tome?" He pressed his hand to his heart.

*Joe's heart.*

"You even nailed the writer's slouch. I'm impressed."

"No you ent." Caralee stood, stretching her sore spine. Her neck still ached from the Son's invisible beating with sandymancy on the day he'd stolen Joe's body, which seemed forever ago but was only two days earlier. Spending the night curled over her journal had only made the neck ache worse. "That don't impress you much."

"True." He slid out of bed bare-assed naked, yawning and stretching his arms, twisting at the waist, legs spread and feet planted.

*This again.* Was he going to show off naked every morning? Caralee supposed that'd be what made it a morning routine, and prepared herself to endure what seemed like such crotch-floppity arrogance. Then again, maybe she should stretch and push herself—with clothes on—to make her body as strong as his was. That would be a good idea, wouldn't it? He certainly looked as though he benefited from the routine.

Caralee didn't feel *one bit* lusty toward the Son, owing to personal preference and the fact that he was evil personified who'd stolen her only friend. She preferred a thicker, rougher-looking fella, and—if she was being honest with herself—one that wasn't smarter than she was. Caralee liked to be the smart one and found herself most drawn to Joe when he was kind, but also when he struggled with simple tasks. She wasn't necessarily proud to admit that, but she didn't see any way to change it. She didn't find silly women attractive, either—with womenfolk, Caralee didn't mind smarts, so long as they were practical smarts and not daydreamy smarts like her own. Caralee wondered if she'd feel lusty toward a woman. Marm-marm was the only woman she'd known who fit the description, but she was Marm-marm and not for lusting after.

The Son, on the other hand, could raise the cock and wet the cunny of just about anyone in the world. Caralee wasn't just anyone, but she knew sexy when she saw it. More than a few wouldn't mind these floppity mornings at all.

If a more beautiful man existed, she'd pay good shekels to see him just to know. The Son's sleek triangular torso, his hard stomach that followed two gutters of muscle to melt into his round thighs—and between them, well, Caralee blushed. His arms, thighs, and chest seemed more muscular than his thin-waisted frame suggested. His dark hair spilled over his shoulders, and his face always seemed to catch the light in the most flattering way possible, looking angular and indestructible.

The Son rinsed himself from the basin of water—dipping his face into that cool mask—and patted himself dry with the bedsheet. He leaned naked against the bed frame and produced a smear of something that looked like silky putty in his palm. He rubbed his hands together, then combed the stuff through his hair with his fingers. He tossed his hair so that it shadowed one eye.

"Come here." He crooked a finger. "You don't get to wash, obviously. I've no desire to ruin my appetite with the sight of your lumpy almost-body, but you can, at least, do *something* with your hair."

"Wossat?" Caralee indicated the stuff that shined in a thin layer on his palms.

"It's from a crock of lard I begged off the bartender while you were being ogled by drunks. We make do with what we have, don't we. Come here, darling worm, and spin around."

She spun around, and around again, before the Son grabbed her by the roots of her hair and tugged till she faced away from him. She yelped like Mag at a startle; he ignored her.

The rest of the grooming process was relatively gentle. He distributed the lard evenly across his palms, then wiped off any excess with the sheet he'd used to dry himself. The Son pulled up some sections of her hair and tugged down others, rolled some around his fingers, and glared at the rest.

"Better, but saccharine. Dip your head down and flip it up as quick as you can without snapping your twiggy neck. Good. Now shake it side to side till I say stop. Stop. Stop! Sap and semen, you are ferocious." He patted her hair like a babby's back. "I was styled since birth, so my technique is flawless. You're hopeless, but I have to say, I do good work. You're almost average. Not quite, but almost."

*Fuck you?* Caralee thought, but didn't say. At least keeping her mouth shut was getting easier.

The Son retied her ribbon belt and re-hiked the hem of her burlap shmata.

"How you people survive without mirrors is a mystery, but it does explain a lot." He straightened Joe's trousers as best he could.

*They're too big now.* The thought hit Caralee like a charging dunderbeast.

"Rich folk got mirrors." Back home, the village shared half a broken hand glass, but Caralee'd never bothered at the ongoing struggle to get a moment with the thing. She wondered if that'd been a mistake. Then she wondered why she got angry at the thought of needing to look in a mirror. She'd gotten this far without one.

"Now tell me about my reward," Caralee demanded of the Son.

"Reward?" He buttoned up Joe's shirt, then unbuttoned it to his satisfaction.

"You remember, you scathole."

"Oh, that." The Son took Joe's jacket from the peg on the wall where he'd hung Joe's things, and slipped into it. The jacket was big as well, but not too much—it had always pulled tight across Joe's round shoulders. "My age is past, my homes long ago fallen to dust. The world, however, finds a way to preserve a bit of everything it has lost. Remember that when you lose something—or someone: all manner of things return." He had one foot out the door, his face obscured. "All manner of things. So follow me."

Caralee trotted after him, cranky but hungry for the bait he'd laid out for her. She wondered which of her drawings would look most like these alleged "ancient ruins."

At first, the Son's generosity had seemed at odds with his character, Caralee mused as they left the Last of the Wine, but now she suspected that he saw generosity as just another tool to control. She raised a fare-thee-well chin at the smiling lump behind the bar, who nodded in return. He didn't appear to have moved all night.

The morning was darkly clear, the eastern half of the sky painted with spears of sunlight that almost turned the crack in the sky a too-bright pinkish gold, and the starbirth clouds had given way to the daytime stars. Caralee stopped to check on the critters after the short walk to yesterday's murder plaza—as promised by the alderman, the cart and its cargo remained unmolested. Three guards dozed under the merchants' stalls beside the cart, and one grunted a surly hello at their approach.

Atu and Oti chirruped happily to see Caralee—she had worried about them, though she knew they'd be fine. Comez was on alert, and Caralee saw other guards in their blue-badged coats patrolling the streets. If there'd been any sign of something unnatural, the criers would have cried—but the night had stayed silent. Caralee indulged the critters, letting each kiss a hand. Both were so dear and loved her so much that she was up to her elbow in the soft tubes of their mouthparts before she knew it, laughing and giggling at their suckling.

The Son pretended to vomit, and Caralee pulled herself out of her burden-critters' mouths, wiping her hands and arms on the side of the cart, then scrubbing them dry on a bagged bushel of cable wicker. The Son basked in the sideways sunlight that brought daytime to the *nihnepsolom,* drenching the murder house in color that matched the painted yellow door and windows. Staring at the crack in the sky, he traced its shape with a finger.

"The world is leaking atmosphere," he said matter-of-factly, turning away from the broken sky. "Slowly, but more and more so if that crack continues to grow. You say it was smaller when Joe's grandmother was young?"

"Ayup." Caralee thought that *atmosphere* was another word for her journal, but she got the gist of it. What else would be leaking through a crack in the sky, if not air?

"There are worse consequences than a dark sky during the daytime—worse even than a suffocating world that's already been dried up nearly past saving. . . . Things could be worse." He said this last to himself and then shot Caralee a shut-up glance. "I know, I know; I'm evil, et cetera. I'm also right; things can always get worse."

The Son rubbed his neck. "Now is not the time for calculations—I'll have to make some, soon, if you'll rip me a page from your journal." The Son looked uneasy. "Few things scare me, Caralee Vinnet—and that"—he cocked his head upward—"is one of them."

He chewed his lip and cracked his knuckles. "When you win our battle and unmake me, and the world is left to fend for itself, then *you* will be in charge, whether the drooling idiots of the world recognize it or not. You will be the alpha idiot. When that day comes, remember that there is always some new apocalypse waiting around the corner."

He paused. "Or maybe *you'll* die, and I'll remember it."

"What good is that gonna do?" Caralee didn't understand.

"Presumably, you will remember to carry out our purpose." He shrugged one shoulder. "I would."

*Now wait one minute. Purpose* was the word that had stunned him yesterday, when talking about harpies.

"You gotta purpose?" This was the first bread crumb that the Son had dropped, the first hint he'd given Caralee of his intentions. "*We* gotta purpose?"

The Son looked her up and down, but not in the way he had when styling her hair or tidying up her shmata.

"I promised you the end to my story, didn't I? Someone has to fix the sky."

"You wanna *fix* the *sky*?" she asked. It wasn't possible, but then neither was anything else about the Son of the Vine. "And you're gonna do it with *me*?"

"Along the way, yes. Someone has to fix the sky." The way the Son repeated himself, Caralee could tell it wasn't the only part of his purpose. As a matter of fact, fixing the sky would be the only part of *anything* he wanted to do after escaping the wasteland. Surely, he'd have designs older than that.

So it did not surprise Caralee that the Son kept his secrets. The sky was a start.

She flared her nostrils. "Then we fix the sky."

The Son took her chin in one hand and leaned in, their gazes locked. "This world needs caretakers. Every caretaker is a beast, whether they be harsh or kind. Even the kindest caretaker knows in her heart that, in times of certain peril, the end does indeed justify the means. One day, such a beast may have to choose between loves and lives, even if it makes a monster of her."

"A beast is a monster."

"*No.* Haven't you been listening to anything I've said up to this point? A beast has purpose. A monster has only passion. The caretakers of the world have purpose—that is what we are. Whether it's reengineering a faulty superstructure or breaking apart carbon dioxide molecules to outgas oxygen, it is the caretakers' duty to persevere. Do you understand?"

"If you talked anything other than fancy jazz, I could tell you."

"Forget I said a single word." He flipped his hair toward her face and sucked his teeth. "You're all doomed."

Though the Son had disturbed Caralee with his talk of purpose and apocalypses, sky missions, caretakers, and beasts and monsters, she pulled herself together and reassured Oti and Atu that she'd be back soon. They gurgled mournfully as the Son led Caralee back to the little alley and whatever secrets it held—or didn't.

The promise of ancient ruins washed away some of her worry.

They walked around the rind of the bowl that nestled Comez—one circular road ringed the gridded streets, and walking along it offered a view of nearly everything below. There was the central, tiered open-air market, half of it bustling with commerce, the other half empty—and there, to the north, the three-keyed gate smiled like a sideways mouth with only three teeth left, and the blue terra-cotta rooftops outshone the morning haze. To the south, where the world stopped, rose a wall of mountains. Back home, those mountains were little more than a line of shadow obscured by dust haze, but here they loomed over Comez, toothy and impassable—her trip with the Son had been mostly eastward, but the road dipped south at the last bit, and by the time they'd reached Comez, they'd grown closer to the barrier mountains. They folded against one another, forming a solid wall, all sheared cliffs and impossible peaks.

No one ever passed through those mountains. The world ended there.

Looking at the town below her, Caralee thought of the tumbledown walls of the cottages in her village. The buildings here in Comez had a similar rectangular footprint, the same three-finger-style cornerstones wherever two walls and the floor met at straight angles. The difference was their condition: the houses back home were little more than ruins made livable in the slapdash fashion of wastelanders. The houses in Comez all still had their original stone archways or had been maintained in their original condition.

Before she'd met the Son of the Vine, Caralee had assumed that all buildings were based on the same template—squares or rectangles arranged this way or that. What else could they look like? For once, she tried her best *not* to imagine, which would spoil her discovery. She'd imagined all night long and had drawings, so she didn't need to hold the images in her head. She let them go and opened up her mind to new ideas. There could be hints all around her.

"The houses here aren't in ruins. Why are ours so dilapidated, back home—is that a word, dilapidated?"

The Son snorted and nodded. "I've not seen your nameless shitfarm, but I imagine it's far away from a decent quarry and you've no masons, nor the numbers for the work."

"We don't farm scat! Why does everybody keep saying that."

"Caralee, focus." That was a fair request.

*So.* If buildings in Comez shared a similar design to the buildings back home, then an unfamiliar design should stand out, if she could spot it. She'd seen the basics of modern construction: square corners, right angles, gray stone from a quarry a day or two north of here—and the Son had been right about her village being too distant from any source of good building rock. Streets laid out in a grid—well, that was a result of square corners and straight walls, wasn't it? Back in the Son's day, the world had dripped green, and the Vine coiled all around. Straight lines wouldn't have been the only option, maybe. What might folk have created in the Vintage world?

Caralee caught herself daydreaming again. With the Son as her companion, she knew she must be the best possible version of herself to stand a chance to foil him. Sands, she couldn't even keep her mind on one thing during a morning stroll. The Son pointed at the three-fingered cornerstones they passed, where two walls met a floor. "You call it a *cornerstone.* In our tongue, the word was *rac opkthene. Rac* means 'first,' and *ob* means 'hard.' *Kthene* means 'earth.' What do you think *rac opkthene* means?"

"First and hard and earth, so maybe it means 'first stone'? Definitely 'first stone.' But why change *ob* to *op*?" She didn't understand the rules, but knew they must exist.

Caralee thought that for someone who'd never heard another language, she had a talent for learning them. She'd impressed herself so far, which was a not-new feeling, but one she felt in a new way, about a new thing.

"Bonus points for the correct answer and an insightful follow-up question." The Son smiled. His brown eyes caught the sunlight at an angle and turned to gold. "Certain sounds fit together. Put your hand on your chest and say the 'phh' sound." She did. "Now say 'bhh.'" She did, and felt her chest vibrate.

"Can you feel how the only difference between those two sounds is that vibrating in your chest?"

"What do you mean?"

"I mean that you kept your tongue in the same place for both sounds, and that vibration in your chest was the only difference between the two."

Caralee nodded.

"That's a manner of articulation called *voicing.* When you put two different kinds of sounds together, one often adopts the manner of articulation of the other. This compromise of sounds happens naturally in the evolution of language, in some ways, because it can make the word easier to pronounce. Thus, *ob* becomes *op* when it comes before the 'khh' sound of *kthene.* Hold your hand to your chest again and say those three sounds."

"Khh. Phh. Bhh." She felt ridiculous.

"Which sounds are voiced?"

Caralee lit up. "Only 'bhh' is voiced! The others don't vibrate."

The Son clapped. "You philologist! My young word-lover. It does make sense—you talk so much that you must have accrued an instinct concerning language."

"Naturally," she agreed. Caralee knew she talked a lot, that much was true. Why pretend it didn't have its benefits?

"If you voice the 'khh' sound, what sound does it make?"

Caralee tried several times to work her mouth and throat correctly, during which she sounded like she was drowning in her own blood, until she found the answer. "It makes the 'ghh' sound."

"Indeed. What if you put *op* in front of a word that began with a voiced sound? For example, *gupp* means 'water.' What word do you get if you put them together, with *op* coming first, and what does it mean?"

Caralee bit her lip. She'd have to stop doing that when in deep thought. The Son controlled himself to keep his secrets safe. If she intended to best him, she'd have to learn to do the same.

"*Op* plus *gupp*. Phh. Ghh. So that'd be *obgupp*, right?" She said it again. "It does come out of my mouth easier than *op-gupp*," she acknowledged.

The Son nodded. "Correct. Its meaning?"

"What it means? Hard water. What's like water, but hard." She resisted the urge to chew her lips, tug on her ears, or frown. "That's a tough one—wait, it's *ice*! Ice is hard water!" This was fun. "Does hard stone mean metal?"

"Yes! Yes, bravo!" the Son exclaimed. "You're far more clever than I was at your age."

*Liar.*

Age, that was another weapon. Caralee could learn anything—she could even learn to control herself, maybe. How, though, could she ever catch up to the Son in terms of time? He'd had a prince's education, and near to forever to teach himself, trapped in his stone *matzeva*.

The Son turned his attention to the doorways. He stopped at one and nodded at the square stones that rose on either side of the entryway, then waved a hand at the curved stones above that formed their arches. He asked Caralee to consider those curved stones. The square stones—the square *opkthene*—rose in a straight line to a point somewhere above Caralee's head but below the Son's. Beyond those, the *opkthene* began, bit by bit, to take on a rounded triangular shape.

The Son said as much. He ran his finger up one side of the arch and stopped at the topmost stone, which was a chunky block that looked like an upside-down, rounded triangle with the tip cut off. Marm-marm would call it a . . . *trap* . . . *trapezoid*. But rounded at the top and bottom.

"*Angkhet opkthene*." This was another vocabulary question. The Son shook his head the way someone does when they've forgotten something obvious. "*Angkhet!* I can't believe I haven't taught you the Auld Vintage word for the Vine—your stupidity must be contagious. The name for the Vine is *Angkhet*. So what is the *Angkhet opkthene*?"

"Vine stone?" Caralee didn't see the connection. "What the scat is a Vine stone? Why would they name a funny part of a building after the most sacred and important thing in the world?" she asked.

"Precisely because the Vine is—was—no, *is* so important. In our mutual common language, the *Angkhet opkthene* is called a 'keystone.' Why do you think that is? What do a key and the Vine have in common?"

"Nothing?" Caralee blurted out before she'd given the question any thought. "I mean, okay. The Vine was the *key* to keeping the world alive, right? And a key closes a lock. Maybe a keystone is the *key* to holding the archway together?"

"Go on." The Son gave no hint of whether she was right or wrong. He wanted her to finish laying out her reasoning. She liked that—it would train her to maintain her focus.

"Well, so if it's the most important stone in the archway, then . . . Hey, if you took away the keystone, both sides of the archway would fall down. Those curvy stones are stacked to fit, but they're unbalanced. If you set them like that, they'd fall inward as soon as you moved your hands. But if you held them up, and if you put the keystone right in the middle, and if they all still fit together just so, then that keystone would catch the curved stones on both side and steady them, while the slanty edges of the stones on either side would hold up the keystone at the same time. It's like a lock, but for stones."

The Son said nothing and strolled along.

"Am I wrong?" Caralee asked.

"Of course not. I've just exhausted my supply of compliments. You'll have to congratulate yourself."

She knew it! How'd she know it? Is this what real learning felt like? Intending no offense to Marm-marm, real learning was almost better than dumplings. Almost.

"Keystone, huh? Why not 'lockstone'? That would make more sense." Caralee thought about home. "Hey, why didn't we just rebuild our doorways whenever they fell down? The stones would be right there, so even if they broke when they fell, you'd still know what was missing. Why'd we forget that? You just balance the stones right—make sure they're all shaped right. That's easy enough to remember."

The Son let out a long breath. "That's not a question I can answer. There's an old cliché, which like most clichés is true, that says the only constant is change. This is change: the result of what you gain and what you lose. My fathers' fathers' fathers built palaces. *Their* fathers' fathers' fathers built the sky, and I haven't any idea how. Everything changes. Everything that begins, ends."

They'd reached the narrow alley from the night before. In the daylight, the alley was better lit and stopped at a plain stone wall, but the ground beneath the dead end had been boarded up with three planks of real wood. Wood was expensive enough that whatever lay below must be important or dangerous or both.

"Hmm." The Son bent at the waist and examined the sturdy boards. "Turn these boards to sawdust."

"Okay? I should use my, you know—sandysense—right?"

"Cock-a-vine! Tell me that's not what your people call your seventh sense."

"Seventh sense. Huh. Aren't you skipping one?"

"Boards, dust, now. Please." He pressed his fingers over his eyes and made a show of his impatience.

Caralee extended her sandysense and felt the precious wood. She hated to destroy it, but she wasn't going to let that stop her—whatever lay beneath—ancient ruins or just some stuff the Comezze didn't want anyone poking through—Caralee intended to see it. To her sense, the wood tasted different from sand and dust. No, it wasn't quite taste, but it was something like the ghost of taste.

Not-tasting wood, Caralee pulled at the first board. The board strained but didn't break. She pulled harder, but nothing happened. Then she tried pulling and pushing at the same time—and with a moan, the boards buckled—just a little bit. So she pulled and pushed, pushed and pulled, until she'd chipped the wood to pieces.

She did the same with the second board, and it fell apart more quickly.

"Clumsy," the Son said. "For the last board, don't try to move the wood one way and then the other, like you would with a physical tool. Sense the cells of the . . . Sense the smallest parts of the wood, the grains of sawdust that make up a piece of wood—and move them away from each other in all directions."

Caralee pushed her sandysense into the wood, deeper than she had before—it felt like digging her fingers into hard-packed sand or straining to see something on the horizon. Maybe sandysense was a seventh sense, after all—it wasn't seeing, and it wasn't tasting, and it wasn't touching.

She sensed little grains, boxy bits that—*yeah*—that could be sawdust. They were glued to each other, the walls of each boxy bit stuck fast to the walls of the boxy bits surrounding it. She imagined that glueyness breaking apart, and the bits spreading out in space. She pictured holding a pile of sawdust in her hand and then blowing on it—and how the sawdust bits would blow away from each other into a cloud.

So Caralee flexed the inner muscle of her sandymancy and reached out. Again, it wasn't touch—it was touch's weird, invisible cousin. She didn't need to see with her eyes to make it happen, but she needed to sense it with something *like* sight in order to know what she was doing.

The board exploded, only *exploded* wasn't the right word. Caralee didn't know the word for more-than-exploded-it-just-went-from-one-solid-thing-to-a-cloud-of-dust-all-at-once, but that was what happened. The sawdust flew up in a cloud and then sifted down, coating her hands.

Caralee couldn't quite believe what she had done. She spat sawdust out of her mouth and wiped her face.

"Thank you." Caralee knew by now that sometimes the Son praised her when she'd done something right, but that when she'd surprised him, he was just as likely to say nothing at all. She smiled to herself and wondered what other things she could more-than-explode.

Scary round chucklers, with their too-wide smiles and sharp white teeth? Could she defend herself with sandymancy? Could she *attack* with sandymancy?

*Fuck the broom. I* am *the broom.* That sounded stupid, but maybe it was true.

The Son stepped up and brushed away the sawdust from a stone relief carved with snakelike coils of stone in a pattern that Caralee's eyes couldn't follow. She stepped forward and ran her fingers over the stonework, smooth as it could be.

"What is it?"

"A doorway, of course."

The Son pressed both of his hands on the stone and flexed his fingers. Caralee felt the tingle of sandymancy, but it smelled different—no, not-quite-smelled—different from the not-quite-smell she'd sensed when the Son had used his sandymancy to make the two sand pillars, back in the cart.

The coils of stone slithered—*moving like snakes*—and looped their coils over one another until they pulled away completely to form a round opening in the ground. Below, a set of stairs led down into darkness. Instead of square, these stairs were round. Spiral.

Caralee had begun to recognize a pattern with the stuff from the age of the Vine: there seemed to be lots of spirals. The only spirals that were around today were things like dust storms, and cable plant, and the stars spinning in the sky, and there were spirals in her fingertips, and in shells you could find in the wasteland, and in the curl of a lizard's tail, and in the hidey-shape of pill bugs . . .

Caralee would have to reconsider spirals.

"Wow," she said. It was only sandymancy, but those slithering coils of stone had not-smelled and not-felt and not-looked different from the wood, which itself felt different from regular sand.

First wood, now stone.

It dawned on Caralee that sandymancy wasn't about *sand* at all.

She looked to the Son to ask him, but all of a sudden, he didn't seem happy at all.

"Whatsamatter?"

"I've figured out where we are." He dropped his chin a bit. "I had *no idea* the wasteland had spread so far. Sap and semen! Only the rind of this world yet lives."

"What? Tell me," Caralee pestered the god-king. "Tell me more."

The Son showed her his left hand, palm up.

"Say for a moment that my hand is a map of the whole world."

"Okay."

"All of *this*?" The Son drew a circle around the meat of his palm, excluding his fingers and thumb. This is the wasteland." He pointed to the first knuckle of his little finger. "We're here. Comez is built upon the ruins of the Guinoisse Baths—that's how the name *Comez* was derived."

He slumped against the alley wall, hand-map still open. "In my day, these baths were a distant retreat between homes. I would come for a soak whenever I visited my grandmother, who lived just a bit farther east." The Son's tone soured. "Father installed Grandmother Athinne as far away from the City of the Vine as he could manage, the coward."

Caralee marked the details about the Son's family and fought the urge to run down the stairs into history and shadows. She focused on the map of the world.

"Oh. This sounds bad." She jabbed his palm with her finger. "All the world used to be like Comez?"

"Don't be absurd. We filled our world with marvels."

Standing by the spiral stairs was making Caralee's muscles ache with inaction. "Are we going down?" she asked.

The Son curled his lip and took a step into the shadows. Caralee kept her mouth shut and she kept close, but by a chuckler's starving grin, it took effort.

Walking down the odd steps, curling away from the daylight, Caralee couldn't see much beyond the first twist. The air was warm and heavy with something that took Caralee a minute to realize was water. She'd never felt so much water in the air before; it was like holding your face over a steaming pot of water.

With the Son taking point, they made their way down the stairs, testing each step, pressing themselves against the wall. The air grew warmer and wetter. The stairs curled enough that Caralee couldn't keep track of how many circles they'd made as they climbed down, but when at last the steps ended and the wall upon which she'd been relying to guide her disappeared, Caralee dropped into a crouch. She faced the darkness, wary and small. Sweat trickled down her back.

"It's so dark," she whispered the obvious.

The Son took a breath. "This is a witchlight," he announced, and with the buzz of sandymancy, a light sparked into being over his head, held in the palm of his upstretched hand. For a moment, the light dazzled Caralee, but when her eyes adjusted, she saw that it was a fizzing, bright kind of fire that seemed to hiss outward from a single point in the air between the Son's fingers. He held the fire in his hand, his arm held steady over his head, and then twisted his wrist. The spark of fire grew to a lick of flame, and the lick of flame weaved around and through itself until it became a ball of fire, like a little wicker ball, if wicker were fire and balls could float.

*Balls.* In the middle of her awe at the witchlight, Caralee missed Joe with a sudden stab that disappeared almost as quickly as it had come. Joe would have something stupid to say about fireballs.

The Son took a breath and let it out with intention—Caralee not-felt another not-vibration of sandymancy, and the wicker-ball of fire shuddered and became a solid sphere of blue-green light. He tossed the witchlight into the air, where it hovered above their heads, drifting a little this way and that.

"Wow," Caralee breathed. "Can you teach me to do that?"

"Will you just *look,* chuckl—Caralee." The Son swept his arm toward the baths, revealed by light.

She'd been so focused on the magick of the witchlight that she hadn't remembered to look at what it was meant to show her: the Guinoisse Baths.

A floor fanned out before them for thirty paces, and it was made of gleaming tiny stones—no, *colored tiles,* flat as could be—laid in both winding whorls and intersecting lines. This would be what you'd get, Caralee thought, if you took Marm-marm's geometry lessons—simple triangles and circles etched in the sand—and transformed them into artwork. Artwork that you walked on.

"Wow," Caralee repeated herself. "Just . . . wow."

Above the tiled floor was a high ceiling with six—no, seven—sides, rather than four. The sides weren't flat, either, but were curved like an onion, and they were also etched with simple shapes that overlapped each other to form dizzying patterns.

The Son's witchlight drifted toward the center of the seven-sided dome-roof-thing, and where the seven angles met, they formed a head-sized drop of stone with seven slit-like openings. The witchlight ball drifted into the slitted stone teardrop, which Caralee realized was a kind of lantern. Was it built for witchlights?

*They didn't even need fire to see in the dark,* she thought, as jealous as she'd ever been.

Lit seven ways from above, the room dazzled as it was designed to do, and Caralee twirled around, sponging up every detail.

There were no square edges to be found anywhere. The walls arced upward and inward, and met the floor in a curve. One wall held a series of wide, flat shelflike holes, but even these were rounded at the corners and didn't line up straight so much as rise up and down across the wall, like waves of sand.

At its widest end, the tiled floor sloped up to cup the baths themselves. Three stone pools grew from the far walls—which were stone, bare but perfectly shaped, more like a body than a building. The three pools each were round with a teardrop corner, and they intersected in some trick of roundness and pointiness, and were staggered in height.

Each held a staggering amount of water, enough to drown in, which had a milky blueness to it that Caralee had never seen before, and a crust of white mineral ringed the pools' lips.

"The kind of art is called *mosaic.*" The Son knelt and ran his fingers over the exactingly cut tiles of the floor, instructing Caralee by what seemed to be force of habit.

"This is . . . This . . ." She pointed to a section of the floor where the intersecting arcs took on a regular repetition. "Why'd we stop making all this?"

He snorted. "Probably the same reason you stopped eating cake."

"Cake?"

That caught him off guard, although Caralee couldn't see why. The Son shook his head and muttered something she couldn't hear.

"What's that?"

"I was only saying that our ancestors could pinch out the stars." He turned to admire the ceiling. "Someone's done that, you know—I'm not being florid. Out there, somewhere, people no different than you have stolen stars." He nursed an almost-shy smile. "They've plundered suns wreathed with briar patch. They've melted moons." He pushed up from the floor like a sprung trap. "Watch out for rats. I hate rats."

Caralee slipped her hand into the closest pool. The water was as warm as a hearth fire, and Caralee could imagine slipping her whole self in to float for hours, pondering the art-floor—no, the *mosaic*—and the mysteries of the universe. *Mosaic.* She rolled the word around in her mouth. Was that his language, or hers, or something older?

Caralee wafted her hand back and forth through the pool. The water was so smooth, so . . . endless, somehow, even though the bath held all of it. Caralee couldn't bring herself to tell the Son that this was the first time she'd ever seen more water than could fill a soup kettle. She felt so small, and he would only make her feel smaller.

The Son wasn't just ancient. He brought with him his own Sonnyvine-tales, stories that were so much older than he that Caralee could never track them. Even the bare details broke her. Were the stars *suns*? All of them? What the jazz was a moon?

*And what's a cake, and what's florid, and what's so wrong with a nice, crispy rat?*

# III

Grandmother returned me to my tower for another year of lessons, accolades, and recriminations. I fell into a dark depression. Only a year of my sentence remained, but to a child, a year is a lifetime, and I felt as if mine had been stolen.

While I terrified my tutors with displays of the magicks they taught me, my nine-year-old thoughts were never far from the instruction of my greatest teacher: the world-beneath that she'd shown me; the histories of our world, both known and forgotten; the wonder of the Beasts of Care; and most of all, though it was the smallest story, the once-lost love between Grandmother Athinne and Grandfather Moysha.

She'd described my grandfather the god-king as a young man, full of curiosity and determined to restore our understanding of the Vine, driven by that ambition to scientific pursuits that would have been considered blasphemy, had he not been a bright young royal.

When would it be my turn for such immunity? The question dogged me then, as it haunts me now.

I worried that Grandmother Athinne would not return the following year. Sometime after he married my mother, Father built Grandmother Athinne a beautiful home in the east, and then exiled her there. As she grew older, Grandmother's quarterly visits became biannual, and then yearly. At nine, I did not have an adult's understanding of the ebb of life in old age, but I had seen her lean more heavily on the gold-knobbed cane upon which I had teethed, and I had followed her sloth's pace down hallways she would once have hurried through. She hummed more often and more loudly, which meant she was in pain.

Over the following months, I visited and revisited my illegal outing with my grandmother and the tales of her youth with which she had soothed me upon our return to my tower, when I was overwhelmed by the world-below and by the crawling worm-creature I had summoned, that could keep our soil healthy if and when the Vine could not.

It was a foreign concept, to imagine the Vine as fallible. It was our divinity——how can the divine fail?

Except the Vine was *not* divine, not essentially, though it would be blasphemy to say so aloud. The Vine was a construct and, as a construct, was subject to failures and restraints as are all other creations of humankind.

Decades earlier, when Grandmother Athinne had been a dark-haired scoundrel and Grandfather Moysha an unfashionably rugged seeker, their romance had changed the fate of the world. With Athinne's skills as a technician and her understanding of the world-below, Moysha found a partner who could help answer his quest to fully understand the health of the Vine and its ramifications for the future stability of our world. In Moysha, Athinne found a lover who listened but was not cowed, and together not only did they investigate the Vine as none had done for centuries——if not longer——but became convinced that the sacrosanctity of the Vine was a mortal flaw in our society.

It was blasphemous to question the Vine and its eternal providence. How, then, could any flaw, any danger, be averted? Our faith had blinded us.

Athinne led Moysha to the deep places, where they discovered and confirmed the sickness that gnawed at the Vine, root-bound and molding. Moysha, a royal, could access the Beasts of Care that Athinne had studied for so long, and with his help, she reached the limits of the knowledge we retained. . . . Of the known Beasts of Care, none were suited for a cure. What was unknown remained unknown. The thousands of years since the building of the world had seen much change, and no knowledge is perfect, especially over time. Lessons were lost, technologies abandoned, and our faith placed increasingly in the Vine that, while a work of wonder, was nevertheless the work of women and men.

Together, they drafted a radical plan. Moysha and Athinne could not marry. Moysha must become the Lord of a Thousand Names in order to succeed his mother, the Most Holy Daughter of the Vine. As god-king, he alone could implement the policy changes, enact religious reformations, and begin the real work to ensure the survival of our world.

As the Bride of Plenty, Athinne would have been little more than a china pattern. So it was decided that she would marry advantageously and operate as an independent activist and patron to select initiatives that just so happened to dovetail with Moysha's efforts within the government.

It would appear that Moysha's and Athinne's progressive notions arose independently, and their separate circles generated such sensible discussion concerning the question of the Vine and its longevity, that what began as a tryst appeared, over the ensuing decades, to be an organic shift in popular thought.

Not everyone agreed, of course. Most struggled to accept the possibility that their safe and beautiful world could ever change, let alone that it might change for the worse. To be fair, it is a frightening thought for those without the discipline to face the abyss.

Hello there, abyss.

If there was a discipline I can be said to have struggled with, I suppose it would be druidic magick. Singing flowers from seeds was no difficult task, but the druids who taught me became my most hated enemies. All druids follow a code so fanatically strict that it appears to outsiders to be simple insanity, but there is nothing simple about the madness of the druids. They are star-thieves, whose stole their powers thousands of years before my world was built, and they are tortured still by paranoia and guilt. That is a tale I can never tell, because the druids exact an oath of secrecy from their initiates, and I hate them for it.

Such a vile, binding promise, for what? They taught me to germinate seeds, one at a time, and killed my plants before they grew more than ten centimeters.

A day came when my druid tutors could teach me no more. Oh, they painted themselves in a more flattering light and claimed that we had reached the limits of my potential to learn their arts any further.

We all knew that for a lie. If my potential had limits, I would not be in prison.

So I chose to end the internment phase of my education.

I threw a handful of morning glory seeds at the iron door that barred the tower, and I sang. I don't know which sound rang sweeter, the shouts of the druids too impotent in their own field to stop the vines that tripped their feet and bound their wrists, or the scream of iron being shredded by crawling leaves and sky-blue flowers as strong as the Beast of Freedom in full bloom.

# 7

The road east from Comez rolled along easily enough at first, toward twin spurs of rock that rose from the plain like two fingers pointing at an angle across the sky, and the pass between them held dangers worse than a broken axle. Height-wise, Twofinger Pass was nothing compared to the barrier mountains scraping the southern sky, but it towered over their tiny cart all the same, casting a narrow shadow across the dying land like a sundial. If Caralee and the Son made it through the narrow road through Twofinger Pass, they'd have easy going afterward. Beyond the pass, the land folded into the grassy Hazel Hills that surrounded Grenshtepple's. Tricky thing was, the journey was a long one on a good day. If they got held up for any reason at all, they might not make it through the pass before nightfall.

That'd be when the dangers worse than a broken axle came out to play. And eat. And other things.

Caralee looked up to the rising peaks of Twofinger Pass, to the rocky hills to the north and to the southern mountains whose rippling fangs marked the edge of the world. "When I swore I'd follow you anywhere to get Joe back," she breathed, "I didn't really think the world was so *big*." She remembered the map of the Son's palm, and the pinkie crease she'd lived on all her life, crisscrossing back and forth over her tiny home range. All that sky, over patches of cable that stretched for miles—the enormous and empty world that Caralee knew accounted for less than a knuckle.

"Well, you're a liar." The Son's answer hit her out of the blue.

"Wh . . . wh . . . what?"

"I don't believe that you're following me to the world's end just to get Joe back."

"Except that's what I'm doing." Caralee tossed him the reins and leaned back, such as she could, the sun warming her shoulders just a little. "Just look at me, I'm following you. Like, that is exactly what I am doing."

"Nobody goes where you're going," he said. "Not anybody who lived, anyway."

"Oh, and where am I going?" It wasn't as if he'd been straightforward with that information.

"*With me.*" There was a warble in the Son's voice. He killed it.

"You don't get it." Caralee thought the Son's ego was too inflated to understand the idea that he was not *every* child's nightmare. "I don't *care* if I survive. I care about Joe, and if I don't try as hard as I can to save the people I love, I'd feel like a monster, and life wouldn't be worth living."

"Oh yes, forgive me—it was never those of us who took drastic action who curried the wrath of history." The Son honeyed his sarcasm with a toss of his hair and threw up his hands in entreaty. "Do you think I was never young? That I never loved a big, dumb oaf who kept me safe? I had siblings. Not all of them were cruel—I did not *want* to kill them all, Caralee."

Caralee had a feeling—a knowing—that inside himself, the Son was beating that warble from his voice into a bloody pulp. "Sometimes, trying to save someone is the worst thing you can do to them or yourself."

Caralee would not let him dissuade her. "Listen to you—'or yourself'—you're so selfish. How can I *not* try? Who cares what I turn into? Not you. You don't care! You stole him. You stole *all* of him, right out from under my nose."

"Ah." The Son whipped the critters from a crawl to a skitter. "So Joe *belongs* to you."

"Scatting right, he does." Twofinger Pass loomed nearer, shadows and sunlight lancing through its narrow amber peaks.

"So Joe is property," the Son agreed. "He is a person who belongs to another person, and that person is you."

Caralee opened her mouth to argue that she hadn't said that *at all,* but the Son kept on:

"Funny." He picked his teeth with a slender nail. "It's just that when Joe was alive, he belonged to nobody but Joe. Now, Joe belongs to me, and you reveal that you've only ever *wanted* to own him. You've always wanted him to belong to you, and he never did, and he never will. Maybe *funny* is the wrong word."

"That's really mean." Caralee held up her hand as if she could banish the Son of the Vine by the force of her shame. "He's not my *property,* like he is to you. He's mine because I'm his." She quickly amended that too-true explanation. "And we're both Mag's, and she's ours—and Atu and Oti, too. Family."

She turned her head and spat onto the road. "You're fulla shatterscat, acting like you don't know what *family* means when you went and murdered all of yours."

"You and I had very different childhoods." The Son didn't flinch. Caralee couldn't hurt him with the truth, not the way he could rake her over coals with a passing insight.

The critters sped from a skitter to a skeet—a swift skeet, too, although the Son hadn't adjusted his hold on the reins. Caralee put their anxiety down to the tone of her voice and tried to match the Son's nonchalance.

"You ent ever loved anybody," she said softly. "That's shatterscat." Caralee knew that she was wrong, that deep, *deep* down the Son was as human as she was, but he'd pissed her off.

*He must have loved, to hate that hard.*

"I have loved before." He snapped around as if to slap her. She'd nicked him. He took a deep breath, and turned away. "I know love. I know a warm breeze, too—but I don't let it set my agenda. *I* choose my path, one step at a time." The Son looked toward Twofinger Pass and fixed his gaze there. The walls around them had begun to slope up on either side as they entered the narrow gap between the fingers of rock, and blocked out the morning sun. The shadows spread. "That was the best lesson I ever learned." The Son nodded to himself. "No matter what happens, you move forward, one foot after the other. Through anything."

He shivered and folded his hands across his lap. "There, a lesson from your monster. Satisfied?"

*Liar. Thief. World-killer.* My *monster.*

"Am I satisfied?" Caralee shook her head. "Nope. Not till I get my Joe back. Not till that."

"Because Joe is *what you want,*" the Son pressed the point. "You talk about love, but love is a scrim for *want.* You want what you want, and you'll do whatever it takes, wait as long as needed, become whatever you must become, to *get* and *keep* what you *want.* Just like me."

"I'm nothing like you!" How could he say that?

The Son chuckled. "You're a far cry more like me than you'd care to think. Why else do you think you aren't a smear of bootsblood on some shitfarm road where I found you? You called to me, and I heard you. If I'm a monster, then you're a part of *our* monstrosity."

"Why are you telling me this?" Caralee felt such guilt at the mention of her summons that she nearly puked. "Is this *fun* for you?"

"Pfft." The Son fixed her with a glare. "I've begun your education, haven't I? The oldest lesson known to humankind is this: *know thyself.*"

He turned to face her in the cart, with an explanation on his lips. Caralee gave him her full attention, practicing against his own. The critters followed the road as they would.

"Listen," the Son began. "If something is true—plainly true—and you choose to ignore it, then that truth becomes your weakness. Tactically, that's an avoidable shortcoming, and the last thing *you* need is another shortcoming. If you are too sentimental to see yourself for what you are, then you will *never* get what you want. The world is full of people competing for the same goals. If you choose at the outset not to outsmart them, then you choose to lose."

Caralee pulled a face. "All this to teach me I'm a selfish loser?"

"Who would you rather be: a Caralee who understands herself and decides for herself who she will become, or a Caralee who refuses to see the world clearly?" The Son's narrow brows were pressed together—he needed her to understand this. "Within each of us sleep our best selves and our worst selves, our strongest selves and our weakest selves. We choose from moment to moment which of our selves will wake to act and which will yield." The Son would not be denied when eager. She admired and feared the way he used his mind like a weapon to fight three moves ahead. "Consider what price you might pay, should you choose to comfort yourself with flattering delusions."

"Comfort?" Caralee stuck out her tongue. "Mister, I ent ever been comfortable."

Soon enough, the shadows bleached away as morning stretched to noon and the sun appeared overhead, peeking into the gulley through which they rode, too slowly, carefully.

Also soon enough, Caralee asked another question.

"Back there. Last night? At the inn? Did you see the way they looked at me?"

"I did."

"I saw how they looked at *you.* Like a handsome gentleman scholar, just passing through. How fucking wonderful for you." Caralee stretched her dressed-up shmata with her elbows, trying to give herself more room in the front. She'd kept the ribbon, but untied the knotted hem.

"Yes, how nice for me." The Son preened, his larded midnight hair managing to gleam in the limited sunlight. "It *is* nice to be recognized for my obvious minor merits, rather than as an apocalyptic menace out of legend. Would you rather they'd come at me with pitchforks?"

"You pretend to be all these things, but what you really are—"

"I know myself precisely. Answer me this, would you rather strangers look at you as a girl or a woman?"

The idea of that choice frustrated Caralee. "Here I am, a nice young person who didn't kill anybody, and *I* get gawked at like Bety Newtits." She tugged out the top of her shmata, looking down at her not-girl body. Each day, her body became *grown,* rather than growing. "I hate it."

"Do you?" She hated it when the Son asked her a thing when she'd *just said that thing.* Especially when it was a good question.

"Naw. Sorta. I just don't like being in between, I guess. Once my head catches up to my body, I'll . . . I dunno. I'll be better about it, I think." Caralee crossed her arms over her chest. "By then, I won't be Bety Newtits anymore. Except every time I go somewhere new."

"So far, all I hear is someone whining about being attractive."

"But I'm not attractive! That's what's creepy." Caralee tried to make herself as small as possible. "You said it yourself—I'm scrawny and lopsy-boobed and ugly." She shook her head to herself. "It doesn't make sense."

The Son wrapped his arm around Caralee's shoulders—just around, not touching, resting it on the divider between the seats and the cargo. He cocked his head toward hers and said, "I have a confession to make."

"What," Caralee pouted.

"I lied about your looks." He wore just a touch of a smile. "The truth is, Caralee, that you look perfectly average. Dead normal."

"I do?" She knew that wasn't a compliment, and that it shouldn't matter in the first place, except that it did. "Why'd you lie to me?"

He pulled his arm away. "Because victory over an enemy who doubts herself is easily accomplished." He almost finished there, but added, "And because, whether it's genuine or not, you display entirely too much confidence."

*Too much confidence? Has he heard a word I said?*

"Just look at your choices. Appallingly bold to be sitting here, next to me. You are in more danger than anyone alive, but here you are, complaining about your breasts and learning how not to die. Who is this Bety Newtits, by the way? Is she worth knowing?"

"She's not a real person?" Caralee scrunched up her face. "It's just a thing people say. Slang, I guess. You ent never heard anybody say, 'Look at Bety Newtits over there,' or suchlike?"

Then she remembered who sat beside her. *Of course he's dumb on slang.*

"That's not slang, you know," he answered instead. "It's an idiom. It's idiomatic. You are idiomatic, Caralee Vinnet."

"Am not!"

His invisible smile was as bothersome as his inaudible laughter. The Son of the Vine was the worst.

"What's Bety Newtits good for, anyway?" Caralee continued the conversation alone. "Gawking at, that's all, and then touching on, or rubbing up on and, listen here: I ent for knocking up, you hear me?" Atu frilled her antennae and chirruped in solidarity. Between she and Oti, Atu was the smarter of the pair.

Caralee was about to ramble on when a black blade sliced across the sky. In the distance beyond Twofinger Pass, a bird rose high before angling back behind the peaks. Again it crossed into view, then disappeared, as the bird winged back and forth in the sky beyond the gap between Twofinger's two fingers.

The Son didn't seem to notice or care, and answered her declaration. "I think you know by now, Caralee, that I certainly do *not* want to knock you up."

"I know it." Oti hissed happily and rubbed antennae with Atu. He was the sweetheart of the two. "So the one man I can trust not to touch me is the monster who stole my only friend?" Caralee kicked the cart, and Oti jumped. "That's messed up."

The Son nodded at an alcove, just a short climb above, that looked fit for a rest stop. "Hey, here's a shady spot. Let's kick out for a bit of lunch, shall we?"

"Sure, I could eat. But we gotta make it quick."

The Son loosed the reins and let the critters slow. She gauged the time by the position of the sun—they were ahead of schedule. Mag wouldn't allow it, but Caralee got so hungry, and Mag wasn't here.

"Good, good—a growing young woman needs every meal." He pulled out a roll of brown paper.

*Did he buy* sausages? Caralee couldn't complain about sausages. Her stomach gurgled in agreement.

"When I kill you, I'm gonna be so lonely." She stared out into the cloudless sky, wondering.

What had looked from a distance like a decent-enough spot for a midday break, with its shady overhang and natural stone steps, proved upon closer examination to be anything but decent. Piles, ropes, and jiggling heaps of jellied mucus stank up the defiled alcove, but that wasn't the worst of it. Scat, all kinds of scat—human scat, animal scat, and gobs upon gobs of white birdscat were mixed in with the pools and lumps of snot.

Worse, there was blood—not blood but *veins* of it, little red lines branching all about, and they were . . . they were *moving.* Strings of capillaries branched off from one another, pulsing and wriggling beneath a skin of snot and shit and puke. It was an actual nightmare come to life, here in the middle of nowhere, just to ruin Caralee's lunch.

She heaved and added her own bile to the muck.

"Curious," said the Son, holding his sleeve to his nose.

"I *hate* snot," Caralee said between retching and scrambling down from the alcove as quickly as she could. She wasn't that fond of blood that moved on its own, either, but these were weird days.

"Mmm." The Son stayed above, studying the nightmare. "That *is* odd."

"You're scatting right, it's odd!" She retched again at the thought and found herself thankful for an empty stomach—which was a first.

"Look at all this shit. And there, the vomit. But it's mostly just mucus." He broke off a crumbling lip of sandstone from the wall and poked at the layers upon layers of snot, quivering on the stone floor like jellied critter brain. "And the . . . animated blood. You cannot know how much the sight of these squirming blood vessels pleases me."

"This *pleases* you?"

"Feh, *pleasure* may be too strong a word. Still . . ." The Son jumped down from the ledge and fanned fresh air into his face. "You have a point on the snot, Caralee."

*Still . . . what?* she thought, but opted to follow along. "Snot is disgusting!"

"Agreed." The Son tucked the sausages back into the cart. "So much for lunch."

So they rode on, and the only movement Caralee saw was the big black bird in the sky and its slashing flight between the tall, flat slabs of Twofinger Pass. Either she and the Son were making even better time than she'd realized, or the bird was circling closer. By its size, it had to be a condor. Only the smaller scavenger birds, like vultures, dared the wasteland. Condors and larger birds kept to the east, where there was enough life to feast on death.

Something about the size and approach of this condor made Caralee nervous, even though they only ate dead animals. By now, it flew nearly overhead.

She'd been eyeing the bird for almost an hour before she mentioned it. Caralee hadn't known scavenger birds to circle more than a few times before realizing that she, Joe, Mag, and the burden-beasts were alive and well. Usually they flew off to find a sandfisher's pit of corpses or a dunder lair. The way it circled didn't concern Caralee so much as make her wonder: Was there a dying creature nearby? If so, had it been limping along ahead or behind them for the better part of an hour? And if so, that was the steadiest, stealthiest dying creature that Caralee had ever seen. Well, *not* seen.

She said so.

"Ignore it." The Son issued an order, not advice. There was an edge to his strictness, some submerged feeling he kept to himself.

Caralee did her best. After what seemed like forever but was probably much sooner, she couldn't help herself. She glanced up.

"Still there?" the Son asked. He didn't seem angry.

Caralee grunted yes. The condor spiraled closer and closer. She could only guess at its wingspan, but it must be huge.

They rolled over a boll of collapsed rock; Oti and Atu's sixteen legs eased the rickety cart across the debris. The path ahead ran straight, but widened for a while, with only a single jut of rock down its middle to block their way. The critters' skittering returned to its usual rhythm.

As the path widened, the condor tightened its spin, and Caralee could make out finer details.

Despite its size, the bird must have been young—thick gray down still collared its throat, though its head was bald—meaning it was an adolescent, at the oldest. The size, though, that was unnatural. Something was odd about its posture, too, like its head was heavier than it should have been. At the same time, its body was longer, arched almost . . . backward? She'd seen a northern bow at market once, curved and then curved again in the other direction, and the condor's posture reminded her of it.

Caralee cooed as the bird flattened out just before the top of its climb, becoming a pencil-thin line in the sky before flaring its wings in a series of powerful beats and leaning into a dive. She imagined what it must feel like to fight the wind and *win*.

"I said *ignore it*." The Son's edge was showing.

As if sensing Caralee's disobedience, the condor winged off its flight path, arrowing closer to their slapdash wooden cart, and Caralee suddenly had a terrible feeling that they were the mighty bird's target. The condor was still far away, but the size of the bird fooled the eye, and Caralee knew that it could slingshot toward them in a heartbeat.

"I, uh . . ." Caralee stammered. "I don't think I'm very good at doing ignoring."

The Son whipped his head up in time to see the condor, with its twenty-foot wingspan—twice as big as Caralee had ever seen or heard of—level out above their widening ravine and soar over the lone jut of rock in the clearing where they'd found themselves vulnerable. The Son startled, expression shifting from guarded secrecy to outright alarm.

"What have they done to you." It wasn't a question, and he didn't say it to Caralee.

On its return, the condor didn't fly *straight* at them—it didn't seem inclined for the swift and brutal kill, which was odd for a raptor, even though the massive thing ought to be scavenging, not hunting. Something about this bird looked wrong and felt wronger. As it swung toward Caralee's side of the cart, she understood. It wasn't a condor.

That wasn't gray down around its neck—down didn't gleam in the sun.

That was some kind of *metal* is what that was.

In a flash of too-fast thoughts, Caralee remembered the claw marks on Dinnal's bed and body and windowsill, and the alderman's mention of the metal folk, and the Son's sudden silence on both the topic of the metal folk and that of the snotty bloody alcove. The thoughts didn't come together into something she understood, but she realized that they were linked, somehow, in the fraction of a second it took for the not-condor to zoom close enough to touch her.

Sweeping past Caralee, the not-condor reached out with one long wing and brushed her shoulder. The wing was black, but the wingtips, true enough, shone with the same metal as the feathers at the creature's throat. While the brush might have looked like a caress, it stung like a chuckler bite—and drew a line of fire along her triceps. Caralee clapped a hand over the wound and yelped in surprise. Blood dripped through her fingers quick and steady as her heartbeat.

"It cut me with its wing!"

Caralee felt pretty certain that condors' wings weren't tipped with razors.

The Son furrowed his brow at the sight of blood dripping between Caralee's fingers, as the not-condor circled around again, low and shady. Its eyes were gray pinpricks of hate.

No, not gray. They reflected the sun, gleaming. Those eyes were polished metal. It circled back around for a second dive. Its beak, too, glinted with metal.

"Sonnyvine, what *is* that thing!"

The Son, still seated, slipped one arm behind Caralee's back and another beneath her knees, and with one swift heave he tossed her over her side of the cart, where she skidded hard on her back as the cart rolled on. Then he vaulted upward and out of the cart himself, in a single liquid leap, and sprinted toward the walls of the pass behind them, which they'd passed through minutes before.

"*Run!*" he shouted at Caralee before diving for cover.

The beast touched the cart with one talon—also metal—and the shabby vehicle disintegrated, emptying its cargo and sending Atu and Oti into somersaults, the reins tangling in their spiky bronze legs.

Caralee and the Son picked themselves up on opposite sides of the clearing, then both sprinted toward the center, where the spur of rock divided it. They crouched behind the weathered stone, putting it between themselves and the direction of the creature's next dive.

"That," the Son gasped, "is no condor."

"No scat!" Caralee heaved. "Did you see its eyes?"

"Steely."

"No, dunderhead—they're made of *metal.*" Caralee was up on an elbow above the rock, looking at the wreckage. Atu was on her back, squirming her legs helplessly. Oti tried to wedge Atu up with four legs, but two of his own were badly injured, which left only two legs on the ground to support the weight of both critters. Sixteen eyes together, the burden-critters saw far more than Caralee. Clutching each other, the critters screamed.

The massive bird didn't dive as Caralee had expected—it had circled around to come at them again from the same side, right where they'd placed themselves. Caralee felt the rush of wind as the creature bore down upon them, but the winged beast missed Caralee and the Son by centimeters.

Only it hadn't missed—it flew straight toward the critters with a screech of tortured hate.

Oti skittered over Atu to protect her from the monster's outstretched talons. Atu wailed in protest, but Oti pinned her down, covering her body with his. The flying terror's shriek held a note not unlike laughter as its metal claws split open Oti's abdomen and crushed his thorax.

"Oti!" Caralee yelled, horrified. She ran to help her family, but the Son caught her, cruel and wise. His hand held her by the back of the neck, and his grip was the grip of the world itself.

"*No.*"

Atu, flipped right side up by the force of the impact, screamed and hissed and scatted herself, keening while she tried to hold Oti's disgorged abdomen together with so many of her legs that she fell down, only to scrabble up and try again. Falling and failing, covered in her life mate's life stuff, wailing a wail that needed no translation.

Caralee shouted and tore at the Son's grip, but he was iron. Oti's death-whistle was raw and wet and desperate not to slip away. Three of his legs met Atu's, and Caralee swore that they gripped each other tight as two lovers holding hands at a parting.

*He knows that it's not sleep. He knows it's forever.* Caralee screamed so hard she thought she'd fly apart into pieces.

"Listen to me. Listen!" The Son pressed his mouth to her ear and spoke in a ragged, gut-wrenched voice. "You are reacting. You are reacting to a murder. You are watching your family be torn apart before your eyes. You can do *nothing* except survive. You *must breathe.* Don't scream, don't struggle, don't move—just *breathe,* or your death will follow in scant seconds."

Her mind heard him, but Caralee's heart overrode her wiser selves, and she screamed again.

The Son gripped her forehead with one hand and willed her saner, willed her still. She felt his intention, felt concern from him and felt love from Atu and Oti—though she couldn't be in their thoughts at this terrible moment—and she felt her love for them, for Joe. Did she feel love from the Son? Did she feel love from Joe? Whatever she felt, it brought her back to herself.

Whatever the Son had done, it was nothing like sandymancy—it was as if he had his hands inside her thoughts, not controlling them so much as moving her agony into the background so that she could feel the love that fueled it. She could decide to turn away from the pain, rather than being carried along by it. A heartbeat passed, and another, and then another, and Caralee sagged against the Son, still desperate, still out of her mind, but no longer suicidal—and the part of her mind that remained detached, because it had to, realized that's what her impulse had been—nothing other than suicide.

"That shatterscat fucker killed my boy!" Caralee begged in a ragged whisper, clawing at his chest while sobbing. "My babby boy, my Oti!" She collapsed into an awful sobbing. "I raised him from a hatchling," she cried. Then, wrack turned to wrath, and Caralee hissed through her sniffling, "What kind of beast has jazzed-up metal wings? I am going to scatting *torture it till it dies.*"

"What beast has metal eyes," the Son said in a hollow voice. He eased the vise grip of his hand and massaged her neck where he'd held it.

Caralee raked her fingers through her hair, horrified at the sight of her dying friend and its maddened mate. "No bird at all, that's scatting what."

"No bird at all," the Son agreed. "That metal is called *steel.* Avoid it."

The creature circled back to swoop and grab Oti's corpse from Atu's frantic embrace, carrying him off overhead—and splattering gray-brown hemolymph onto the Son's face and shoulders. The god-king scraped the gray goo out of his eyes, balled his hands into fists, and bellowed.

Dust rose in billows as wings beat overhead. Whatever the beast was, it was landing. Caralee pissed herself.

Through the haze, she saw a bird-shaped mammoth scooping out slobbery gobbets from Oti's insides. It shredded his fist-thick exoskeleton as it stepped from one steel-taloned foot to the other, clawing at its food. Hanging from the underside of the bird-monster's chest, small and shriveled, were two drooping glands. Resembling a bizarre marriage of teats and testicles, the pulsing glands sweated and squirted the ground with snot, scat, and sulfur. Bloody lines snaked from its glands to the ground, squirming.

Each time the creature dove its head into Oti's corpse, it junked more of the stuff from its glands. Its own blood pooled around it. The stench was overwhelming.

"Are we going to die?" Caralee tugged at the Son in despair.

At that, the monstrous bird-beast turned its head toward Caralee. Its steel eyes matched the steel feathers at the tips of its black wings, and the ruffle of steel below its bald neck, and the steel talons smeared with the gore of Caralee's friend, poor Oti. Atu screamed while the steely bird-thing took steps toward Caralee and the Son.

The creature cocked its head in the worst way. Oti's carcass lay still. He was gone.

"Oh, don't you fucking dare," Caralee seethed.

It took another step and, eyes on Caralee, opened its beak to screech a sound like laughing knives. So loud, so piercing that it burned Caralee's eyes and staggered her thinking. The beast laughed on.

*No.* She pushed through the hazy feeling. How did it slow her thoughts like that?

Caralee balled her fists and took a breath, ready to die. Fuck the Son's orders. Joe was gone and so was Oti, and now she'd go, too, but she'd take this monster with her.

The monster was a harpy. Caralee had riddled out that much. But what kind of harpy had metal parts?

She reached out with her sandysense and not-felt the rock beneath their feet, remembering how the Son's stone-working sandymancy had not-felt, back when he'd opened the way down to the Guinoisse Baths in Comez. She not-felt the rock beneath her and she stretched that feeling till she not-felt the rock beneath the beast's feet. With a call to the stone, Caralee grabbed a slice of rock from below. She heaved as mightily as she could through the harpy's mind-numbing haze, and a wall of stone ripped itself out of the ground at the beast's feet, tripping it. The harpy fell forward, landing on its face so hard that its steel beak sank half a meter into the rocky ground.

"A tactic?" The Son clapped her on the back, wiping gore-grimed hair from his face. "You genius! Now kill it."

"You kill it!" Caralee pushed him away. "I'm a girl! Ent you a monster?"

"Oh, *now* you're a girl."

The harpy was scrabbling to pry its face from the ground while its steel-tipped wings scored the earth like two plows. It worked its legs, one foot and then the other, until its beak slipped free from the ground and cast its shadow over them both.

"If you think me incapable of feeling fear, Caralee, you are wrong, wrong, wrong." He spoke true. She had that, at least. "It's a monster. Beast. *Monster.*"

The thing retrained its gaze upon Caralee. The harpy screamed that knife-scream, the laughter inside it cutting deep. The haze inside Caralee's head grew stronger. She slapped herself in the face and ground her teeth.

"But *you're* the monster!" she begged the Son.

"Well." He considered that.

"Please!" Caralee begged, knees giving out. She sank to the ground, prepared to die.

The harpy stalked toward them, perhaps three of its paces away. Less, maybe.

"Stop calling me that." The Son stood up and squared his shoulders. "I am a beast, not a monster. Fucking remember that." He sounded just like she did. Then, "Let this be your second lesson in fire today, Caralee Vinnet."

Two paces.

The Son relaxed his posture, his breathing deep and steady.

One pace.

"*Molten.*" His voice held all the strength in the world. No one could possibly argue with that word and win. The whole world really *would* answer his call.

The steel-infused harpy screamed once, rearing up and flaring its wings wide—and they burst into flaming slag, their tips melting and dripping to the ground with popping hisses, setting its wings afire. It staggered as its talons turned to grease beneath its feet, and its gleaming silver collar melted through its chest, severing its wings first and then the spine. Its beak melted, gullet-hole gaping in its skull. Beak-melt sizzled down its chest, and the harpy fell to the ground, dead. Its steel eyes poured out their sockets, frying its brain while its head burned bright as a bonfire.

Molten metal and smoking sulfur consumed the flesh and bones of the beast, the stench of burning feathers and charred snot.

Caralee stared at the glorious carnage with disbelief. She had no words.

The Son turned from the wreckage and extended his hand to Caralee.

"If you are no girl, then I am no monster." As if he hadn't just defeated a massive beast that was impossible in at least three ways? Caralee's bones felt like jelly.

"Is that fair?" he asked her. "Woman to beast, and beast to woman?"

She shook his hand, nodded breathlessly, and let him haul her to her feet, one arm under hers to support her jellybones.

The ground burned, and still Atu screamed.

Caralee didn't know what steel was, but she fucking hated it.

Then, looking to the Son, whose attention had returned to the slag, a question. Could she still hate him?

"So you come in steel, these days." The Son curled his lip at the toxic flame-toilet. He kicked a piece of charred bone away, and it exploded into cinders midair. He snarled. "Who did this to you?" He looked to the sky, and then he looked to his feet, but his eyes were unfocused, like he was looking *beneath* his feet. Pretty far beneath his feet.

Were there options? Caralee thought it would be pretty clear that the *metal* people would have put *metal* in a harpy where no *metal* belonged. Did the Son think otherwise?

"What happened to you?"

Caralee wondered more what *he* had done. The Son's killing stroke all but punched Caralee in the gut. That was the strength of her enemy? She was fucked. How would it feel when the Son turned on her? One day, he would pivot toward her in a sudden twist of hate. He would utter some vile word and erase her forever. Still, Caralee sobbed. Atu shrieked.

The Son cast a look toward the cracked sky and growled. "I wonder if a stranger has been playing in my garden. I hope . . . I *think* that I hope it's a stranger." Did he look sad, or proud, or angry?

He shook his head at the harpy's corpse, his expression brimming with competing emotions. "Who's Bety Newtits now, I wonder?"

# 8

After the blast of furnace-wind and sandyfire had seared the air, and all that remained of the steel harpy was bitter flaming slag and charred fluids smoking like the foulest incense, Caralee coughed black tar onto her fingers and, shuddering, began to sob from deep inside her gut—from below her gut, from her hips, from her bloodied knees still on the ground. The sob shook and shivered into a wail louder than Atu's helpless keening, and Caralee barely noticed her sandymancy as she sucked in noxious air and screamed so hard that it shook her teeth. Pebbles rattled across the ground like bits of ore in a miner's pan. Charred bone popped back into flame as the ground cracked beneath Caralee's anguish, and flat puddles of cooling metal cracked, their still-molten insides oozing forge orange.

Caralee pounded the earth with her fists and screamed and screamed. The walls of Twofinger Pass rang like a tuning fork, shedding flakes of axe-sharp rock that sliced the air and embedded themselves into the ground.

She felt a warm hand on the small of her back, and that sense of love-concern-*whatever* stilled her again. More gently this time, a feeling that Caralee could only describe as *family* brought her back to herself, though the madness of her grief—her *nihnepsolom*—fought against the calming, loving sanity. It felt like two types of love, one kind, one wicked, warred against each other inside her, but the strange non-magick sapped the strength of her sandymancy until she was just a wounded, miserable person weeping on her knees, and the song of sorrow that shook the tines of Twofinger Pass grew still.

Her senses returned to her in time to see Atu's own *nihnepsolom* rage and fade on its own. Atu skeeted toward Oti's remains at the other end of the ravine, where she kissed his mutilated body with her long, wet mouthparts, keening. There wasn't enough left of Oti for Atu to hold together, and she made no attempt. Atu knew her life mate was dead, but loved him still the best she could. Her keening fell to a huffing, repetitive gurgle-sob.

Atu wouldn't let her sorrow drive her mad. Critters had a wisdom.

Caralee stumbled over to kneel next to Atu and sob alongside what was left of her family. She stayed that way until she stopped shuddering and Atu pulled away from Oti's steaming corpse, resting her heavy bronze head on Caralee's thigh, mandibles slack, drooling from the proboscis that hung limp from below them.

When at last Caralee pulled herself up to lead Atu from the nightmare scene, the critter turned away willingly, slowly, hissing the melody of a dear, rhythmic song of grief. It was an old song, a variation of which critters always hissed at the death of a life mate or a friend—the song and its variations were as old as the world, and if the Son was to be believed about stolen suns, maybe it was older than that.

Atu cupped Caralee's face with her antennae, frilling like feathers over Caralee's skin, looking up at Caralee through a funnel of green-and-gold fronds. Atu's eight black eyes held no expression, but to Caralee, they were far from unreadable. With her long, elastic proboscis, Atu reached up past her mandibles and through the curtain of her antennae and found Caralee's face. The critter hissed and gurgled the song against Caralee's lips and cheeks, kissing Caralee in time with the wordless dirge. Sobbing over Atu's eyes, cocooned in the song of Atu's pain, Caralee had never felt such closeness with another living being.

Her mind couldn't grasp the concept: these circumstances were near to the worst possible, but somehow made for the most precious moment of her life.

The Son gave them space, and Caralee knew that to be a mighty kindness. Instead, he busied himself salvaging what he could from the wreckage of their cart. Most of the cargo had been shredded and now littered the ravine.

Atu would follow Caralee like a babe to the teat. That was good and that was bad.

*What do we do now?*

"Anything make it?" she asked when they neared the Son.

"Here." He handed Caralee the sack with her journal. "I am sorry about your friend." The Son nodded to both Caralee and Atu. He sounded genuine. "I am sorry for your family's loss."

"Thank you." Caralee shouldered the sack and turned to pet Atu. "Get us away from here."

Caralee leaned on the Son's arm and shuffled toward the northeastern end of the ravine, toward the exit from Twofinger Pass. Atu followed just behind. They limped forward without speaking, exhausted and torn inside and out.

"So that's what a harpy looks like?" Caralee asked the Son when she couldn't take the silence anymore. "But without the metal parts?"

"I take your meaning, and yes." He hid his face. "I knew the ones who made her. They were dear to me."

Caralee knew well enough to leave that topic alone. The violence and loss had dulled her curiosity, at least for the moment. "What do we do now?"

"I haven't riddled that out yet." The Son combed his fingers through his dusty hair. "What do you suggest? Is Grenshtepple's the closest settlement, or is there somewhere more convenient?" he asked her, then gave his own answer. "We have to get rid of this spiderbeetle."

"Get rid of Atu?" The idea struck Caralee as a horror. "She needs care."

*Care I can't give her. Scat.* He wasn't wrong.

"Then we'll find someone to care for her. I've shekels enough left to make sure the nearest candidate for crittertender will welcome Atu."

*The nearest crittertender.* The Son was right; Atu would be little trouble to anyone, and everybody needed shekels.

"Naw. Keep your shekels," Caralee said.

"Why's that?"

"Oh, you'll see . . ." It was Caralee's turn to tease out a secret.

The Son picked dirt from his nails and measured Caralee with his gaze. "There's nothing more adult than leaving family behind, Caralee. You've done that thrice—first Joe and Mag, now Oti—I wish you didn't have to do it again."

Caralee didn't know what to make of that, except the echo of her determination, which said that she had *not* left Joe behind, not at all.

Twofinger Pass narrowed again as they left behind the gruesome remains of the clearing. With only a ribbon of sky overhead, the narrowness of the pass flushed them forward to the open world, as if it was finished with them.

"So tell me about steel, I guess. You said it's iron? But it's not?" Caralee asked, needing a distraction.

"Did you ever play with blocks as a girl?"

"Sure. We have blockums. You can make all kinda little things with 'em. Come to think, they're just like the square stonework in Comez and back home, only smaller."

"*Blockums?*" The Son seemed torn between lingering respectfulness and his actual personality.

"What's wrong with blockums?"

"You have blockums. *Blockums.* That . . . will have to do. So: imagine blockums that are so small that you can't see them with your eyes. Imagine that there are different . . . let's say, colored types of blockums. There are three hundred and seventy-two colors of blockums."

Caralee pictured all that. She'd have to be awfully small herself to play with blockums that wee, and she said so. "Also three hundred and seventy-two colors is a lot."

"Don't worry, there are only about forty that you'll ever encounter. In fact, you and I—our entire bodies—are composed mainly of three colors of blockums."

"Wait, we're *made* of blockums?" That was shatterscat. "If anybody was made of blockums, they couldn't move, and if they did, they'd just topple over into a pile of blockums. Like sawdust. Is sawdust blockums? I'm *not* sawdust."

She could all but hear the Son roll his eyes at her questions. "Forget about those questions for now. Imagine that everything, *everything,* even the air we breathe, is made of blockums. All that you see and feel is made of many, many simple arrangements of blockums. Can you picture that? Little blockum arrangements floating around in empty space?"

You stacked blockums on top of each other, and put them side by side—Caralee tried to imagine blockum arrangements that held themselves together and somehow made everything. If the arrangements stuck together, how could anything move? Was it chaos or order?

*It's both.*

"Like little pyramids floating around in the air for me to breathe, or a bunch of crosses stacked together to make a table? A lot of sloppy shapes tumbling and making up my blood?"

"Um. Yes? Yes. Yes, almost exactly." The Son looked concerned.

"Whatsamatter?" Caralee worried what she'd done wrong. She clocked the sky for another jazzed-up harpy, but it was clear.

"Well . . ." The Son found the words. "You learned elementary particle physics in five steps."

"Whatever you just said, I don't think it's all that true?" Caralee could imagine all sorts of things, but that didn't make them fact. Invisible blockums included.

"It's all true." The Son pressed the advantage Caralee didn't believe she had. "Blockums are why blood is red. One particular blockum arrangement tumbling through your blood looks like a flower with four petals. In the center of each of the four petals sits *one* blockum of iron. Imagine that iron blockums are painted red. That iron blockum, just as iron does when it rusts, turns the whole flower red, and there are so many red flowers in your blood that all of it looks red, even though it's mostly water."

Invisibly small red flowers tumbling through her veins. Such a pretty notion that Caralee pictured it at once and said so.

The Son muttered in disbelief. "You might *not* be the alpha idiot, Caralee. I might go so far as to dub thee a low-grade simpleton." Then, "That's a step up, in case you—"

"I got it. So steel?" She tried not to picture Atu holding together Oti's sausage-split abdomen. "Steel, *please.*"

"Steel is a metal, made almost entirely out of iron. Red iron blockums arranged in a mostly regular pattern—"

"So it *is* both order *and* chaos!" she cut in without meaning to.

"What? Yes, but . . . what?" The Son blinked. He looked Caralee in the eyes, searching for something. "Did you hit your head?"

Was she really impressing him, or was he just softening the blows of the . . . of what happened? She pushed away the memories of Oti's screams and focused on blockums.

"The blockum arrangements." Caralee held out her hands, miming shapes with her fingers and waving her wrists to twist those shapes this way and that. "You say they make me, they make the ground, they make my blood. So it seems to me that some gotta be real regular, like in a sword or a stone. Others gotta be bendy, like rope, but they all have to hold together just so. But then the held-together arrangements have to be able to tumble about all willybilly. That's what Marm-marm called Fanny Sweatvasser, who's all over the place. I mean she will say *anything* like *whenever.*"

The Son shook his head to dismiss the very idea of Fanny Sweatvasser. "Steel. At the start we have the iron blockums arranged in a neat little pattern, like you said. Then we take some blockums of what's called *carbon*—that's the black stuff inside your pencil. If you add a certain amount of carbon blockums to the iron, it changes the pattern in which the iron blockums are arranged. This new arrangement of mostly iron and a little carbon, that's steel. It's stronger than iron, even though it's still mostly iron."

"So you make steel with a pencil, and blood with iron?"

Silence. The ravine widened, and they could see the end of Twofinger Pass at last. Below the hill of rock and rubble that spilled out of the pass, Caralee saw rolling hills of yellow green.

"Finally, life!" The Son exhaled.

Even Atu, who still followed Caralee close as could be, seemed to relax at the sight of open land and air. The Hazel Hills rolled like sand dunes for miles and miles, only they didn't shift, fixed into place as they were by grass and root.

"Caralee. You've just expressed an actual understanding of how *everything* works at a level that is only a few orders larger than the smallest level possible."

"You're not gonna tell me that *blockums* are made out of even smaller blockums?" Smart or not, Caralee had a limit.

"Not yet, no. *Culono!*" The Son swore in Auld Vintage or something older—he never did that. "You're not a simpleton at all, are you? You sly kitten. You . . . I do believe that you're 'forgettably adequate'!" He took a deep breath. "That's more than a few steps up from a simpleton. Can you guess how many forgettably adequate people I've known in eight-hundred-plus years?"

"Um." Guessing seemed futile.

"Six."

"Six?"

"Six."

"Not a lot, then." Caralee kept her reaction neutral and returned to the subject of tiny blockums. The end of Twofinger Pass sloped downhill—steeply. Sweet Atu skittered forward to catch them if they stumbled.

*This is gonna break my heart all over again,* Caralee thought of parting with Atu.

"Carbon, huh?" Caralee liked the names of these tiny blockums. Could it all really be true? She looked at her hands and wondered how much of her was iron, and whether she really had any pencil-stuff inside her.

"How much?" she asked. "How much of the black carbon blockums do you add to red iron blockums to make whatever steel is?" Already, that sounded simplistic.

The Son slapped his thighs. "You're kidding me."

"How much?"

"About two percent, depending on the method and the available technology." He held up two fingers. "Do you even know what a percent is?"

Caralee shook her head.

"One percent is one out of a hundred. Two percent is two out of a hundred."

"Why don't you just say that?"

"Look," the Son snapped, "you don't *actually* know everything."

"Two percent seems like not that much."

"In any system, small changes can shift everything. Think of poisons and antidotes, medicine and drink—a few sips or less, and you're dead or drunk or cured. If we assume we're working with purified iron, then adding carbon changes the way the iron atoms fit together like . . . Think of pushing individual blockums into a larger patten, without toppling the whole assembly of blockums. If you do that with iron and two percent carbon, the result is a metal that's harder, sharper, less brittle, and less prone to rust." The Son stopped, shielded his eyes, and took in the world beyond Twofinger Pass.

"Do you think the steel came from the metal folk?" Caralee asked. "We don't make steel, and they're metal, so . . . ?"

The Son said nothing for a minute, looking due east and taking deep breaths. "That is one of a few possibilities," he said after some time, but elaborated no further. "Look there, at that line of light reflecting the sun." The Son turned his gaze to the north and pointed. Sure enough, a line of something bright ran off to the northeast. "Another of their metal roads."

"Will we follow it?" Caralee asked, not at all opposed to the idea of seeing a bunch of *metal people.*

"Not yet," the Son answered plainly. "But soon, I think."

"Speaking of I-thinking, I think it's time you told me where we're headed." Caralee was limping and bleeding and miles from home, her friends were dead or stolen or alone forever. She needed better answers than she was getting, when the Son gave her answers at all.

"Look, I know how this started." She wanted to say this right. "I don't know what it is now. I don't hate you. I don't like you, but I can't hate you even though I want to. Scat, I promised I wouldn't call you a *monster,* though I don't see how *beast* is that much better. Whatever we are, it isn't just enemies, and it isn't just about Joe, and it isn't just about learning, and I don't think it's just about *you,* either. So we're together, going somewhere."

"We are? We?"

"Don't play stupid." Caralee twisted the point. "You said that *we* needed to get rid of Atu. That was mean and true and you said *we.* So tell me where we're going."

"I said that?" the Son asked, before answering himself. "I suppose I did."

He swept his hand toward the day.

"Among other things, we're off to fix the sky." He wriggled an eyebrow. "Didn't I tell you that already?"

"Well, yeah, but I thought you weren't telling me everything."

"You are correct. I am not telling you everything. Are you not used to that yet?"

"Do you mean it, though? Can you really *fix* the *sky*?" Even the words sounded wrong.

"I do mean it." He sighed. "I don't know if I can fix it, but I have to try, don't I? What are we without purpose? What am I?"

Caralee hadn't expected him to give her a real answer. She wasn't sure this *was* a real answer, but it had the tang of truth to it, and he'd mentioned it before. It didn't explain their march east, though. The sky wasn't east, it was up. Maybe he'd make for the Metal Duchy and that would explain things.

"When you say 'fix the sky,' do you mean repairing the crack or making the sky bright again?"

"Both, if possible. Either will give the world more time." The Son ran his hand across Atu's gleaming bronze-green thorax, and Atu gurgle-purred. "But first, your friend." He sighed, looking like a man who'd gone soft.

Caralee watched the Son with a sideways eye, thinking of Joe despite the mind-spinning notion of *doing* anything at all to the sky.

"Atu's not so bad, is she?" she asked him after a while.

"Naw," purred the Son, then shook his head as if to clear it. "No. No, she is not. She is brave and loyal and bereaved. Oti sacrificed his life for us, and Atu knows it." He smiled sadly. "She reminds me of a person I knew. Someone brave and loyal and bereaved. One of my brothers. Neither of them gave up in the face of danger. Foolhardy or not, I cannot help but honor Atu's bravery."

Caralee hung her head, silenced at last. She and Atu forged ahead, the legendary beast in tow. She wondered, though, what drew him to the east? What manner of beast was he?

They followed a road that was more of a downhill trail that rippled over folds in the ground that made for little hills. Yellow grass grew on either side. Caralee hoped that taking Atu to Grenshtepple's was the right decision. They had a friend there.

*Please let Thomb say yes.*

The hills leveled out and their trail became a hard-packed road wide enough for two carts to ride side by side. Even though their cart was gone, the wider road made for easier walking, as it was swept clean by one of the guilds from Grenshtepple's. The population of Grenshtepple's was big enough to support guilds and shops that competed for business. It had more than one blacksmith, two functioning mills, *six* wells, a candy shop, a haberdashery, three apothecaries, and even a bookstore.

Those were more driblets of wisdom from Joe Dunes. Caralee never thought she'd be grateful for his detailed teasing. Now, Atu's life depended on it. Caralee couldn't bear it if anything happened to the critter on their journey, wherever it led.

The grass on either side of the road grew thicker with every kilometer. Even the air felt less chilly. The road ran straight, but the long hills on either side folded deeper and taller, wrinkled like a bedsheet, and—best of all—they were safe. No sandfisher's maw hid underfoot, no chucklers disguised as rocks waited to bounce and smile and swallow. The dopey shoulders of a dunderbeast wouldn't blend into the surroundings here, and their too-long arms wouldn't reach out from seemingly nowhere to rip your face off.

Caralee spotted a squarish block of dark stone in the distance. "Look, it's one of the jotunankles!" Caralee tugged the Son's sleeve. "You know the ankles?"

The Son shook his head.

"Just wait. They're . . . Hey, here's a thought. You might actually know what they are."

The going was slow, if steady. Eventually, the road followed a hill to its top, beyond which lay what Caralee called a jotunankle. It was the size of four or five of the buildings from Comez stacked atop and side by side, but made from a single piece of green stone. The jotunankle looked not totally unlike a cornerstone—a *rac opkthene*—but was curved like a keystone—an *Angkhet opkthene*—with two arms jutting almost sideways from the ground and another leaning backward toward the sky. Where the arms met, the jotunankle was buried in the ground, with grass growing over its weathered edges. That grass hid thousands of smaller stones that could fit in Caralee's hand, and they had to watch their steps. The stones were all tumbled smooth, but the way they hid half-buried in the ground made walking tricky.

You could break your ankle, which is how Joe said they got their name.

"Look familiar?" Caralee asked the beast, tickling Atu's antennae.

"Hmm." Rather than answer, the Son kicked at the lichen-furred rocks at his feet. Then, still less answeringly, he doubled over and dug his hands into the ground. He sifted through what seemed to be dozens of pieces of tumbled stone, pulling a few aside and tossing the others in every direction.

"Ouch." Caralee caught an unworthy stone in the shin. "Watch it."

"Look here." The Son held several stones in his hands. He held one up to the sun, which transformed it into a brilliant pale jewel, translucent blue within its rough skin. It was the color of Wet Sam's milky eye.

The next stone was similar, but glowed a firelit orange with the sun behind it.

"What are those?"

"Pieces of broken glass." He nodded toward Grenshtepple's, following the angle of the ankle.

"Pieces of glass from what? Did Grenshtepple's used to be something else, like Comez and its baths?"

The Son smiled as wide as a chuckler, but he didn't answer, instead climbing the other side of the hill toward town. The road was meters off to the side, but the view was best here.

From this distance, Grenshtepple's beauty showed itself clear as critterscat. Broken arcs of ancient stone protected the town in spirals of fallen stonework. The gaps between were patched with modern gray masonry, except for two gaps that served as gates, facing east and west. Unlike the deliberate walls and purpose-built gates of Comez, Grenshtepple's had cobbled itself together with Vintage ruins. It wrapped around and across itself like a maze.

Closer up, Caralee saw still-standing curls of massive stone, half-broken bridges and shattered mammoths that weren't jotunankles, but close cousins. Dry moss hung from the curled fingers of an enormous curved stone that was stuck at an upright but odd angle, as if it had fallen that way. The whole city looked like the work of a child's play castle that had been kicked over, with the remaining used and broken pieces hauled together and interlocked or supporting each other. It was a beautiful pile, and at its moss-furred peak, a massive stone head lay faceup, sheared away from the rock just behind it. If the stories were true, a *stream* of water bubbled up from inside that rock.

If the stories were true, Caralee bet her only ribbon that there was sandymancy at work. Water from rocks couldn't just . . . happen, could it?

"Can we see Grenshtepple's the way we saw Comez?" she asked, half begging, half scrupulous.

"That depends on your plan for Atu, I think." The Son sounded like he was giving her a choice, but Caralee didn't think the answer would be yes, whomever ended up making the choice. They had a sky to fix, after all—"among other things."

After the slope down from Twofinger Pass, Grenshtepple's was surrounded by the rolling Hazel Hills—as if the bedsheet hills had been rippled into circles by the falling stones that had made the city. Rather than make her way to the gates, Caralee led them around to the right, to the south—aiming for a meadow that she knew, and hoping that Joe's crittertender friend still kept his flock there.

Her heart jumped in her chest when she saw the man in a dirty smock standing between two sturdy tents. His brown trousers were rolled up past buxom calves that were hairy and tanned. Behind him stretched a fenced-in square of meadow where a dozen or so critters of different breeds wandered, mostly in pairs.

Thombthumb the crittertender waved with both arms as soon as he saw them. He'd know straightaway that two travelers with one lone critter wasn't likely to be good news, and if folk had critter problems, they were sure to be looking for Thombthumb.

Caralee picked up her pace, all but running toward the man who was Joe's friend, with Atu clacking at her heels. Thombthumb's scruff was thicker than Joe's fuzz and darker, and his eyes were a shadowed brown that was almost black. Caralee noticed at once that while Thombthumb looked about the same as he'd looked a few years earlier, she saw him now in an entirely new light. His broad shoulders, thick thighs all the way down—those calves, that grin.

Thomb was the same, but Caralee wasn't.

Thombthumb's hands were huge, and dark from working in the sun, and he wore a big ring on his middle finger that was ridged and hooked to help him with his work. His smock was open halfway, where dark hair fanned across his chest.

"Well, if it ent Thombthumb the crittertender!" Caralee greeted him with more enthusiasm than she'd meant to. "How've you been, critter-man?"

Thombthumb—who'd been watching Caralee approach with a curious anticipation—blushed when he recognized the little woman from three days' journey west, who showed up all of a sudden looking so grown. For just a moment, his face darkened, maybe wondering where Joe was—Thomb had only ever known Caralee as Joe's tagalong—but when the Son caught up to them, Thombthumb flashed the god-king that same flirty grin.

"That you, Caralee Vinnet?" Thombthumb squinted, like the sun was in his eyes, although it was squarely above him. "Well, I'll be knocked up, aren't *you* a different sight than you were, when was it, two years ago? You'll be a woman grown now, entcha?" He put his hand over his heart and just so happened to brush his half-open shirt aside to reveal one brown nipple, soft and hairy. Caralee felt an exaggerated edge to his good cheer, but couldn't keep herself from wondering if he was the nipple sort or the other kind.

*How would I go about asking him, exactly?*

The Son groaned. "I know this man."

"You *do*?" she asked aside. "And is it hot all of a sudden?"

"I'll be *knocked up*?" The Son rolled his eyes, but stood a little straighter and smoothed his hair with both hands. "I know his type."

"Caralee, what are you doing all the way out here? Where's Mag? Where's my lad Joe?" The night before, at the Last of the Wine, Caralee hadn't *loved* being looked at like Bety Newtits. That approval on Thombthumb's face, however, gave her a new appreciation for her body. She noticed that Thomb spared an appraising look toward the Son, too, while hiding behind the masklike smile of a yokel—and wondered if everyone wore masks, and how many they wore, and if they ever took them off, and when, and for whom.

"Who is this darling critter?" Thomb turned to Atu, crouching and holding his hands out for the critter to suckle. Shy for only a moment, Atu crawled forward and all but plopped her head onto Thombthumb's hand. He supported its weight and nodded, looking at the scratches in her exoskeleton and sniffing the drool that leaked out of her flaccid proboscis.

"There's a good girl. Aren't you the sweetest one?" he reassured the critter, scratching between her antennae with his thorny ring. He listened to the faint trill Atu made and to the hiss and gurgle of her song, which had now faded so as to be imperceptible to anyone other than a crittertender.

"What happened to Oti?" From his crouch, he looked at Caralee with a clouded expression.

Caralee shook her head. She didn't trust her voice.

Thombthumb inhaled sharply, but stood and introduced himself to the Son. "Thombthumb the crittertender, at your many services." He flicked the Son a casual two-finger salute, and asked Caralee, "Who's this fancy-looking fella you're going with?"

"This is my tutor. I'm gonna be a sandymancer, Thomb." Caralee tried not to lie, but that meant tippa-toeing across the truth.

"Why's he wearing Joe's jacket?" Thombthumb asked the question easily enough, but fixed Caralee with a tight smile. "It's still got that cableshine stain on the collar. Bleached it right yellow. We got to drinking, once or twice. I'd know the smell of Joe's old sweat anywhere. A person's fresh scent is a whole other experience, you see."

Thombthumb stared at the Son, who yawned.

"Joe lent it to me," the Son said. "We've become close. Extremely close."

Thombthumb pricked his ears up, listening to something Caralee couldn't hear. He wrinkled his nose, inhaling and exhaling quickly like a dust hare sniffing the wind.

*Please, Thomb, don't smell too keenly.* Something sorrowful rolled across Thombthumb's expression. He ground his teeth.

"Well, sandymancy, eh? Ent that a thing." Thombthumb returned his attention to Caralee, his concern obvious. He had a big heart, which got him into some of his troubles. "Funny thing to walk out of the wasteland, though."

*Back off.* Caralee cleared her throat.

"Atu, then." Thomb sacrificed his curiosity entirely too easily. "What happened and where?" he asked Caralee in a soft voice, shaking his head. "She's leaking fluid from her joints. It's how critters cry. That's not too healthy for her, but we can patch her up with dirt clods and a big meal of scat." Thomb's eyes watered—that was real. Critters felt their emotions deeply, and a good tender like Thomb had a hard time not sharing those feelings. "She's been through something violent, and she's still singing. Oti died real recent?"

Caralee couldn't bring herself to answer. Something in her throat seemed lumpy, and her eyes welled with tears. Thombthumb wiped one away with a dirty knuckle. "I'm so sorry, Caralee." This time, his gaze met hers, tits or no. "I am so, so sorry. Was it quick? Was it painless?" Then, in a lower voice, "Are you hurt? Are you *safe*, Caralee?"

"I'm not hurt," Caralee shook her head. Thomb lowered his chin, twisting his crittertending ring with worry—and purpose.

"A harpy killed Oti," the Son said, his voice neutral. "Atu here tried to hold him together as he died. She is a brave soul."

Thombthumb sniffed the air again. The Son was upwind, and Thomb's eyes went wide, then narrow, then wide again. His breath was rapid, but she saw him force himself to take deep breaths and relax his clenched jaw.

Not for one second did Thomb stop sniffing the air.

*Sometimes it's not the folk who know the most who are the smartest,* Caralee mused, thinking about their encounter with Eusebius.

"Harpies? This far west? That ent right." Thombthumb shook his head. "Must be starving."

"Starving?" The Son tugged at his sleeves.

"Ayup. The world is changing again. The critters can feel it. I can feel it. The good dirt is drying out into dust. Each season, more and more critter eggs don't hatch, and those that do are scrawnier than I've ever seen." Thomb stared down the Son. "That scatsucker the Sonnyvine really did kill the world, didn't he? Slow and painful. Almost like torture. Stole just about everything from us, didn't he? Just look at what we got left."

Caralee turned the conversation on a shekel. “Not just a harpy, it was—”

“Unusually aggressive,” the Son interrupted Caralee and flashed Thomb a strange look that might have been a warning. “Too aggressive. It had to be put down. For Caralee’s safety and my own. You understand.”

Caralee took Thombthumb’s hand, which was big and warm, spreading her fingers around the sharp crittertending ring. It sported hooks and bristles that came in handy wrangling critters. Joe had bragged that Thombthumb could speak to the critters with rings like that—and do more, besides. Critter broodmums could manage all sorts of wonders with just a little sample of hemolymph, even if their species didn’t match up. As Caralee took his hand, Thomb looked down at his ring and frowned. He had a notion, she could see it.

“Thomb, we’re headed east, and I might not return . . . for a while.” Saying it out loud sent a chill up Caralee’s spine.

*I might not return at all.*

“I’ll heal up Atu till then. She’ll be safe here, on my life, she will.” Thomb’s eyes watered. Whatever people said about Thombthumb the crittertender, he *was* kind. He might be odd, but he cared for Atu as much as Caralee did. He cared for everyone.

*And what’s so bad about sharing your body? He should share his body.*

Caralee felt thirsty.

“Oh, Thombthumb. Thank you.” Thombthumb caught Caralee in an absolutely massive hug, sparing a lingering look over her shoulder. She could feel that look by the angle of their bodies and the slight turn of Thomb’s chin when he brought her in close enough that he thought she wouldn’t notice.

So Thomb was suspicious of the Son. What of it? What could a crittertender do with suspicions?

Caralee relaxed into Thombthumb’s hug, and she didn’t deny that she wished it could be more than a hug. When it came to affection, Thombthumb took no prisoners.

“Anything you want or need, Caralee.” Thomb meant it. “I’ll keep Atu safe, feed her well, let her play with other critters if she’s the sort.” He released Caralee from the hug that was as strong as a dunderbeast’s, but he kept his hands on her shoulders. “I’ll bunk with her in the triage yurt for as long as it takes for her to settle in.” He bit his lip with a glance toward the Son. “Till you come back safe and sound, you hear? You and *Joe’s close friend* and Joe’s jacket.”

Caralee understood and kept the conversation strictly to bronzebacks:

“Been my critters since I was wee. Atu offered me her hind midleg the first time I got into the cart, to lift me up—and she steadied me with her fore mid-leg, like I'd raised her myself." Caralee sniffled. "She's a good critter."

The Son cleared his throat. "She truly is." He sounded bored, but struck a pose. He stood there, all long, dark hair and slim waist and cocked posture.

"Oh, poor thing!" Thomb scrubbed the shining lines of Atu's exoskeleton with the bristles on his ring, and Atu kissed him once, sweet and sloppy. She treated Thomb as if he were family, like Caralee or Mag or Joe. Thombthumb looked up at the Son with big, black eyes and a smile that was anything but coy. "Thank you, friend. She's in good hands now. Thombthumb has good hands, you know." He held both hands out for the Son to take.

"You have my name, sir." Thombthumb winked, turning one of his rings just so. "Might I have the pleasure of yours?"

The Son, looking offended and pleased at the same time, allowed Thombthumb to shake his hand.

"Ouch!" The Son snapped his hand from Thomb's. "You cut me, you swine!"

"My pardon, sir!" Thomb recovered easily—Caralee reckoned he could flirt with a whole caravan of Patchfolk all at once and not miss a beat. He held his arm behind his back as if to keep it at a safe distance, but Caralee saw him twist the ring again—it was bright with blood.

Whatever mischief Thomb was up to, it could get him killed. Still, Thomb *would* be expert with his hands, wouldn't he? "Damn it, I'm sorry—always forgetting to take my crittertending ring off before I shake hands. Stupid Thombthumb."

True enough, a spot of bright red blood welled up from the Son's palm. It looked more like a gouge than a cut. Caralee figured that the Son's dedication to their cover story prevented him from melting Thomb as easily as he'd destroyed the steel harpy, and she had never been so thankful for lies and lying liars like the Son and herself.

"Apology accepted." The Son took the offense in stride, although Caralee could tell it enraged him. "The tools of husbandry, I suppose? Clever."

"Bronzeback critters are born in pairs, ent they?" Thomb ribbed his knuckles down the center of Atu's head, between the stalks of her tall, furry antennae, massaging the almost gold folds where her exoskeleton thickened between them. Her whimper came as a soft trilling of her antennae. "Usually one male and one female, not always—either way, they're born sterile, but they're mates for life. Well, best friends for life, if there's a difference. Poor Atu. Hate to see family torn apart by ill deeds, don't you think?" he asked the Son. "Ah, it's a shame, ennit? Most don't get over it."

Caralee slumped her shoulders.

Thomb shook his head. "Who's to swoop in and bring a loved one back from death?" Thombthumb returned his attention to the critter, examining Atu closely, muttering under his breath.

Caralee avoided looking at Joe's jacket hanging from the Son's slim shoulders.

"What can we do for you, I wonder?" Thombthumb stuck his hand deep into Atu's proboscis, feeling around. "You're a strong girl, aren't you? You and me are gonna get along just fine, Atu. Just fine."

"Joe always said they were gonna have babbies one day," Caralee lied. Joe knew as well as everyone that only critter broodmums laid eggs.

"I just bet he did! Well, Joe may have babbies one day, but not Atu." Thombthumb corrected her, then hid his face. She heard him sniffing the air again. "That Joe, I tell you. Can't wait to see that big blond brick again. We have our share of fun together!" He laughed out loud, but Caralee could feel his tension. "Think Joe and Mag'll visit us soon? Their visits are as regular as the sunrise."

"No," Caralee said, wishing she could tell someone, *anyone,* the truth. "Mag's cart broke an axle—she and Joe went back to Comez for a fix."

*"Joe may have babbies one day,"* Caralee thought, feeling terrible. *And here I am talking critter husbandry with Thombthumb and Joe's body's thief.*

The Son inhaled sharply, right on cue with Caralee's thoughts. "Isn't it rather difficult, my dirty friend, to husband critters who cannot mate?"

Thomb straightened his back and twisted his shoulders one way and then the other, cracking his spine. For the first time, he took an attitude. "I got three broodmums burrowed into these hills. Abdomen three times as long as I am tall." He cleared his throat. "Ghost-white bellies and no eyes at all. She don't need eyes to know you, though, right down to your bones."

"I see."

"She'll hear the truth of you. Smell it, too."

"Is that so."

"It's a shame my best broodmum is senile." Thomb scratched behind his ear. "She could help, you know. Bring her a critter who's lost its mate, and the broodmum can clone the dead critter with just a taste of the live one's hemolymph."

The Son nodded as if regrowing the exact same critter was nothing special. To him, it probably wasn't, but Caralee would have to see it to believe it.

"Doesn't always work, but the new critter hatches near full-grown born, and the surviving critter treats the clone as if it were the original mate. It's truly a magickal means to preserve the hive." Thombthumb looked at Caralee, one eye narrowed fiercely. "All it takes is a drop of hemolymph."

Owing to their positions, it was the eye the Son couldn't see.

The thought of Atu nurturing a new Oti made Caralee smile. A new start for the both of them. That Oti wouldn't really be Oti, not the same Oti, anyway, but Atu wouldn't care—and Caralee bet that Atu would catch him up to speed in no time.

It was a lovely fantasy, but it was a fantasy. The broodmums were going sterile. Soon there might not be enough burden-critters to do all the work that needed doing, and what would folk do then?

*Die, I guess. Die a little more.*

"There's no way your other broodmums could . . . try?" she asked Thomb.

He narrowed his eyes. "For you, Caralee, I'll ask. I can't guarantee that either one will hear me or remember how." He cleared his throat. "I'll feed the good broodmums fresh scat for a week, spike the scat with cattanippy leaves and cabbages and see if that doesn't perk one of them up." He took a deep breath. "I'll try to fix this, Caralee."

The Son pretended to fail to restrain a smile and then dismissed the crittertender from his attention. "I approve," he said to Caralee, "of leaving Atu in this muddy man's care. I see that he is nothing if not attendant to the needs of creatures small and great."

Caralee's gaze flicked back and forth between the two men.

"I'll let you three say your farewells." The Son turned away. "You have one minute."

# IV

Heights are no one's friend. Gravity works in one direction only, and nothing and no one is too high to fall. Ask a pair of binary stars. Ask my sweet sister's skull. Ask the Vine; ask the world; ask me.

I was almost ten years old when I freed myself from my father's fourth-favorite pleasure tower. I hope that Father intended it as a kindness when he decided upon the place of my imprisonment; it was, after all, a lovely building. Built atop a barbican that encircled one of the highest-built baileys in the palace complex. I suspect, however, that it was not kindness that led me to the remotest of the palace's satellite complexes. His little banishment.

Refitted as a school and prison, the tower's seventeen floors were repurposed to support the staff required to provide me a complete education and the skills I would need to not accidentally destroy anything with the brush of a finger. I was installed upon the seventeenth floor——I had access to the rooftop pleasure dome, with its inlaid pool ringed with cushioned steps. The ceiling of the dome had been enchanted with a suite of astrolabe effects so that I could look through it at night and learn the stars. Arabesque windows looked out over my city, thousands of feet below, huddled against the mountainous body of the Vine. Beyond them was a ledge of peach stone where I could dangle my feet over the frightful fall and daydream.

No one objected when I freed myself with a handful of seeds. I'm not sure whether that was the goal all along——that I would earn my freedom by taking it——or if Father's gambit to render me docile had backfired so spectacularly that no one dared to make another attempt. Perhaps my grandfather, the Most Holy Son of the Vine, intervened.

My siblings received me with their usual diversity. Esk-Ettu cried and almost crushed me with his big bear hug. Sweet Ester had written a song in advance and stood nervously as she performed it for me, her voice the sweetest clarion. Raclette glared and said nothing. Tilcept-Arri called me fearless and approved of my tactic. Zincy, firstborn, couldn't be bothered——they took after our father in their crimped, uninterested demeanor.

I turned ten within weeks. Life appeared to normalize. Grandfather Moysha left the city for weeks at a time, working on a secret project in the east, by the coast. Grandmother Athinne never again returned to the capital. By the next year, her frailty had turned to illness, and Mother visited her once, alone, and returned quiet and pale.

Not long after my twelfth birthday, Mother planned a final visit to Grandmother Athinne's home, the Tower-That-Floats, which Father had built to keep her distant and which was, of course, a gilded cage much like my tower. He enjoyed locking his problems away in pretty things, so that he could forget that any ugliness had ever existed at all.

Father stayed in the capital while the children traveled east. Athinne, at last, had become a problem that my father could outlive. Her death would be the penultimate problem of its like, after which I made certain that Father could outlive nothing.

At twelve years old, with two yet-living grandparents——one from either side of the family——I possessed no such vinegar. I moped, staring over the railing of our galleon, losing my thoughts in the prim-loom of skyrachnid-silk strands threaded through the ship's rigging. Above and around the parchment ship, five hundred goldbelly windspiders glided their paperweight bodies through the sky, bearing us toward the setting sun, where our grandmother waited to see her family for a final time. With the sun below them, the spiders' mirror-bright bellies formed our own little constellation.

My siblings were scattered across the deck when the Tower-That-Floats appeared to slouch up from the darkening ground below. Mother gathered the babes around her and cried at the sight of the great seven-sided structure. Arches of industrial malachite rose hundreds of feet into the air. They formed seven facets, alternatingly open-aired and paneled with stained glass. Ester and Stimenne oohed at the colors that painted their faces when they leaned over the railing, dazzled by hundreds of tons of colored glass backlit by the last of the day. Raclette and Zincy argued over something I can't remember, and Tilcept-Arri shushed them.

Our ship drifted to the zenith of the malachite arcs, where they joined to form the Tower-proper, a lozenge of stone suspended above the ground with no support beneath it. Father had built Grandmother a replica of the sky itself, and installed her at the point farthest from the land.

Forbid and forget. Father had his theme.

My twin sisters, Shara and E-Shara, helped Mother with the little ones, and

Esk-Ettu pulled me onto the slick green stone of the landing. He didn't share my connection with Athinne, but the boy loved his grandmother.

What is this sting, my wasteland? I have no eyes, but I want to blink away tears. I have no breath, so why do I feel as though I cannot catch it?

My brother. My sweet brother. You were not the first beloved sibling whom I killed, but if I had my breast I would beat it. If we had hands, I would hold yours.

We saw Grandmother the next day, all at once and then in groups of twos or threes. She asked to speak to Zincy alone, which made sense, for they were the eldest and would one day be Child of the Vine. She made the same request of me, and I could feel the others bristle.

"Fucking nightmare baby," Raclette growled into her fists. Mother looked bereft.

"Eat a bowl of assholes, Rack." Esk crossed his big arms and stared our sister down. She rolled her eyes, and some green-uniformed nurse led me through Grandmother's suite and into the oak-paneled rotunda where her bed had been moved closer to the windows.

Flowers choked the circular bedroom——cut flowers in vases, dried flowers hung from the ceiling with ribbons, potted palms packed as densely as a bespoke rain forest.

In her huge bed, Grandmother looked small as a child. She wore her wig of snowy curls and a gray herringbone robe, but her neck brace was bare. That hit me hard to see——it was a sign of the coming finality that Grandmother Athinne's strict standards were breaking down. I had never seen her neck brace without some splendid scarf covering its yellowed padding.

Her face was wimpled with skin, as if her skull had shrunk, with tiny black eyes and gray lips. No lipstick was another blow to Grandmother's pride.

She shifted her arm, and I realized that she could not lift it, so I took her hand in mine. It was smooth, as if the markers of old age no longer served their purpose and had withdrawn. When she squeezed, her grip was still strong.

Iron within rot; even dying, she was all I aspired to be.

"Amaunti . . . my boy." She moved her neck some. Like her arm, it was as close as she could come to raising her head to greet me. "It is so good to see you, child of mine."

I kissed her hand. I kissed her cheek. Her perfume smelled the same. I did not understand why a scent should outlive a woman.

"I will miss you," I said out of nowhere. I winced at the words.

Athinne smiled, took a breath, and nodded. She was running out of words, with too much still to say. As her heart failed, her lungs filled up with fluid. Each breath came shorter than the last.

"Listen, listen." She shook my hand side to side, weak but urgent. "Do you remember when we walked beneath the roots of the World-Tree?"

I nodded, although I'd never heard the Vine described so. "Yes," I said. "Yes, yes, yes."

"Ah, you are mine. Yes." She rolled her head; her neck ached.

Then she looked into my eyes, and her expression grew stern. She summoned some of her remaining energy.

"It must be you, Amaunti." Her voice crackled like static, but it rolled over me as if it were thunder. "You *must* rule."

I must have made some noise, for she shushed me.

"Your father will doom you all. We know how the truth terrifies him, and he will bury Moysha's work if he becomes god-king."

"Grandmother?" Of course I understood her.

"It's worse than that." She squeezed my hand again. "It must be *you,* not Zincy, not Tilcept-Arri, not Raclette or either of the twins."

"Why?" I knew why. I was the only sevenfold-adept in the family, the strongest in any magick; I had been groomed to understand my world and not to flinch from its secrets; but, ultimately, because I was the least-worst choice.

"It will be hard, Amauntilpisharai, my treasure. It will be grim. Your siblings will not understand. You will have to ensure your apotheosis by any means necessary. Or the world will surely die."

I was crying now.

"The Son of the Vine is as old as I am. Your father may replace him before you are old enough to act. If this happens, Amaunti——if your father becomes the Son of the Vine——then we may lose a lifetime of work. When you become Son of the Vine yourself, you cannot risk usurpation. No one, not even our angel Stimenne, can be allowed to threaten your authority. Your father is not the only coward in the kingdom, and there will be those who would prefer a puppet queen to you, who are no one's toy."

"I can't do that . . ." I could. I would.

"You will. You can." She coughed, sinking back into her pillows. "I am so sorry. To leave you. With such a bloody fortune."

I wiped my eyes and kissed her cheek, then looked out the windows through the palms at the rainbow gardens below, where acres of flowers were stained with sunlight that shone through a thousand different shades of colored glass. This beautiful place and all the land around it——the sky above and the encircling seas, the barrier mountains and the wild places——they were worth any price, weren't they? My family, their blood, my soul?

After dinner, outside on a malachite balcony wet with rain, I argued with my sisters Raclette and Stimenne. The night was black, the stars and nebulae were hidden by clouds.

"She's drowning in her own body," I argued, "and she's not going to get any better. Do you want her to lie there and suffer for weeks? Is your love for her so selfish that you would not let her go as a mercy, when she is already gone?"

Stimenne cried to herself, turning away from me to hide her tears.

"You are every bloody bit the monster that Father calls you." Raclette hid her tenderness behind a wall of rage. "I won't let you do it. I won't let you kill her. You're a murderer!"

"I am not! For starters, this is just a conversation. We should ask the doctors to do it, Rack. I'm only trying to——"

"She's right, you are a monster!" Stimenne found her spine and turned on me. She spat in my face. "You are a monster!"

"I am not!" My face felt hot. I stepped toward her. The rain had picked up again. "Stop saying that!"

"Murderer!" Why wouldn't she listen to me? Why did she keep calling me what I was not?

"Stop calling me a monster!" I was crying, too, now, though the downpour hid my tears. "I love my grandmother and that does not make me——"

"A monster!" Stimenne and Raclette screamed together.

"I. Am. Not!" My hands shoved Stimenne, hard. It seemed that my hands moved of their own accord, but I know that they did not. Stimenne fell backward with a shriek, striking the railing with the small of her back, flipping her over the railing and off the balcony. I saw her little body tumble once, head over heels, and then she was gone. The night and the wind and the rain stole away her screams.

Raclette and I rushed to the railing, but the ground was too far below and hidden well by the elements. I could not see Stimenne hit the ground, nor hear the impact.

Raclette wailed.

"I didn't do it," I stammered. I didn't push my sister off the tower. I couldn't have. I looked at my bare hands, long-fingered, strong but smooth. I had lovely hands.

I turned away from the balcony and climbed the stairs to the upper-level terrace where Grandmother lay abed within the central rotunda. I was crying and hyperventilating, so I knew that I might be believed when I ran inside to tell my lie:

Stimenne had behaved foolishly, playing on the railing. Raclette's ill temper rendered her accusations less believable——she'd never liked me, and the circumstances were already tragic enough. Children are prone to overreaction and misadventure. Amaunti was many things but not a liar.

My lie grew inside my head, and I clung to the lie with all my strength.

From that moment on, the truth was as much an enemy as a friend. Raclette raged against me every moment of every day since. I could hardly blame her.

What had I become? An enemy of the truth, like my father? Or a monster, at last?

No, Grandmother Athinne had taught me well. I was not a monster. There was work to be done. I swore to myself that I would do anything I could to spare my family. Perhaps I could offer them a choice?

So I hoped. If not, then I would teach Raclette the difference between a monster and a beast, and fulfill my wretched purpose.

# 9

Caralee and Thombthumb stood together, alone for a moment. The critter-tender's brown eyes were wide with worry. She didn't think she could stand his questions or keep herself from telling the truth.

"Caralee." Thomb ducked his head level with hers to look her in the eyes, the mask of an oafish yokel gone. "You know you can trust me, right? Who is this person? Where is Joe? Joe would never, ever, *ever* let you come all the way out here on your own."

That much was the naked truth, and Caralee looked away, worrying the ribbon around her waist with nervous fingers.

"And not with some fancy man leading you off to who knows where. Caralee . . . what happened to Joe? He would sooner die than let you off alone or give up his daddy's jacket."

"His what?" *His what?* "His daddy's . . ."

"Don't you know? How don't you know?" Thombthumb shook his head like they were both idiots. "Of course he didn't tell you. Caralee, that jacket is all Joe has left of his daddy."

*But . . .*

"It was?" She caught herself too late. "Is?"

Caralee never imagined she could feel so much shame.

Thomb's full lips turned down at the corners when he looked toward the Son, who'd walked due north across the road and past the gates, leaving Grenshtepple's behind. "What the fuck happened to Oti? This man is putting you in danger, Caralee. And he smells wrong, sounds wrong. All kinds of wrong."

"Thomb, it's . . ." What could she say? Thombthumb was right about everything.

"Caralee, you know my nose is sharp as tacks, but it's not just my nose. I can hear it, Caralee. Like music, too much music all at once . . ." Thomb trailed off and Caralee wondered if Thombthumb possessed other gifts as well.

Caralee's eyes began to water again. She changed the subject harder and faster than she'd ever done in her life. "Thomb, listen. I can't learn anything at home. I'm trapped." She looked at the fractured sky. "And . . ." She couldn't possibly tell Thomb that she was off to save Joe and fix the sky. "And back home, I'm nobody."

"That ent true, and you know it." He sucked his teeth and looked to the sky for a while before he spoke again. She thought Thomb was trying to keep his eyes dry, too. "You really gonna be a sandymancer?"

She nodded. Everything important went unsaid, too risky or too frightening or too sorrowful for words.

You know I've got the sandysense, Thomb. I . . . I gotta go." She wanted to tell him everything. She wanted to throw her arms around Thombthumb and sob for days, pound her fists on his chest and beg forgiveness for her crimes. For the Son's crimes. For her silence and her complicity. "Lemme go, sweet Thomb."

Thomb loosened his grip on Caralee's hands, but they laced their fingers together. Thomb was frowning, grinding his jaw, tense as a dust hare at twilight.

"Caralee, you trust me with Atu, right?" he asked.

Caralee nodded and poured all she'd left unspoken into her answer.

"Listen, if you need anything—anything—I'm right here. If . . . when Joe and Mag get that cart fixed up and come in for business, I'll be sure to tell them which way you're headed."

"Thank you, Thomb." *For pretending to believe my lie.*

"You gonna promise me that you'll come back?"

Caralee held back her tears through sheer self-loathing. She bit the inside of her cheek till she tasted blood.

"If I can, Thomb, I will. I promise I'll come back if I can." That much, at least, was the truth.

She pulled away, her fingers slipping through his. Thomb shadowed his eyes and rolled his shoulder as he loped away.

*He's so scared for me. Maybe worse for Joe. Everyone I love is gone, and I'm following the Son of the Vine like some heartbroke critter. I'm a worm.* I *chose to be a worm. I should eat scat for the rest of my days.*

Caralee fell apart inside, but she put one foot in front of the other as she let the tears come. That was the Son of the Vine's shatterscat advice, to keep her feet moving. It worked, and she cursed him for it.

Letting herself sob, Caralee followed the beastly god-king into the unknown. So she'd chosen, and so she'd follow. Let Mag and Thomb fret as they would—Caralee had vowed to undo the Son's wicked deed, and vows should never be broken. It didn't matter what happened to her along the way, or whether she became a beast or a monster herself.

Caralee tried to pull her thoughts back to something small enough to be merely awful. So she was following the Son of the Vine, who said he was off to fix the sky. Caralee didn't believe that was the whole of it, not any more than Thomb believed her excuse about leaving home to be a sandymancer. But, she supposed, if the Son *did* fix the sky along the way, that wasn't something she'd want to miss.

*Mostly cuz it's not possible.*

Neither was getting back Joe, according to the Son, but Caralee didn't plan on letting that stop her. The impossible was their joint purpose, hers and the Son's, if they had one. If purpose was the difference between a beast and a monster, then they were both beasts.

With that terrible purpose bristling in her mind, Caralee marched past the gate that led into Grenshtepple's without so much as a glance toward the city's emerald interior, where spring-fed ferns grew and stones sang. She'd given up the right to such things. Only her promise or her want to save Joe kept her feet moving. She didn't think herself worth a song, let alone a garden.

The Son kept a steady pace—well, Caralee thought, more of a pouty stalk than a pace—with his head down and his fists clenched. When Caralee caught up to him, his tone was caustic.

"Have yourself a goodbye grope?"

She didn't reward him with an answer. Today, Caralee decided, hating the Son as much as herself, was the day that Caralee Vinnet would keep her mouth shut.

*Fuck my questions. Fuck the monster. Fuck that shatterscat steel harpy.*

The Son didn't alter his stride or turn his head, but she felt his attention sharpen a bit.

"Hmm. You aren't whinging about skipping the ruins of the Tower-That-Floats and whatever the squatters defiling them have built for themselves."

*The Tower-That-Floats?* Caralee's eyes narrowed to dagger-blade slits. She wasn't even curious. She wanted to puke.

"Really. Nothing?" He shrugged, then elbowed her in the ribs as if they were on speaking terms. "Are you feeling ill?"

*Fuck that. Fuck you. Fuck me. Fucks all around.*

They marched maybe a kilometer more in silence before the Son grumbled and kicked a stone. It flew in a perfect arc down the hard-packed road and hit another stone, which skidded in a straight line until it smacked a third stone, which hopped into the air and fell back right where it had started.

"Say *something.*" He sounded bored. Was it possible that the Son bored as easily as she did?

Instead, Caralee looked around for something to occupy her thoughts. It wasn't that she wanted to talk so much as she worried she'd say something out of habit without realizing it.

The walls of Grenshtepple's were a kind of stone that Caralee hadn't seen anywhere else, not even in the bins of assorted jewelry at the market outside Comez or in the trinkets that the Patchfolk brought to trade. The smooth stone was a swirl of dark greens, none of which Caralee had ever seen in the natural world—all of them darker by far than the bright stalk of aloe vera that the Son kept in Joe's daddy's jacket.

Here and there, the swirls took on the appearance of loopy, goony faces, which reminded Caralee of Eusebius, and she wondered how the old wizard was faring and if he'd gotten lost again. However nasty he'd been to her back home, he'd seemed so lost when they found him outside Comez—and to have discovered his own mother slaughtered in her bed. . . . Caralee wondered if he'd actually encountered the steel harpy or just its bloody aftermath.

She brought herself back to the green stones of Grenshtepple's. The ancients-made walls were smoothed in a way that was similar to but more weathered than the baths at Comez. They did look like they'd fallen into place, all askew and cracked, but they still rippled with the same edgeless style that confounded the eye and reminded Caralee of the curves of the human body. She tried to extend her distraction by counting how many body parts she could find in the piled walls of the green city. There, a fat hip curled around the crook of an elbow and flexing triceps; there, a shoulder sagging from the tendons of a neck.

She couldn't see the stone face at the top of the city, mouth open to the sky. If Joe could be trusted, water bubbled out of the statue's mouth.

"I can't believe that your bugfucking oaf drew my blood." The Son shoved his palm out so that Caralee couldn't avoid looking at it. "Once upon a time, such a crime would have seen him tortured to death. Is he always that careless?"

Caralee said nothing, wishing Thombthumb had gouged out the Son's scatting eyeballs.

The Son took a different tack.

"Want to learn how to conjure a witchlight?"

Tempted, Caralee bit her tongue. They walked side by side with no distractions, no critters to rein, no cart to protect, no goods to sell. Caralee had pushed past the initial shock of losing Joe, pushed past that first roar of anger and the sandpit of fear that came with it. She had put her soul on the line, befriending the enemy. Now it was her hatred of that friendship that she slogged through. When she'd swore she'd do anything to bring back Joe, she imagined all sorts of awful things would stand in her way. Never in her nightmares did Caralee think that caring for the Son would be one of those dangers.

He stopped walking and turned to face his mortal enemy. Caralee's feet stopped almost on their own, but she kept her jaw clenched tightly.

"Hello." The Son smiled, victorious at capturing Caralee's attention. "First, cup your hand."

She resisted—she really did—but not with her whole heart. Caralee looked at her hand. With hesitation and a spike of self-hate, she curled her fingers.

*Use that fondness, and use that hate. Look obedient. Turn his false friendship against him.*

Caralee was learning magick and learning how to be ruthless.

"Think of the way you summon Dustbutt. Imagine the feeling of the sand, the way you can sculpt it with your seventh sense, seeing Dustbutt in your mind's eye before bringing it into being. Now listen: earth is a fixed element, which for the sake of this lesson means that it's inert—in simpler terms, it won't move without some external force. It's *still.*" He picked up a clod of black dirt from beneath the grass. "It's also a tangible element, meaning you can touch it, carry it, throw it around."

Caralee pictured the way she pulled Dustbutt up from the ground and the way the Son had lifted those twin pillars of whirling sand, back in the cart, ages ago and two days earlier—even the way he'd kicked the stone down the road, which had skidded into a second stone, which had popped a third into the air. He'd moved them, and they'd moved each other, and they'd all stayed where they'd landed.

The Son moved on. "Fire is different in both aspects; it is neither fixed nor tangible. It's the opposite of fixed—mutable—which means it changes from moment to moment. Whereas a rock will stay the same rock even after you kick it, the flame from a single misplaced candle can grow big enough to consume a house or a harvest's entire crop."

*Okay . . .*

"You're wondering, 'So what?' and I'll get there. Sap my vine, you're insufferable even when you're mute." The Son cupped his own hand, mirroring

Caralee. "Fire is also intangible, unlike earth, meaning you can't touch it. It will burn your hand, but your hand cannot hold it. Every babe learns that lesson early, don't they?"

He looked to Caralee, still mute, then rolled his eyes. "Yes, they do. Concerning pyromancy, remember that you're working with an element that cannot be physically controlled—it is intangible—and that will also change on its own if not controlled—mutable. These are two dangers that you must manage at once.

"With earth, you just move it about, really. Juggling is harder to learn. Fire, on the other hand, requires a deeper level of control before, during, and after you summon it. One errant thought and you can die like that contaminated harpy. Hold the fire you summon lightly, but wrap your seventh sense around the heat. Keep its shape contained and keep its temperature controlled. Whereas your ability to control earth depends on your understanding of simple physics and a modicum of attention, your strength with fire depends on a total focus and a nimbler use of your imagination.

"You can see how pyromancy is a more advanced form of elemancy than geomancy. How do you summon fire to your hand on a cold night? Where does it come from, and how do you call it?"

*Elemancy, that's what sandymancy's really called. Pyromancy and geomancy. What other 'mancies are there?* Caralee remembered the Son had said there were seven magicks. If sandymancy was just one of the magicks, there were six other *entirely different* types of magick besides sandymancy. What could they possibly be?

"Think of fire—of all heat—as motion," the Son went on. "Think about your blockums, in fact. Imagine that you create fire by moving blockums faster and faster until they're moving faster than anything you've ever seen. Until they begin to glow.

"To summon a witchlight, first visualize an invisible sphere of air through which the fire cannot escape. Go ahead, summon that sphere now. Imagine holding an unseen ball in your hand. Reinforce that visualization with your seventh sense—what you call your 'sandysense.' Conjure up the idea that your ball is hollow and inescapable. That nothing inside it can ever get out."

Caralee did so, forcing her imagination to comply until she could feel—no, *not-feel*—the tingle of the conjured sphere. She could see it, even, with her actual eyes, shimmering in her hands like the air above a campfire.

"Well done," the Son approved. "Now, don't call to fire from outside the sphere—that is an easy way to burn your face off—besides which, if you've made the sphere correctly, the fire won't be able to get inside it. Remember that heat is motion. I want you to visualize the blockums inside your sphere—air blockums, blockums of dust, blockums of moisture—whatever's inside. Picture those blockums all moving faster and faster, colliding against each other and bouncing off the inside of your inescapable sphere. *Don't* let go of the visualization of that sphere—or, again, you'll burn your face off. Just try to add the idea of motion to whatever's inside the sphere."

Caralee followed his instructions, careful not to burn off her face, and felt the sphere vibrate more forcefully, though it still looked empty.

"Good. Faster, faster—ever faster, until you see the results you've intended. This part is tricky: visualize those blockums moving so fast that you can no longer see them—imagining something you can't see, while also controlling it. You want to create and control *chaos* inside the sphere—while maintaining the *order* you've created with the sphere on the outside of what will be your witchlight. Chaos inside order."

Caralee didn't want to die like that harpy or learn to live without a face, so she forced her attention entirely into the task. Maybe this was how the Son honed that knife-sharp focus that made her feel so uncomfortable when he aimed it at her.

The sphere shimmered, and the air inside it vibrated, and Caralee whipped up the blockums inside faster and faster. Nothing happened, and nothing happened, and nothing happened, and then the air above her hand exploded like a burning log, sparking a fire so sudden that it shocked Caralee out of her focus.

The spark rebounded off the top of the sphere, which startled her into losing control of the sphere, which evaporated. The rebounded spark landed in her cupped hand, searing her palm. The shock of the pain wrecked her focus. "Scat!" she cried, breaking her silence and shaking the pain away from her injured hand. At least it hadn't been her face.

The Son roared with laughter and victory.

"Well done, all around! You summoned fire, and I summoned your voice. Hello again, my chatty student."

"Fuck you," Caralee all but whispered, looking at her burned hand. "I did it. I didn't do it right, but I *did* it."

"Thus a true 'sandymancer' is born. You're no mere dust-witch, Caralee Vinnet; you have the will and the intention to control all the elements—and more. To tell the truth, I wasn't sure you had it in you. Oh, you had bluster, but this—this is *progress*."

"Progress fucking hurts." Her hand hurt *so bad*.

"Here." The Son rummaged through the pockets of his jacket and produced the spiny, thick stalk of aloe vera that he'd stolen from the window box of the murder house in Comez. "After you defeat me, and you tell them all that I was wicked *and* correct, add *prepared* to the list. Wicked, correct, and prepared." He flashed a charming smile. "We'll build the list as we go, and maybe you will come to know me, after all."

He scratched at the dried end of the stalk, scraping off a brown crust, then showed the end to Caralee. The end of the pointed stem was wet inside, wet like drool or snot but with a smell like . . . It was a new kind of smell. Fresh, somehow.

Cable plant was never wet. It was hardly even damp, with just a string of sap at its core. Certainly, it could never be called *fresh*.

"Now give me your hand. This won't hurt."

Caralee held out her burned hand, and with a light touch, the Son dabbed the goo from the stalk onto her wound. Caralee inhaled sharply, expecting the gel to sting, but instead, it felt cool and eased the pain.

"Unlike most everything in this world, my forebears did not design or alter aloe vera at all. It comes to us directly from our origin, out there among the stars. Its name is older than our world. Naturally, that makes it a sacred plant. If I am the Son of the Vine, consider this one of the Vine's great-great-grandparents."

"It's that old?" Caralee tested out the name. "Aloe vera."

"It was one of the seven tines of the Grown Crown." The Son pointed to his left temple, just past his hairline. "It grew right here."

"You said that before, but it's hard to picture."

"Survive me, and you'll live to see it yourself." The Son surprised Caralee with reverence as he kissed the wet end of the stalk of aloe vera and returned it to his pockets.

*Those aren't his pockets, they're Joe's pockets. Joe's* daddy's *pockets. I'm such a git.*

Joe had never talked about his parents much, which Caralee understood—her parents died when she was wee, too—but Caralee still felt the sting of not knowing that the jacket had belonged to his daddy. She'd thought she knew everything there was to know about Joe, and she'd been wrong.

They continued their march away from Grenshtepple's and would soon pick up the road. Questions tumbled through Caralee's head like fallen blocks of stained glass. Would they head north to the Metal Duchy or continue heading east? What lay east, anyway? Caralee knew the Son would reckon with the metal folk eventually. Would he really grow a crown from his head? How was that for sleeping?

"Don't stop trying to conjure your own witchlight," the Son said, perhaps sensing that Caralee's thoughts needed corralling. "Once you get the ball of fire started, we'll work on things like multiple witchlights, and changing color, and setting them to float. That's all much less dangerous. Don't be afraid of burning yourself—you *will be* burnt, if you are the promising wizardling that I know you to be. Whatever you do, don't give up."

Caralee elbowed the Son. "What was the first thing I told you, Son?"

He held one finger to the corner of his mouth and cocked his head. "Hmm. I believe you said, 'I know you, Sonnyvine,' am I right?"

Caralee screwed up her face, cupping her hands again. "Not that. The other thing."

"You told me that I talk weird."

"You do—but the other-other thing." The firewall sphere popped in to place as if she'd been practicing all her life.

"That it's been eight centuries since my downfall."

"No! The *other* other-other thing," Caralee crowed. Something about a slight distraction made it easier to focus on her sandymancy.

"Ah, that. You declared that you were intelligent, then disproved that declaration by telling me that you don't ever, ever, ever give up. Was it three evers or four? Maybe only two—but it felt like four."

"So?" A spark of something tiny and dense appeared in her sphere. It grew, the light low but evenly distributed.

"Look, you've almost got it," the Son approved. "I am merely dispensing some ancient wisdom. You've no idea how many aspirants burn their faces off and give up. They return home to live ordinary lives, disfigured and powerless." He corrected himself with a growl. "*Gave* up, I suppose. Who knows how they trained that candle-backed moron."

"So how do I make it change color?" she asked. "And float."

"Some color comes from heat, but for the prettiest palettes . . . You've more particle physics to learn before color. . . . I do not look forward to teaching you about noble gases and electron states."

"Right." She let the fiery motion inside the sphere slow down, and the witchlight dimmed from yellow to orange to red before winking out. "Only thing going with heat is how fast the blockums are moving, innit? Like the colors of a candle."

"Incandescence, yes," he muttered. "Just like a candle. Aptly observed."

"If I'm that great you should tell me where we're headed, don't you think?" Caralee dared. "I mean, I know you wanna fix the sky, but where do we *go* for that?"

The Son nodded, kicking the dirt like Joe but without stubbing anything.

"You've earned it, yes, and since you won't understand at all, I don't see the harm in sharing."

"Thanks?"

"Our first destination is—or used to be—a little bay out east. Once it was nameless, then it was not, and now I suppose it must be nameless again."

"You're right, I don't understand. If the metal folk broke the sky, why aren't you swaggering into their city or whatever and slaughtering them all?"

"We'll get there, tiger. There is an order to things."

"Like what kinda order, and what's a tiger?"

"Here's a related question." The Son held out his hands and cocked his head. "Why would a whole armed force—squadron, patrol, whatever scale in which these metal soldiers are deployed—wear heavy metal armor? They've got fast and presumably well-protected transportation, and by our limited collection of evidence, their only actions have been to establish infrastructure and attempt to trade. Skyfuck aside, their only transgression seems to be quarrying my stone without permission. They've been awake for three decades, but have only moved outside the boundaries of their estate within the last few years."

"What's the question?"

"If a group of people have only soldiers to accomplish non-soldiery things, does that make them *less* dangerous or *more* dangerous?"

"More or less dangerous than what?"

"If our newcomers are all soldiers, are they an army? Are they here on purpose, or is their arrival the result of some folly of war? If the latter, do they have enemies? Will their enemies follow? If the former . . ." The Son put a hand across his flat stomach. "I may have quite a bit more metal to melt."

Caralee harrumphed. "Maybe it's more about who's in charge of the soldiers?" she offered. "I mean, who's telling them to build metal roads and start cutting up stone without asking anyone? Who's smart idea was it to steel-up a harpy? Isn't the person in charge the one you want to get to? Metal clothes or not, if soldiers are anything like plain old guards, then they have a big boss making decisions."

The Son declined to answer, but Caralee knew she was right.

Something that she saw over the next hill snagged her attention. A black treebone in the distance, where the road picked up. A black treebone the size of a man, crooked and thin. Caralee rolled her eyes and spat, and the Son followed her line of sight.

"Are you kidding me?" Caralee pointed out the unsteady form of Eusebius.

"This cannot be happening," the Son complained. "Does he spend all of his time loitering?"

They closed the distance. True enough, Eusebius stood—again—not far outside of town. He looked more haggard, more lost, if that was possible.

His body looked thinner, stooped in dark robes and black plumage, streaked with white wax from the tapers that burned on his shoulder pads. Stringy black hair was combed down over his balding head, and the wrinkles crisscrossing his face were made all the more prominent by the thick white makeup smeared into his skin. His hands crawled like critters, restless and long-fingered.

Beside Eusebius stood what seemed to be the carpet from his wheelbarrow, rolled up and tied with twine. He'd propped it up against one of the many green stones that littered the perimeter of Grenshtepple's. The remains of the wheelbarrow lay not far away—it had booted a wheel and its handle was cracked.

"Hail, fellow travelers!" Eusebius called out, waving his arms. "This is your lucky day!"

"In what possible way." The Son sounded irritated, but less enraged by the wizard's mere existence than he had been before. It was hard to hate such a sad man, and Eusebius looked to have gotten even sadder since last they met.

"Why, this astounding heirloom carpet—only seven shekels. What a savings!" He threw his spider hands into the air and tilted his face to the sky. Only tilting his face to the sky demanded that Eusebius arch his back as far as it could go, plus bending back at his knees and hips. He looked ready to topple backward—all painful angles and nothing on him that rested straight or still. Caralee couldn't figure out how much of Eusebius's strange body owed itself to his unfortunate natural condition—which Willum the alderman had mentioned—and how much was theatrics. He'd learned to use what he had, that much was clear.

Caralee also recalled the carpet-shaped outline on the floor of Eusebius's mother's kitchen. Of all the valuables in that house—Dinnal had owned good, sharp knives, and she'd grown aloe vera in her window boxes, and probably had jewelry somewhere—why would Eusebius take something as bulky as a carpet? Through a *window*?

Eusebius looked at Caralee and the Son without recognition.

"Hello." Caralee frowned. "It's me, Caralee Vinnet."

Eusebius blinked. "Seven shekels, a legendary bargain!"

*Does he not remember us? Me?*

"Please, fair strangers! Let my ill fortune cushion your feet for a hundred years, with craftsmanship the like not seen since Amauntilpisharai of the Thousand Names destroyed the world and murdered all the sweet babbies of the Land of the Vine!"

*Who? Oh. Uh-oh.*

The Son lashed out with his arm and grabbed Eusebius by the throat.

"*Where did you learn my name?*" The Son squeezed his hand, and the sandymancer's hawking cry died in his throat.

Caralee recalled how the Son had choked her like that, when he'd lifted her off the ground and taught her precisely how worthless she was. Caralee had been given the chance to prove him wrong—and she had, one step at a time. This, though, was different, and Eusebius would fare even worse. He clawed at his throat.

"He can't answer you if you crack his voice box, can he?" Caralee tried to recapture the Son's name from the ether, but Eusebius had spoken so fast, and the name was so foreign. *Amau* something.

The Son released Eusebius from his grip but not from his question.

"Eh? Ah!" Eusebius coughed. "You have heard of the Lord of a Thousand Names? What a pleasure to meet a fellow scholar of the bygone days!"

The Son flew Caralee a glance. "What is wrong with him?"

She shrugged.

"Hey," she said to Eusebius. "Your name is Eusebius, right?"

The gangly crow opened his black-rimmed eyes wide. "It is. May I ask how . . ."

"We met outside Comez," said the Son, narrowing his eyes.

"Did we? No, we didn't. I'm sure of it." Eusebius blinked. "Comez, you say? I was born in Comez. I meant to visit. I . . ."

"How 'bout me?" Caralee asked. "You met me even earlier. Back in my nameless village, remember?"

"Yes!" Eusebius clapped, his expression brightening. "Caralee Vinnet! The shitfarmer who fancies herself a sandymancer!"

Caralee growled. The Son pressed the matter. "You really have no recollection of our encounter outside of your birthplace? I threatened to kill you then, too."

Eusebius held a hand to his head as if it ached. "Many pardons, most kind sir—I have, that is . . . my memory of recent events seems to have slipped away since . . . Well, if I made it to Comez, it's a muddle. I remember my name and my life and this rude shitfarmer, but the past few days are just . . . empty."

If the sandymancer's face went white beneath his makeup, it didn't show, but Caralee could sense it, and he trembled. "I had a horrible dream. My beloved mommy . . ." He shook his head to clear it of shadows. "I missed my chance to visit, I think. Too busy with less important matters, such as recovering my things." He patted the carpet that stood rolled up beside him. "Only . . . all my things were with Mommy. It is a mystery."

His eyes watered, and watered honestly. Caralee saw dried blood in the cracks of Eusebius's face paint, all along one side of his head. Of course he was innocent.

"You remember meeting Caralee at her village? You remember your sandymancy?" The Son shot questions. "You remember growing up a rickety boy in Comez? You remember those things, but not what happened yesterday?"

"How do you—"

"Answer the questions."

Eusebius nodded, mostly to himself. "My bones, yes. I remember, I remember—everything, don't I?" He looked to Caralee, for some reason. "But then . . . wings? Horrible metal eyes?" He wrung his hands. "And pressure, a headache like none I've ever felt. I told you, my memory . . . since I had that nightmare . . ."

"You saw it?" The Son pressed the question too sharply, and Eusebius recoiled.

"My . . . I saw my mommy." The wizard's voice cracked. "I missed my mommy."

"Hey," Caralee said, taking his hand—his skin was silky soft despite his gnarled, lumpy, shaking bones. "It's gonna be all right, ent it?" She stroked the veins on his hand, like she'd do for Mag whenever she became upset. "You ent so bad, are you?"

The Son had cast his gaze eastward. "What have you been up to?" He wasn't talking to Caralee or the befuddled wizard. "Do you have *purpose* now?"

"Wossat?" Caralee asked. The Son kept on about purpose. It didn't make any sense.

"Nothing a merely adequate person could understand."

Caralee rolled her eyes and pointed to the blood caked on one side of Eusebius's forehead. The Son squinted, took a serious breath, and nodded to Caralee that her observation was a clever one.

"What have we here?" he asked.

The Son tapped one finger on Eusebius's forehead and closed his own eyes. Caralee not-felt the tingle of sandysense as the Son probed the wizard's brain. She extended her own sandysense to watch what the Son did, exactly. He seemed to be not-pulling back skin-thin layers of the wizard's brain—but without actually *moving* anything.

This level of sandymancy was far, far beyond her. Caralee watched as the Son burrowed toward a dense, spiraled structure at the center of Eusebius's brain, which glowed with constant activity. It projected connections to every part of the brain and pulsed to a dozen beats at once—except for a strip of dark along its center. The projections from the dark strip of the spiral structure were few and pulsing weakly.

"This is awesome." Caralee watched rapt as the Son showed her the inside of a living human brain. "Are we really that . . . complicated? There are more lights in him than stars in the sky."

"Be quiet," the Son snapped. "This is . . . very . . . delicate." He exhaled sharply. "Oh my. This is a rare and rather delicious brain trauma." The Son dropped his finger and rocked back on his heels. "Do you remember how the harpy dulled your senses, staggered you with a kind of a mind fog?"

"Yeah . . ." She did, barely. Parts of that day were impossible to forget, like the screams of the critters and the smell of burning slag. Other parts of their encounter with the harpy were hard to remember.

"Long story short, your friend here got a full blast. Even longer story short, the harpy can manipulate the blood of animals. Somehow—during the fracas with what we can now assume was the steel harpy—this wizard suffered a stroke. Part of his brain went without blood for too long. He's probably lucky to be alive." The Son weighed his hands in the air. It looked like he was preparing a lesson. "Have you heard of amnesia?"

"Mag said her brother's wife had a fit one day and couldn't remember her own name."

"Yes," the Son clipped. "That's retrograde amnesia, which means you forget your past. This, however, is anterograde amnesia, and it works in the other direction—you forget your future."

"What?" Caralee and Eusebius asked as one.

The Son addressed the wizard. "Your brain is injured. You suffered some kind of damage in Comez, I believe, and you no longer have the ability to form new memories."

Eusebius thought about that. "I have never heard of such a thing. Most kind sir, how is it, then, that I remember your questions enough to answer them?"

"Different sorts of memory." The Son waved away the difficulty of the question. "Your short-term memory remains intact—what's damaged is the process that converts recent events into long-term memory. You can hold ideas in your mind while we talk, but you cannot *keep* those ideas. In a few moments, or when you sleep, you will forget again. You are stuck at that moment, forever. Your life before is all you have." The Son's eyes narrowed. "Which means you can answer my question: Where did you learn the name Amauntilpisharai?"

*Amauntil . . . pish . . . arai.* Caralee didn't lose the name this time.

"Oh." Eusebius looked lost. "I didn't see Mommy, then? I shall have to visit her. She worries."

"She worries no longer."

Eusebius nodded, muddying his eyeliner with tears, despite his permanent ignorance.

Caralee wondered if there were even more types of memory. Eusebius seemed to know the sorrow of losing his mother, but without remembering her loss. Maybe feelings and memories lived in different places.

"Answer my question, please," the Son asked as gently as Caralee had ever heard him speak. "Where did you learn my name and first title, Amauntilpisharai of the Thousand Names?"

"I . . . I read many tomes at the Sevenfold Redoubt and precious few elsewhere." Caralee never imagined she'd feel sorry for the sandymancer, but he looked so broken—and she understood how he felt, sort of. Caralee's former life back home was crystallized in her mind, but every moment with the Son challenged her such that she couldn't quite grasp everything that had happened since they'd met.

Her life before the Son and her life after the Son did not fit together at all.

*Since he stole Joe.*

"Yes," Eusebius said to himself. "It was within an illuminated manuscript, from which I deciphered the thousand names of the Son of the Vine." His shoulders slumped unevenly.

"You translated *all* of the thousand names?" The Son looked skeptical. "The title is meant to be more evocative than literal, but there *are* a thousand actual—"

"I translated all of the names, yes—does that answer your question, most kind . . . Forgive me, but have we been introduced? I don't believe I have the pleasure of your name."

The Son flared his nostrils. "You've the pleasure of a thousand."

"Hehe." Eusebius chuckled and wagged a finger. "Fear not, most mysterious sir, I understand the needs of discretion! Now, may I interest you in a fantastic carpet? I might not have mentioned, but it's worth considerably more than seven shekels. Thanks to my ruthless bartering, I was able to acquire it at a fraction of the cost and am delighted to share my good fortune with any discerning customer." Eusebius had the audacity to lie.

"Shatterscat," Caralee hissed. "You got that carpet off your ma's kitchen floor, longshanks."

"Calumny!" Eusebius recoiled in false distress—or not, if he'd forgotten that part. "How dare you deliver such an accusation! How *very* dare!"

"Cuz it's true?"

"Ah." Eusebius calmed immediately, smoothing the waxed feathers on his shoulder pads. "Did I mention that I am able to offer you a low, low price of a mere seven shekels?"

"Are you kidding me?" Caralee asked Eusebius. "Do we look like we need a carpet? I'm not gonna carry it, I'll tell you that much right now."

The Son clucked. "Not so fast, Caralee." The Son peeled back a corner of the carpet and examined the pile.

The Son hummed with sandymancy, and Caralee not-felt the tingle again—but not just from the Son. She not-felt the tingle of sandymancy *from the carpet.* It echoed back, a fainter version of the Son's not-humming.

"Unroll it, please," the Son commanded the wizard, who'd recoiled from the carpet like a sandviper. He'd have sensed the sandymancy, too.

"I, er . . ." Eusebius made an attempt to untie the twine knot that kept the carpet bound, but his fingers weren't up to the task. "Perhaps, that is, you might . . ."

"Give it here." Caralee pulled the knot apart easily, caught the rolled up thing on her shoulder, and eased the carpet onto the dry grass. "Ooh, it's pretty," she added as she unrolled it. Blues and reds and golds swirled in a similar teardrop pattern as the baths at Comez.

"Aha! Oho!" The Son's sudden smile beamed with solar energy. "You're well preserved, aren't you?" He knelt and traced the patterns with his fingers, almost giddy.

"Wossit?"

"Our lucky day, is what it is." The Son's good mood was infectious. "One shekel."

Eusebius pantomimed distress. "Alas, most kind sir, I would be flat broke at that price!"

"Ent you flat broke now?" Caralee asked with a doubtful frown.

The Son chuckled. "Two shekels."

"For five shekels, I'll accept the loss."

"Three." The Son flashed Caralee a look, his lips pressed into a line of a smile. "And you'll tutor my ward for two weeks."

"Tutor? Ah, yes, the wee sandymancer. I'm afraid I'm headed east."

"As are we."

"Eh." Eusebius looked at his feet. "I'm afraid I would only slow you down."

"Four shekels, and I promise: we'll make *excellent* time." The Son's sly smile promised to show Caralee something new.

*What is he about now?* Caralee wondered, then looked at the carpet. *How we gonna make good time with a lame wizard and a stupid carpet?* It was a hard question to answer without knowing where, exactly, the Son was headed. He'd said that their "first stop" would be a bay in the far east, but Caralee didn't have the first clue as to why or what the Son would do when he got there. Was he ever going to confront the Metal Folk? Could he really fix the sky?

"Four shekels it is—most kind sir, we have a deal."

They shook hands, and the Son dropped two shekels into Eusebius's other hand.

"Eh?" A white-caked eyebrow raised itself in polite enquiry. His tears were drying, black streaks down his white face, caked on one side with rust-colored blood.

"You will receive the remainder of your fee upon your dismissal, of course," the Son purred. "*Arepa enquis tonnara,* of course?"

Eusebius hissed, then inhaled sharply, and then smiled a manic smile. "*Tonnare arepito, enquisale!* 'May the buyer's word be legal, and may be the terms of the broker be law.' So few who speak Auld Vintage these days!"

The Son looked at Caralee with a secret smile and eyebrows raised in delight. "I didn't kill a language! Huzzah for me." He pointed to Eusebius and to the carpet. "You will fly it for us, of course."

Eusebius's eyes appeared to roll full circle twice in his skull before settling on the carpet he'd just sold. "But it's not. It just looks. I couldn't awaken it. How did . . . You truly know what it . . . is?"

The Son nodded, smirking. "We used to call them *nepeculim.*"

*Air-something.* Caralee tried to puzzle that out, but she was missing a word.

Eusebius looked down at the carpet and screamed, "You *shatterscat* textile!" He clapped both hands over his mouth when he heard his own outburst. Carefully, Eusebius parted his fingers one at a time and whispered out from behind them: "That is, I used every application, to no avail. Surely you jest, most kind sir. Yet how could you possibly know it at a glance?"

"Oh, you know, from a *book*." The Son allowed himself a good deal of sarcasm.

"Alas, your eye is excellent, Master, but this carpet is inert." Eusebius waved his arms uselessly, a barren tree in a sandstorm. "I could not awaken the enchantments, if indeed this is no false artifact." He clasped his chest as if his heart ached. "Four shekels!" he lamented.

"Mommy was right," the wizard added. "I shouldn't be surprised. Mommy was always right." His voice caught on the word *was,* but Caralee didn't see the signs of any deeper understanding.

"Yes, this is one of ours. Beautifully preserved," the Son said to himself. "Caralee, would you like to learn how to fly?"

Eusebius looked like he was about to go into shock.

"That's a pile of scat." Caralee couldn't believe what she was hearing. "I mean, yes? But how the fuck?"

"Do you remember our lesson comparing earth and fire?" the Son asked; she nodded. "When I said that earth was safe? This is a potent exception!" He looked downright giddy. "There's no trouble of exploding witchlights or another incident of melting metal into slag. But once we're finished, you had best not fear heights."

Eusebius's eyebrows grew even higher, and Caralee wondered if his eyebrows would be happier if they left his face entirely.

"Did you say *witchlights*? The young miss has already learned witchlights?" The wizard held his feather collar to his chin and peered over it at Caralee. Was he afraid she would bite him? "And what's this about slag?"

"Oh yes," the Son bragged, clearly intent on giving Caralee as much credit as he could. "My darling ward is becoming quite the battlemage. You should see her crack heads with her quarterstaff. Why, she slew the harpy—she slew a harpy in Twofinger Pass."

"A harpy!" Eusebius sat in a huff onto a green rock behind him, holding his head in his hands. "If there was ever a wonder, it must surely be you, most kind sir. Your ease with Auld Vintage—pray, most kind sir, whence do you hail?" He'd forgotten that he'd already asked that question.

The Son looked Eusebius square in the eyes and told the truth.

"I come from the heart of the wasteland, where everything you've ever longed to know sleeps beneath the sand."

Eusebius's laughter came out thready. "Such japes! I see I'm not like to get the truth from you straightaway." He waggled a rheumatic finger at the Son. "So be it, most kind sir! So be it!"

Caralee didn't get it. Thombthumb—a crittertender—had all but named the Son of the Vine after one meeting. At the very least, he suspected *something* out of the ordinary. And yet, Eusebius the sandymancer, man of the world, an *actual* scholar who had read *actual* books, wouldn't see what was right before his nose. The Son hid nothing from the wizard, and Eusebius refused to see it. His pride blinded him.

Caralee saw here an example of a fellow's strengths turned to weakness. Also some brain damage.

She also wondered if just maybe there was more to Thombthumb the crittertender than she knew. How much more could there be?

"Now, Caralee, let's begin." The Son cleared his throat.

"Okay."

"Kneel here"—he indicated the ground at one of the narrow ends of the carpet—"and follow my instructions just so."

"Okay." She knelt and held her hands over the carpet, ready.

"I want you to extend your seventh sense and pluck the blue threads. Leave the others alone for now."

She did just that. Dipping her sandysense into the weave of the carpet, at first she felt like she was grasping at loose cable hay. Then she found a blue thread and held on to it. It had its own vibration, which resonated with her sandysense. Following it, she soon held all the blue threads in her mind's eye, a secret pattern hidden inside the carpet's weave. Just by holding them—by not-holding them—she seemed to bring the blue threads to life. They buzzed back at her with an echo of her own sandysense.

A fringed corner of the carpet tugged itself up, flapping as if it were blown by a tiny wind. Tassels frilled, and Eusebius made a sound like wood creaking in a gale.

"Unexpected!" he crowed. "Woe to the witchtides, this girl has true potency! Is the world so vast now that children go untested and magickal adepts simply wander out of the wastes with hands that vibrate with the voice of the world?"

*You have no idea.*

The Son ignored Eusebius and continued instructing Caralee. "Now, the gold threads along the edges, while keeping the blue threads active."

That was simpler—the gold threads were also woven throughout the carpet, but began at the edges and so were easier to find. After conjuring witchlights, holding the weaves of two differently colored threads was almost as easy as breathing.

"I'm doing it!" Caralee howled, solidifying her hold over the threads of blue and gold. The entire edge of the carpet rose up, not blown this time by wind but straight and level, ramp-like. As she completed the work of touching every thread, the carpet rose along its length, gliding up from the earth, steady and even.

The Son clapped. "Finally, take hold of the reds."

Caralee found the reds more slippery, but once she'd seized one, the rest of the pattern snapped into place, not-blazing in three colors that were also not-colors.

Nothing new happened.

"What did the red threads do?" she asked, keeping control of all three colors of threads.

"You can stop," the Son said. "You've awakened it. The three colors are like a key. Blue gives the carpet buoyancy, gold provides stability, and the reds are flight controls, which you aren't using right now. The carpet will answer to you, now, whether you're using your 'sandymancy' or not."

Caralee imagined the carpet moving up and down, a stray thought, but a stray thought that the carpet answered. It rose till it reached Caralee's eyes, and then descended again to the level of her knees.

"I am moving a magick carpet." Caralee said it aloud, and the words sounded ridiculous, but the carpet seemed to understand what she wanted it to do.

"I am flying a flying carpet." The idea sounded absurd no matter how she said it.

"This is my flying carpet, and I fly it with magick."

"Okay, fine." The Son moved her along. "Now, as long as you don't think suicidal thoughts, we won't plummet out of the sky."

"We won't—what?"

"What do you think this beautiful piece was made to do, merely hover?" The Son stroked a gold edge before leaping onto the floating carpet—which bore his weight without so much as bobbing. "Well then, sandymancers one and all—climb aboard. We've a ways east to travel."

The Son's commands were light, indifferent, and he leaned down and offered the wizard his arm. Eusebius took it with a flash of gratitude, and put a swollen foot on the carpet. Soon, both men stood looking down at Caralee.

"Are you kidding me? We're going to *ride* it?" She stepped back. "Won't we fall off?"

"That's the dangerous bit, isn't it? Are you *afraid,* Caralee Vinnet?"

"Not one bit!" Caralee threw herself onto the carpet, landing on her stomach. It felt as solid beneath her feet as stone.

"We head east for now." His expression was something new, a personal curiosity, without his usual detachment. "Yes, east we go."

And so they did.

# 10

Kneeling at the edge of the flying carpet, its fringe flapping wildly in the wind, Caralee whooped with delight and alarm as they rose ever higher, past the walls of Grenshtepple's, till she could see the whole town from the top down—its intertwined walls of dark green stone, with even more stone fallen or hauled into a pile in the center of the city. It looked like an accidental castle.

In the center of the green stone maze, Caralee caught a glimpse of Grenshtepple's famed stone face, hollow eyes to the sky, mouth open and frothing with dark water. Its nose had been cleaved away, and the simple shape gave no indication of gender. As they raced east, the face disappeared beneath a crisscross of standing stones. Those stones defined Grenshtepple's streets but also climbed over the walls in random arches and simple columns of stone balanced upon stone. Those looked to have been done recently, as no two stones in a column were of the same size, but all were balanced just so. Joe had shown Caralee how to make tiny towers out of fieldstones when they were wee. From up this high up on the flying carpet, Grenshtepple's balanced-stone towers looked just as small.

*From up this high on the flying carpet!* Caralee couldn't believe her own thoughts, so she said it out loud.

She couldn't keep the joy from her voice and she didn't try, singing, "*I'm flyyyyying—what?—I'm flyyying! I'm a-flying up today!*" She giggled, then whooped into the wind. Even her whoop sounded like a song.

Eusebius groaned from the middle-most spot that he could find and pressed his hands over his eyes.

"Yes, you are," the Son said, sounding pleased himself. Behind her, he stood at ease on the carpet, which flew steadily enough that Caralee thought that, with practice, she could do the same thing. The carpet seemed to have a pull of its own, a solid downward tug that anchored her to its pile.

*"I'm a-flyyyying! I'm a-scatting-flying up today!"*

"Yes, I think that's an entirely appropriate reaction: *Imma fly, Imma fly-fly,* et cetera." The Son didn't even sneer when he mocked her song. "You know, Caralee, I think you should bard. Barding is for you."

Caralee paid him no mind.

"I never knew the world could look so big and so little all at once." The sensations of flying forced such awe upon her that she couldn't put the feeling into words. The way her stomach dropped when they rose, the way the wind rushed *beneath* her, the smell of fresh air purified of dirt and shit, the sight of the land she'd only ever walked upon falling away like a blanket out of a window, while the sky grew larger to fill the space left empty by the shrinking land . . . flying was a revelation.

"Grenshtepple's looks so beautiful down there. Did it look like this way back when?"

Still kneeling—she wouldn't dare stand yet—Caralee braced herself with her hands on the carpet, elbows locked, and leaned as far out as her nerve allowed.

"Entirely different. Eight centuries ago, this place was a seven-sided geodesic dome formed of malachite arches. Every alternating side was filled in with stained glass, with open air between them for the rain to water the gardens below. We found fragments of the glass earlier, beside your jotunankle. All that green stone you see, those were the arches."

Caralee struggled to imagine the green stones below put together to form a seven-sided whatsit. Dome-thing. It was like Jemima Sand's stone puzzles, but a thousand times more complicated.

"And the face? What about the stone face?" Caralee shouted into the wind.

"Stone face?" The Son turned back to look. "I don't see any stone face."

"It was just there!"

"Well, I can't see it now, and, anyway, there were no stone faces. Vintage artwork was rarely anthropomorphic. We paid homage to nature and mathematics."

"So then where did it come from?"

"I can only theorize." The Son didn't seem troubled by the gap in his knowledge. "I would venture to say that there are eight centuries of stories between my time and yours, and this 'face' belongs to some bygone latter era."

As they sped away from Grenshtepple's, Caralee pictured some less-ancient people carving a rocky spring into the shape of a face and wondered why they'd do such a thing. She saw time flowing backward, lifting those broken stones into seven arches, and tried to imagine glass windows higher than any building and awash with colors. She pictured a window hundreds of meters tall and almost laughed.

*That'd be a scatsucker to clean, I bet.*

Behind them, the late-afternoon sun lit the greening hills below with streaks of gold while the light faded from the sky. The carpet couldn't be flying more than fifty meters high, but the whole entire world seemed to spread out before her, and the night seemed to be waiting for them just up ahead. She could see through the last of daylit sky toward a growing darkness that shined with stars and their cloudy cradles. To the southeast, the sky looked darkest, and the horizon looked somehow . . . lumpy.

"What was it for?" she asked. "Grenshtepple's, I mean."

"It was a garden, built to house a darling exile." The Son's fondness was plain in his voice, even though Caralee couldn't see his face. "An exile whom I loved very much."

"Sure, but who was it, and why were they exiled?" The passing-by of the Hazel Hills below became rhythmic, hypnotic rather than sickening. The stars above appeared motionless as the ground raced by—the scale of it all dwarfed Caralee.

The Son sat next to her, relaxing as if they were resting on the ground and not a carpet in the sky.

"Grandmother Athinne was banished for sharing her opinions with my father, who was at his most cowardly when confronted with good sense." He took a deep breath and massaged his thighs, legs draped over the side of the carpet, feet swinging in the open sky. "I was here when she died. I was twelve."

*That is not what I thought he'd say,* Caralee thought before admitting she hadn't known what to expect in the first place. She couldn't imagine the Son at twelve years old. Like most twelve-year-olds she'd known, Caralee reckoned he'd be somewhere between a sweet babby and a bratty terror, only he actually *was* a terror. So she gave up on imagining.

"I'm sorry about your gran," she said.

"Thank you, Caralee." The Son held his hands in his lap and turned them palm up and palm down and back again, staring at them. Was that guilt?

The hills rolled on, and in the distance southeastward—increasingly southward—something shadowier than the night pushed up past the horizon. That's what was lumpy.

"Did it have to do with the Vine? Is that what they argued about?"

"Yes," the Son answered briskly. "The Vine and me. They always argued about the Vine and me."

"Was your gran dangerous or something?"

"Grandmother Athinne, dangerous?" He barked out a charming, condescending laugh. "*Absolutely.* In an argument, she was an assassin. Father *hated* her, and she reveled in it. Mother thew a fit when he sent Grandmother into exile, but Grandmother didn't put up a fight at all, which terrified Father, because he couldn't understand it. Which, of course, delighted Grandmother, who took pleasure in confounding her son-in-law. It was all very dynastic."

Caralee couldn't imagine the Son having parents at all, with all of his sins and his title—let alone a gran.

"She lived at the very top, in a swirl of pagodas and terraces called the Tower-That-Floats. It's a shame that it's collapsed. You could see the pinnacle for days away. I came here whenever I could and whenever Father pushed me to my limits. My sister Stimenne spent much of the year here, cutting herbs below and climbing the long stairs to bring them to Grandmother, whose gardens rivaled my father's thousand towers. There were cultivated gardens in the ringed terraces above, but the ground below was an absolute *jungle* of flowers. We loved it."

Caralee didn't ask how the Son crossed the world to see his gran, though she was dying to know. By carpet or something even stranger? She used her elbow to hold fast to the sack with her journal, slung over one shoulder, wishing she could put pencil to paper *right this very minute.*

"That must have been hard, your daddy hating your gran."

"Not at all. I agreed with her entirely." The Son shook his head. "It happens. Family and politics each have their casualties. Political families can be the most unkind."

A beat followed. Caralee wasn't sure what he meant. She'd never met a politician before.

They flew on in darkening silence, punctuated by Caralee's periodic refrain—"*I'm flying! I'm flying! I'm a-flying up today!*"

"Oho!" Eusebius spoke up for the first time since he bunkered down for liftoff. "Friends and strangers, I'm afraid I have terrible news."

"Wossit?" Caralee asked, risking their lives to crane her neck and look behind her at the wizard, in case it was important.

"Brace yourselves, strangers and friends . . ." he said, holding out his hands as if to forestall a riot. "It appears that we are, well, *flying.*" Eusebius nodded as if to console children. "I know, I know—it is alarming. I am alarmed. Have no fear, I shall concoct a solution. I am certain of it."

"But you sold us the—" Caralee made to explain, before catching herself. "*Ohhh.* I get it now." He'd forgotten and would do so again.

Eusebius pressed his fingertips to his temples and began to think, visibly so. Caralee returned her attention to the flight and the flying.

As late afternoon became twilight, the Son asked Caralee to—carefully—bring them to the ground. She slowed their pace and closed their distance from the ground, which she could barely see for the darkness, and marveled at how the carpet responded to her intentions without her having to use sandymancy. The dark lumpiness to the south grew nearer and larger, and as they landed, it formed a black wall that rose above them, taller than the walls of Comez or Grenshtepple's. The climbing shadows scared her, and she said so.

"What is it?" she added.

"I've an idea, but we'll wait till the morning to confirm, and in the meanwhile, you shall dazzle us with your patience," the Son answered. "By the by, you landed this decoration with astonishing skill. Slowed the speed before you lowered the altitude, didn't dash all of our heads in, the whole affair, root to bud."

"Dash our *heads in*? That's a thing? Now you tell me?" Caralee sat up straight.

"These dangers slip your mind whenever you're immortal."

Caralee, who thought herself fair-minded, didn't argue.

She wasn't keen on bunking down so close to that shadowy, lumpy wall-thing, but better a scat than a shatterscat, as Brid the toiletteer used to say before she fell into the scat pit and died. Wet Sam never said that.

"Well done in any event." The Son stepped off the carpet, which Caralee kept at a hover just a pace above the ground. "I mean, who deserves to die of poor carpeting?"

*I'll tell you who,* Caralee thought.

"How's this carpet even *work*, anyway? What holds it up, what makes it respond to me when I'm not using any sandymancy?"

"Oho!" Eusebius coughed. "A question from my . . . Are you by chance a prospective student? The carpet, yes, 'tis one of the lesser mysteries." The wizard raised his head from his huddle of robes and feathers. "I say 'lesser,' alas, only because we've lost the arts and sciences of so many ancient marvels. . . . Even a wonder such as this, I am afraid, is a mere footnote in our catalog of diminishments."

The Son sniffed. "I'm glad to hear that you recognize your wretchedness, hedge-witch." He didn't look to the wizard, but shook his head to Caralee.

"Honestly, it's as if I awoke to find that astronomers have all decided to study their toes. As to your question, I can explain how it works—it's an easy explanation, if not a brief one." He paused. "Oh, but wouldn't that ruin all the *fun*?"

The night wind carried away his laughter.

Eusebius jerked as if he'd startled himself. He squawked and looked concerned. "Who are you people? Wherever are we? And why is Mommy's carpet with us?"

Caralee implored the Son with a look.

"It's an heirloom, you see," Eusebius muttered to himself more than them. "We . . . we're quite a ways from Mommy's house, aren't we?" he announced. "Thank goodness you two are with me, yes? The effort of awakening a Vintage relic must have taken quite a toll on this poor old wizard. I'm *almost* surprised that I managed the feat!" He offered his hands and smiled with the acceptance of due congratulations. His teeth were yellowed and broken. "You are welcome."

Caralee elbowed the Son's ribs. "Can you fix him?"

"No, of course I can't fix brain damage," the Son snapped as if she'd asked the dumbest question on earth. "I'm a god-king, not a doctor, Caralee."

"I thought you owned the world and it answered you?"

The Son wrinkled his nose. "My neuroscience is conversational, which means it's passingly inaccurate at best. All I know is there's a lesion on his hippocampus—please don't bother asking—" He forestalled her questions with a swipe of his hand. "It is a structure that manages our memories like, say, a librarian. . . . A *library* is a house filled with books. The librarian takes new books and stores them, and can find them for you upon request. It keeps the record of all the books—memories—you've ever made. If the hippocampus gets damaged, the librarian might lose all the memories—or, in this case, might keep the old memories but no longer have room to store new memories.

"So." The Son tapped Eusebius on the head. The wizard looked up with a feeble smile. "His ignorance is stuck being ignorant. It's a special hell, because the hellishness of it renders him unable to appreciate the hellishness of it. On some level, he knows."

Eusebius nodded, his smile fading.

To Caralee, the Son asked, "Did any of that make sense?"

Caralee shook her head and lowered the carpet the last few paces to the ground. "But it's okay. If you can't fix him, can you magick it somehow? He's forgotten everything that's happened a buncha times already, and he's gonna get *really* annoying."

"That he is." The Son nodded, but turned his attention to the earth in front of the carpet. "First, some comfort." He crossed his arms and looked around, nodding at the solid dry ground beneath the grass. Caralee had landed them in a vale between three hills that nestled them against the lumpy, dark wall.

"*Filkapyth.*" The Son snapped his fingers, and the center of the little valley erupted with a spur of orange-hot rock, with smaller spurs jutting out around it with pops of magick. The sudden light and heat illuminated the dale in which they'd landed, and turned it into an instant campsite.

Caralee oohed. Eusebius made a sound like a bird being strangled and plucked at the same time.

"*Filk*—'people'; *pythe*—'fire.' Campfire." The Son paused. "Also sometimes it means 'a wonderful way to massacre an entire population,' but that usage is less . . . popular?" He cleared his throat.

"*Culyob.*" With another grumble from beneath their feet, three stone knobs with flat tops rose from the ground around the campfire. The Son sat on one and warmed his hands by the glow of the orange earth crystals. "*Culi,* 'ass'; *ob,* 'hard.' Again, there are, eh, other usages?—but here the word functions as a colloquialism for seat, chair, bench, stool, et cetera."

Caralee stifled a giggle, taking her seat. "You're a *culi.*" She glanced at Eusebius, and her merriment faded.

The sandymancer stood still as stone by the far corner of the carpet, concealed in the night save for the two tapers burning on his shoulder pads, his face as white as a ghost between their tiny flames. Caralee shivered at the sight.

"Sit down, crookbones," she tried to cajole him. He spooked her. The night spooked her. The light from the *filkapyth* didn't extend more than a few meters—the hills and the lumpy wall all remained cloaked in darkness, and Caralee felt exposed.

Eusebius walked forward, eyes flickering between the strange campfire and the sudden stone chairs as if he didn't believe what he saw. Trembling, he braced himself and slid down to the ground, leaning his back against the stone stool but keeping his bottom on good earth.

"Have I mentioned my fantastic heirloom carpet?" Eusebius asked the night in a small voice. He looked up to the multicolored night sky with a wistful, dreamy expression.

Caralee's skin fair to crawled, watching the ghost of a man in nightmare paint forget himself again and again. The stars twinkled in his teary eyes.

"I look forward to passing my savings along . . ." He swiveled his head at Caralee. "To you!"

She jumped. “Stop!” Caralee held out her hand. To the Son, “Do something, please?”

The Son cast Caralee a questing look. “I could just *scar* a memory or two into his mind, but it’d reduce him to drooling faster than his poisoned face paint.”

“You have to do *something.* He’s annoying *and* scaring the scat outta me.” She didn’t hide her fear.

“Someone’s afraid of the dark?” The Son pursed his lips.

“Shaddup and fix him, okay? Or *I’ll* try, and suck the blood outta everybody’s head again.”

The Son blinked, then chortled. “Excellent gambit, Vinnet! A wonderful threat. I’ll contrive something immediately.” He moved to the wizard and squatted low, looking Eusebius square in the eyes. She didn’t fancy the Son’s narrow backside, but knowing—somehow—that it was Joe’s thick thighs and head-sized calves squatting like that, Caralee had to take a deep breath. If only she could *see* them.

“My cognoscence is out of practice by several centuries—I haven’t met a mind worth knowing since the world went boom. But I suppose if my effort goes sideways, we’ll just leave him here.”

“We will not!” Caralee wasn’t sure when she’d decided to keep Eusebius safe, but it seemed that she had.

“You can put him out of his misery first, if you like. You need a murder or two under your belt.”

“Yeah.” Caralee hung her head. “I’ve kinda already got one.”

The Son had the decency not to respond.

“Psychic surgery it is, then,” he said after a moment. “Do you have cognoscents? Never mind. This is a different sort of magick from elemancy.”

The Son brushed one thumb down Eusebius’s white-caked, pockmarked, wrinkled cheek, and again across the wizard’s knotted brow. Caralee didn’t sense any sandymancy, but she could tell that something was happening by the way Eusebius’s eyes went wide.

The Son held his hands a centimeter apart and whispered rapidly to the air between them.

Now Caralee not-felt the tingle of sandymancy. Whatever the Son was doing, he’d added sandymancy to his working.

Arcs of lightning furred the space between the Son’s palms, like little threads from tiny thunderclouds. He pressed his palms together, and the lightning flickered into a point of gold light that he held between his two middle fingers. He twisted his steepled palms this way and that, drawing a line of gold and weaving it into a triangle as wide as Eusebius's shoulders, flickering in midair. The triangle came to a point at each of the tapers burning on Eusebius's shoulders and again at the wizard's brow.

With a sigh of effort expended, the Son dropped his hands. The golden triangle remained, shimmering in the night air. The Son swirled a finger in the center of the triangle, and the sacred geometry pulsed from gold to green. Gold light darkened and cooled.

When the Son spoke, it was with the calm, measured power of utter authority.

"Your mother—sorry, your mommy—was murdered by a harpy with steel eyes and steel claws. Your encounter with the monster caused you to be unable to form any new memories. You are traveling with myself and my ward, Caralee Vinnet. You are Caralee's tutor for the next two weeks and have been paid in full, up front, to your satisfaction. It has been two days since your mommy's death and your injury. You will remember this and count the days moving forward as well. When your work is done, you will return to your superiors and tell them nothing."

The Son flicked his fingers upward, and the triangle faded away, leaving the wizard's tapers burning a steady green glow.

"I won't bother to explain cognoscence to you, but I've enchanted the flames of his candles to repeat the message. Magicks can work together—*should* work together. Pyromancy and a rough job of psychic surgery . . . it's not a cure, and it's not much."

Caralee was too surprised to say a thing.

"As long as his tapers stay lit, he won't wake up every hour with the same idiot questions. He'll know how long it's been and, at least, will recognize us." The Son shrugged. "Or he'll drool."

Eusebius moaned and held his head in his hands.

"I suppose he might recognize us *and* drool." The Son stepped back. "There's no reason one should exclude the other."

Caralee bedded down on the soft carpet, the air evenly warm. It seemed like her whole life she'd been cold, and the whims of the winds could tug away a fire's heat or pull smoke over her till her lungs burned—but these glowing earth crystals radiated an even heat for ten paces all around. Her head felt so heavy, but she resisted sleep.

Caralee took out her journal instead, to scribble in the orange light and attempt to sketch what the Son had done to Eusebius.

Eusebius, meanwhile, rocked himself and stared into the crystals' fiery gleam. His tapers burned ghostly green in the dark.

"There's an old technique for divination that calls for these crystals," Eusebius said, not looking away from the *filkapyth*. "But no one at the Redoubt knows how to summon them. I could ask you to teach me, most kind sir, but I wouldn't retain it, would I?" Eusebius laughed to himself, squirming on his seat. "Did I least have the honor of your name, most kind sir?"

"An elemancer cannot perform divinations. We'd need a priest for that, and, blessedly, they are all very dead." The Son kicked out his heels to warm his feet. "To your second question, Eusebius, you claim to know all of my names, although that connection seems to elude you."

*The carpet should have a name,* Caralee decided and began jotting down ideas.

*Maybe Flighty?*

"Serves me right." Eusebius tilted his head back against the *culyob*. He creaked as much as he groaned. "Though I suspect I guessed the truth as soon as I saw you. I did, didn't I? No, don't tell—I'm certain I knew you at the very once."

*Wanda?*

The Son, chin ducked toward the fire, looked up through heavy lids and scrutinized the wretch.

*Breezy?*

"Is that what you think?" asked the Son. "That you know who I am?"

*Sunny.*

Eusebius's eyes flickered to one side as the memory enchantment whispered the Son's reminder over and over and over. "Yes," he said in a small voice. "I think I should know the Lord of a Thousand Names upon sight."

He closed his eyes to sleep, a loser unaware of his victory.

Caralee didn't smile, but she relaxed, exhaling a breath that seemed to last forever. If the Son wasn't concerned by the shadow-wall fifty paces south, Caralee supposed she shouldn't be, either. And the *filkapyth* radiated such warmth.

A bone-deep tension between her shoulder blades unknotted itself as Caralee accepted the truth of the battlefield. She could be friends with her enemy. That wasn't a contradiction, not the way she'd thought it was. It wasn't weakness—it wasn't anything at all related to warfare. They knew each other well enough now not to need to plumb for weakness or test for strength. They could enjoy the lull before their duel—after all, both were unique in ways known only to each other. Because she'd taken on the Son and lived, Caralee had declared herself to be more like him—and less like everyone else in the world.

Most folk were ignorant and helpless in a world that was slowly dying. They knew a fraction of their history and a few scraps about the man who'd ruined everything. Caralee *knew* him, was learning from him, was locked in battle with him, cared for him in some way she didn't yet understand, hated him in a way she understood too well, and she followed him for so many reasons. All that was wrapped up in whatever he felt for her, which wasn't nothing.

Together they were headed to the ruins of some ancient bay, and to fix the scatting sky, and who knew what else.

She was going to kill the Son of the Vine. Or something.

She set the journal away and curled up on the carpet, between the *culyob* and the *filkapyth*. She needed sleep as badly as Eusebius.

The Son lay at the opposite end of the carpet and stretched out with a sleepy sigh.

"This carpet really is much more comfortable than your cart, you know."

"Thanks." Caralee grinned at the night. "I named it Sunny."

Caralee woke to sunlight, though she swore she'd only just closed her eyes. Where the lump of darkness had huddled in the night, she now saw a place of legend. Treebones, brown as her eyes, holding up clouds of green leaves, and beyond those, treebones taller and taller still. Taller even than the Vintage steles—so tall that smaller treebones grew beneath them, and beneath those, saplings and vines and ferns that shimmered with all the colors of the rainy-bow wheel.

She made a sound of wonder.

The Son rolled over to look at her, only to gape at the same sight that rendered Caralee wordless. He pulled himself from the ground with that unnatural grace and was parting branches before she could stand. Eusebius snored, still resting against his stone seat, green tapers burning.

"I've never seen a living treebone." Caralee breathed, drinking up the experience. "Let alone a wall of them."

"It's not a wall, it's a tree line marking the boundary of a forest." The Son held a huge leaf in his hand, its broken stem dripping sap as white as Eusebius's face paint. Caralee approached from behind as the Son ran his fingers across the rippling veins of the leaf—it was bigger than her head. He tested the leaf's curled, drooling edges with his fingertips. The treebone—tree?—from which he'd snapped the leaf was a tower of lumps and burls, bubbles of warped growth. It didn't look at all like the simple treebones she knew.

"And a very strange forest at that." Something in the Son's voice tempered Caralee's wide-eyed wonder.

The two stepped through the veil of dripping green, and Caralee found herself in a shifting labyrinth of emerald lights and a new smell—that of dark, wet soil. The Son knelt to examine the rainbow ferns that grew in numbers among the roots of the great trees.

Caralee didn't understand how the greening but still dry Hazel Hills could give way so suddenly to this moist wonderland. No path existed for them to follow into the interior, and they both gawped at the tangled impasse.

Tripping over root and stem, Caralee ventured back to the carpet to grab her journal. She had to sketch this or she'd never forgive herself.

As she tiptoed around the sleeping wizard, Eusebius's snoring stopped, and he opened his black-caked eyelids—he was alert in an instant. His eyes clocked left and right, remembering nothing of the night before—or since Comez—until the green fire from the tapers on his shoulders whispered memories into his ears. He nodded to himself, as though the facts the Son had placed in the flames were the wizard's own thoughts.

Eusebius all but cock-a-crowed as he coughed and shook his body to life. Caralee wondered how he'd ever managed on his own and whether the Patchfolk caravan were glad to be rid of him.

"How's this sad git gonna tutor me up?" Caralee muttered to herself.

"Oh, look," he said, pointing toward the wall of green. "It's a forest!"

"There, he can tutor you on basic nouns. Satisfied?" the Son sassed, walking back from the tree line.

"Oho!" Eusebius tried to stand, but struggled. Caralee gave him her arm and helped haul him to his feet. "Thank you, young miss. Aren't we fortunate? Few enough in this dusty world can say they've walked among the rainbow ferns of the Wildest Wood! Make sure you don't touch them, though. Burn you through your skin and melt your fat into soap, they will."

The Son spun Eusebius around by his shoulder and then stopped him from spinning in a complete circle. Eusebius looked dizzy.

"You *know* these woods?"

"Know them?" Eusebius clapped and danced a little jig with his shoulders although his bloated feet and creaking knees couldn't jig along. "I have slept here many nights. The roots of the trees slope like my bones, and with a little trial and error, I could always find a place here to rest myself without the ache." He smiled to himself, then cocked his head.

"Have you ever seen Lastgrown, most kind sir? The Wildest Wood is one of the wonders of the world, and it harbors an even greater world-wonder. Lastgrown hides itself well, but surely a gentleman of your caliber has toured the world thrice over."

The Son's eyes went electric at the word *Lastgrown*. Caralee's heart skipped a beat at the mention of the hidden settlement that few believed was real, but she hadn't thought that the Son would know the name. Maybe he didn't?

The Son relaxed the muscles of his face and groused over the plants. "This growth is crazy. The mutation rates must have been spiking here for hundreds of years. The system is trying to maintain habitability, but it wasn't designed to survive multiple catastrophes. My grandfather understood that, but my father never did. The world all but died for it." He scowled. "So here we are."

Caralee pulled her lip. "But you. . . . *You* destroyed the Vine."

"I almost saved it. I tried to save it. I can still save it." His voice held the same impossible determination that Caralee felt about Joe.

The Son pointed to the shimmering ferns growing in the shade. "The ferns are covered with urea crystals. That's what makes them refract the light—but these plants should all be dead. Nothing can metabolize that much nitrogen without becoming so acidic that it dissolves itself from the inside out." He sniffed his hands. "The ammonia smell is masked well. The aromatic compounds must be massively alkaloid."

"So don't eat it?"

"I would avoid it entirely, yes. What an unpleasant way for a plant to live, scoured with lye on one side and scalded with acid on the other. How did this . . ." He trailed off, but his eyes lit up. "I need to see the heart of this forest."

"What about that bay and the metal folk?" Caralee asked. "What about the sky?"

"You don't understand." The Son waved at the poison rainbows below their knees. "*This* is a working Vintage system, doing what it was designed to do." His eyes went wide. "Grandfather. Sly goat."

"*Grandfather?*" Caralee shouted. "I see why you killed your family—they're fucking everywhere."

"Oho!" Eusebius limped toward the trees, but Caralee and the Son walked faster and met him by the carpet. "The Wildest Wood! Have we been here long? I used to come here, you know."

The Son waved away the wizard's refrain. "How do we reach the interior? Is there a path?"

"Tsk-tsk." Eusebius shook his head. "Alas, that's a sworn secret known only to a few select merchants and ambassadors, such as myself. However, with your delightfully airborne carpet—again, you are most welcome!—we may simply fly over the wood. What a sight that would be!" The wizard began to hum, then sing. "*I'm flying, I'm flying, I'm a-flying today!*" He shook his head a little, like he had an earipede crawling into his ear to lay its eggs.

"He remembered!" Caralee tugged the Son's hand to turn him away from the wood. "Eusebius *remembered* that song I sang just to annoy you!"

"So?"

"So he remembered something that happened after his injury. You said that was impossible. I didn't use your psychotic surgery or green candlelights or anything."

"I'm aware of the circumstances, Caralee; I just don't see any benefit."

"But if I sing to him, he might remember the song?"

"Maybe. The brain processes music differently from speech. But what's the use of teaching him an awful jingle?" The Son looked at Caralee like a puzzle. "Aha. You are either annoyingly compassionate or impressively clever."

"I'm both." She shrugged. His expression was withering. "You're the one who said so. I can be both."

He shook his head. "I can't believe you named the carpet Sunny."

"Sure. Sunny the Carpet. You got a thousand names, can't she get one?"

"Shut up and fly her, please." And then, "We are *not* naming the carpet Sunny. That offends me."

*Duh.*

Eusebius lowered himself onto Sunny the Carpet, eager to visit his old stomping grounds.

The Son sat cross-legged and looked to Caralee.

She expected that awakening the carpet again would involve some more sandymancy, but the carpet rose from the ground the moment she intended it to. Not at any errant thought, but when she focused her will and decided upon an intention, the carpet obeyed.

The Son had told the truth—Caralee had awoken the carpet, and it answered to her now. It hovered, waiting for instructions.

She leapt on and crawled to the front. Her knees were sore from all the kneeling the day before, so she dared to sit on her bottom, cross-legged like the Son. Again, Sunny seemed to pull Caralee close to itself, a kind of second gravity.

As they rose above the first tier of treetops, Caralee could see that the farther one went into the Wildest Wood, the taller the trees grew. She held her breath—the wood looked like a green thundercloud, roiling all across the land and climbing ever higher.

"That way." The Son pointed toward the tallest trees, toward the southeast. It seemed that they were at the foot of a green mountain, flying toward its peak. Clouds, mountains, rainbows—the Wildest Wood had already proved itself worthy of the name.

Caralee could see no path through the wood below. She shuddered at the thought that the whole world was once this wet, this intricate, this colorful.

The rolling green fantasy climbed higher and higher, and Caralee lost herself in the raw thrill of flight and forest. The world had become a sea of leaves. She relished soaring toward the sky, and the idea of reaching the crack in the firmament was less of a fantasy now.

*We can* fix *the* sky. All these revelations from a single carpet—what else lay in store for her?

"Fuck," the Son cursed, pulling Caralee away from her wonderment. He pointed to the north.

A swath of trees had been broken—towers toppled—revealing sand-colored splinters and a path of ruin nearly as deep and sheer as Twofinger Pass.

"Caralee, bring us down immediately," the Son commanded.

"What is that?"

"Devastation," he answered, sounding brittle and tense. "Quickly, please. You won't be able to maneuver among the trees, and you must not land us amid the toppled trees. The splintered wood will be sharp, and who knows how treacherous the fallen branches may be."

"But—how will I fit Sunny through there? How do I land when there's no land?"

"You'll figure it out. Just bring us down, and *now.*"

Caralee lowered Sunny to a hover just above the treetops. The leaves were everywhere—blazingly green—and they hid branches that would poke holes in anyone or anything. Caralee had to skitter the carpet back and forth as she made her way down, corkscrewing around branches that grew thicker and thicker the lower they got. It was a lurching, painstaking task.

Once they were safely below the surface layer of leaves, Caralee relaxed a little and realized that Sunny could spiral down around a single tree, more or less, rather than trying to fly her through the trees on a clear path that didn't exist.

When they reached the ground at last, Caralee parked Sunny the Carpet in a clear patch a few paces off to the side of the valley of fallen trees. There was barely enough room between the fallen logs and the thorny underbrush, but Caralee made do, then helped Eusebius climb off Sunny while looking to the ceiling of green treestuff that hid the sky.

"Roll up the carpet," the Son commanded.

"Roll up *who*?"

"I am not going to call it—"

"Her. Her name's Sunny the Carpet. Deal with it."

"Roll up *the carpet* and rotate it so that it points the same way as the tree trunks. How else do you plan to get it through the trees?"

Caralee tried. On instinct, she could roll one end of the carpet tightly toward the other end. The rolled-up carpet lifted one end, but hovered at an incline. Gently, she urged the lower end to point lower still, until the carpet hovered at her shoulder, straight and as narrow as could be.

She'd landed them near enough to the path of devastation that they could step between the trunks of the more massively broken trees, like spiders crawling across a delicate mess without disturbing it.

The trees had been torn in a single direction, ripped down like a curtain—but why?

"What happened?" Caralee asked the Son.

"Look there." He stopped her from moving forward with an arm, but pointed with the other toward something shiny in the center of the path of destruction.

"What is it?" She stood on her tiptoes to get a better look and saw what looked like shining metal hats and something that looked like—no, *was*, a metal arm, with fingers, holding a metal spear. "Are those—"

"Metal folk, yes, I believe they are." The Son did not sound happy. "Look there and there."

Caralee saw more of them, perhaps a dozen. Men and women both, with the faces of real men and real women, mouths and eyes open with the surprised expression of the dead. Their metal outfits were just that, merely armor, like Willum Amos, the alderman of Comez, had claimed. Caralee said as much.

"Our alderman told us the truth." The Son pointed again, this time to the chest plate of one of the metal soldiers. "Look at how they died."

Great gouging claw marks had torn through the man's armor.

"They must have been investigating the wood when she saw them?" The Son ran a hand through his hair. "Their armor is etched and corroded from the rainbow ferns—they ran this far, and they would not run this far for any good reason that I can imagine."

He was right, their armor wasn't *all* shiny, but dull and blackened in spots, especially the boots, where Caralee could see boots.

"When do you think this happened?" she asked the Son. The faces of the metal soldiers were bloated, and their gaping eyes were shrunken. She thought it might have been days.

The Son agreed.

"So before we fought the harpy, then?"

"I would think so. It killed these men and then flew west to Comez, after which we found it in Twofinger Pass. At least, that is what I can glean from the three data points we've found." He paused. "It is odd, and hateful, and I fear the bastard Beast will be reborn again all too soon."

Caralee tugged on his arm and squinted. "What the scat is that? What do you mean, 'reborn again'?"

"Never mind." The Son shrugged her off and shook his head. "Come on. Let's pick our way through this place. I wonder what else is hidden beneath the canopy of the Wildest Wood."

"I *do* mind!"

"Then shut up, because you'll need to pay attention to where you're walking." The Son did as he said, stepping carefully over the splintered stumps and into the forest proper, green and heavy. "Unless you'd like to be corroded into pus like some alien's armor."

"Um . . ."

"So on we go." The Son continued working his way through the underbrush, maintaining their bearing toward the heart of the Wildest Wood.

"Was that . . ." Eusebius looked shaken. "I have a terrible feeling that I've encountered . . ."

"The harpy, yes." The Son gritted his teeth.

"Why do you talk about it like it's just one thing?" Caralee asked, edging her way around a clump of rainbow ferns. "Harpies have always been around—are you saying it's been *one* harpy, flying about for centuries?"

"It might seem that way, but not really, no. How . . . how do I explain this?"

Caralee not-felt the tingle of his sandymancy, and a sycamore leaf as big as her torso plucked itself off of a branch above and drifted down until it hovered above their heads. It folded in half longwise, then folded down wings—folded up a neck and a little leaf head, with a sycamore stem tail. When the Son was done, the leaf had folded and refolded in so many different directions, in so many little corners, that it didn't look at all like a leaf folded to look like a bird but like a bird grown from a leaf.

"Once," the Son began, "there was a special creature called the Beast of Wind, and they were the only one of their kind. Whenever they grew old, just before they died, they reproduced: and they were reborn as a baby. No one had ever seen the Beast of Wind, but they knew that they were very old and very important, and so two scholars asked another creature, called the Beast of Blood, to seek out the Beast of Wind and to see what she could see, and then return directly to report."

The Son's sandysense stirred the ground, and a mass of tough little roots wiggled into the air, untangling themselves from the soil, being shaped into . . . what? The Beast of Blood looked like a web of wriggling tendrils, as thin as a spiderweb, whose shape shifted as its little ropes stretched and contracted like restless fingers.

"The Beast of Blood never returned, and the two scholars eventually gave up hope. The Beasts' ways were mysterious, and while they had hoped that their investigation would bear fruit, it was only ever just that—a hope."

The bleeding finger-roots that made up the body of the Beast of Blood, dripping white root sap—which with a twist of new sandymancy the Son turned the color of blood—reached for the flying leaf, and grabbed ahold, and pulled both Beasts toward each other. The Beast of Blood wrapped up the Beast of Wind in a blanket of red lace.

Caralee remembered the crawling blood vessels that slithered across the snotty harpy's nest.

"The scholars moved on, their gambit abandoned. One married and had children, while the other did the same—and became god-king as well. Eventually, two of their children married one another and, after a fashion, gave the two scholars grandchildren, after all.

"But the scholars had not forgotten their work, for they believed that the mysteries of the Beasts of Care were as important to the survival of the world as the Vine itself.

"More than thirty years after the two scholars sent the Beast of Blood on its mission to find the Beast of Wind, stories spread of something strange happening in the eastern provinces. Tales of a strange new creature—a *monster*—roaming the skies above the Morning Glory Sea. Can you guess what this new monster looked like?"

The Son gestured, and his two conjured "Beasts" resumed their struggle.

The red sap spread across the leafy surface of the Beast of Wind's wings, and the veins of the Beast of Blood dove in and out of the leafy body, weaving the two beasts together. The Beast of Wind's wings sagged, torn and punctured, and white sycamore leaf sap and blood and whatever other juices dripped from the mingled creatures. The conjoined creatures became a single body, dripping sap and blood, and it flapped its strange new wings. If a bloody leaf-bird could look agonized and confused, the new creature looked just so. It raised its little leaf beak to the forest canopy and opened its maw as if to scream—and Caralee remembered the horrible, mind-killing scream of the steel harpy. The Son had said the harpy could still the blood in your veins.

The Son waved his hands, and the roots and the leaf dropped to the ground. The rootsap turned white again, and the leaf unfolded itself, looking merely crumpled.

"The Beasts of Care were engineered to self-reproduce or self-repair—designed to function for perhaps hundreds of thousands of years. Our ancestors thought further ahead than even I can fathom, but perhaps not far ahead enough . . .

"The Beasts are also each unique in design. Entangled, Blood and Wind were in no way compatible, their purposes utterly different from one another, yet they were each compelled by programmed primal instinct to regenerate themselves. Thus was born the harpy, a bastard Beast with no true purpose, which of course makes it a monster."

Caralee stared at the Son, not realizing her eyes had all but dried out. Her jaw had nearly fallen off. She waited for more and, when the Son was not forthcoming, asked for it.

"What happened next?"

"What do you mean?"

"That can't be the end of the story. What's the harpy up to? Do you think it found its purpose?"

"It doesn't have a purpose." That worried the Son.

"Then why'd it attack Eusebius and his ma, or us?"

"Hmm." The Son didn't answer.

"I have so many questions." Caralee squared herself to begin when the Son cut her off with a swipe of his palm.

"No. I'm tired of sharing."

*Beasts of Care. How many are there? What are their names? What do they do? Can I find one? How will I know if I find one? If I find one, will it help me or will it try to eat me like the scatting harpy?*

"Most kind sir?" Eusebius raised his hand to ask a question like a kid at Marm-marm's lessons. "What are their purposes, the Beast of Blood and the Beast of Wind?"

"I said no more questions."

"Could it be looking for *you*?" Caralee asked. "The world answering to your call and everything?"

The Son blinked rapidly. "Well, that's stupid, but . . . if it's looking for *me*, because I'm its god-king. And instead, it's just finding ordinary *sons*?" He looked at Eusebius. "That's not a plausible theory. I refuse to accept it."

Eusebius pulled himself through the forest with Caralee's help. He muttered to himself.

"I swear, I was just looking for something. . . . Oh, what was it?"

Caralee patted his arm. "It's okay. You're all right."

Eusebius nodded, frowning, then stopped in his tracks to look at the trunks of the trees around them. His gaze flickered upward.

"Oho," he whispered. "*Uh-oh*."

Something red and round fell from above. It looked to be the size of a cart wheel, and it exploded upon impact. Caralee screamed and covered her face with her hands.

Cockroaches erupted from the half-pulped red thing. Flying cockroaches, which buzzed up in a filthy swarm and clotted Caralee's lips and eyes and nostrils. She coughed as one of the roaches flew through her fingers and crawled into her mouth. She bit down hard, then chewed and swallowed it.

The Son swatted at the cloud of fat brown bugs that flew and crawled upon his skin. A tingle of sandysense from him and the roaches fell to the forest floor, crushed dead.

"Shank shou," Caralee thanked the Son through her surprise snack.

The Son saw her and recoiled. "That's disgusting!"

"I didn't hear you complain when you were eating critter dumplings." Caralee smiled and licked roach legs from her teeth.

"You are disgusting."

"My, my, I must have forgotten to mention the dire apples." Eusebius hid himself behind his robes. "They're quite unpleasant and will crush you if you're not careful."

Caralee asked for an explanation, craning her neck to look up. Huge red fruit hung from the boughs of the trees above them, bobbing as the branches swayed in the wind.

"Best guess?" The Son picked a dire apple seed out of a half-rotted mess of fruit. The seed was longer than his hand was wide. "This was once an apple orchard, before it mutated." He frowned hard. "But why an apple orchard should survive my apocalypse, let alone thrive in this admittedly bizarre way—that is a mystery." The way the Son said it, Caralee didn't think it was as much a mystery as he was letting on.

"So that thing was an apple?" she asked. "What's an apple?"

"Not apples," Eusebius said, haunted eyes ghostly in the gloom. "*Dire* apples."

"Right." The Son scraped pulped dire apple from his hair. "Well, whatever manner of apples they are now, I can assure you that they began as ordinary apples. Not that anyone alive is likely to take my meaning."

Caralee shook her head—he was right, she didn't know what he meant.

These dire apples shone like ruby giants, fat and sweet beneath the boughs of the mutated orchard trees. They looked like towers of knuckles, those dire apple trees, all kinks and burls as they stretched toward the canopy, branches heavy with dire fruit.

The forest floor beneath them smelled sweet and rotten, and dire apples rotted in rich soil, where snaked treacherous roots as gnarled as the branches above. Caralee realized that they'd entered a dangerous area of the wood. The sight of big red fruits so dangerously high was a bit unnerving. One could fall at any moment, to crush them or explode with critters.

"Do apples always explode?" she asked the Son.

"Absolutely never."

"What happened to them?"

"They changed. We'll cover evolution sometime else, when we're not dodging cockroach bombs." The Son looked up also, scanning the trees for wicked fruit. "Dire apples, indeed."

They inched their way toward the heart of the Wildest Wood. Caralee helped Eusebius pick his way through as the trees towered taller and taller, their dire apples growing farther and farther from the ground. At places, their roots kicked up higher than Caralee's head, and she could walk through them like doorways. She marveled at more plant life than she'd seen in all her life, ten times over—from mossy clumps the size of dunderbeasts to the ceiling of green leaves overhead. Climbing vines tried to choke the indomitable dire apple trees, some with leaves so waxy they shed piles of wax shavings, others that grew so shaggy they furred the tree trunks. Caralee did *not* marvel at the dire apples but kept an eye out for falling fruits, and walked very, very carefully. This would be an easy place to break an ankle.

Hours passed as they picked their way carefully through the forest, and all three found themselves sweating profusely. Eusebius's white face paint dripped onto his feathered collar. At some point, they must have left the orchard, because dire apples no longer rotted beneath their feet. As the trees grew ever taller, the forest floor became easier to manage, drowned of light as it was, and in time, they stumbled into a deep glen where the trees parted completely. Not far ahead into the clearing stood a square shed. A *perfectly* square shed.

The Son gasped a real gasp.

Half sliding, half stumbling, they descended into the grassy ditch, which ran ahead in a straight line for some distance past the square shed before ending in a drop-off. Beyond the drop-off, Caralee saw only green-veiled shadow.

The shed was covered with moss and ivy, but its perfect corners were uneroded by time.

The Son tore at the ivy and scraped off the moss with his bare hands, eyes wide with delight.

"I had thought the centuries would have buried them all!" he exclaimed. "This is a wonderful find."

"What *is* it?" If it excited the Son so, Caralee thought it must be a wonder far more impressive than the Wildest Wood, and she couldn't quite imagine that.

"It's a way down."

"To what?"

"If I told you, I doubt you'd believe me." The Son shook his head. "This leads down to the world-beneath."

"The—"

"—world beneath the world. A realm of machines and the old magick of our ancestors, most of which proved a mystery to those of my age, just as our knowledge is lost to you modern-day primitives. Beneath our feet, seas of poison surge through massive plastic caverns, and great gyroscopes spin forever on pylons that hang above bottomless pits. The world-beneath exists to support the world above. Along with the Vine and the Beasts of Care, it is one of the three pillars of the world." The Son ran his hands along the smooth square edges and pressed his sweat-soaked forehead against the metal. "Oh, what a lucky find."

"Can I see?"

"Ordinarily, I'd deny you the pleasure out of spite, but today, I'll deny you out of necessity. We'll come back, I can't split my focus any more than I already—"

"Come *back*? No way! Please?"

"Yes, come back. I'm nowhere near ready to begin work belowground." The Son looked at Caralee, frowned, and relented. "A peek, only."

He pushed a round bubble set into the odd metal wall, and the bubble flickered with light. After a few flashes, the light shone dim but steady, and the wall parted like curtains. Eusebius snorted with shock, but after the snaky stone portal to the baths in Comez, Caralee was growing used to the fact that Vintage folk built some jazzed-up doors.

Ordering Sunny the Carpet to float outside, Caralee stepped inside with the Son and saw that the interior was just an empty metal room, a simple metal box. On the inside wall, by the door, there was a whole array of bubbles. She reached for one.

The Son slapped her hand away. "Don't be stupid! I told you, just a peek. We'll go down when we . . . when we have time. Or when we don't have any time left."

He pulled Caralee out of the metal cube, and the door closed behind them. When it did, Eusebius snortled in surprise again, and Caralee wondered if that was just how he sounded when shocked or if he'd forgotten about the door between them opening and closing again.

"Down?" she asked the Son. "It takes you *down*?"

"That's what an elevator does, isn't it?"

"I would know how?"

"It's called the world-*beneath,* you idiot." The Son brushed her aside, sniffing the air like a dust hare. "I smell . . . salt water. Let's continue on." He was thirsty to see Lastgrown, and so was she.

The dale-ditch ended in a cliff that jutted out over a drop deeper than Caralee could see through the leaves below. The fall could have been two meters or fifty. The Son kept sniffing at the air.

The edge of the cliff was tangled on both sides by thorny, tightly coiled roots. Beneath one caul of the briarroots, something black and wet glistened. Sunny returned to her position hovering just above Caralee's shoulder, and Caralee walked away from the two men.

"Hey, what's this?" she asked.

The Son stepped around to get a closer look. He froze.

"Stay away from it, Caralee." The Son's voice held a sudden tension.

"What is it?"

"I said *stay away.*"

"But I wanna see what it is," Caralee whined.

"And I want a traveling chef, so we're both disappointed." The Son didn't sound like he was trying to be funny. "Get back here."

She ignored him.

"Caralee, *don't* touch it."

Caralee pulled at the thorny roots, which tore the skin of her hands but allowed her to get the job done quickly. Only when she finished did it occur to her that she could have used sandymancy and saved herself the blood.

She'd revealed the wet black thing to be a statue of dark stone, which rested at the lip of the precipice. Caralee had to lean out, holding on to a branch, to examine it.

"Caralee Vinnet, stop that right this minute!" the Son shouted, sounding half like Mag.

*Mag.* Caralee missed Mag.

The statue looked like a fat man, sitting legs out and head down, as if drunk, or asleep, or dead. The figure cradled oversized, three-fingered hands in his lap, big oval feet turned outward, his jowls so pendulous that they half-buried his downturned face and ran around the back of his neck, a fat statue of blubber in black stone. Caralee thought it a queer thing to find in the middle of a forest, but then, she didn't know anything about forests. Maybe this was a thing that happened a lot in forests, like exploding dire apples filled with giant cockroaches or rainbow ferns that would melt your face off.

She brushed away more dirt from the statue's neck and the shoulder, but neither her eyes nor her fingers could find any seams or gaps between the curved angles of the figure. It was carved out of a single block of stone. What Caralee had mistaken for jowls was in fact the lower ridge of a flared helmet, with a dark recess in its face, where the eyes should be.

"Mistress, if I might suggest?" Eusebius spoke up, leaning against the steep wall of the ditch.

Caralee flashed him an arch look. "I'm hanging on by a handful of leaves. What is it?"

"Grok it, as you did the fibers of yon carpet. Mayhap your sandysense will prove more elucidating."

"*Grok?*"

"Forgive me, Caralee, I had forgotten where you came from. Of course you're vocabulary is limited."

*Tell me about it.*

"To *grok* is to know, to understand a thing from many angles. You grokked the carpet, did you not? I remember something about a-flying? It hovers at your shoulder? In any event, you are welcome. Grok it!"

"Absolutely not. That is a terrible idea." The Son's voice brooked no dissent. "Keep your hands off, and *do not* grok it. Besides, I already told you *no more today—*"

Ignoring the Son's demands, Caralee supposed grokking the statue was a fine idea, and extended her sandysense toward the figure, as she had with Sunny.

When she'd grokked Sunny the Carpet, it had awoken in steps—but when her sandysense touched the statue, it awoke all at once, from asleep to awake in a heartbeat. The head lifted up, nothing but blackness in its deep, eye-level recess.

*Shatterscat!*

Then an indigo symbol pulsed across the recess where the statue's eyes should be, and with a voice like stone scraping against stone, the statue spoke:

"Greetings, mistress. I am your man, Sazerac."

It was then that Caralee's hand slipped on the wet branch, and she fell backward into the ravine below.

# V

Time passes. I don't remember how. I killed my sister; Grandmother died; and if I was not entirely shunned by my remaining family, then I grew incrementally less welcome. The only consequence for my role in Stimenne's death was a distance that would make it easier to walk the path which Athinne had set before me: to rule and to trade the lives of my family for the life of the world.

I wonder, if my siblings had known how our grandmother conspired toward their deaths, whether they might not have offered me more compassion. I wonder if it would have changed anything. Certainly, I would still have killed Father. I wouldn't have needed permission for an act of good sense.

Time conspires. The years following Athinne's death saw me transferred from my tower to an invisible prison. I lived alone amid a dozen palaces and the Thousand Gardens whose names belonged to the heir to the Grown Crown, my father. I visited the city that lay a kilometer below, where I met lovers and dealers and hangers-on, few of whom comforted me. I met with cranky officials for lightweight duties like smiling at the birthdays of important people, their gallery and library openings, their dead eyes. My family ignored me, barring Esk-Ettu and occasional gifts from the twins, and I was happy for it.

Without my family, I was not constantly reminded about Athinne's plea to slaughter them all. My reprieve would not last. Again, it was a grandparent who freed me. As if passing a baton, my grandmother's absence was filled by my grandfather, the god-king himself.

He did not appear in my doorway, herringboned and snowy-curled like some gallant hero clutching her gold-knobbed cane. Grandfather Moysha moved more carefully, out of necessity——a god-king does not have the freedom one might imagine. Ask my matzeva.

It was Esk-Ettu, of all people, who knocked on the door to my library as he let himself in. He wore camping khakis and carried his own duffel bag, his dark eyebrows animated with good cheer and his cheeks split into triple dimples by his wild grin.

I was sixteen, and Esk was seventeen.

"Grab what's clean," Esk drawled. "And if anybody asks, don't say a thing."

"Nobody's going to ask me anything."

A land carriage waited for us in the city below, tucked behind a privy hedge in one of our forgettable city estates. The staff had followed the instructions delivered with the vehicle, and Esk and I left the city within the hour.

We took turns driving as we made our way east, again. The trip was not a short one, and we'd spent several nights sleeping beneath the stars by the time we passed the Tower-That-Floats. Its gardens bloomed more beautifully than ever, but in an overgrown way that spoke of neglect. Our boisterousness guttered into silence for a while, but not for long, and a few days later, we reached the god-king, our grandfather, and his great and secret project.

At the edge of one of the eastern coast's many nameless bays rose a great house constructed from good green stone, surrounded by sandy flats spotted with low palms and trailing ground vines. Two smaller stone buildings flanked the great house, and beyond, by lapping waters of the sea, were pitched a half-dozen wooden *obisolim*, or sleeping-booths——a standardized structure made to accommodate ten adults. Two ships were anchored just offshore, with ancient-style wooden hulls and lateen sails. At the edge of the white beach, tall palms arced toward the sea and then away again, as if they'd changed their minds halfway through growing.

Time distorts. I wonder what Grandfather's bay looks like now? Is it a sun-caked salt pit, or does some briny remainder of the Morning Glory Sea still hug its tideless shores?

Sun at our backs, Esk-Ettu and I were met with cheers from sailors and botanists who'd just left off for the evening and had opened their mezcal casks before their bread baskets. Welcome hands helped us out of our prehistoric land carriage and pressed us with food and liquor. There was plenty for all.

We asked after our grandfather, the Most Holy Son of the Vine, and saw his people's affection for him reflected in their smiles. We were told not to expect him till the morning, even noon.

"Ol' Mr. Vine has his head fulla bark tonight," drawled a man taller and thicker than he had any right to be, with hands bigger than my skull. "His Mostiness bade the two captains and the forewomen to celebrate the arrival of his beloveds in his stead, and by vim and venom, that's what we intend to do!"

"Oy-oy, Broadsides!" hooted one of the tall man's fellows, and the workers, sailors, engineers, and botanists set about to do their god-king's bidding.

Four or five campfires linked a curl of the bay together in that kind of blaze-against-the-night that surprises the wilderness with the ferocity of human joy. Our calls out-called the night birds and the frogs and the insect string section that shrank against the din of party people and their happy sins. Guitar and song and drumbeat rolled out across the still sea.

Esk and I left our untouched beds in one of the *obisolim* and unrolled our sleeping bags on the soft white sand, staking out a sweet spot twenty meters from the most distant campfire, and with a conspiratorial wink, we agreed upon the evening's rules of engagement: there weren't any.

A dark-curled sailor named Mae came to retrieve us and led us to a copse of tall elbow-palms between fires. A looming shadow growled hello and flared back muscles the size and shape of wings——Broadsides waited in the cup of a palm with a spliff of rolled tobacco and skunk weed between two thick fingers, and a bottle of mezcal squeezed between his long, rocky thighs. Mae shrugged off her work shirt and revealed two dark cups of her own. Smoky treats, all around.

Esk strutted his bowlegged Esk-strut and relieved the big man of his bottle, while the hyena-shadows of other revelers loped around us, joining their honored guests between campfires. Two princes were among the revelers, but in the smoke-light, I could have been anyone, dancing in the throng by the bent-over palms that were perfect for so much of what we did.

The nebulae were at their brightest——and so the night was at its deepest——and Esk had a breast in his mouth, a lad's mouth on his cock, and a bottle in his hand——it was a perfect night by the seaside for him.

Mae and Broadsides sandwiched me——lucky me——and as we moved together, we braced ourselves across the bent palm tree's smooth trunk. Mae stretched like a cat, cradled by the tree, arching her back. Broadsides had me barrel-bent over the branch where Mae shuddered, and he blanketed the back of my whole body with his torso. Like nesting dolls, there was more of Broadsides than there was of me, and there was more of me than there was of Mae.

"Sap and stem!" Mae hissed, then laughed out loud, face to the stars.

Taking the initiative, Broadsides reached beneath my knees and buckled them, lifting me off my feet and pushing me up the branch toward Mae. He used each of his hands in a different way, and each made me moan into Mae. Mae reached down to pull me up on top of her, and Broadsides slid forward with me. I kissed Mae's breasts and her shoulders, inching forward until she grabbed my thigh with one hand and pulled me inside her. Her other hand remained where it had been, fingers splayed and pleasuring herself.

Broadsides bent over me, nuzzling my neck and kissing my ear. Without withdrawing entirely from Mae, I pushed back against him and growled. With a few thrusting strokes, we three found a rhythm.

Mae made sounds but no words. Broadsides, too, at first remained wordless.

"You're a little monster, aren't you?" Broadsides snarled, and Mae growled happily. "A monster born to fuck."

That was a mistake.

Don't call me a monster.

I shrugged off Broadsides, rolling him to one side and dropping him to the ground. I felt a slick of emptiness as he pulled out of me, and the equal, opposite feeling as I rolled away from Mae. She looked disappointed as I stumbled to the water.

"I'm sorry." Broadsides reached out an arm almost long enough to catch me. "I forgot myself." I didn't have to turn and look to know the expression on his face. Sweet spider eyes, black and vulnerable despite a face like carved stone. Mae abandoned us with a sigh, slipping off the tree and onto the sand.

"*You're* sorry," she said, frustrated, but kissed Broadsides goodbye.

I left Broadsides behind, stumbling away from the beach and toward the stone great houses. I passed Esk-Ettu on the way, who called out a hello that was muffled by some pound of happy flesh.

Time refines. I must have searched for Grandfather——I was fucked up enough to have stumbled and skinned my elbows, or was that from Mae and Broadsides? Next I knew, I closed a sturdy wooden door behind me, thankful to shut out the sound of music and the crowd.

I had a question for him, but I didn't know it. I needed permission, I think, not forgiveness. I think.

Am I a monster?

Grandfather's bald, square head remained bent over his workbench. He kept the seven tines of the Grown Crown pruned or filed to nubs, in the military style. The great house was lit by stark white witchlights, concentrated above the workbench, where he tugged apart a curl of brown bark with forceps and a needle.

Grandfather hummed a hello, warmly, without looking away from his work. He spent every possible moment trying to solve a problem that no one wanted to admit existed. The world belonged to him, but it so often seemed the other way around.

I wasn't sure how to ask my question. How do you ask a question like that?

"Should I do it?"

The Son of the Vine took a breath and kept working. That wasn't regular bark.

"Grandfather?" My saltslick breeches were all I had on, and they barely covered me; my grandfather didn't object, but my short hairs stood on end at the thought of what my father's reaction would be, were he our god-king. "Grandmother Athinne——"

"I know everything there is to know about that woman, Amaunti." He straightened his shoulders and pulled himself away from the work. I couldn't read his bright eyes.

"Is it . . . ? The Vine . . . What if, what if, what——"

"You loved your grandmother?" He nodded. "Then you'll do what she asked you."

"I love all my family." It wasn't back talk, strictly. Just another truth, offered up . . .

Grandfather Moysha bit his lip, nodded, and cocked his head toward the door. "Do you know what I call this place?" He shrugged. "You don't know; it's classified. Would you like to know what I call it here, this warm little inlet where my sailors come to fuck my grandsons, and not the other way around?"

"Of course I want to know!" I bleated, still drunk.

He told me. It took a minute for my hazy mind to translate from Auld Vintage and, afterward, to process what the name meant. Xylem and phloem! Athinne was right. I wouldn't have doubted her except to save myself. It *was* blasphemy.

Time reveals. I must have sobbed, because Grandfather's hands found my shoulders, and his deeply wrinkled face commanded my attention. I could not look away.

"Get ahold of yourself, Amaunti."

"You're young——"

"I am not, and even if I were . . . I am not you."

"What?" That was absurd. Look at me, I thought, covered in cum and mezcal. I couldn't find my shoes, let alone murder my family and save the world.

"We all have our talents." How many times had I heard this line? When would my talents be anything but a burden and worse? "No, listen. Hear me, Amaunti. I could mend the world, given lifetimes, but not alone. You, a sevenfold prodigy *and* an heir——you can cut through seven layers of confounding magicks and carry on recovering the science of it, you see . . ." He pulled himself away from the temptation of the work at hand.

I'd been right——that wasn't bark.

It was dead Vine.

"We can keep this secret——I can keep it from Father——and Zincy will, will listen to me, you know they will. Zincy is better than I am, who cares if I'm——"

"You are the heir that your grandmother and I have chosen." Grandfather flicked his eyes to the dead graft of Vine behind him. "Do you really believe that the world's government has endured for thousands of years based on the merit of blood and birth order alone?" Of course I didn't——my education was rife with dynastic usurpations and power struggles, many of which were classified. "You know better than that."

"What do you want from me?" I asked, knowing the starting price for the future. What else would it cost? "How much are you going to ask of me?"

It was my first good question.

Grandfather held my gaze and did not reply.

That was my first honest answer.

"You can't know the future." I have never felt such fury. He stilled it with a nod.

"And I do not. Athinne and I, one of our duties has been to prepare you for yours. Do I hope that you will not need to fulfill that duty? Amaunti, I pray every night that you do not! That some shining paragon of the human diaspora won't find me, save me, and relieve me? Or for some unexpected variable to treasure your soul while you whittle it down, because we asked it of you?"

The pain was clear in his voice. I felt hot shame. Of course my dear ones would not lightly ask this of me. Not without exhausting all other possibilities. I was their grandchild, but more to the point, I was a gamble. A final bid. Grandfather played out the last few hands of a desperate round of the highest-stakes game. Knowing what I knew, I couldn't bring myself to hate him for casting me in my role. Knowing what I know now, I'm amazed he spared me a moment for any tenderness at all.

The Son of the Vine was right: he was not young. He died in his sleep within the year, of a stroke. My father became god, and I became something even worse.

# 11

Caralee awoke alone in a wooden cabin, with slashes of sunlight cutting through the gaps between the planks. Her head throbbed as soon as she moved, so when she sat up in bed, Caralee yelped and held her hands to her ears. She lay on a cot, and a small blanket was draped over her feet and legs that was fashioned from squares of different types of cloth stitched together—all faded but not all faded equally. That was Patchfolk handicraft.

But they'd been miles from the wasteland, and this wasn't a Patchfolk cart.

They'd been . . . flying and . . . dodging red lumps. Dire apples. Eating cockroaches. It seemed a dream.

Caralee turned to the side, wincing at the pain in her head, and slipped her legs off the cot until her feet found the floor. She realized with a startle that she was naked and pulled the quilt over her chest. The only other occupants of the little room were a wooden chair by a small table and a pisspot. Someone had draped a change of clothes over the top of the chair.

She stood with a little effort, snatched the clothes from the chair, and sat back down on the bed, hard. Her body didn't want to cooperate, but Caralee unfolded a worn red-and-green-striped sweater and a pair of brown trousers with a belt. Not wanting to stand up and expose herself, she scrambled into the sweater before slipping on the trousers, one leg at a time. Steadying herself, Caralee stood again, and managed to stay upright. Her sandals, like her shmata, were nowhere to be found, but a pair of boots drooped against the wall beside the chair.

Caralee couldn't see herself, but the sweater fit well, she supposed. The trousers were big in the waist, but the belt worked so much better than a ribbon! She liked the way the trousers had loops for the belt, and it wasn't as complicated as she'd always thought trousers would be. All she had to do is rip the belt one way and then the other, and her trousers would drop straight to the floor. It wasn't as convenient as lifting up her shmata to piss, but that seemed a small trade-off for real clothes.

On the table she found her journal leaning up against a worn but durable leather satchel. Who had given her these new things? Who had taken her here, and how? Who had undressed her—and why? Caralee slipped the journal into the satchel, then slung it over her shoulder, holding to its sturdy strap.

She took a breath and pushed open the door to a world of colors.

The first color that Caralee saw was green. A thousand different greens, mottling great walls and tendrils of . . . what? It rose up in front of her and towered, arced, coiled and curled all around her. Stalks as thick as a house, tiny root systems as fine as her own hair—curlicues of green dipped in the wind above and around her. It was *everywhere,* whatever it was. Above her, below her.

Caralee realized what she was looking at—what she *must* be looking at—and her heart leapt. Pieces of the whole, a budding stem here, a vine there . . .

*It's the Vine.*

Her jaw dropped open so far she half expected it to bounce off her collarbone. Her hand scrabbled into the satchel, ripping out her journal and opening its wraparound binding without looking down.

Had she traveled back in time? Was this some kind of time magick? She looked at the sky, shadowy blue and crossed with the daytime stars—and beneath those stars, white as chalk, was the forked-lightning crack in the sky, and it was the same size and place it had been the last time she'd looked. In the distance, all around her, walls of trees packed side to side, guarding the heart of the Wildest Wood.

The second color that Caralee saw was blue. There was water down there. Water! She heard it lapping all around, like coins falling. Dark blue, spattered with brilliant spots that came and went. A huge body of water sparkled below her—she'd never seen so much water before. Thick with the winding Vine, the water of the bay was as many shades of blue and blue green as Caralee had ever imagined. The blues of the water below and the blues of the sky above seemed to mirror each other or dance with each other, keeping them together and apart at the same time.

The next color that Caralee saw was *all of them.* Yellow-painted wooden buildings sprouted wherever a stable coil of Vine or an older building could support the weight. One of the biggest buildings spanned two thick coils of vine—somehow—and sported a weather vane on its sloped roof. The roof was rust red and the weather vane was bright white. There were orange and purple houses below that looked like they were floating on the water. The air smelled sharp and a new kind of funky.

Caralee flipped to the first two blank pages and sketched across both of them, trying to capture all of what she saw. As before, her hand followed her eye with a pleasant ease: wooden planks, all warped, never quite fitting together properly; ropes and ladders and walkways and bridges; some people, but not many—some were working with their heads down, others napped in the sun; a flat segment of Vine with two people standing on top of it, digging into the thick skin of Vine beneath them, harvesting something into baskets. Caralee spun around, trying to capture every angle, but there was too much to be seen at one time—she needed a better view.

She stopped spinning and found herself face-to-face with a cheery, chubby, white-haired woman wearing a pink suit.

"Hello, Caralee? You had quite a fall." The woman's voice was pinched but her manner warm.

Seeing such a jolly woman in such a bright pink suit so jarred Caralee that she stared without making any response at all. First boots, then the Vine—now this pink lady—just how hard had Caralee hit her head?

"Hello, dear? Caralee?"

"Y-ya-your clothes." Caralee found her tongue still sleepy. "Are loud? I mean bright."

The kindly woman tilted her head to one side. Her pink beret didn't slip a hair.

Caralee made a partial recovery, but continued to fumble. "I'm sorry. I think I hit my head." Then a random thought terrified her: "Am I like Eusebius! Have I met you a lot?"

The pink woman put one of her very small hands on Caralee's elbow. "Just twice, dear."

"Twice?" Caralee put her hand to her chest. "*Twice?*"

"That's right." She looked concerned. "Although you were *very* unconscious the first time. I suppose you won't remember. You've been asleep for two days, dear."

"Oh, good. I mean, not that I was asleep. Never mind." Then, "Did I fall? I was in a crazy place and, I think—did I fall?"

"Right onto your noggin." She patted Caralee's hand.

Caralee nodded and winced.

"My name is Biddle Becky, and it's a pleasure to meet you alive and walking." The merry woman introduced herself, smiling at the eyes despite her pursed lips. "Much improved from meeting you bleeding and carried by two *unusual* gentlemen and one . . . one other visitor." At that last, Becky's mouth twitched.

*That thing. That statue who called himself my man.*

"It said it—he—was my man."

"Yes, I have heard that refrain quite often over the past two days." Biddle Becky offered Caralee her hand and led her down a plank to the platform below. The wind blew, and the water lapped, and the Vine rocked gently, and the platforms groaned like starved animals.

Biddle Becky seemed friendly enough—but Caralee knew better than to give the woman her trust just because of the appearance of friendliness and a new set of clothes. Color-dazzled and upended as Caralee was, she was still walking hand in hand with a stranger.

*Again.*

"It is a good thing for us that one of your unusual gentlemen friends is an arch-sandymancer! No one here has *ever* heard of such a leaf-green flame atop a sandymancer's tapers. He's restrained your so-called man with invisible bonds. Marvels upon marvels." Biddle Becky laughed, nervous but careful to contain it. "How the stone man's purple eye does flare!" She laughed again, less convincingly.

"Right," Caralee said. "Marvels." The plank ended, and they turned around to find another plank descending below the first. So, just like stairs. Stairs that wailed whenever the Vine gently rocked. "It's not purple, you know, it's indigo."

Biddle Becky smiled and held on to a wooden banister to steady herself. Caralee caught herself tripping and did the same. The little she'd seen of Lastgrown thus far was beastly beautiful and overwhelming—and unsteady.

Wherever the Son was, Caralee felt desperate to get to him. What would he say about all *this*?

The lower tiers of Lastgrown were a maze of scaffolded plank-stairs, rope ladders, and fragments of secured wooden flooring. As they crisscrossed their way down, the Vine grew ever thicker—and Caralee saw that the individual stalks all grew from a single mass that pushed itself up from beneath the waters of the bay. Tunnels bored through this mass—and into lower reaches of the thicker vines that drooped down and touched the shores of the bay—made for shortcuts, and other carved-out spaces created cozy green bungalows.

"It really is the *Vine,*" Caralee breathed.

"Yes. Yes, it is." Biddle Becky squeezed her hand. "How are you feeling, dear—how, exactly, are you feeling?"

"My head hurts and I'm . . . definitely not in the wasteland anymore. How did you . . . How is there . . . Vine here?"

Biddle Becky raised her eyebrows to acknowledge the mystery, and she pulled Caralee down another ramp. "We haven't a clue, if I'm being honest. We Lastgroovians have been here for generations—when my great-great-great-grandfather founded the settlement here at Lastgrown, the Vine looked much smaller than it does today. It grows and grows, but however much it grows, it won't *spread.* We've been vexed by that for over a hundred years. Even the fruits have turned to poison . . . I'm sure you noticed that the flora of the Wildest Wood are not all merely large, but—well, *wild.*"

"The rainybow ferns, yeah. Dire apples, too—and, I guess, a stone guy."

"Yes." Biddle Becky's smile turned brittle. "The Vine gives us what it can, but the Wildest Wood doesn't nourish us as it should."

Caralee thought of the whorls of aloe in Dinnal's window boxes, how the big plant sprouted smaller plants—hens and chicks. Was this a chick of the Vine?

Could this Vine grow? Could it nourish the world? Caralee had never known hope like that, and it felt like a kind of danger. You could get lost in hopes like this, like the *Vine.*

"There's so much water."

"Yes, though not nearly as much as there once was, I reckon." They turned again—their fourth ramp. "The body of the Vine has displaced the bay's water almost entirely—its underwater mass is nearly as big as what you see above."

Caralee craned her neck to watch the Vine as it towered and arced, dipped and curled. Did it curl and dip and arc beneath the surface of the water? The Vine had pushed its limbs through the earth, pushed up the trees and given them their look of crooked teeth. The Vine snaked over ground and formed a maze of walls, terraced by the loose soil of the rain forest, where tidy lines of crops grew in the black dirt.

"What's a bay?"

"A bay is a cup-shaped body of water where the shoreline curves in on itself, leaving only one side open to the water. You can't see it from here, but there's a little rind of sea remaining to the east, salty and dead, but wet enough—and the bay opens right up to it."

"Got it." Caralee dithered over the matter of her new things. "Hey, Biddle Becky. Thank you for . . . Are these someone's things? They were laid out by my book, and I was pretty naked, so . . ."

"They're entirely yours, dear. We've plenty to spare."

"Thank you." The clothes and the satchel made for the second-greatest gift of her lifetime, but Caralee's trust couldn't be bought. "I only ever had burlap sacks to wear, so—thank you."

At the end of the last plank, Caralee followed Biddle Becky across a rope bridge—which swung nauseatingly and looked like a death trap—into a great room that had been carved into a bulky section of the Vine, stretching open-sided along the water. Thick-woven mats overlapped on the plank wood floor, and three tall archways led in and out. Plants in buckets grew as tall as treebones—others hung in woven nets from above, and still others grew from pockets carved from the walls of the Vine itself. People stood here and there in twos and threes, bent over tables with maps, diagrams, and miniature designs. Caralee almost tripped over her own feet looking at the Lastgroovians: some wore brightly colored accessories, others a kind of drab brown uniform that must be the town guard.

Biddle Becky guided Caralee toward an alcove with cushioned chairs and a small wooden table. The fat statue sat black and bulky near Eusebius, who rested uncomfortably in one of the soft chairs. His tapers burned with green light, and Caralee had to admit, it kind of made him look like the king of the plant wizards. Small wonder that he commanded Biddle Becky's respect.

The statue, which had called himself Sazerac, sat near the wizard in the same position in which Caralee had found him: legs splayed wide, head and shoulders slumped forward. Like a sleeping drunk or an abandoned doll. He didn't raise his head—or move at all—upon her entry. She didn't have a good reason to trust him—just like Biddle Becky, Sazerac was new.

*We'll see soon enough, I guess.*

Eusebius squawked himself awake at Caralee's approach. Evidently, the Lastgroovians trusted that a simple nap couldn't keep a green-tapered sandymancer from maintaining the binding on a moving statue. They must not have many sandymancers among them, to be so credulous. Eusebius flapped his elbows and stretched his back—his spine made a series of popping sounds.

"Oho! It is my faithful student!" He clapped in delight at the sight of Caralee. "How are you, my dear? Might you perhaps tell me where we are? I feel a bit overwhelmed, of a sudden."

"We're in Last—" Caralee caught herself. She wanted to come up with a new tune for a new memory—it seemed at cross-purposes to use the same tune for multiple memories. She didn't want to stuff too many thoughts into one little jingle, and she was far from musically inclined. Still, she did her warbly best.

"*We're in Lastgrown, Lastgrown, and we're fine-fine, fine-fine!*" Caralee began singing softly, and mimed a jig with her shoulders. "Sing it with me? *We're in Lastgrown, Lastgrown, and we're fine-fine, fine-fine!*"

"*We're in Lastgrown, Lastgrown . . .*" Eusebius sang along, looking lost but curious. "*And we're fine-fine, fine-fine!*"

He dropped his head for a moment, then lifted it, smiling anew.

"Oho, apprentice! Did I not tell you we'd find it?" Eusebius cheered himself into awareness, glancing about with delight. "It's been decades since I was last here—Biddle Becky's father, Rabb, was Biddle then. It's lovely to be back at Lastgrown. Try not to slip, though. You'll drown."

"I'll . . . try . . ." Caralee began. She saw Sunny the Carpet, rolled up and stuck into an empty barrel, beyond which the Son stood in an archway overlooking the bay, staring at the wall of Vine beside him, tracing his fingers across its dimpled skin. The way he moved his fingers was odd; each finger moved on its own, like a guitar player's, with purpose.

Eusebius rustled and clucked. "God has been petting his plant all morning. He must feel quite glad to see it. Still, it's odd, don't you think? I'm glad to see you alive and well, young miss. *Are* you well?"

*God?* Eusebius had finally grokked his employer's identity.

"I think I'm okay. Thank you, Eusebius, for looking out for me and for being sweet." She petted his soft-skinned, gnarled hand. "There you go."

"Ah, so." He cracked the joints in his neck, and lost himself again. "There I went. I'm certain that I did, if you say it." Eusebius was clever enough to make himself agreeable whenever he realized that he'd lost the trail of the conversation. He kept some dignity for himself, even if he didn't know why. "You've always been bright, Caralee. Ever since I saw your wee mannikin, Sandass, I knew—I said to myself, 'Eusebius, that young woman is a prodigy.' I did!" He smiled at her, teeth yellowed and lips wide. He seemed to believe what he said.

Maybe it was true and it was his vanity that he'd forgotten, unable to maintain it since his injury.

Caralee blushed and checked a growl, not sure how she should feel.

"Would you summon it for me?" he asked.

"What, Dustbutt?"

"Just so. I think I'd find Sandass a comfort, here among the legendary." He looked around at nothing in particular. "I think you'll join the living myths, you know. I really do. You're a mountain among us, Caralee." Eusebius cocked his head sideways toward the Son. "*He* thinks so, too."

*I am such a scathole.* Caralee cursed herself for ever being cruel to this . . . what? Sweet, diminished, learned, unloved . . . Now that she knew the man a little, it was hard to dislike him. With a smile and a nod, Caralee lifted the dust from the floor. The floors and decks of Lastgrown were oft-scrubbed and well-cleaned, so she had to reach farther away to carry what dust and sand and dry dirt she could find.

Slowly, the dilute particulates came together into the slope of Dustbutt's backside, the wrinkle of his little nose. His hopping feet and towering ears, twice taller than his head. He looked too ghostly, so Caralee reached out to the mud and grit below, where the land met the water.

It was so easy, she discovered, to lift the earth up and leave the water behind—as if the water *wanted* to be left behind. What had the Son called it? Fixed. Like the earth, water was happiest however you found it. Both elements sought their level.

"Hello, friend!" Eusebius raised his eyebrows and reached out to pat Caralee's mannikin. Dustbutt jumped into Eusebius's lap. Caralee flinched, worried the wizard was more fragile than the mannikin, but he waved away her concern. She felt the vibration of sandysense at work. "Excellent dual-element approach! Were you a student at the Redoubt, you'd be blazing through the mysteries. Now run along—Sandass and I will keep each other company, won't we?"

Without instruction from Caralee, Dustbutt lifted his little nose and kissed Eusebius on the chin. The wizard was capable enough to take over control of her conjuration, at least.

Caralee walked away dazed. She hadn't hit her head at all, she decided. She'd died and gone to some impossibly weird afterlife. Topsy was turvy, while turvy had gone *entirely* topsy.

She found the Son in his archway of the Vine hall, where he stared out at the bay and the towering-yet-drooping trunks of Vine that sprung from it. From this angle, a beefy stem of vine lifted up from the water and curled skyward, and beyond it, Caralee saw a horizon that reeled away forever.

Lastgrown kept astonishing her at every new turn. The city was woven like a spiderweb from sailor's rope, linking permanently moored ships—lofted above the bay by the mountain-thick mass of the Vine—with semipermanent buildings made out of rope and wood and Vine, slung under the thickest passes of Vine stalks. Below those suspended houses, house-thick tendrils of Vine climbed out of the displaced bay and slithered into the forest.

The Son stood there, fingers tracing the Vine, eyes glazed. His mind must be eight hundred years away.

Caralee tried to imagine what seeing the Vine would be like for its Son, and failed. Their worlds were too far apart—no, their times. She had no frame of reference. The thoughts and feelings of the Lord of a Thousand Names were protected by history itself.

Behind her, Eusebius sang a little jingle.

"Stop singing to the animals, Caralee." The Son dropped his hand from the wall as she approached. His face became that perfect, powerful mask.

"No," she said and pointed to the green of the Vine. The bulk beneath and around them, the tendrils and stalks above, any piece she could see from their vantage beneath the scaffolding that supported Lastgrown. "Is this really what I think it is?"

For a beat, the Son said nothing. Then, his lovely face twisted with sudden hate: "It is."

Caralee felt the Son's mood like a kick to the chest. She wouldn't get the flood of wonder she wanted, not right now. That was okay, though. She'd get answers in time, and for now, she had *all this* to see for herself. That wasn't a bad idea, actually—to experience the Vine herself, without the Son, might give her some advantage she never dreamed she'd be lucky enough to gain.

Eusebius's song came again. Caralee caught the words.

"*We're in Lastgrown, Lastgrown! And we're fine-fine, fine-fine!*"

The Son growled, but Caralee clapped.

"He's doing it! He's remembering my song!"

"That gargled doggerel is a far cry from song." The Son pulled away from their view of the Vine and returned to the common room behind them. Caralee stretched her neck to see the green of the ceiling, while the Son kept his gaze fixed, straight ahead. "It is as I suggested: the mind processes music and song through different pathways than it does ordinary spoken language—just as it processes spoken language through different pathways than the written word."

"Okay, brain, pathways . . . other stuff." Caralee had wearied of her ignorance, though she still longed to learn more and more. "So if I sing, then I can keep him, you know . . ."

"It doesn't matter. A song is not enough to restore a man to himself."

"How can you say it doesn't matter?" Caralee pushed back. "Of course it matters."

"Why help him? He remembers his training, everything before. Anything he can teach you, he already knows."

"No. *Wrong.*" Caralee planted her feet and stood her ground. She was a mountain in this world, and *he knew it.* So she wagged her finger and told him some starbirth-cloud truth: "I need to help him because it's the right thing to do, and if I do the right thing, then maybe other people will do the right thing, too. Even if nobody even notices me, I've still done something to help someone. Me helping Eusebius makes the world a little better, and no offense, but we gotta start doing that instead of, you know: *you*."

"You'll get a knife in the back before you inspire the world to stoop to generosity."

"Maybe, but what did you ever do for the world?" She threw that in the Son's face. "Besides, he hasn't taught me a thing. It's all been your—wait . . ." Caralee realized the Son's trickery. "You're using his failures to teach me what he can't."

The Son shushed her. "You are not supposed to know that." He smiled sideways. "Cheeky misbehaver."

"So, I'm gonna keep singing to him." Caralee scratched her neck.

He changed the subject. "Did you know they have druids here? I hate druids. I don't often bother myself to hate. But fucking druids . . ."

"Droods?" Not many could say they'd met a drood. Caralee had heard tales of men and women gathering in the night to dance around treebones naked, who could speak to the grass and hear the voices of animals. "Really? Are they naked?"

"Are they *what*?"

"Uh. Never mind. I've never seen a drood before, that's all."

"The word is 'dru-*id*,' with two syllables. Now, druids are awful, you should know that. Terrible people—paranoid, fanatical, often insane, might kill you for picking the wrong flowers." The Son let out a breath of tension. "You people. 'Droods.' At least they don't call themselves treezards or soilcerers."

"Blarp bloop blip? Blarp *blip*?" Mocking him didn't stop Caralee from taking mental notes to journal.

"I'm killing you as soon as we leave this place," the Son cracked. "We can't stay, but we'll be back. Lastgrown changes everything."

It did—a piece of living Vine—that had to change everything.

*He really wants to put things right.* Caralee didn't want to believe it; she could kill a wicked man.

The Son clapped his hand to his heart, suddenly sentimental. "Oh, but I don't *want* to leave. This farce is as close as I'll ever come to home." He reached out to touch the archway of pale green Vine, lit by the sun, but pulled his hand away at the last moment.

"I'm sorry." She was.

"It's all my fault, anyway." His bitterness returned.

"Hey. Yeah, it is," Caralee admitted. "First of all, tossing yourself into the pity pit doesn't help anyone, and it's kind of annoying. And second, Son, we're standing in some *Vine*. I think that's the important thing here? You don't *have* to make yourself the center of everything, even if you might be."

"If it's that easy, why don't you try it?"

"And third, you're just jealous."

"Me? Of what, I cannot imagine." The Son looked amused, but also shadowed.

"You're jealous cuz you spent all those years not able to do a single thing, but here, ordinary people performed a miracle, didn't they? They saved a piece of what you destroyed. They helped it grow so big, and they protected it from the world and made it their own."

The Son let out a breath, but didn't argue. Instead, he changed the subject again—as Caralee had noticed he did when she said something about him that cut too close to the truth.

"You should have listened to me, back there. You should have left that thing alone." He cocked his head behind him, toward the slumped stone form of Sazerac.

"What is it?"

"I'm not finished." He was stern, but Caralee noticed that he kept himself from looking at the Vine. It was subtle but deliberate. "That was dangerous. I *cannot* risk failure a second time, or this world will truly die. If you cross me like that again, I will put you down."

She knew that he meant it. He'd kill anyone who posed any threat at all to his purpose.

"These Lastgroovians—a collective noun could not be more absurd—know more about your stone friend than they've let on, but nothing useful. I don't believe for one minute their professed ignorance about an ancient statue all but standing guard at their perimeter."

"Why *were* you so hot under the collar about me touching him?" Caralee asked.

"You were hanging out over the edge of a cliff, hanging on by a wet branch, and you *fell*. I think my concern speaks for itself."

"Shatterscat." Caralee didn't buy that. "You had me kneeling at the front of a flying carpet, and all of a sudden you're worried I'm gonna fall? No, you didn't shout at me to get back away from the edge; you were afraid of *it*. Him. Sazerac. Whatever. Why? What is he?"

"Why, Caralee, he is your man. I believe Sazerac made that clear from the start."

"You know what he is. What is he?"

"No. I didn't know what he is, not yesterday."

"So you know today?"

"Today?" The Son sneered through a smile. "Today, I know many things that I did not know before." He waved toward the Vine all around them. "Don't you?"

That signaled the end of the Son's helpfulness, for now, on the subject of stone creatures.

"So, fine. Whatever. Will you tell me anything about the Vine here? How did it survive, and if it did, why aren't we all saved? Becky said the Vine wouldn't spread past the wood."

"So I've heard. Every available system is in a panic, and I'll need to—"

"*We're in Lastgrown, Lastgrown . . .*" Eusebius jingle-jangled from behind them, interrupting. "*And we're fine-fine, fine-fine.*" He looked around with confidence. "Oho! Lastgrown again. We've been here for some time, you know. I don't know if you knew that." He chewed a hangnail with yellow teeth. "I used to visit Lastgrown, you know. I was an ambassador of sorts. We're hidden by crafty trees and cunning dales. They shift, did you know that? I don't know if you knew that."

"Crawling trees, is it?" the Son addressed the diminished wizard. "Prehensile root systems. Entirely his style. Amazing."

"Whose style?" Caralee asked.

"Walk this way." The Son all but trotted ahead of Caralee. She followed him, miming his nose-in-the-air carriage and long swinging arms. They descended another array of planks into an older stone building, until Caralee's newly booted feet rested on solid stone.

"Look around. What do you see?"

Caralee did so. "We're standing on a stone floor, and the walls are bricked, too. It's the same green stone from Grenshtepple's." There had been a settlement here long before the Lastgroovians came here, that much was clear—though much of the stonework was covered with wet green ivy. Most of the masonry was tumbled into ruins or tilted askew, but some still in use—there an archway that led to the water, there a path that led to a little herb garden.

"About the same period, too," the Son concurred. "Mother's mother was installed at what is now Grenshtepple's. Father's father, the Most Holy Son of the Vine, constructed a project here that consumed him. This new Vine was his vision. A second Vine! It was blasphemy. Grandfather Moysha insisted on constructing new systems to protect against multiple catastrophic failures and unforeseeable calamities, such as metal people breaking his sky. He knew that the Vine was not . . . infallible? Perfect? Immortal? All the things we were told. When Grandfather died, his successor—my father, the Most Holy Son of the Vine, shuttered all the work here and abandoned the site. Grandfather failed, it had seemed. Now it seems he did not." The Most Holy Son of the Vine paused.

"Your *gramps* planted all this?"

"He tried. Budding the Vine was—technically—treason and blasphemy, but the Son of the Vine cannot—also technically—commit either crime. So this place was kept a secret. But the project failed, and Grandfather Moysha died." The Son pointed to a sandy field that retreated to the wood, where a towering palm tree grew so thick that the husks of its trunk were shaggier and more matted than a dunderbeast's fur. "I last saw him here. Right beneath that monstrous palm, there by the tree line. The water level was higher then, and the palm was merely a palm. Grandfather was securing line on a sailing ship. I was sixteen and standing about where we stand now."

Caralee didn't know what to say. If she were eight hundred years old, the world would be full of ghosts, too.

The Son turned away, and Caralee followed him back up to the Vine hall.

"It is time we discussed what to do about your new guardian," the Son said, meaning Sazerac. "You do collect them, don't you?"

"Set him free?" she asked the Son, thumbs in her belt loops like she'd seen folk in pants do.

"Free? The purpose of this Beast does not allow him freedom." The Son waved his hand and Caralee not-felt a brief tingle. "There, he can move again."

Without a beat in between, Sazerac pulled his splayed legs into a squat and stood, then marched to stand beside Caralee, pounding bass through the floorboards. It startled her, but she stood her ground.

"So you're Sazerac, and I'm Caralee Vinnet." She had to start somewhere. "Do you want to stay here, Sazerac?"

"I will follow you, mistress."

"Okay, but why?"

"I am your man, mistress." Sazerac bowed, his stone body bending—the effect did not seem possible, but Caralee could no longer rely on her common sense to recognize the impossible.

"Sazerac? You don't have to call me *mistress*. I'm nobody's mistress."

"Begging your pardon, mistress. How shall I address you?"

"Caralee is just fine."

"Of course, Caralee." When Sazerac spoke, the indigo symbol in the recess of his visor pulsed in time to his voice. He bowed to her.

"What . . . what *are* you?"

"I am your man." He held out his hands, three-fingered and huge. "I am Sazerac. I am yours." He bowed again.

"Stop bowing and what do you mean, you are my man?"

"I am your man."

"Yeah, stop saying that." She took one of his stone hands in her own. His touch was hard like stone, but warm. She squeezed his hand slightly, and Sazerac squeezed back with the same amount of force.

"Of course, Caralee. I offer anything that you request and which is in my power to provide, Caralee," Sazerac pledged. "I will protect you, obey you, and perform any task that you may require. I belong to you."

"You're not *mine,* Sazerac. I just found you, is all."

"You woke me, Caralee, and so—begging your pardon—I am your man. I will do what you ask and not say so again, but that is my purpose." Sazerac's armor-shaped body looked to be carved from a single piece of black stone. If he really was her protector—if he really answered to her alone—that could give Caralee a major new advantage against the Son.

She bit her lip. This was a lot to take on. "So you're not going to hurt anyone or anything?"

"Only those who attempt to harm you." The stone man sounded offended, which was reassuring, only Caralee wasn't ready to be reassured just yet.

"O-okay. Okay, then." Caralee considered that this conversation might be a little too much for her just now. Her head ached; the Vine lived—that was enough for her brain to chew on.

A polite clearing of the throat announced the presence of Biddle Becky, who smiled too sweetly when Caralee turned around. The white-haired Biddle in the pink suit patted her hands together and nodded to the Son.

"Kind sir," she said, "I have consulted with my deputies and made preparations for your departure, as requested." As hospitable and generous as Biddle Becky had been, she didn't seem keen for her guests to stay on.

"You won't need a map—once the droods open the path, your way will be plain to see." She pressed her hand into his arm. "I've carved out a bit of time tomorrow morning. The droods have agreed to my request. We don't often get visitors, and we like to keep it that way." She paused, revealing the determination she hid beneath her cheerful eyes. "Lastgrown is the world's last hope, as you must have realized. The Wildest Wood is our only protection from a starving, thirsty present—but the future, if we can stomach the now, will be wet and good."

"Thank you." The Son said nothing about the Vine or what he thought of the Lastgroovian mission. "Tomorrow morning, then."

Becky nodded once, polite, curt—all tight smiles.

"As you pointed out, Caralee, Lastgrown doesn't need me." The Son looked to the sky, then said in a stage whisper, "But now I know where I need to go."

# 12

As the foursome walked along the shoreline to meet the droods, Caralee wondered how she might make use of Eusebius and Sazerac in her struggles with the Son. Eusebius had grown fonder of her, but now that he seemed to know the Son's identity, Caralee couldn't count on fondness to win out over fear or fealty. Sazerac had promised to defend her, but the Son had easily dominated the kindly statue to put the Lastgroovians at ease.

Caralee didn't think that she and the Son would turn on each other anytime soon, but she needed to reach for new options—she had to educate herself as fast as possible.

Could she sing instructions into Eusebius's memory? Her singsong memories seemed to be taking hold, in a lurching, warbly way.

Could she use Sazerac for a single distraction?

She needed a moment alone with each of them. Orchestrating that became her next goal.

*Step by step, forward into the dark.*

Caralee liked the Son. Maybe even she loved him—the Son had allowed Caralee to see the world, learn about history and blockums and sandymancy that surpassed anything she could learn at the Sevenfold Redoubt. The Son had gotten her out of the Nameless Run, even if he'd done so in the most horrible way possible.

The Son claimed he wasn't a monster. He called himself a beast, and said that beasts were monsters with purpose. If that proved true—if he really wanted to put right his ancient wrong—well, that wouldn't sway her from her ambition, either. She would kill him dead and damn the world.

Did her heart shrivel that easily? If she had to become monstrous, Caralee would choose to be a beast instead, and conquering the Son would be her purpose.

Caralee's awareness of her surroundings didn't flicker, despite her thoughts. That became easier, too. She wasn't as easily distracted as she had once been. She juggled multiple problems and honed her mind to a fine point, called elements to her command, and consorted with wizards, kings, and legends. She flew a carpet. She'd seen the Vine.

*Will Joe even recognize me?*

Caralee helped Eusebius across the wet sand of the shoreline. Biddle Becky and four droods awaited them at the tree line some distance away. The four droods had chlorophyll eyes, and the two men had mossy stubble instead of beards. All had long grass knotted into their hair and shawls woven with red and yellow sycamore leaves as large as Sazerac's head.

"I'm afraid our goodbyes will be brief." Biddle Becky wore big brown boots like Caralee's and a brown coat over her pink trousers.

"Hey, Biddle Becky? I gotta question if it's okay." Caralee didn't really mind if her question was offensive. A good person would, but an ambitious person might not.

"Go ahead, Caralee."

"Why do you wear pink so much?"

"Because I *like* pink." Biddle Becky raised her eyebrows and did not elaborate further. She looked to the droods to begin their plant-magick.

The Son stepped forward and graced Biddle Becky with a shallow bow.

"You have shown us hospitality, generosity, and trust." He looked from Biddle Becky to the droods. "Do your people know the name of this place, in Auld Vintage?"

"Of course not." Biddle Becky almost laughed at the idea. "We're a maze of guesses, we are. Not a lot of hard facts. Some rumors, some puzzles." She eyed Sazerac.

The droods looked to one another.

"If it pleases," the Son said carefully, "I can offer you the name of this place—what it was called during the Age of the Vine, long before your last-growth appeared."

"How? That is, how can you possibly know?" Biddle Becky blinked. "Wherever could you have—"

"Oh, you know." The Son winked at Eusebius. "In a *book*."

The wizard tittered, all but blushing beneath his face paint.

The Son swept a hand across the view of Lastgrown, backlit by the sunrise. "We stand in *Angksef-Seysef*, and its age is over eight hundred years old. It was built by *a* Son of the Vine, but not *your* Son of the Vine."

The four droods looked like they'd just passed their stools.

"Yes." The Son approved of the droods' reaction. "The name means 'Granddaughter of the Vine.'"

"Granddaughter of the Vine." Biddle Becky breathed. "How apt. What a revelation, if true."

"It's true and like you said," Caralee spoke up. "You've trusted us this far."

"So I have," Biddle Becky answered almost to herself. "So it's true—the Vine really did reach across the entire world? And this was a little bud, was it? Perhaps? Asleep for so long, I suppose . . ."

Caralee worked her tongue and tried to find the words hidden in the quickly spoken word. *Angkhet* meant "Vine," she knew that much. *Sef-Seysef* would mean "daughter-of-daughter," she reckoned, since *sef* showed up twice and *seysef* meant "daughter" or maybe "daughter-of."

"I won't ask again how you claim to know this, sir, so I bid you a swift farewell."

The Son swanned his hands in acceptance.

*Cocky git.*

At that, the four droods curled their hands toward the tree line and began to chant. One sang a high-pitched melody that echoed off the wall of crooked trees.

It wasn't just song, but a green mist that snaked out from between their lips. Four serpents of green fog chased each other overhead, darting tongues as sharp and small as thorns, before slipping off into the wood.

"Ooh," she said. The Son rolled his eyes.

Caralee expected trees would move slowly, being trees, but their roots jumped up and began to squirm like critter legs, plowing through the earth, trunks tilting outward from the emerging path to lean on their sturdy, densely grown neighbors. Within minutes, a road ran straight ahead into the Wildest Wood, black and clear of underbrush.

"Shatterscat!" Caralee said to herself. One of the droods snickered.

The entire wood had parted at the droods' command. No sandymancer could command trees. Small wonder that Lastgrown kept itself well hidden.

"You've no idea how much I loathe druids. I might have mentioned." The Son looked to Caralee. "But the magick of the treefuckers is an extraordinary one. Long before this garden world was built, the first druids found a star wreathed in briar, and they stole the secrets of their order."

"Okay," Caralee said. Her head didn't have room for any more amazement just then.

The Son sighed and looked down the lane of trees, then back to the Vine. "They are just awful."

"Right. Off we go, I guess," Caralee said to Sazerac, who held the rolled-up carpet under one bulky, rounded arm.

"The sooner so, the sooner we can close the gap in our perimeter," Biddle Becky urged them on. "I mean no offense and wish you luck and safety in your travels."

Wary of the crawling trees, Caralee led the others onto the path through the Wildest Wood. They'd walked but fifty paces down the path when the trees behind them righted themselves and skittered back together. The wood would flush them out and seal itself in their wake.

"She's really serious about the trees," Caralee muttered. "What was that scat?" she asked the Son. "Granddaughter of the Vine? Really?"

"Granddaughter of the Vine, yes. It was a project of my grandfather's, the Most Holy Son of the Vine. He considered it prudent to cultivate and restore long-damaged redundancies that would, among other functions, protect the world in the event of a catastrophe. *Angksef-Seysef* was his prototype of an entirely new type of approach—a redundancy of the Vine itself."

"What's a redundancy?"

"A backup plan for a backup plan. Something that isn't vital until some more important system is damaged. Take, for instance, your critters. Insects have taken over many roles in the ecosystem that were once played by mammals. Food, clothing, prey—we had cows and tigers; you have critters and chucklers. Obviously, everything was better in my age, but insects survived in harsher conditions and mutated as programmed to fill what gaps they could. Without the Beast of Blood to maintain the animal populations and keep them capable of sustaining their respective ecological roles . . . It's possible that other Beasts stepped in. Who knows, maybe there's a Beast of Critters . . ." The Son scrubbed his face with both hands and stretched his spine.

"Don't *you* know?"

"Grandfather hoped that *Angksef-Seysef* could serve alongside a dying Vine as its eventual replacement." The Son ignored her question, which was an answer of its own. "He was entirely incorrect—the system was designed for *the* Vine, not a flower bed of Vines. If the Vine fell ill—and it did—it would have to be completely destroyed before a new Vine could be cultivated. Grandfather would have learned from his mistake, but the project was never completed in his lifetime."

"Sadly, no." Sazerac spoke for the first time. Caralee and the Son turned around to stare. "The endeavor was doomed."

"That's right," the Son said slowly, walking in a circle around Sazerac, hypervigilant. "My father scrapped the project as a failure. He thought it impious to doubt the perdurance of the Vine. Yet while the Vine at Lastgrown has, indeed, grown—it has not spread. It occurs to me now that perhaps Father was right, in his petty way."

Eusebius nodded solemnly, either following the conversation or clever enough to nod along all the same.

"I am sorry for your loss, Amauntilpisharai, the Lord of a Thousand Names and the Most Holy Son of the Vine." Sazerac accepted without hesitation that the Son was who he claimed to be, but how did he know so much?

The Son offered no reply, but turned to resume the trek out of the wood. The trees resumed sealing themselves behind them. Caralee picked up her pace.

"So if there's only one Vine now, why ent it everywhere?"

"I'm getting to that. Everything that lives, dies, doesn't it? There are cycles for all living things, even the Vine." He pointed to the displaced rainbow ferns on either side of the road. "The world is empty enough of the Vine that the chick at Lastgrown grew—but as it grew, it met something that stopped it from growing. What could that be, Caralee?"

"Okay." The question was an instructive one. "Well, if the Vine is dead, then the Vine around here should just spread, right? Unless the Vine *isn't* dead, which is stupid because . . . naw, that can't be, right?" It was an insane notion, if Caralee understood correctly.

"As I said, perhaps the original Vine endures." The Son chewed his lip. "Somewhere out there—somewhere—some part of my Vine lives on. The Vine at Lastgrown spreads as far as it can until it detects the presence of the original Vine. Maybe some lingering root system or antibodies? Biomarkers hijacked by microbial life? The Vine clearly can't be *alive* . . . I remember killing it."

Eusebius cleared his throat. "How might that be, most kind sir? Surely if any piece of the original Vine lived on, even a vestige, wouldn't we know—as we know of Lastgrown?"

It was Sazerac who shook his head. "No, Eusebius. The world has many unseen crevices, caverns, ruins, and bowels, within which any number of ancient things may hide. Perhaps the last bit of the true Vine struggles to survive in an inhospitable world. Perhaps it, too, has changed over the centuries, and no one has recognized it for what it is. Perhaps it feeds them dust and twigs, and they are grateful for it."

*Feeds them dust and twigs . . .*

Something in Sazerac's boulder-voiced pronouncement gave Caralee the chills. She had a knack for finding those hidden, ancient things. With her luck, it would be Caralee who'd find the half-dead Vine, and who knew what jazzed-up misery *that* would turn out to be.

Hours later, they stepped out of the Wildest Wood—but much farther north and east than where they'd first slept beside its boundary. Not three paces out of the wood, the trees folded back upright, and with a skittering of roots, the path out of Lastgrown closed completely, as if it were never there.

Caralee tried to orient herself and failed. To the north was a high ring of grassy hills, and to the east three mountains rose tall and rocky, snowcapped and imposing. Beyond the mountains rose the walls at the ends of the world.

The terrain here was flat but stony, with only brown scrub growing here and there. The sharp distinction from the Wildest Wood unnerved Caralee.

"All right, Sazerac," Caralee asked nicely. "Would you lay out Sunny the Carpet, please?"

Sazerac dropped Sunny the Carpet to the dirt, then unrolled her with a flick of one stone finger.

The Son, Caralee, and Eusebius took their places on Sunny, but Sazerac didn't move.

"Come on, Sazerac," Caralee urged.

"Are you certain that the carpet will bear my weight?" His indigo eye pulsed when he spoke.

*How's he know Sunny flies?* Caralee wondered. *Or is Sazerac not stupid and he sees three people sitting on a carpet in the middle of nowhere?*

Sazerac took his spot at the rear of the carpet, sitting in what was apparently his usual position—legs splayed, hands palms up in his lap. A chubby doll—a sleeping sentinel.

Caralee raised Sunny the Carpet from the ground, but not very high.

"Let's stay low to avoid—" the Son began before Caralee interrupted.

"A new harpy? Not a problem."

The Son harrumphed. Caralee wondered how quickly the corrupted Beasts of Blood and Wind would hatch a new harpy.

They skirted the edge of the wood, and Caralee urged Sunny to fly as fast as she could into the east. She had to shield her eyes from the sunrise.

When the dark green mountain range of the Wildest Wood lay behind them, Caralee allowed Sunny to rise high enough that they could speed over the terrain. The fierceness of the wind told her how fast they flew, and Caralee relaxed into the meditation of travel. It was just like long, boring trips with Atu and Oti—poor Oti!—she held the reins but freed her mind to soar. The sunrise painted their faces with gold light.

To the north, wrinkles of rocky foothills lay as far as she could see, and barrier mountains to the south were just a tiny line at the horizon behind them. As the sun rose, Caralee could see lone mountains here and there ahead of them, craggy but lonely. If there were barrier mountains out east, they were far away.

She howled out to the sky, *"Oh, we went down to Lastygrown, to see what we could see! I touched me a stony man and fell into a ravine!"*

"Oho!" Eusebius spoke up from his huddle. "We did? She did. What a gauntlet we run!"

It wasn't long before two shining lines appeared along the ground in the distance, running north, where they met and became a single line. As they grew closer, Caralee recognized the lines for what they were: the roads of the metal folk.

"Look," she said to the Son.

"I see," the Son clipped. "Turn this ill-named thing and follow the steel road."

"But I thought you said that you knew where you were going, all of a sudden?" Caralee asked, while doing as the Son ordered, circling around to follow the tracks.

"Detours will happen. Look closer. What aren't you seeing?" the Son called out in answer. "Use your attention, Caralee."

*Right. Steel lines, meeting in the north—are we close to the Metal Duchy?* Looking south, Caralee noticed a little bump that seemed to slide up one of the lines. The little bump left a cloud of dirt behind it.

"Is that a cart?" she asked.

"We're going to find out." The Son raised an eyebrow.

"Okay, but for the record, that seems like a really stupid idea." Caralee pressed Sunny the Carpet toward the ever-closer maybe-cart.

"How is it stupid?" the Son asked. He'd joined Caralee at the head of the carpet, lying on his stomach, propped up on crossed arms, peering over and out. His hair flew a black banner behind him.

Caralee nodded toward a ring of earth in the distance, into which the metal road disappeared. She couldn't see beyond the wall of stone and grass, but the closer they approached, the bigger Caralee understood it to be. If the Duchy lay beyond, it was surrounded by a *massive* earthen ring-wall. "You gonna melt 'em all? Me, I'm pretty vulnerable to swords and stuff. Maybe you're not, but if you are, and you get my Joe killed—then we are *over.*"

"We?" He smiled.

"Shaddup." The steel road ran north around what Caralee could now see was indeed a circle of earth. She wondered how the metal folk built walls of hill and asked the Son how'd they'd done so.

"They didn't build it, stupid." The Son shook his head. "It made itself when they fell from the sky. That's a crater."

Caralee imagined dropping a stone into the sand and how the stone threw up a circle of sand around it. Fuck him for being so right all the time.

"Huh." Caralee thought about the size of the crack in the sky. "That's one big circle of sand—or dirt or whatever. How come the crack in the sky is so small?"

The Son looked at Caralee like she'd become a fresh sort of idiot, and she remembered her observation about whether or not barrier mountains existed out east.

"It's a *lot* farther away, isn't it?" She answered her own question.

"Whether they landed here deliberately or crashed, the story of the Metal Duchy—so far—seems one of desperation and last resort, rather than one of invasion and conquest. Since they landed, they *slept* for what, a hundred years and more? Awoke just a few decades ago?"

"Correct, most kind sir." Eusebius nodded with his eyes closed, playing the sage.

"They must have been in cold-sleep or some other form of deep stasis appropriate for travel between the stars. Since they awoke, they've done little but build roads that lead to lumber and stone, and make overtures for simple trade." The Son paused. "I don't know what to think of them—don't you wonder what *they* think of *us*?"

"I wonder about everything, so of course I do? But I don't want to *find out.*"

"That makes no sense."

"It makes perfect sense! Say I wanna know what's at the bottom of a deep, dark pit. I'm not gonna throw myself in to find out."

"But I'm *me,*" groaned the Son. "Lower our altitude. Keep us flying as close to the ground as you can."

"Okay, but—"

"*Quickly.*"

"Sure, but—"

"How close do you think we are from that . . . cart?" the Son asked. It was also headed north, but lagged a ways behind them.

"Not so close."

"Right. We've time to stage ourselves. Full stop, please," the Son chirruped. "Right here, yes."

Caralee brought Sunny the Carpet to a stop beside the steel road and hopped off. She could feel the steel road vibrating the ground. Staring southerly, down the long run of the steel road and across the diminishing distance, Caralee could make out a chain of individual carts approaching. They must have been connected to each other, like a caravan.

"You want Sunny the Carpet grounded or hovering?" Caralee asked, not sure what the Son had in mind but certain that he'd have an answer to her question.

"Hovering. Let them see the surprises this world holds in store for them." He pointed to the approaching snake of metal carts. "But let's not give them the opportunity to blast us out of the sky. Eusebius, you stay seated, where you are. I will stand nearby. Caralee, you step forward and take lead. Sazerac, I imagine, will follow on your heels."

"I shall, unless directed otherwise."

"*I'm* up front?" That came as a surprise, but not an unwelcome one.

Though it was still a good distance away, the caravan of metal carts looked fair to bristling with shiny steel helmets and shiny weapons that Caralee imagined were at least as sharp as the harpy feathers that had sliced her triceps.

"Caralee? Do you not feel ready for your first lesson in diplomacy?" She hated it when the Son answered a question with another question. That was supposed to be *her* trick. "If you're afraid, you can stand behind me—along with the invalid and animated statuary."

The metal caravan started screeching something awful, and the sound rang Caralee's head like a bell.

"Oh, good." The Son exhaled like a man who hadn't just said, *Oh, good.* "They've seen us."

"What is that sound?" Caralee shouted over the screeching.

"The sound of a train of metal carts pulling to a sudden stop on a metal road, I should imagine."

The sound of metal on metal—like the harpy's laughter.

The caravan slid to a stop some hundred paces away, and the screeching stopped with it. Two dozen gleaming figures leapt over the sides of their linked carts and began sprinting toward the foursome. They carried long steel spears and tiny steel shields.

"Okay, so, diplomacy. What it is: lesson away." Caralee readied herself for melting. "Do I slag them first, or do I wait for them to kill somebody like last time?" She winced at her own question, remembering Atu's screams as she tried to hold Oti together. "Actually, fuck that right in the eyeballs. Imma melt them first."

"Sap and syrup, no!" The Son held his fingers to his temples. "You *talk* to them, Caralee. Diplomacy is *talking* to people before you melt them. Please, let's remember that."

*Shatterscat.* "You want me to talk to them? What's that gonna do?"

"Look at them." The Son sounded so calm. "You can stay silent while these armored off-worlders decide what to do with us, or you can speak first and steer the encounter as best you can. Which sounds like the wiser choice to you?"

The metal-armored soldiers sprinted toward her, the Son, Eusebius, Sazerac, and Sunny the Carpet. Caralee snarled and stood, clenching her fists. "I lost one friend. I'm not about to lose four more."

The metal soldiers fanned out in a fighting formation. They moved to surround Sunny in a wide arc, still fifty paces away. Those tall steel spears they carried didn't exactly look like walking sticks. For one thing, Caralee had never heard of a walking stick that spat fire.

"Saz, don't try anything weird, okay? Just do whatever these steel gits say."

"As you wish, Caralee." Sazerac sounded as uncertain as Caralee thought a statue could sound.

Someone shouted something in a language Caralee couldn't understand—it was a soldier whose armor was more decorated than the others, set with barbed hooks pinned with red ribbons. He barked orders at Caralee, but his accent was too thick to understand.

Caralee crossed her arms. She tried to make her face as stony as possible.

"Oho!" Eusebius remembered himself again. "Such armor! Young miss, you mustn't provoke them, I beg you. By their armor, I do believe they hail from the Metal Duchy. Why, look at this one with the ribbons on his razors. Fascinating plumage." The sandymancer looked down at his own black-feathered shoulders and chewed his lip.

"Don't try to help her, wizard. I want to observe." The Son leaned back, holding his arms above his head. Was that what the soldier had been shouting, for them to raise their arms over their heads? Why would he want them to do that? "Caralee has been training for this moment."

Eusebius held his arms out to either side, but his shoulders were unable to raise his arms any higher. "She has?"

"I have?"

The metal sentinel shouted again. Caralee could make out the words this time, sort of.

"Oho, footpads!" Eusebius exclaimed. "Well-armored footpads! I might have mentioned, I *cannot* raise my arms over my head. I am ever so sorry, but my joints will not permit me to do as you ask."

The Son remained impassive as six guards flanked him. Six more faced Eusebius, who crooked his elbows upward to raise his hands as high as he could manage. They barked at Sunny, who hovered in mute defiance.

Caralee shot her arms into the air, not wanting to be poked by any of the *dozen* burning spear tips pointed at her. Sazerac raised his arms, too, as a dozen more spearmen hissed at him.

"Oho!" Eusebius wailed. "Please don't slaughter me, brave metal warriors!"

The six guards surrounding him—already spooked by the carpet—looked to one another, uncertain what to make of the painted creature with candles on his shoulders. Caralee was glad for their open-faced helmets. Dozens of angry soldiers were daunting enough—she'd have soiled her trousers if they'd had metal faces.

"Oy, you lot!" Caralee shouted at the soldiers surrounding Eusebius. "Back off my friend there! He can't lift his arms over his head—he'll crack a shoulder," Caralee called out to the approaching metal captain. "You've all but shattered the sky, and now you'll abuse my poor old . . . um . . . tutor, I guess? Rude."

With a signal from the captain, the soldiers relented, and Eusebius held his hands out in front of him instead.

*Huh.* Caralee hadn't at all expected that to work. Did throwing tantrums work when people no longer saw you as a child?

The half dozen charged with Sazerac spat alien curses at the armored man and struck sparks off his shoulders with their spears. Sazerac stood perfectly still, his head angled toward Caralee but otherwise docile.

"We don't understand you!" Caralee shouted, forcing authority into her voice. "You talk funny and way too fast."

They hissed the same curse words, again and again, until their red-ribboned captain called out to someone behind him, who was out of sight.

"I said, we *don't understand you.*" Caralee spat in someone's face on accident.

A clarion voice called out from behind the ranks of metal soldiers—it rang across the air and issued orders in a tone that sounded both formal and brutal. From behind her, Eusebius begged the Son to reconsider.

"Are you quite certain, milord of the Thousand Names?"

“Please don’t call me that in public. I am just a simple patron, traveling with his ward and her tutor.”

“But the young woman is quite outnumbered by an army from another world. She must be terrified.”

The Son only laughed.

“Do you see how her mouth moves, and can you hear how words come out of it?” He pointed to Caralee with his chin. “It’s the army who’ll be terrorized.”

“But—”

“You’re a sweet wretch. Give her a minute.”

“Come and get me, you sky-cracking, road-building, harpy-steeling cowards!” Caralee howled at a squadron of heavily armored soldiers. Shielding Sazerac with her own body, she faced down two dozen metal folk without showing a stitch of the fear that she felt. The soldiers seemed paralyzed, and she hadn’t heard that dominating voice issue any more orders.

Caralee growled through her teeth. The soldiers, for their part, flinched. Now, that was interesting.

*Why would a buncha soldiers be scared of one young woman?*

“Torchjets off!” Ordered the likely answer, as she slid through guards who parted for her like sand for a snake. A steel woman with a dark brown neck, dark brown hands, and a shining steel face. Unlike the others, her *face* was made of metal. The stranger’s bell-clear voice called out in that alien dialect.

The soldiers repeated her orders with one voice. That impressed Caralee, who had never seen a trained fighting unit before. The flames at the tips of their spears guttered out.

The metal woman strode forward on legs long and thick with muscle and steel. The commander—that’s what Caralee thought she must be—was a bizarre mix of ordinary deep brown skin and steel. Not just steel armor but steel *skin.*

*Just like the harpy,* Caralee thought with a shiver.

The tall woman glared at Caralee from steel eyes set in a steel face, then she slipped her—metal—fingers underneath her face, and pulled it off entirely.

So the face was a mask. Were the hands gloves?

Beneath the mask, the metal commander’s face was stern but human, her expression blank and her eyes flashing. Her long hair was rolled into locs more lovely than Mag’s had ever been, and studded with steel. Her armor was unreal—the woman sprouted steel from her skin, below and above every major joint. Staggered petals of steel rose from her biceps and thighs as if they’d grown there. Her breastplate was a ripple of steel that began at her pelvis and ended flat beneath her armpits. Her collarbone was reinforced with a torque of shining metal—no, not a torque, it was the collarbone itself, pushed up through the skin and revealed as metal, or so it appeared.

Upon her brow she wore a wire-thin circlet that would have appeared simple, had it not been growing from her scalp.

The commander and Caralee assessed each other, and the commander saw Caralee's eyes flit toward the mask and the commander's face and back again. The steely woman tossed the mask toward Caralee, who snatched it from the air and held on to it without breaking eye contact. Her sparring with the Son had hardened her focus, and the steel woman could not stare Caralee down.

"What witch brings a demon onto my lands?" the woman demanded of Caralee in an accent that was clipped but less garbled than that of her soldiers. The commander wasn't old, but she carried herself like a veteran. "Speak up, witch!"

Caralee didn't answer straightaway. This woman unnerved her in a way that her spear-bristling soldiers did not, though she carried no weapon that Caralee could see.

"You walk with the soulless!" The woman pointed at Sazerac. "Demon!"

"Ex . . . excuse me?" Caralee found her voice. "What are you on about?"

"Your name and rank, filth!" She slid her hand along the petals of steel at her hips, and the metal *moved like liquid.* She drew from it—was that the right word?—a slender blade with a slight bend before the tip, which she pointed at Caralee's collarbone. "This particular blade is made to sever the spines of animals, and I will put you down like a bull should you continue to growl as one."

Caralee glared. She bit her cheek to keep quiet.

"Good girl." The woman almost smiled. "Name, now."

"Names, right," Caralee said. "How 'bout you go first."

The metal woman's lips twitched. "If you like." She allowed a small smile. "I am Duke Elinor of Meroë, called Elinor the Ashamed by some, Lady Steel, Daughter of Apocalypse, High Prentice to the Holy Forge, Last of the Blood Metallic, and I have been generous with you."

"Right. So, I'm Caralee Vinnet, and I really, *really* thank you for your hospitality. All these weapons, from all these big, strong strangers, pointed right at little me! Thank you. Really, from the bottom of my scathole, *thank you.*"

Steel Elinor glared and opened her mouth, but Caralee interrupted her. That was, after all, Caralee's specialty.

"Do I have to remember your whole name? Because it's a lot. You're a lot. This is a lot. Has anyone ever told you that you're a *lot*?"

The duke blinked. "You may call me Steel Elinor."

"Hi, Steel Elinor. I'm basically sixteen years old, by the way," Caralee added. "So is this, like, a spear for each month? I'm not too great at numbers yet."

Steel Elinor held her sword high and steady. "Are you sane, child? Do you have any idea who and what I am?"

"Are you stupid?" Caralee didn't need another bully with a title in her life. "How the fuck would I know that?"

Steel Elinor sputtered. "I command the greatest army on this pathetic world!"

*This again. Do I attract despots?*

"Shut. Up." Caralee took a breath and flared her nostrils. Her words startled Steel Elinor, who stepped back. "I have *been through this conversation before,* okay?" It was Caralee's turn to sneer.

"Even a brittle alloy can be smelted." Elinor shrugged Caralee away entirely. "As any pony can be broken."

"What's a pony?" Caralee said while thinking, *Fuck you.*

Steel Elinor looked over Caralee's shoulder to address Sazerac, who sat fat and impassive at the center of an arc of spear tips, Caralee and Elinor between them.

"What is your hour, demon?" Elinor demanded.

Sazerac said nothing, adhering to Caralee's orders.

"Speak!"

"Go—go ahead, Saz." Caralee edged Sazerac toward freedom. "Just your mouth or your eye-light; you know what I mean."

"I repeat." Elinor's fierceness knew some patience. "What is your hour, demon?"

"Par-pardon me?" Saz stood stock-still, his indigo eye pulsing at each spear in turn. He looked to Caralee for instructions.

"Look at me, demon! Do not look to your witch for answers." Elinor's eyes flickered toward Caralee's resentment at the word, but she kept on. "I'll ask you once more, and then I'll have you incinerated. *What is your hour?*"

"He doesn't know what you mean, and neither do we, and why would we, because you're from wherever?"

Elinor faltered. The Son chuckled. When the duke found her voice, it came soft as a licking tongue. "What are you?" Elinor looked to Sazerac. Her voice trembled. "Tell me, please, are you one of the devils? If there are more of them, then I must know."

Sazerac's head dipped in a kind of an upside-down shrug. "I am none of these things, Steel Elinor. I know none of these questions. I am Sazerac, and I am Caralee's man."

"Devils lie!" Elinor cried. "Devils slaughter!" Elinor held her sword arm high at her shoulder, angled down to point at Caralee's throat.

"I do not lie, and I do not slaughter." Sazerac's eye pulsed in time to his voice, steady and true. "I do not know any devils or demons. I belong to Caralee Vinnet, and she is my only concern." Saz paused. "I must confess, Steel Elinor: I am concerned."

"As am I." Steel shining, her eyes bright with violence.

Caralee had never met a fanatic before. She found it immediately exhausting. "Look, lady. Kill me or don't, but can we get on with it?"

The captain in red-ribboned armor cleared his throat and offered some suggestion, but Elinor turned on him so fast that Caralee's eyes buzzed. Elinor shouted him down as he cringed, answering her anger with whinging apologies.

"Rawntallion here seems to think I should treat you gently because of your age." Elinor turned to Caralee, teeth bared. "I reminded him—'twas a *child* who destroyed our home. 'Twas a *child* who ignored all sense and ancient warnings and befouled the mercury springs. 'Twas a *child* whose blasphemy set free the demons who drove us here, to exile. Rawntallion understands, girl—do you?"

Caralee shook her head. "What part of 'from another world' are you not hearing?"

"I was a girl, too, when I released the demons who drove us from our world!" Elinor raged. "Do not think me sentimental."

*Shatterscat.* Caralee didn't believe that for a second. Nobody who kept a cool head got this worked up.

Elinor angled her shoulders, pulling away with her sword arm and leaning in with her other to rest her fingertips on Caralee's face. Caralee saw that her hands were a mix of steel and flesh. The duke's fingers were warm—hot, maybe—but her open-fingered steel gauntlet was as cold as the wind from the west.

Caralee looked up to Elinor.

"Look." Caralee made her voice small. Quiet, so Elinor had to strain to listen. "I'm just trying to find my friend." Caralee opened her brown eyes wide. "I got two men, a talking statue, and an old carpet. You got the biggest army in the world." She slumped her shoulders.

*Let this sentimental bully hang on her own rope.*

When Steel Elinor spoke next, her tone had softened. "'Twas a girl who freed the Twelve of Morning, each the devil of an hour." She ground her jaw, edging her blade closer. "I'll not mistake danger for whimsy again."

Caralee dug her heels into the dirt.

"I ent a *girl,* and I ent *you,* and Saz ent no divvil." She reached out and touched the sharp edge of Elinor's sword. "So you go on ahead and kill me for no reason. Start killing young folk, that'll be the perfect message to send to your new neighbors, won't it? First you take our harpies—harpy?—which were terrifying enough already, thank you—and you give them steel insides, and now you come at *me* for being dangerous?" Caralee screwed up her face. "Lady, *fuck you.*"

Elinor winced at the mention of the harpy, but it wasn't the kind of straightforward wince that might have told Caralee she'd hit the mark. There might be more to the tale of the steeling-up of the harpy. Elinor recovered as easily as Caralee had come to expect from regal types.

"Finding your friend?" The duke smiled a smile Caralee knew well and loathed, the smile of dismissal. "Your friend must be important, for you to dare to bring a devil onto my lands."

"You don't know scat about me, and you don't know scat about my Joe. You don't know any of us, and if you're gonna judge us for that, then folks—" She looked to the soldiers behind Elinor, the ones ringing Saz, and back to Elinor. "How you think *you're* gonna be judged for breaking our sky?"

The steel lady sheathed her sword, which melted into the metal armor. Only the pommel remained, jutting out from the steel at her hip. Elinor all but slew the four strangers with her gaze as she barked orders to her troops.

The soldiers pulled back their spears but corralled the four toward their clockwork caravan. Elinor folded her arms and looked from Caralee to Sazerac and back again. "We will take you two onto the train. We shall see if your demon is tame, Caralee Vinnet. If it moves a hair, I will have the both of you incinerated where you stand." Elinor kept her eyes toward the carts as liquid steel flowed up from her shoulder to her neck, and up her neck to re-form the mask she'd tossed away.

Caralee looked behind her. The Son's face was a calm mask of its own, one that indicated to Caralee to submit for now. She trusted him that far.

"Saz, come along and do what they say, okay? Don't give them any reason to think that you're . . . whatever they think you are." She took a deep breath and willed her next words to be true. "You're with me, so everything will be fine."

Sazerac nodded once. Behind the mask, Elinor narrowed her eyes.

Eusebius looked around him, at the metal soldiers, at their duke, at Caralee.

"I'm just fine, young miss! Don't you worry about this old fellow! Not one bit . . ." He tried to sound carefree. "You take care of yourself, won't you? I don't mind saying that I do *not* care for that woman—that one there." Without moving his arms, Eusebius pointed a crooked finger at Steel Elinor. "That one, with the armor growing out of her skin? No—no, I do not care for her, *not one bit.*"

# VI

My older sister Ester loved games. Sport games, lawn games, parlor games, puzzles, and mysteries. It came as little surprise, then, when she married our brother, Amau-Alua, also my elder, who was a champion football player and a terror at dominoes. They lived away from the city on a country estate surrounded by orange groves and apple orchards, with fields and courts for every sport imaginable, and the most intricate hedge maze I'd ever seen.

Grandfather Moysha had died, and my father became the Son of the Vine. Moysha's work was scuttled as soon as the seven superlatives grew the crown from Father's wrinkled head. Those associated with the late Son's efforts were disappeared or bought off. The work at Angksef-Seysef was abandoned, and by all accounts, only I knew why.

While I stared in horror, my siblings continued their little pursuits, unconcerned and, to be fair, entirely ignorant that our father's cowardice would doom their great-grandchildren to die of thirst or starvation or asphyxiation.

Ester asked me to visit often, though I rarely did. When next she passed along an invitation, however, I accepted immediately. I held back tears as my valet packed my bags. I bit my lip as my driver took me away.

My worst fears had come true, exactly as Athinne and Moysha had predicted. I knew in my gut that my work couldn't begin until I was certain not to be interrupted, and now I understood why. I saw that the fate of the world depended upon my nerve. I would like to say that I had no choice, but that is almost never true.

I am the tenth child of seventeen. That is too much to ask of any Beast, no matter the purpose. Even in a dynastic world where murder was considered an appropriate method of self-advancement, sixteen siblings and one father is too much blood to spill without consequences. I was never certain that I would succeed. I forced myself to hope that I would slay them all, which was torture.

Viewed from the countryside, the body of the Vine was a marvel. It began like any mountain, rising up from the plains with walls of green almost as dark as the malachite of Athinne's tower or the ordinary greenstone basalt of Angksef-Seysef. The City of the Vine pattered white walls and terra-cotta roofs around the body's base and crawled up switchback roads carved into the rind, which was thick as bedrock. As the Vine rose, its body narrowed, bulblike, before splitting into a dozen stalks: three reached to the sun, trained to grow straight and tall enough to serve as towers; four stalks arced nearly as high before curling over themselves and bending to brush the ground like a god's willow, their tendrils coiled above the city, shading the land with snakes of shadow that shifted from sunrise to sunset; the lowest seven stalks were the eldest and the thickest, and they lay nearly flat to the soil where they were still taller than any of the city's ground-level towers. Those seven cables of plant meat and magick spanned the entire world——at places, they snaked across the land; at others, they were lofted like ancient aqueducts.

Ester and Amau-Alua's estate sat beside one of the seven world-spanning Vine tendrils, just at the point where it split into three smaller stalks that snaked beneath the soil and ran for miles in different directions. I was invited for a private visit, which suited my purposes.

It was not unusual for squabbles to break out among the heirs of a new Child of the Vine. The time after coronation was inherently unstable. Any number of tragedies would be overlooked as a hazard of life as an heir to the world.

Ester was always full of energy and good cheer, and she met me at the gates with a sandwich and a bottle of scented water. She joined me in the back seat as we drove the last kilometer from the entrance to the estate to the manor itself, and she hugged me as I devoured white cheese and spicy greens rubbed with mustard, thick tomatoes as dark as blood, pressed between crunchy-soft bread baked that morning.

We passed the hedge maze, tall and dark even in the daytime, and I wondered at the possibilities.

Amau-Alua was built like me, lean but strong, dark of color, though he kept his hair shaved short and his beard long. He hugged me with one arm, happy to see me, if not as gleeful as his sister-wife.

We drank and ate more. We played cards on a table beneath the orange trees, where the air smelled of their bright flavor. We kicked the ball back and forth, laughing when I tripped over my own feet, pretending to be clumsier than I was. We ran through the hedge maze, hooting and chirruping to throw each other off course, racing to be first to reach the fountain at the center of the maze. We were children again.

Murder is an art and a science, and I was a novice. Though I'd steeled myself, I did not perform well. I did not know how unclean death could be or how to administer mercy and cruelty with the same stroke.

I cannot forget the look on Ester's face when I found her between two rows of boxwoods, surprise and happiness to see me that turned to some gaping hollowness when I used elemancy to break her legs both above and below the knee. I summoned those druidic mysteries that I have sworn never to speak of and filled her mouth with leaves and branches so that her cries could not be heard. Then I fled.

Amau-Alua didn't appear worried when Ester failed to appear at the fountain, but by nighttime, he was beside himself. I cast witchlights across the massive field of hedge, and I withered the maze as dozens of servants, Amau-Alua, and myself searched for our missing sister.

He found her first, trapped beneath a tumble of dead hedge, barely alive. She'd lain there for hours, suffering and mute because of my bungling ignorance.

My brother looked at me with the strangest mixture of rage and acceptance. Nothing in the natural world could have shattered Ester's legs and gagged her with hedge.

"Raclette was right," he said. "You are a monster."

I slipped a blade into his guts, quick but messy. My hand disappeared inside his stomach until the blade found his spine. I jabbed, and my shaking hand somehow managed to slip between his vertebrae. Amau-Alua collapsed beside his bride.

The servants were easy to kill or mesmerize. The minds of those inclined to obey are easy to manipulate, and the magick of cognoscence was a rare talent. It would be difficult to detect.

When the inhabitants of the estate remembered who they were, they found their masters. Ester had died of exposure, and Amau-Alua suffered the slow agony of a mortal gut wound. They died where I left them.

My father asked Zincy, now the Lir of the Thousand Names, to eulogize the dead couple at their joint funeral. Zincy, in their samite robe, long beard, and rose-painted eyes, the future Child of the Vine, painted the perfect picture of nobility. Whether Lord or Lady or Lir, the Thousand Names suited my eldest sibling, and I couldn't help but love them for it. How I hated myself for wanting them dead.

My role in Ester's and Amau-Alua's deaths was treated as a matter of fact, accepted quietly by everyone, even Raclette, who could do nothing but glare at me across the aisle as our brother and sister were returned to the soil.

Father possessed no talent for druidry, so one of the seven superlatives performed the ritual. Naked, the druid laid her hands on the ground and closed her eyes. The white hairs of growing roots bristled up from the ground and picked at the dead, who were also naked. She proceeded slowly, and it took several long minutes for the soil to open up and tear the bodies apart as the crawling roots pulled Amau-Alua and Ester below, until all that was left was freshly grown grass.

I used elemancy to wick away my tears and steadied my breath. I was the eighth of fifteen children, now, but not for very long.

# 13

The "train," as Steel Elinor had called the metal caravan, rumbled to life as Caralee and Sazerac stepped inside it. The carriage shook with such an energy that Caralee worried the contraption would burst its steel seams, but when the train lurched and began to move, she almost laughed at how slowly it rolled on its tracks.

But the train gained speed, and the faster it went, the less the carriage shook—the thrumming vibration evened out, and Caralee sat herself on a bare steel bench, near to the doorway through which she'd entered—Sazerac stood there, looking lost, if a statue could look lost.

Caralee reached out and took Sazerac's three-fingered stone hand in hers. His hand wasn't cold the way stone would be cold, but it wasn't warm the way skin would be, either. He felt more like a hot stone that had been set beside a fire. She squeezed it, and he squeezed back with equal force.

Above them, a metal roof kept out the sun and, presumably, the occasional mist that passed for rain. Heat radiated from the floor and kept away much of the chill of the wind, even though they now sped along at a speed that awed Caralee. She let her vision blur and the passing of the crossbeams on the tracks outside mesmerized her. They blurred into something else, a flickering of what the train left in its wake: speed.

Caralee would never have dared fly Sunny the Carpet this fast. How did a metal caravan speed across a metal road? Was it magick? Did they have big metal critters to pull it? She hadn't seen any critters, but if it *was* critters, then they must be huge—and eat a *lot* of scat.

Caralee felt for her satchel and opened it just a bit to peek at the silvery mask that Elinor had torn from her face and tossed to Caralee. Why did she do that? It was a funny thing to do, if you thought you'd caught a witch and a divvil—wasn't it?

She looked up from her satchel into a dozen empty faces. She was wasting time she could spend wringing these metal morons for information, clues—even their insults might teach her something of their nature.

"So," Caralee said as if their spears didn't exist. "You all from beyond the sky, huh?"

Nothing.

"Sounds fancy. What was it like, where you came from? I bet it was a lot different than the world. Our world. Was your home a world? I mean, I dunno what the options are. Can people live beyond the sky without a world? It looks awfully dark."

Still nothing.

"I mean, except where it doesn't. Do you all live in the starbirth clouds or on a star? Your armor's shiny, so maybe you lived on a star. I bet it's real shiny there."

Someone sighed.

"Another thing—do you all grow your own armor, or is it just that awful lady who yells at you? She the only one who makes her sword disappear? For someone who seems dead set to believe that *I'm* a bad witch, you'd think she'd act like a good one. Does she always shout like that? I think if I was gonna order a buncha people with spears and torchjets—what's a torchjet, anyway?—So, anyway, if I was gonna tell a buncha scary gits what to do, I might be nicer about it. That's just me, you know. I'm sure she's got her own thing, so . . ." Caralee smiled and nodded her head, wondering if Elinor let them keep their tongues.

"Do you eat metal food?"

*Can't they talk and hold a spear at the same time?*

"Hey, Sazerac? Don't move or anything, but I think you can talk without us getting torchjetted and ansannerated. Anyway I am kinda done with this shatterscat, and if they wanna burn me, honestly, right now, I'd be happy to be done with these gits and their bully boss." One of the guards growled, which Caralee counted a win. "Yeah, I said it." She shook her head. Metal people were the worst.

"Oh, you *can* understand me? That's nice, real nice, because I wouldn't wanna just talk at a metal wall. Might be frustrating. I think I'm frustrated. Hey, Sazerac, do I sound frustrated?"

Despite his size and, well, rockiness, Sazerac looked vulnerable—especially if these metal scatholes could destroy him like their Steel Elinor had threatened. Caralee wouldn't let that happen; she'd keep Saz safe. They were in it together now.

"No, Caralee," Sazerac answered without turning his head. "You sound dangerous."

"Yeah, yeah. Well . . . Hey, Saz?"

*If they're gonna ignore me, fine. Gits.*

"Yes, Caralee?" His voice was kind gravel.

"Where do you come from? I mean, she's probably gonna yell at us again and ask all sorts of questions that I don't understand. Also, I want to know."

The metal soldiers looked to one another. They'd been given strict instructions, none of which covered the event of Caralee Vinnet's sass-mouth. One grumbled and got an elbow in her rib from her compatriot for her trouble.

Caralee realized why the Son had given her the task of being the diplomat: it really *was* her mouth.

"I am sorry, Caralee. My hand belongs to you—indeed, my whole self is yours—but the answer to your question is not mine, and I cannot give it."

"*Please?*"

"I cannot. As I said, the answer is not mine. If I could tell you, I would tell you."

"Huh. What's that about?"

"I wish that I could say."

"Do you know and you can't say—or do you not know at all?"

"Like anyone else, Caralee, I do not always know what I do not know."

*Huh.*

"Did you follow someone else around, before you started following me?" She thought about it. "You knew about *Angksef-Seysef.* What else do you know? About that. Or then. Or anything."

"*Angksef-Seysef* was under construction when I fell dormant." He paused. "I knew a man who was kind and wise, but he must have died, or I would not have slept. In my sleep atop the cliff by the bay, I dreamt that *Angksef-Seysef* was abandoned. For many years nothing happened. Then I dreamt that the Vine grew and that people came but were afraid of me, and they could not awaken me."

That was quite a story.

"Okay, wow. So you were around during the building of *Angksef-Seysef*?"

"Yes. Eight hundred and ninety-seven years, four months, six days, five hours, thirty-seven minutes, and six seconds ago. Seven. Eight. Nine."

"So you can count." Caralee had no reason not to believe Sazerac, but that was quite the tale. Could Sazerac have worked for the Son's gramps? "What about before that? What's the furthest back thing you know?"

"Caralee? Sleep always comes before awakening. Before I awoke, I slept. My clock did not count that time, but external cues indicate it was for thousands of years, not hundreds. My oldest memory? Hmm." Sazerac thought for a while. "Void and starlight. Yes, I remember stars and their vacuum, as if from high above. Is that helpful?"

*Not by half.* Sazerac answered her questions without hesitation, as well as he could. Caralee still felt troubled by his instant connection to her, that immediate obedience, but she liked him. Out of her three companions, the statue was the warmest.

"Sazerac, you know that nobody can own anyone else, right? You ent *mine*, and you ent *nobody's* except your own."

"That is a noble belief, Caralee. I do not gainsay your wisdom, but my whole self is yours. That is my purpose. I serve, simply. I am one who *belongs-to*."

"You're *not mine*! That ent a gainsay, it's a lose-say, Saz!"

Saz made a sound like a gentleman poked in the gut.

"But . . . it is my purpose, Caralee." The way he said it, you'd think it was Caralee who'd said something wrong.

The red-ribboned captain cleared his throat. "Shut your mouth, witch," he demanded in that thick accent.

Caralee stuck out her tongue and gave the man a nasty look.

She stared out the open window behind her, slipping one elbow outside the cart. Almost immediately, she allowed herself to forget the scene inside the train and let her mind float free.

Moving this fast, the wind became a thing that she could actually *touch*, the way the force of it blew her fingers back and pushed against her palm, like the water in the baths at Comez. She imagined how fast they must be going to scoop up so many blockums of air that the wind filled her hands like water.

The metal caravan ran so straight that Caralee didn't see the massive earthen ring up ahead, although she knew that was where the train must be headed. When darkness dropped like a curtain, Caralee startled and pulled her arm back inside the train. For a minute, the train rumbled forward on its tracks through the darkness, but before Caralee had time to imagine anything horrible, the darkness lifted as quickly as it had fallen. Caralee shielded her eyes as the train sped through the sunlight again, across a blinding plain.

Her eyes adjusted, and through her fingers, she saw steel treebones sprouting black leaves on branches that grew apart from one another in simple angles, not crowded and overlapped like the leaves on the trees in the Wildest Wood. Here and there were circular beds of shining metallic plants with bright red petals, and square rows of green plants with dark fruit. Along the edges of the plain, the metal folk had built silver bowls each the size of a house, perfectly round and aimed at different angles toward the sky. Silver tents pushed up from the earth in the same rounded silver petal-shapes as Steel Elinor's armor—and the crisscross of train tracks mazed across all the remaining land that Caralee could see.

Around and between all these strange things grew a lawn so green and manicured that it took Caralee a while to recognize that it was real grass and not another alien thing, like some green outdoor carpet that went on for kilometers.

Her eyes darted from lawn to cups to tents to fruits and back.

The train ran straight ahead, so Caralee couldn't see where they were headed. She stifled the impulse to climb halfway out the window, to whoop into the wind and feed her curiosity. As they grew closer to what must be the center of the plain, the buildings increased in density and height, and the tracks all started pointing the same way. All the roads seemed to lead to the same place.

*What would the Son say if he were here?* Caralee asked herself, feeling alone. *Would he recognize any of this stuff? Or would all of this be just as strange to him as it is to me?*

The train screeched and slowed with so sudden a lurch that Caralee almost threw up. Metal rang off metal as the train shook even more fiercely than it had before. Caralee clapped her hands to her ears as a piercing whistle joined the awful tremor. Just as the whistling died and the shuddering eased, soldiers from other carts began jumping over the edge of the train's open windows—Caralee saw them roll behind her as they sprinted onto a causeway that looked like stone, if stone could be poured and smoothed like clay.

The metal caravan shuddered to a stop beneath a rounded metal half roof, and the soldiers goaded Sazerac and Caralee toward the exit. The air smelled of oil and grease.

"Come on, Saz. It's okay if I call you Saz, isn't it?" Caralee beckoned, ignoring the steel cohort. "So, Saz, just follow real close to me and do what they say, and definitely, don't do anything else." Someone snarled. "I mean you can answer questions if you—"

"Yes, Caralee, it is okay to call me Saz," Sazerac cut her off. "May I suggest we do as these stalwart soldiers command, until you are safer?"

"Yeah, yeah." Caralee did as Saz suggested. Apparently *her man* wasn't above telling her to shut up like everyone else.

*So far, so good, Saz.* Caralee figured that Sazerac was an unexpected comfort—one that proved true to his word in the face of the largest fighting force that Caralee had ever seen. He hadn't left her side or disobeyed her once, but he had enough of himself to speak up just now, to make a suggestion he thought might keep her out of danger. . . . Even if that suggestion was to be quiet.

Peeking outside the train, Caralee looked up to see that the ceiling was high enough to be hidden in shadow, but if she looked back toward the sunlight behind the train, she could see the strange steel trees and the shadow of some kind of tall building—were they underneath it? Jostled as she was by spears and soldiers, Caralee didn't gripe or fuss as the soldiers hustled her up a corner of the poured-stone causeway and onto a metal stairway that for some reason hypnotized Caralee.

*Is it moving?* The stairs looked like they were rising up from the floor, which was ridiculous, but so was poured stone and silvery trees and a crater full of metal strangers and their metallic shatterscat.

The soldiers in front of her, who walked backward to keep their eyes on Caralee and her divvil, stepped backward onto the stairs in pairs. Immediately, they began to rise up without moving their legs. The soldiers behind her urged her on, and, taking Sazerac's hand again, the two of them took a step onto what were *definitely* stairs that *moved.*

They were the longest stairs Caralee had ever seen, and the straightest. She could look up for a hundred meters and still not see their end as the stairs climbed into the guts of the building above.

"Have you ever seen anything like this, Saz?"

"Not for a long while." His voice sounded small in the huge open space. Lights as bright as small suns glared white in spots here and there, above and below them.

"Like *Angksef-Seysef*? Or, you know, before that . . ."

"Long before." Saz didn't go on. Caralee wondered if he could.

When the stairs finally came to an end, her forward guards stepped backward off it—they had to hustle upon their first step off the stairs, since the ground beyond them didn't move the way the stairs did. The steps below her feet collapsed upon one another, then disappeared beneath the floor. She stumbled, but righted herself with Sazerac's help—he crossed the threshold with one steady step, increasing his speed for a few steps farther than Caralee would have thought necessary.

*Oh,* she realized. *We have to make room for the people behind us.* Sazerac really did know what he was doing.

The guards marched Caralee and Sazerac down a hallway nearly as long as the moving stairway. A half-pipe ceiling obscured the tower above, but angled glass windows looked out over the land below, and Caralee had to shield her eyes from the reflection of the sun in a thousand mirror-bowls.

*We're that high up?*

They reached a set of huge double doors made from metal and glass, and Caralee jumped back when they slid open on their own. Why did everything about the metal folk insist on startling her?

The floor thrummed with a constant vibration and what sounded like the pounding of hammers. Caralee heard the coughs and complaints of people hard at work.

The steel soldiers brought Caralee into a three-story open space with metal walkways along all sides, and giant pincers, wedges, and forks that held constructions of metal and other materials. Some were the size of a person, others as tall as the room itself. Some had legs—two, three, four, or more; some had arms of a similar variety of numbers; others had limb-like attachments that Caralee couldn't recognize at all.

Not all the metal folk wore metal, which came as a surprise even though it made sense. Along the floor and walkways were folk wearing ordinary clothes—Caralee saw a number of different uniforms in gray and black and red cloth and leather—who hurried from one of the odd constructions to the next. Others wore workshirts that seemed color-coded. Some held strange tools and pressed them to the creations, sparks flying. The noises that filled the room were worse even than the train, as was the stink of grease and . . . sharp smells, unfamiliar. Burning tar, almost, and lye.

The soldiers prodded Caralee and Sazerac through the sparking workroom and into the relative silence of a corridor—red-striped metal walls and a ceiling that glowed with warm light. They marched down one corridor, then another, and another—all carpeted with bright red runners laid over a metal floor made from some metal darker than steel or silver.

The group turned at a wide doorway and entered a windowed vault of a parlor—a cavernous room with steely pillars and window-bubbles that pushed out from the walls, to better see the land below and beyond. It was quiet here, and the air smelled sweeter. Benches and chairs ringed some of the pillars and were set in little circles near the walls, not unlike Biddle Becky's staging area, where Caralee had found her friends after she'd woken up in Lastgrown.

Some of the cushions were red and dark gray, others kept to peaches and gold. The furniture itself, Caralee noticed, was a mix of wood and metal. In the middle of the room hung a chandelier in the shape of a twelve-pointed star—it was as wide as a house, and set with lights that were neither candles nor witch-lights. Beneath the chandelier sat a table the same exact size and shape, which was crowded with silver pitchers and bowls of black clay that rested on brightly beaded coasters. Some of the pitchers held bouquets of those silver plants with bright red petals—up close, she could see they were made of six overlapping floppity petals, with a dark eye at the center. Other pitchers sat on trays and were surrounded by black clay cups and clay bowls that held the dark fruit that Caralee had seen growing in patches outside.

She felt the footsteps of her guards, booted feet on the dark red carpet. Caralee figured they could take any formation they wanted—they wouldn't stop her from enjoying the flowers. She leaned forward to smell them—she'd heard that flowers smelled pretty—but these had no scent. The air itself must have been perfumed.

She plucked a flower and tucked it behind her ear. The silvery stem was easy to pinch off. Caralee sniffed her fingers, her nose twitching like Dustbutt—unlike the sap of the aloe vera plant, this flower hardly smelled of anything.

Looking around to make sure no one was watching, Caralee slipped a beaded coaster from underneath one silver pitcher and hid it in her satchel. Those beads would fetch a *fortune* just about anywhere.

*Well, now it looks uneven.* Caralee grabbed five more coasters, walking around the table and pretending to inspect the pottery and the spread.

"So what's the deal?" she asked the guards behind her. "Is the duke gonna kill me or what?"

Caralee realized she couldn't feel the boot steps anymore. She assumed they'd been marching toward the walls to stand guard, but when she turned around, she saw that they were gone.

"Sazerac?" she asked. He was standing by the door where they'd entered. If he'd been curious about the twelve-pointed table or the bubble windows, he'd obeyed Caralee and not indulged his curiosity. "Saz? Where'd everybody go?"

"Caralee?" Sazerac asked. He sounded worried. Was he shorter? "Caralee? I seem to be sinking."

It was true. A circular hole had been burned into the carpet, and the floor beneath was dropping at a steady pace.

"Saz!" she cried out, though it sounded like a squeak.

"Caralee? Please take care of yourslllfff." The floor closed over Sazerac's great big head, cutting him off. The edges of the circular cutout in the carpet frilled and seemed to crawl inward, little fingers of dark red pulling themselves toward the center until the hole was no longer visible at all.

"What the—"

Behind her, a section of the curved metal wall rippled, and a panel slid open. Inside was a round little room that Caralee had no intention of entering. A bell chimed from within.

"I am going to melt your face off, lady," Caralee said to the ceiling.

With a series of machine whines, the lights in the hall shut off. The bubbly windows darkened, and for a second, Caralee wondered if it was sunset, but no—the windows themselves were turning not-windowy. Soon they were as opaque as the walls. Caralee found herself alone in the darkened hall—her one source of light was the little round room itself, its light white and cool against her face.

"You know, this seems like a lot of work!" she shouted, sure that Elinor was watching. "You could have just locked us up the regular way . . ."

Caralee was *not* getting into that tiny little cage.

"Or put me in a cage yourself," she muttered. "You coward."

She eyed one of the arrangements of chairs and couches, and she dragged one gray-cushioned footstool toward the light of the cage, as if the bright room was a campfire or an orange crystal of the Son's *filkapyths.*

Trying her best to keep from being intimidated, Caralee forced herself to admire the way the cushion was stapled together, in neat crosswise lines that formed diamond shapes.

"Ooh," Caralee said, sitting on the footstool and discovering it made her bottom happy.

She faced the cage and the cage faced her.

"I am not getting in. I can probably survive on water from those pitchers for a while. Whatever those purply fruits are, too. I don't need much. The flowers are probably poison. You seem like the type who'd grow poison flowers just because you can."

No one answered her.

"I really don't have time for this?" Caralee complained to the darkness surrounding her. "But I guarantee I'm stubborner than any of you." She wiggled on the cushion, setting in for a long watch.

*I can wait.* Caralee didn't feel as certain about that as she thought she ought to feel. *What if it's not a cage?*

She resisted the urge to stick her head in and take a look. The little room looked featureless from the outside, but for the glow of its walls.

Caralee took her journal out of her satchel, unwrapped it, and turned to a blank page. She started sketching the round cage-room, which gave off just enough light for the task. She sketched the stapled footstool, and the flower from behind her ear, and the train tracks, and the train. She sketched a metal soldier's armor and Elinor's spiked hips and her silver-studded ropes of hair. Time passed with only the scratching of her pencil to keep her company. Minutes, hours—with the windows dimmed, she had no way to gauge the passage of time.

Then came a low rumble from above. Caralee thought she heard someone clear their throat, but it was far too loud and too . . . machiney. She looked up and saw nothing but vaulted ceiling. The rumble sounded again—it was definitely someone clearing their throat. Where did the sound come from? Where was the scathole clearing their throat at her?

"Ugh," Caralee complained to the distant ceiling. "You're awful."

The lighted wall of the cage pulsed on and off, as if it were growing anxious. Caralee stood and walked to the door. Chewing her cheek from nerves, she stuck her head inside, looked around quickly, and ducked her head out before that strange door could close and slice her head clean off.

Were those round lights to one side of the cage?

Caralee stuck her head in for a second, longer look. On the inside and beside the door to the cage were bubbles similar to the ones she'd seen in the square metal room they'd found uncovered in the ditch by Lastgrown. What had the Son said about it?

*It moves up and down.* And then, *Curiosity is gonna kill me dead.*

"Fine. I'm getting in. Have it your way. But if you kill me, I'm gonna haunt you and clear *my* throat till *you* die."

The bubbles were labeled with letters that Caralee didn't recognize.

*No, wait. Those are numbers.* Overly stylized and a bit different from the numbers she'd been taught, but obvious after a closer look. *There's ten, and twenty, and—shatterscat—thirty?*

The bubble at the top, marked thirty, was blinking, while all the others glowed steadily. So Caralee pressed the top bubble and jumped at a chiming of the bell she'd heard before. The door closed, the moving room shuddered, and Caralee felt her stomach drop. Was she moving upward? The process happened quickly—she had little time to worry over her fate, when the door slid open, and the bell chimed again.

The first thing Caralee saw were the stars twinkling in the cracked sky. Whorls of starbirth clouds spun all around, and for a moment, Caralee felt like she was standing at the top of the sky. Then the notion of thirty stories hit home, and she understood that it was only height that made her feel that way.

The day had passed quickly—that is, there'd been a lot of shouting and threats and metal cart rides and moving stairs and huge, nice rooms that went suddenly dark, and then she'd drawn for forever . . . it was nighttime, and Caralee felt both cheated and relieved to be done with this outrage of a day.

If only she *were* done.

She stood alone on a terrace that looked built for leisure rather than industry, with long, low chairs to either side and dark climbing plants wrapping around the narrow pillars between them. White, five-petaled flowers gave off the prettiest smell that Caralee had ever smelled—finally, flowers that smelled pretty!

Caralee supposed she was still somewhere in the ducal complex, only thirty stories up. Behind her, the door to the moving room slid shut.

The arc of a metal railing guarded her against a perilous fall, and leaning over it, Caralee whistled at the view. Below, she could see the earthen walls of the crater that defined the ducal province proper, created over a hundred years earlier when the ducal palace dropped through the sky and landed here.

The palace—which she had yet to see from the outside—had fallen from the sky with such force that it had plowed straight into the ground, throwing up an enormous circle of earth. The Son's analogy of dropping stones into sand held up.

A little sand pocket would blow away soon enough, but a hundred and thirty years later, the crater that the metal folk had made still scarred the land. Its outline remained a perfect circle, although the bowl inside the ring of earth had filled in and been flattened by time and, more recently, by the metal folk themselves. They'd carpeted their enclosure with green and silver and steel.

Once the metal folk woke up from their hundred-year nap, they tamped the ground down flat for their roads and those sky-pointed cups and their flower beds and fruit patches. The plain they'd made shimmered with the ovals of those sun-bright but focused lights she'd seen earlier in the causeway beneath the palace—the lights weren't witchlights, and they weren't fires. These were brighter by far and shone without so much as a flicker. Caralee had never known that a light could form a beam, and wondered if light was made out of blockums, too. The light beams pointed all kinds of directions, some of which made sense—lighting up buildings, for instance—and some of which didn't make sense, like the moving lights that roved across empty patches of ground and sky.

Someone cleared their throat. Caralee closed her eyes and took a deep breath to steady her annoyance.

"You look like one thing, but you're really another thing, aren't you, Caralee Vinnet?" the falcon-clear voice of Steel Elinor called out from the shadows. Even in a conversational tone, Elinor's voice rang with authority. Had the duke been there the whole time, watching Caralee? That would be creepy, but *of course* she had.

Caralee had treated Elinor with contempt earlier, but despite Caralee's sass and scat, she realized that Steel Elinor might well be the only person alive who could rival the Son of the Vine in power. Caralee should treat Elinor like the Son at his worst, and so she deadened her expression. Caralee pulled on her mask of skin.

"Because you *look,* Caralee Vinnet, like an ordinary young person." Elinor spoke from the shadows. "But you *aren't* an ordinary young person, are you, Caralee Vinnet?"

Elinor stepped into the starlight. Her dark brown shoulders were bare beneath a peach silk blouse and high-waisted trousers in a pale color that caught the light of the evening. In the night, her skin was the color of the precious, rich earth of the Wildest Wood. Whether from face paint or some subtler steel magick, her upper eyeshadow and eyelids looked dusted with silver. Her feet were bare despite the chill. Caralee couldn't feel through her boots, but maybe the floor was warmed, like the seats in the metal caravan. Maybe the duke didn't feel the cold.

Elinor shimmered. Her oval face was smooth and perfect, and her eyes drank all the light, leaving nothing but the night. She was without doubt the most beautiful sight that Caralee had ever seen.

"Tell me, Steel Elinor." Caralee kept her voice as dead as her expression, remembering to answer questions with questions, or at least answer them at odd angles. "What's 'ordinary' for a half-metal duke who fell from the stars?"

"You prove my point." Elinor smiled and held her hands palms up. "Would an ordinary young person act so at ease, alone in the clutches of a half-metal duke who fell from the stars?"

*No reason to answer that.*

"Would an ordinary young person, as I understand it, cross the world to save a mere friend?"

"*Mere?*" Caralee asked, taken aback.

"I told you that I wasn't sentimental."

"Actually, you shouted it at me while screaming filth at me and my friends, threatening to whatever me with your whatever jets, and calling us divvils and witches. How unsentimental can a person be when they're throwing a tantrum?"

"But you *are* a witch, Caralee." Elinor ignored Caralee's observation.

"*I'm* a witch?" Elinor's backward thinking continued to unnerve Caralee. "You *grow metal swords* and you *fell from the sky.*"

Elinor said nothing. She was certainly convenient with the truth.

"Look," Caralee began, "I'm not trying to be a scathole, but you can't honestly expect me to believe a word you say. All this?" She waved her hand toward the land below, where bright lights punctured the night and soldiers scurried back and forth. "This is real interesting stuff. And you're impressive. I'm impressed. Look at how impressed I am." Caralee pointed at her own blank face.

"Thank you." Elinor humored Caralee with a small smile.

"Shatterscat. Of course your shiny alien city is impressive. You don't seem like a moron, so I'm sure you know that. Instead of trying to dazzle someone who doesn't much want to know you, why don't you just get to the point. Please."

Elinor shook her head, and her smile grew. "Someone has taught you *well.* Was it your demon familiar? Your tutor, broken in mind and body? Or perhaps your handsome friend, who was entirely too pleased at allowing himself to be taken prisoner?"

"You make a lotta assumptions." Caralee balled her fists. "If you only knew what I've faced down, lady, you would shut the fuck up."

"Oh?" Elinor regarded Caralee through lidded eyes. "For the moment, you may relax without fear for yourself or your companions, although I understand you may not take me at my word."

"You kidnapped us."

"You are safer here than anywhere else in your world." Elinor held out her hands like some kind of shield. "I am as human as you are, I swear to you," Elinor said, misreading Caralee's wariness. "'Tis but applied knowledge that separates us, just as it would separate you from the people of the Land of the Vine in its prime."

"I know that you're human," Caralee admitted. "You come from another . . . place we made, or settled, or whatever."

Elinor allowed her eyes to widen. Caralee had just made herself a more difficult rube for Elinor to work over.

"I know a little about our ancestors, yours and mine." Caralee ran her fingers through the dark leaves of the pretty-smelling flowers. "People have stolen suns." The Son had said that. It sounded as awesome and as stupid coming out of her mouth as it had coming out of his. "So what did *you* steal?"

"We didn't steal, we trespassed." Elinor didn't flinch, but she didn't *not* flinch, either. "There *are* monsters, Caralee, and not all of them are human. I thought your world to be a paradise, but you've ruined it, and all I've found are more monsters."

"You know about the Land of the Vine?" Caralee moved to the railing, the sky full of nighttime colors.

"Only through tales passed down through time and from records that are, by now, only semi-historical." Elinor looked to the stars. "Tales of marvels from the early days of humanity's Grand Diaspora, if they can be believed. Now we can believe the tale of the Glass Gardens."

Elinor's words cast Caralee's imagination reeling into an abyss.

"What—where did we all come from?"

Elinor stifled a laugh. "I'm sorry, I'm not laughing at you. It's just so rarely does that question have an answer.

"I'll do my best," Elinor stroked a jeweled loc, her silver-shadowed eyes unreadable. "My best, yes. Once, there was a world where our kind were born. Evolved, if by some chance you should understand what that means." She leaned against the rail to share Caralee's view of the stars. "We left our home to follow a thousand different paths to a thousand different homes. For the most part, we have settled so far away from one another that we may each seem to be alone in the universe."

*Universe.* Caralee couldn't wrap her head around much of that but was immediately gripped by the legend. One world, then many, fanning across the *stars.*

"You really cracked the sky?"

"We did." There wasn't a note of shame in her voice, but responsibility—plain and unaffected.

"You came from outside? Outside the sky? Outside the sky that you cracked?" Caralee found that as she clarified her question, she better prepared herself for its answer.

"I did. We did. 'Twas our arrival that compromised your habitat—your sky."

"Some nerve, telling me that *we* ruined our paradise, when you don't even know the story *and* you're the ones who broke the scatting sky."

Elinor took a breath, but Caralee didn't let her use it to speak.

"You gonna fix it? The sky?"

The duke lifted her eyebrows and turned away, as if to agree that the question was a good one. "When we escaped the destruction of our home, we reached out to the sky for a new place to live. You must understand that this was ages ago, Caralee. Thousands of years we slept as this vessel crossed the void to our neighbor, an emerald paradise beneath an oval dome, set atop an orbital station half as long as a moon . . ."

Caralee wondered what a moon was.

"Imagine our despair upon waking." Elinor clenched her jaw—her frustration wasn't feigned. "Thirty-four years of desperation. Paradise all but dead. Your world will limp along until it dries up and freezes solid."

Caralee understood what the duke implied. Elinor didn't want this world; why would she save it?

"Our voyage took tens of centuries. We slept."

"And when you landed here," Caralee said, "instead of the Land of the Vine, you found *us*."

"We found a dying world—but not a dead one." Elinor laced her fingers together and looked at her hands. "To you, we may seem splendid, even mighty—"

"I didn't say that. Who said that? Did anyone *actually* say that?"

Elinor cut eyes at Caralee with a little smile of victory. "An ordinary person would say that, Caralee Vinnet. A person not trained in the extraordinary. A person not fed stories of stolen suns . . . stories of which we have found no evidence in this world's present. Perhaps you've learned from an older source . . ."

"You don't know everything." Caralee's heart beat faster. This was close.

"Too true. Neither my capabilities nor my resources are infinite. This world faces imminent ecological collapse, and now, thanks to me, it's bleeding atmosphere. My people could help, yes. . . . Or we could *leave* and pray to find another home. If we do commit to this world, I *must* know its every instability. Its history and its present condition." Elinor spoke with fervor, but also a clear vision. "The truth is, I haven't decided whether this world is worth saving."

"You want to know if you can live here or if you should run." Caralee accepted that. "If I could run, I'd wonder the same thing."

"So you understand." Elinor dropped her voice, nodding once, and reached out to rest her hand on Caralee's arm. Wherever this conversation was headed, Elinor was steering it to a particular destination.

"I've another story to tell you," Elinor said. "Before I show you to your room."

*I know you do.* Caralee didn't know just what the story would be, only that it would appear to be a confession, something personal, and that Elinor would use it to try to get what she really wanted out of Caralee.

"When I was young, my world was beautiful."

*You were bad, weren't you, Elinor?*

"Nothing like the Land of the Vine, of course—or what you see of us here in the crater, for that matter. Here we make do. My home—Meroë—was a planet of mountains that looked as if it were painted with the colors of flowers. We build cities from rose gold spun no thicker than my locks. The labyrinth-continent of bismuth, where the metal lead was forbidden. Clear lakes still as mirrors beneath snowy peaks carved with the faces of my family."

*And you need to tell me* all *about it.*

"Worlds ago and ages past, I was not so different from you. Powerful, though I felt it not. The most dangerous symptom of youth, which is doubt, plagued me always. Truth be told, it plagues me still. One never conquers doubt, but if one remains vigilant, one can hold it at bay." Elinor took a breath. "Doubt brings disaster."

"It does?" A lifetime and a week ago, Caralee might have been entranced by this outright sentimental bid to lower her emotional wall. Now, Caralee knew better. "Yeah, I guess it does."

Elinor opened her palm, fingers adorned with rings of a half dozen different metals. Without a tingle of sandysense, Elinor's rings sprouted wires as thin as hairs. The wires spiraled around each other as they rose up from her hand and wove together into the shape of a tower, a plain circular tower with a flat top and little square teeth across the roof.

Then Elinor curled her fingers, the wires unwound, and the metal returned to her rings exactly as it had emerged.

"Our arts were perfect. We built a heaven of metal and mountaintops, and the members of my family were its keepers. Only we work metal without a forge. The gift is in our blood."

*That's how she made her sword out of her hip-guard.*

The Steel Duke nodded with her head and shoulders, leaning on the rail. "Twelve devils there were—are—who sought to undo what we had wrought. They were not demons of the dark, but devils of the bright daylight. The Twelve of Morning, they are called, and hundreds of years before I was born my ancestors trapped them in a clockwork vault, on the mountain beside our family hold."

*A dozen demons trapped next to your home? What could possibly go wrong?*

"All of my young life, I had been warned of the grave charge that accompanied our family's gift, for we were jailors of forces which, if released, might unmake the world. We guarded the prison of the Twelve of Morning. We had warnings not to profane it. But the dancing metal moved so beautifully, like mist, like limbs . . ." Elinor let her words trail off a little too artfully, and Caralee realized that Elinor had given this speech before.

"The clocks burst open at the barest brush of my fingers through the air. I didn't even touch the lock, you see—just passed my blood-cursed hand through an open space of its endless swirling. Oh, it danced! And then the mountain shook, and I saw the horror I unleashed. The Twelve of Morning erupted from their prison and cracked the continent with the force of their escape."

Elinor pointed to an ugly scar underneath her upper arm. "Rosy-Fingered Slaughter, the devil of the dawn hour, caught me in her claws and held me close with four of her arms. She howled cruel laughter into my ear and forced me to watch five of the six cities upon our mountain home collapse beneath the twelvefold terror I had unleashed. The Twelve of Morning are sleepless, and they live for murder—if they can be said to be truly alive. Slaughter dropped me at the steps to the ducal palace—this palace—perched at the lip of newly shorn cliffs. Even in their chaos, the twelve invented new cruelties. My city had not fallen, and harbored what remained of our navy. I abandoned my family and fled, and now I am the last of the metalbloods.

"I was safe; my world burned. It happened in a trice, faster than you can think it." Elinor took a breath. "We seized our flagship and abandoned our world as it burned. We put ourselves to sleep, and when we woke, we were here. No one punished me. No one yelled, or hit me. There was no time, and no reason—I was duke. Father died with the mountain. Rosy-Fingered Slaughter was cruel to save me."

Another rehearsed look to the sky, and Caralee wondered whether Elinor's story was true. Did she deserve Caralee's sympathy at all?

"'Twas a child's error, a simple thing, but it killed everyone I ever loved. I ignored dire warnings, and it destroyed my world."

Caralee gave Elinor the moment of silent reflection she'd crafted.

"That's a sad story. It is." Caralee tried not to sound like a scathole, but she had to navigate this mess and was losing what patience she had. "And I'm super sorry that you destroyed everything, and hey, aren't we both just two women up here on a palace ship having a little chat about our jazzed-up worlds? It's nice." Caralee strained a smile. "Thing is: I'm not you; I didn't do anything to my world; we don't have hidden demons; and please, please just tell me what you want from me. These games give me a headache, and *I'm not interested*."

"Who did? Break your world, I mean." Elinor exhaled.

"Ask around." Caralee pulled back. "We got some stories. What do you think about them?"

Elinor ignored that too perfectly.

*Hmm.*

"Your . . . companion, Sazerac. He is no threat? He does not seek to bleed humanity dry? Perhaps now you understand our vigilance? Why I acted with such . . . concern?"

Caralee put her hand on her chest. "On my *life,* Saz is not a world-murdering scathole. He's sweet, and he's sworn to protect me. He thinks I own him."

Elinor kept still, looking over her dukedom from thirty stories up. "Good," she said after some time.

*Ugh.*

"I've one more question, and then I'll show you to your quarters."

"Okay." Caralee felt ready to sleep for days.

"I *have* heard the stories about the collapse of this world. Were it not for my own crime, I would not credit the tales." She pointed to the west. "Yet there is nothing natural about your wasteland. You, Caralee, know things that the rest of your world does not—that intrigues me. Tell me, what truly befell your world? The Son of the Vine—is he real?"

*There it is. That's what she wants.* Caralee felt insulted but not surprised. This had never been about her at all—why would it be? One world-dooming narcissist sussing out another. *And that's why the Son put me here instead of himself. He has to hide from her. I have to help him.* Caralee couldn't imagine what would happen to them all if Elinor caught on to the Son's true identity the way Thombthumb seemed to have done.

"You don't really *believe* that old ghost story, do you?" Caralee laughed with all her exhaustion, turning it to her purpose. She went slaphappy, like she had when she'd first met the Son—letting the ideas of what Elinor would do to them fuel a kind of crazy, unstoppable river of laughter. Caralee bent over, crying, and found that she really couldn't stop. Her sides hurt, and her head grew light, and Elinor looked at her like Caralee was a broken doll, which made the fact that Caralee was the one who was in control all the funnier . . . until she stopped, and wiped her eyes, and her breathing returned to normal.

"Sorry," Caralee lied. "It's just that it's such a stupid idea, no matter what stories people tell to scare each other. One brat prince *can't* ruin the world like that. You don't seem stupid, but hey, folk are fulla surprises."

Elinor's expression flickered with the impulsive passion she'd shown earlier with her sword in hand. That tiny blockum of emotion was the first unrehearsed moment of the whole bizarre back-and-forth terrace game that Elinor played.

"I mean, sorry if that's what *you* did? But around here we don't build things so that one little kid can kill everyone. It just doesn't fit with our, like, design sensibilities?"

Elinor clenched a fist. "Tell me true. Does the Son of the Vine still walk the world, as your people fear?"

Caralee shrugged, then smiled as wide as she could. "I hope not! He's not *real,* Duke Steel Elinor. Our Vine died. Everything dies, Duke. Everything ends in its time." Quoting the Son again.

"Thank you, Caralee." Elinor nodded and unclenched her fist, worrying her knuckles. Whether she believed Caralee or not was an open question, but it was clear that Elinor believed in the existence of the Son and that his crimes were history, not fiction. "In your journey east, you have not heard or seen anything at all of this 'brat' prince? Or, if not, any remainder of his age?"

"No." Caralee shook her head and held her hands behind her back in case they got nervous. "Nothing at all. People only ever tell the same old story, and it never changes. I haven't seen anything from way back then but standing stones and treebones."

"Thank you, Caralee." Elinor's expression was impenetrable. "Thank you for your honesty."

Elinor kept her peace as she and Caralee took the moving room down to the twenty-third floor. The door opened onto a corridor tiled with interlocking blocks of black and white ceramic. Caralee supposed that designing a palace was its own discipline: everything in the ducal palace seemed round, but it wasn't really a palace, was it? It was some kind of ship. Again, Caralee wished that she could see it properly from the outside, and also she wondered where the flags were.

*This palace flew through the void.* The void was hard to imagine. A ship in the void was even harder—what would traveling through nothingness feel like? She would try to sketch it later, anyway. If Elinor ever let them leave, Caralee would draw everything she'd seen in the ducal crater.

The door to Caralee's room slid open at their approach. Elinor waved for Caralee to enter.

*This is my cage.*

The room was a hollow block of metal, but curved like a keystone. The far wall was cushioned black fabric with silver studs, like the three-legged bench she'd sat on earlier, and the other walls were a simple white that wasn't metal or ceramic. A sloped recess in one wall held a mattress with thick white pillows and a fluffy gray blanket.

"The privy is behind that panel. Just press to open. And you can close your door by tapping here, against the frame. Our furnishings are stark, but I'm certain you will find them comfortable." Elinor hesitated. "We will speak more tomorrow."

"Thank you, Duke Steel Elinor." Caralee wasn't lying, not technically. Elinor had answered some of Caralee's questions, after all.

"'Tis my pleasure, Caralee Vinnet."

"There's just one thing that I've been meaning to ask."

"Of course." Elinor smiled. Caralee put her hand on Elinor's arm exactly the way Elinor had done on the terrace above, and the duke's smile slipped.

"Why did you put your metal inside that harpy?"

The look on Elinor's face was a treasure that Caralee would keep forever. The duke opened her mouth but said nothing.

"It's just, now that you've told me your story—how you, you know? Unleashed twelve metal divvils? And how they destroyed your world?" Caralee stepped into her room, turned around, and held her finger to her chin. "I gotta wonder why a woman so ashamed of unleashing monsters would go and do that, a second time, on a second world?"

"Pardon?"

"Your steely harpy. I killed it."

"You—" True shock shattered Elinor's mask. The duke looked stunned, then sad—deeply sad.

"—cleaned up your mess. Fought off your monster." Caralee couldn't figure why Elinor was sad. "What did you send it flying off to do, shake hands? It killed people, and I melted it to slag." Caralee didn't mind the lie, and the Son had already given her credit for the kill.

Elinor held her hands against her chest. "I didn't . . . I meant—I only—"

"I, I, I. Always about *you*." All of the Son's wicked talk about owning the world came hand in hand with talk of restoring it, but Elinor's games seemed personal. "Why are *you* playing with monsters instead of leading your people?"

Caralee had no idea what it meant to "lead" anybody's "people," but she could imagine what would've happened to Joe and herself if Mag hadn't been around to feed them and teach them how not to get themselves killed.

All of a sudden, Elinor didn't look sad at all, but terrified. "It was a mistake. I needed a weapon, and I . . ." Her voice was tiny, a child's. "You must understand. If *he* exists—if the Son of the Vine somehow lives—I must find him. I must crush him."

*What?*

Caralee bit back her surprise. She took a deep breath and tapped the side of the doorway, closing the door in Elinor's face.

# 14

Caralee had never slept in utter darkness before, and her sleep was dreamless but not featureless, layered with a sense of floating in a cradle of nothingness, neither hot nor cold but safe in sleep's senselessness. Above, below, all around her—empty silence. If there were walls or ceilings or creatures they were as far away as the stars, in every direction. She was alone with her beating heart in the black.

Then the door to her room slid open, and the cool light from the hall cut through the pitch and woke Caralee at once. The Son leaned against the doorway, his long hair hanging over his eyes. Without the sky by which to judge, Caralee had no idea what hour it could be. Her head felt stuffed with cable hay—she must have needed sleep badly, but that came as no surprise.

"Pssst," he psssted.

"Huh?" Caralee scrubbed her face with her woolly sleeves, stitching together the memory of who and where she was. Sleep had been *good*.

"Rise and shine, wee diplomat!" sang out the Son. "It's time to wake up."

"I'm up. Look at me, I'm up. I see you. Look at me, seeing you." She fussed with her hair, gave up, and was glad that she'd fallen asleep with her clothes on. "How did you get here? Did you follow the train?"

"Elinor's a liar. They put us in the caboose. That's the last cart." He looked behind him, down either side of the curved hallway. "You slept in your boots?"

Caralee snorted and shouldered her satchel. She'd passed out without sketching a single insane thing.

Outside, in the looping hallway, three guards lay unmoving on the black-and-white-tiled floor. Eusebius huddled just beyond the door, eyes wide and staring at the bodies. When he saw Caralee, he showed his yellowed teeth in a smile that cracked the caked-on makeup at the corners of his mouth.

"Oho." Eusebius nodded politely, holding one rickety finger to his white-painted lips to mime silence. He clocked the corridor, up and down, before giving one of the guards a kick to the face. The wizard winced through a grin.

"So much for metal?" Caralee stepped over the bodies, wondering how many shekels she could get off one of their helmets.

"Relax, they're not dead," the Son attempted to reassure Caralee, who just then needed nothing of the sort. "Just a little asphyxiated."

"Son, I gotta fess up. About not killing people? I think I've turned a corner." Caralee didn't care about the guards. She'd happily burn this shiny, cold palace to the ground. "You can kill *everyone* if it gets me outta here. Or even if it doesn't. Buncha scatholes."

"Really?" The Son looked less grumpy at the thought. "You have? I *can*?"

"Most kind sir? Which way do we go, I very much wonder?" Eusebius held a jittery vigil over the corridor. "Up or down?" he wondered aloud.

"Caralee, there are terraces and repurposed docking ports above—can you find one?" The Son had his sandysense up and ready. "Anything open to the air."

"Left or right?" Eusebius continued on his own.

"You don't have a way out?" Caralee pressed the Son.

"Within . . . or without?"

"I do, damn it—the way out is a terrace or an open docking port. The longer we spend searching, the more we risk a full alarm—"

"Backward or forward?" Eusebius muttered to a green flame.

"Silence, you waste of biomass!" the Son hissed, and poor Eusebius jumped back. The sound echoed down the coiled hallway.

"Yeah, okay, I have an idea." Caralee just wanted out. "Yeah, um . . . this way. If I can find the moving room, there's a terrace that Elinor took me to, seven floors up. I mean, I guess it's a terrace . . . We could look around, but—"

"We don't have time, miss," Eusebius wheezed.

"Yeah, I figured." She looked at him, white-faced and earnest. "You okay? They hurt you?"

"Oh, don't you worry about me. Your tutor knows a little something about self-preservation, yes, I do." Eusebius blinked—an exaggerated event upon his painted face. His thoughts turned away from the moment, and Eusebius hummed to himself. "*Save the little wretch, wretch, ohhh save the little wretch, wretch from the big metal betch, betch . . .*"

The Son glared at Eusebius. That wasn't one of Caralee's songs.

"Naw." Caralee grinned, leading the way to the moving room. "You did *not*."

"Fine," the Son growled at Caralee. "You've softened me up. I fucking sang to him."

Caralee snickered, pointing the way she'd come with Elinor the night before. "Elinor brought me up. I could see the whole crater from there, almost. That what we want?"

The Son scrubbed his hair with his hands. "It will have to do. This ship is huge, and I still can't get my bearings."

Caralee headed toward the moving room. Thanks to the curve of the hallway and its sourceless light, Caralee felt like she was walking in place—while exposed, at that. There were no corners to hide behind, just the endless curve that seemed to move backward beneath her feet like the climbing staircase in the guts of the palace, but in reverse.

Despite her fear, Caralee felt electric. If this wasn't adventure, what was? She looked back over her shoulder and grinned hugely.

The three hurried down the hallway. She could hear Eusebius's joints pop as they hustled and hoped he wasn't hurting himself. She saw the wrinkle in the wall where the door to the moving room was hidden. There were two of the light-bubble buttons on the outside, one with an arrow pointing up, the other pointing down.

"Here." Caralee held her arms out in victory. "I present to you, the moving room."

"The . . . moving room . . ." The Son flared his nostrils. "It might trigger an alarm. But let me . . ." He pressed Up, and the wall shivered as the moving room rose from below. The door slid open with a chime.

"*Ohhh, that makes sense.*" Caralee clapped her hand to her face. One button told the moving room that you wanted to go *up,* the other, that you wanted to go *down.*

Inside, the Son took a look at the number board and clucked. "Our numerical scripts share a common ancestor. Given our millennia-old population drifts, that's a good sign. These aliens have taught themselves our language, but if we're both using the same numerical script, perhaps we may not be irreconcilably foreign to one another."

The Son tapped the bubble labeled 30, and the door closed, the room rising swiftly.

"Elinor said they came here expecting a green world. She called it the Glass Gardens."

"So she knows her history," the Son grumbled.

"Is that what you called the world, the Glass Gardens?" Caralee rolled the name of her world off her tongue. "Elinor said that her lot slept for thousands of years while their ship sailed, so they're *all* older than anyone alive, including you."

If the Son had any response, he kept it to himself and sighed with relief when the moving room stilled and the door opened to the sweet-flowered terrace where Elinor had interrogated Caralee. She was surprised to see that it was still nighttime.

"Have we arrived, then?" Eusebius hobbled out of the moving room. His hand was clammy as Caralee took it. "*Wretch, wretch!*" he sang, smiling at her and wiggling his fingers to either side like a busker. "*Betch, betch!*"

The sky was still dark, but the eastmost corner had began to glow. Still, the lights and gardens of the Metal Duchy outshone the stars above for brilliance. Caralee figured there could only be one good reason to reach open air when they were this high up. She pointed past the railing. "You *didn't* forget about Sunny, did you? Or Saz?"

"Spot on, Caralee." He winked.

"Sunny?" The Son snapped his fingers. "Your cue."

Rising like a sweet black moon with an indigo crater, Sazerac's head hovered into view at the railing. Beneath his splayed legs flew none other than Sunny the Carpet, flat as a board, her tassels dancing in the wind.

"I thought you said that Sunny answered only to me?" Caralee wasn't above complaining, even while escaping from a crazy alien starship.

The Son pulled a mock-sheepish expression. "It turns out that I have a way of persuading those who otherwise answer only to you."

Eusebius nodded enthusiastically. "It is true, Caralee! The most kind sir has indeed explained that, though you might initially protest, my aid facilitating the exchange will, in fact—"

"Shut. Up," the Son cut him off.

*What is Eusebius talking about?*

"What exchange?" Caralee asked, distracted.

"Nothing." The Son waved away the question. "Sazerac wouldn't leave without you, that's all—until I explained that we weren't leaving you. He got a little dramatic. You know how he gets when it comes to you."

Then Sunny the Carpet did the strangest thing. She raised one of her front corners and waved hello to Caralee.

Caralee waved back.

"Sunny!" Eusebius called out gladly, then turned to Caralee. "We're a-flying today, you know."

Caralee clapped him on the arm, wobbling the taper attached to his shoulder pad.

"How'd you bust Saz out?" she asked the Son. "Figured he'd be under, like, *all* the guards."

"Well . . ." The Son bit his knuckle and grimaced. "Remember when you said I could kill everyone?" He batted his eyelashes. "I might have started already."

*Right.* "Like I said, I don't care. I hope they suffered."

The Son looked pleased, briefly, then laced his hands low and offered them to Eusebius to step upon. Caralee held the wizard's hand as he put one foot up onto the Son's hands and then, with some difficulty, turned around and sat on the carpet. Caralee lifted his legs one at a time onto Sunny's pile. Saz lent a hand as well, and scooted Eusebius toward the center of the carpet. The Son hopped to the front, but made room beside him for Caralee. With a glance over her shoulder to make sure they hadn't been followed, Caralee scrambled aboard her carpet friend, who had waved hello.

"Avoid the lights as best you can, Caralee, then press east fast." The Son pointed toward the shimmering dawn that already pushed away the bruised night. "You'll see the three mountains soon enough."

Caralee angled Sunny toward the east. The Duchy's searching lights waved across the sky and the ground, but not so quickly that Caralee couldn't wind between them, she gauged. Caralee had a thought.

"Wait." She cocked her head at the Son. "Did you get any of the answers you were looking for? I mean, about the sky and stuff?"

"Some. Not enough. However, I did slaughter two dozen of their people, so we should probably shove off for now and worry about diplomacy later."

"Can you still get what you want after you killed all those people?" It sounded dicey.

"Caralee, that's what diplomacy *is*."

Caralee thought that diplomacy seemed to be an awfully convenient lot of things, but she did her duty and shoved off all the same, the carpet drifting away from the terrace before picking up some speed. Sunny seemed to know to stay out of the light, or she knew that staying out of the light was what Caralee wanted.

The carpet showed more and more evidence of a personality, which made Caralee wonder if Sunny was similar to Saz, but mute. Saz seemed . . . unique? And the Son and Eusebius both had referred to Sunny as if there were—or had been—more than one, but maybe they were alike in some way. Could magick bring objects to life—or put life into objects?

Now that Caralee thought about it, hadn't the Son's soul been put into stone by magick? He used some kind of magick to transfer himself between bodies, so at least some of these things did happen.

She wondered what type of magick could move a man's soul. How did he turn ordinary people into his full-body flesh masks?

Caralee brought Sunny as high as she dared, to avoid the lights, and sped away from the Duchy as fast as possible. The metal land rushed past them, while the sky remained constant.

Sunny flew over the ring of earth that was all that remained of the crater the metal folk had made when they landed. For a moment, at a safe distance from the Metal Duchy bristling with its sharp lights and steely armaments, Caralee carefully turned herself around on the carpet to see the ducal palace in its full glory. It did not disappoint.

The palace stood as several smaller towers cleaved to a single central tower of silver-white metal, fat and massive at the base, bulging outward before arcing to an array of slender rods high, high above. Judging by the dark lines of the terraces, they'd been less than halfway to the top of the palace when they flew away.

Caralee was awestruck by the round pointiness of the palace, its tower, and the ring of similar towers that surrounded it, each attached by arms of black metal. The dawn—which rose behind the direction in which Caralee was facing—though Sunny the Carpet flew toward the dawn—lit the complex into full relief: surrounding the central towers was a second ring of lower buildings that leaned out and away from the center. They looked more like petals than towers and were attached to the inner ring by still more black metal braces.

Caralee wondered if those arms could move, and if they'd pull the rings of towers into its bulk, like babes to the teat. If the palace was a ship, maybe it could move its towers at will, to soar through the sky and the void beyond them.

Despite Elinor's unwelcome welcome, Caralee wished she'd had time and freedom to explore its bowels and its heights. Maybe with the diplomacy, she would be able to. She turned her attention back to flying and lowered them from this insane height.

"Good, a lower altitude will make us harder to see at a distance—but don't slow us, not yet." The Son approved of the maneuver, then looked to Caralee for acknowledgment, and she nodded.

"I was wondering," Caralee asked him, "how'd you get Sazerac to follow you, and what else did you sing to Eusebius?"

The Son smiled, which told Caralee that she wouldn't get the straight answer. "We had a chat together, the three of us. Didn't we, Sazerac?"

"Yes, Most Holy," Sazerac said. It seemed impossible that such a massive stone man could sit, splayed so casually, on Sunny's back end, but the carpet bore his weight as easily as she carried the rest of them.

Eusebius dithered, shaking, looking this way and that but never toward the Son. His forest-green candles burned as still as if there were no wind at all, whispering some of himself back into his damaged brain.

"I suppose we're all glad to be away from her?" the Son cajoled his fellow carpet fliers. "We don't need her and her starship, do we?" He rallied himself, but glared at the stars. "We'll fix the sky ourselves."

Ahead of them ran a lifeless stretch of stone called the Deadsteppes, which wasn't as dangerous as the wasteland, largely because it was too lifeless to harbor much danger. In the distance were two jagged mountains. The morning rose behind them, and the Son distributed some sausages.

"Biddle Becky's best," he said through a mouthful.

Caralee agreed, taking a bite of the hard gray mince, although for once, she had little appetite.

"Oho! What is this?" Eusebius clucked himself together again. After he'd listened to his candles, he smiled at Caralee with that empty, almost goony look. His new memories drifted further away, a little bit with every nap. Eusebius's fondness for Caralee, however, didn't drift. Even when his mind was empty, his heart knew her face and her name. It was hard for Caralee to believe that they'd ever been at odds. Her face felt hot with shame when she remembered how she'd hated him.

The wizard hummed. Caralee hoped he was remembering some of the bread crumb trail of jingle-facts that she or the Son had sung for him.

"That metal duke cut a dashing figure, don't you think?" Eusebius asked and nodded, agreeing with himself. "I don't like her one bit, *not at all*—but I will admit, she cut quite the figure, all silver and steel and thighs up to—" He cleared his throat. The bedraggled sandymancer didn't seem to need any help remembering Elinor's thighs. "I must say, however, that I think she is an unhappy person. I don't care at all for the way she treated Caralee. In fact, it made me feel bad." He crossed his arms, sort of.

The Son laughed at that. "Better that she toy with Caralee and give me the opportunity to case the palace alone, without baggage."

"Just so, quite indeed!" Eusebius nodded exaggeratedly, like his neck bones had gone floppity. "Indeed quite, so just!" He cocked his head toward the Son.

"Most kind sir, did your most ancient and dire self discover anything of substance? It's possible that I might have done so myself, but I am afraid that if so, I have forgotten again." He looked off to one side, where low but jagged hills obscured the northerly lands. Somewhere, kilometers to the northwest, lay the Sevenfold Redoubt—the home of the sandymancers—and beyond that, another city with another school that taught everything *except* sandymancy. West of those were the Jazzfoot Shallows—miles and miles of brackish swampland.

Caralee had reached the limit of her knowledge of the world. The rest she'd have to see for herself.

"Discoveries? I made some." The Son's eyes were bright with a rollicking, jolly anger. "For one, the reason that the Duchy's resources are stretched thin is that they did not *land* here, they crashed. They managed a controlled crash, or we'd all be very, very dead, but doing so crushed the ship's drives. A number of other systems that would prove crucial to interstellar travel as well—maneuvering thrusters, carbon dioxide scrubbers, fuel reserves. Whatever choices she's weighing, leaving this world isn't one of them."

"That *ent* what she said!" Caralee cursed, annoyed. "She said she had a choice to make."

"It's not surprising that she lied, Caralee. You should not be surprised by that." The Son turned away. "She *is* weighing her choices, though; that was no lie."

Caralee supposed that he was right. Diplomacy was trickier than blockums or witchlights or Auld Vintage.

"I'll tell you what ent surprising—is that she talked about herself nonstop. It was all 'Oh, it's all my fault that we're here and so you should trust me,' which is plain nonsense."

"Absolute power bores absolutely. I should know. What did she ask you?"

"After she finished her own story, which took a *while*—then she pretended we were just two gals out for a stroll halfway up a flying palace. She quizzed me about Saz, but to be honest she didn't seem that worried anymore. When she was finished toying with me—"

"What did you tell her about Sazerac?"

"I told her the truth, that he's a new friend and that he ent bad."

The Son raised a devastating eyebrow.

"Look, before you start"—Caralee held out her hands—"Saz hasn't hurt anyone and he's nicer than we are. He just *looks* scary. But do I think he's tough? Sure. Do I think he can pack a mean punch if I'm in trouble? You betcha."

They locked eyes, and the Son kept his peace. Not for the first time, Caralee wondered how this could possibly end for her. Flying this far east, they couldn't have much farther to go before they found the Son's birthplace or ran out of land, and Caralee felt no closer to saving Joe than she'd been at the start.

"I am glad to hear you speak kindly of me, Caralee." Saz spoke up; his voice was gentle thunder. "I have never liked being dangerous. I enjoy everyone, my owner the most. I am loyal and strong, but I carry no weapon. Protection is a service, but I am happiest when serving peacefully."

"Hey, you *don't* carry a weapon, do you?" Caralee liked that. "You're armored, but not armed. That's on purpose, ennit?"

"I can only speculate, but I do hope so." Saz looked at one of his black boulder hands.

"Sazerac?" asked the Son out of nowhere, and his voice sounded more vulnerable than sly. "What *is* your purpose?"

"Simply to serve," Sazerac answered straightaway. He shrugged his basalt shoulders.

The Son's eyebrows knitted together, amused and impressed with himself, but not surprised. Sazerac couldn't be a Beast—there was nothing beastly about him!

*Lots of people have purpose,* Caralee thought. *Mag and Thombthumb. Even Wet Sam gets up before sunrise to muck out the shatterscat ditch.*

"Anyway, you didn't let me finish about Steel Elinor." Caralee snapped back to the Son. "I was gonna say, the last thing Elinor asked about was *you,* and I was gonna say—that's one of only two things she gave a scat about."

"What did she ask about me, and what did you tell her?" The shift in the Son's attention was subtle, but Caralee could see through his masks now, sometimes.

"Well, she asked if you were real, which is something that, like, everyone wants to know. She asked what happened to the world—I gave her the answer I'd have given her before I met you." Caralee paused. "Then she asked me if I knew you. Which. How did she know? I didn't say anything, but I think she's too paranoid to give it up."

"Well done. Thank you." Whatever the Son thought about that, he didn't let on.

"Like I'm gonna tell her about you—" Caralee scoffed.

"It's considered generous to accept a compliment, Caralee—"

"Yeah, okay. It's considered generous not to steal people's bodies. Why in the world would she think that *I* know *you*? I mean, we're not exactly your average traveling foursome—sorry, Sunny the Carpet, I meant fivesome—but how she got from 'some weirdos' to 'Son of the Vine' seems like a stretch."

The Son tongued his cheek, and his eyes grew heavy-lidded. "Maybe Elinor can smell another noble disgrace," was all he said.

"I want a better answer soon," Caralee said, but talked right on over herself. "Also I'm still not done. About the second thing that Steel Elinor gave a scat about?"

"Ohoho my." Eusebius chuckled, jabbing the air with a finger. "I do *not* like that duke!"

"All I did was, I asked Elinor why she'd made that steel harpy."

The Son barked a laugh and smacked Caralee on the back. "Of course you did!"

Caralee flashed the Son a wild look, and continued, "She steeled-up the harpy, for sure—but she said it was a mistake. She got real sad, and it wasn't like her other masks. She looked like a little girl."

"A *mistake*?" The Son sobered. "And you believe her?"

"I didn't say that exactly, but . . . her reaction was honest." Just thinking about Elinor made Caralee mad. "I dunno what she's about, but she didn't expect to hear about the harpy from me, and when she did, it embarrassed her. When I told her that it was dead, she looked at *me* like *I* was the creep from beyond the sky." Caralee hesitated. Elinor had confirmed a theory that the Son had had regarding the harpy's killing spree. "And she said she did it to find *you*. She said that if you were real, she wanted to be able crush you if she decided that's what needed doing."

The Son kneaded his forehead, saying nothing, giving nothing.

Sazerac's shoulders stirred, and he rolled his boulder head to look at the stars.

Below Sunny the Carpet's dancing tassels, the Deadsteppes raced past, a series of featureless stone plateaus that climbed northeastward. Only the morning sun relieved the steppes of their suffocating lifelessness—painting the flat stone with gold and purple. By the time that morning grew into daylight, though, the display of colors had faded back to gray.

Eusebius asked for more sausages, and Caralee took one as well, appetite or no appetite.

"Caralee!" Saz spoke up. "Ahead."

From the severity of the Deadsteppes, a road had emerged—almost impossible to see at first, just a line of flat rock that was slightly lighter than the rest. As the road grew easier to see—it was cut into the bedrock and was a lighter, yellowish color—Caralee brought Sunny the Carpet low enough to see that the road had been cut and bricked as well, and looking down its length, the brick road led straight to the two mountains that were no longer on the horizon, but at a middle distance.

Beyond the two mountains, in a haze of heat and distance, a third mountain rose—though at places it seemed to do unmountainly things, like grow towers, and at other places, it didn't seem to exist at all. Maybe it was an illusion of distance and light.

"You can see the third mountain now, or what we made of it," the Son said without needing to point. "Keep us close to the road, and fly *straight through* the passage no matter what."

Caralee nodded. "What kind of 'what' are we talking about?"

"The kind we've all faced down, except for Sazerac."

"Pardon, Caralee's friend?" Saz asked—friendly, obedient, and not at all intimidating, no matter what people thought at first sight.

"He means a harpy, Saz," Caralee growled into the wind. Facing monsters *that she expected to face,* which made a big difference, and doing so with friends at her back—well, if she was going to die trying to save Joe, this would be how Caralee would choose to do it.

"Harpies? Harpies are fictional creatures from primary-world mythologies," Saz said, confused. "Finding a mythological fable here is . . . unlikely."

"Ent no fable." Caralee shook her head. "We've seen 'em."

Saz dropped his head a bit, and Caralee wasn't sure he believed her.

"Consider the human tendency to assign the names of preexisting archetypes to novel phenomena." The Son spoke to Sazerac in what Caralee was sure was perfectly clear language, if you were an ancient god-king or an ancient Sazerac. "Consider the druids, for instance, whose power was stolen from a distant star and who bear little resemblance to their ancient Earthbound namesakes. Consider the Metal Duchy—in ancient times, long before humanity found the stars, dukes were suzerains to their kings, and a duchy was a fixed measurement of land, the management of which fell to the duke. Our Elinor has no relation to any of these long-dead kingdoms; at some point, her ancestors adopted a system of government that was merely patterned after the original."

"So Caralee is not mistaken or lying?" Sazerac sounded happy about that, rather than disturbed about the *scatting harpy,* which Caralee now knew was the creation of two of what the Son called Beasts of Care, which were monsters that took care of the world.

*Not monsters*—beasts. *The Beasts of Care. Taking care of us is their purpose.* Caralee understood the Son now and some of what he thought of himself. *Whether its name is the Beast of Blood or the Beast of Wind or the Beast of Scat, the Beasts exist to tend to the world and the people in it.* That's *why the Son is so down on being called a monster: he thinks he's a Beast of Care. Or he wants to.*

Caralee chewed over that thought and notions of Beasts and care as noon grew to afternoon. Eventually, she asked for more sausages. The mountains were close enough to loom overhead, and the thoroughfare between them, a gate of shadows.

Twofinger Pass had been a narrow ditch between two craggy outcrops, but Caralee wasn't surprised to see that the ends of the world held surprises for her: the pass wasn't a craggy *pass* at all but a beautiful broadening of the road, cut and hewn where the toes of two mountains met.

The road was carved straight through, wide enough for giants, and where it passed through the slopes of each mountain, walls were cut on either side as sheer and perfect as the golden road itself. The walls of the road rose high here and low there, but hadn't been leveled at their tops—instead, they rose and dropped without symmetry from one wall to the other, cross sections of the hewn mountains.

The eerie quiet spooked Caralee—the empty hugeness of the road, and the ghostly silent Deadsteppes that surrounded them. Caralee had never seen a road this square-cut, and out here where no one could use it . . . The mountains and their road gave Caralee chills.

Caralee flew Sunny down the long, straight road to their destination—taking the straight shot the road gave them. There was no point in trying to hide now. The sun was up, directly overhead—*It's noon already?*—and anything lurking in those mountains would be able to track them easily.

This was it—this was where the Son had been headed since he'd stolen Joe. Since before, even, and yet he'd given Caralee *so little* about this moment.

Thinking back on the Son's palm-map of the world, she and he had circumscribed less than one-eighth of the world's edge, from pinkie finger to middle finger, always a few days away from the true end: the barrier mountains to the south, the Morning Glory Sea to the east—perhaps some of that sea lay beyond these three mountains. Maybe the seabed ended at a clear wall, like the sky—and beyond the wall, the void.

Caralee had said she'd follow the Son to the edge of the world if she had to. Instead, she'd followed him *around* the edge of the world.

*A mountain near the edge of the world, where the Son was born and where two Beasts are stuck together making the harpy, over and over again. Whatever could go wrong?*

"The harpy," Caralee said to the Son. "This is where it keeps coming from? Is this where Blood and Wind got caught up in each other?"

"Yes." The Son clipped a nod and kept his eyes fixed ahead. "I believed they nested in this region. With the Vine at Lastgrown, I was able to confirm their exact location. The Beast of Blood traveled as far east as this place, then farther to the sea. The harpy was first seen out here, and continues to be, though it ranges farther afield. As a corruption of the Beast of Wind, it will prefer a high altitude, and as a degradation of the Beast of Blood, it is likely to gravitate toward any remainder of the Child of the Vine." He paused. "I didn't understand, earlier, but the harpy seeks my *aid*, not to harm me. The instincts of the Beasts will send it to me for help, for commands, even if the harpy is incapable of understanding its own behavior. Elinor is less clever than she believes."

"Most kind sir—"

"We may now at last dispense with the euphemisms and aliases, Eusebius. Sazerac."

"Yes . . . Most Holy." Eusebius bobbed his torso, trying to bow with his body—his leaf-green tapers flickering. The wizard smiled to himself and then continued, "Are you saying that the harpy has been hunting you?"

The Son raised his hands over his head and looked to the sky, maybe for answers. "In my long absence, the harpy may have gravitated toward a *place* it associated with the Child of the Vine, which would be yon palace, where I was born. If any of this is right at all, the palace will be close to where the harpy was born—made—miscarried, whatever—as well."

"You're guessing." Caralee crossed her arms. "And that *mountain* is a palace?"

"My guesses are commensurate with my status, Caralee. I shan't be making shitfarmer mistakes. I will err like a god-king. . . . So, brace yourselves."

"Most Holy, if I may?" Sazerac asked. The Son swept his arm as if to welcome all questions, though he didn't mean it. "If you *are* the harpy's . . . primary attachment, to use the parlance of child psychology—"

"Fine, let's use that parlance. It's . . . it's actually an incredibly apt way to look at the Beasts, Sazerac." The Son looked more than surprised, but how much more or in what direction, Caralee could not tell.

"Thank you, Most Holy. I wish I could offer more insight, but I do not know these ones—Blood and Wind." Sazerac paused, then his indigo eye resumed blinking in time to his crushed-rock voice. "I am given to understand that, as the Most Holy Son of the Vine, the world and its components respond to you in a unique fashion. Might it not be possible that the harpy can sense your presence? Might not the harpy have known that you have left the wasteland and are traveling now through lands more accessible?"

The Son reached out to touch Sazerac's helmet-head, but stopped just short of doing so. He looked pleasantly surprised.

"Yes. Those things—any or all of them—may be possible. Probable, even. As I said, Elinor may have merely lucked into—"

"So . . ." Eusebius played with his fingers, hiding his gaze from the Son. "I was attacked because you returned to the world? That's why . . . why Mommy died?"

"Yes." The Son nodded and looked to his lap. Nobody spoke.

They flew on in that silence, and Caralee could feel each of them wondering what they'd gotten themselves into, and with whom—except, perhaps, for Sazerac. Saz could calm a dust storm.

The afternoon stretched on as they flew toward the mountains, and Caralee wondered how many sausages she would eat before they reached the harpy's nest.

*Measuring time in sausages. We should measure time in sausages. Maybe then Elinor woulda had twelve sausages insteadda twelve hour-divvils.*

Caralee felt something judder the carpet, something that wasn't wind, but looking down she saw nothing. She turned to look behind her—still nothing. Something shook her again, from her shoulder? The judder grew stronger, and with dread, Caralee realized that it came from the satchel slung over her shoulder.

*Scat.* Caralee doubted that her journal had suddenly gone wobbly, nor the fruit she'd stolen from Elinor's laden tables . . . *The mask?* "The mask!"

The Son caught a glimpse of the struggle and was immediately on his feet. His balance was expert, even given Sunny's gravity—if he felt a lick of fear at jumping to his feet while riding a flying carpet, it did not show. "What's wrong?" he demanded.

"Elinor's stupid mask, it's . . ." She reached into the bag and grabbed hold of Elinor's discarded mask, which the duke had tossed to Caralee at their first encounter. Caralee had kept it—stupid, *stupid*! She'd only been curious and had all but forgotten about it. Now the *shatterscat magickal* mask shook, its steely face stretching this way and that. Mouth yawning open. "It's going all crazy."

Elinor's mask uttered a low, inhuman howl.

Caralee felt like an idiot who'd just murdered her family for the second time in a matter of days.

"What did I do?" she cried, scrambling with the mask as it awoke. Its steel eye holes *blinked,* and its mouth curled in a smile. "I took the scatting jazzed-up magickal mask that she scatting *gave* me, like I'm some idiot shitfarmer!"

"No, no, Caralee!" Eusebius reached out for Caralee's arm, but his reach fell far too short, and he just barely caught himself before falling onto his side. "Don't ever call yourself that—I don't ever want to hear you say something so unkind about yourself again. It simply isn't true!" The wizard nodded to himself, green tapers still despite the rushing wind, and only then did he notice the source of the upset.

"Set us down, *now*!" the Son shouted, snatching the mask from Caralee. It writhed in his hands.

"What madness is this?" Eusebius crowed, pointing a clubbed finger at the wriggling mask. "The face of the wicked duke, but wrought in vilest steel!"

Beside Caralee, wrestling against the Son's grip, the mask sprouted four arcs of metal, thin as her bootlaces, that touched down on Sunny's surface. Thus braced, the mask began to pull away from the Son's grip.

*It's growing legs and arms.*

"World-killer!" the mask screamed, mimicking Elinor's voice through the sound of tortured metal. Its legs found purchase, and the mask slipped from the Son's grip, recoiling overhead. "Monster! Son of *nothing*!"

He sighed.

Caralee had flown Sunny as low to the ground as she dared, and as fast. Distracted by the alien mask, Caralee's focus slipped, leaving Sunny undirected for a moment. The carpet seemed to recognize the dangerous angle of the fast-approaching ground—Sunny twisted to compensate, of her own accord, but even the most well-intentioned flying carpet can do only so much.

With a heave and a sizzle, Sunny the Carpet tossed off her riders and was scraped into the ground alongside them.

The impact sent Caralee into a wheeling chaos—a splatter of tumbling, rolling, rock-bone-crunching, and screaming. Her head spun round and round as she rolled across the ground so fast that she shut her eyes tight and held her breath, till she hit something hard with her back, and her arms and legs snapped to a stop.

Caralee heard a metallic shriek; her body tried to gasp, but the fall had knocked the wind out of her chest, and darkness crawled at the edges of her vision. Caralee tried to force her lungs to operate, but they weren't working. Reaching for her sandysense, Caralee gathered air and snaked it down her throat, filling up her lungs. She coughed the air out, inhaled on her own, then pushed herself to her hands and knees.

It was a column that she'd hit, and wrapped herself around—they'd reached the end of the road. Columns marked the end of the road like sentries, supporting nothing but marking some important border, like the tree line that bordered the Wildest Wood. Beyond, a valley lay in shadows below, cradled between the three mountains.

Panicked, looking all around, Caralee saw her friends scattered and bloodied. Eusebius lay splayed out on the stones, the lower half of his face covered in blood, one taper crushed beneath him, its whispering flame extinguished.

The Son growled, facedown, pushing himself up from beneath the cracked slab of a toppled column.

Sazerac had been flung into a wall, half of which now lay atop him. Unstoppable, Saz was using his free hand to remove the debris that pinned the rest of him, one piece at a time.

A skittering sound came from behind the columns, and Elinor's mask crawled into view, walking on four short legs, face to the sky. It stepped first one way and then another, uncertain.

One moment, Elinor's mask had four legs, and the next—eight. Caralee watched as the mask's four legs stepped *out of themselves,* splitting in two. She found the odd dance mesmerizing.

Elinor's mask walked on eight legs now like a critter, but it didn't do so for long. The four legs nearest the mask's forehead doubled in length and then tripled. They lifted the mask upright, facing toward Caralee, and turned just so—and formed the impression of a human body:

The four legs near the mask's chin waved briefly in the air before sliding down to become a neck and then the curve of Elinor's shoulders. They sprouted arcs of their own that assembled into the outline of Elinor's arms, hands, fingers. Wire arcs grew and met to form the shape of Elinor's armored torso.

The taller arcs behind the mask dropped down to form hips, wide thighs, long shins, lovely feet.

The outline of the steel duke stood before them in wire-frame, full-hipped and square-shouldered. The steel mask was the only solid piece of her—the rest of Elinor's conjuration was air and wire, coiled and tense. Steel Elinor looked to Caralee and screamed a steel scream.

Caralee struggled to find her voice. When she found it, she screamed back, raw and hateful.

"*What the scat is wrong with you, Elinor?*"

From the corner of Caralee's vision, Sazerac dashed a black blur toward Elinor, driving the wire-frame duke back dozens of feet and pinning her against the polished wall. Dust and rock spattered everywhere.

"Yeah, Saz!" Caralee cheered. Wire-tipped fingers chipped at Sazerac's back.

Caralee extended her sandysense so hard, so fast, that the magickal world burst into clarity at once, and with it, she could know the world around her in ways that her eyes and hands and ears and tongue could never do.

Caralee reached out to know the great weight of rock that was the sculpted mountain. The smaller, living rock that was Sazerac. Somewhere deep below, the heat of fire. Somewhere far, far away, the light of the sun. The air, thinner than a veil but everywhere. And water? It was everywhere, too—the thick blood inside her, even misted in the cold air.

And Elinor. Dense as metal that had been spun like cable fibers. Spun, sung, grown, forged—Caralee didn't care. What mattered was that this mannikin of Elinor was made from steel.

*Let's see how this steel really works.*

Caralee called to the water. It had never come before, like the air—but where the air felt as if it were almost giddy, water was merely stubborn. It could be coaxed, bullied. Mutable *and* tangible. She'd used that stubbornness to keep mud out of the dirt when she'd summoned Dustbutt for Eusebius back at Lastgrown. Now Caralee bent her will to fuss at the water relentlessly, begging and ranting with the silent voice of her sandysense until the air grew so heavy with wetness that it began to fog.

The water obeyed her, but not quickly enough. Sazerac had Elinor pinned to the wall, but Elinor's body kept sprouting new wires, and Caralee realized that Elinor could just *regrow* herself behind Sazerac and walk away from him, like Caralee could step over a pebble.

The damp air became thick. It was almost water-laden enough that the water would clump together and fall to the ground.

*Oh. . . .* That's *how rain happens!*

Caralee remembered her lessons. The elements were real, but there was a truth deeper than fire, water, sand, air, metal, plant, and void. There was physics, pesky physics, which had just scraped half of Caralee's thigh across blond stone.

*Scatting blockums.*

Caralee could feel the blockums that made Elinor's steel. Most of them were sharp and pointy, solid and fluid at once, and arranged in a pattern. Here and there were blockums like black stars, just enough of them to offset the pattern of the iron blockums to create a new pattern. Those would be carbon. Charcoal, the secret to steel! Now that she saw how it worked, steel made sense. The carbon wrinkled the iron's regularly repeating pattern just enough to give it a new pattern—a pattern that happened to have the properties of steel.

Caralee was a sandymancer. She could work around the pattern that made steel and reach the iron within.

Holding the waterlogged air around her, Caralee reached into Elinor's steel wires. Elinor had finished reassembling herself behind Sazerac and had wrapped her wire arms about him.

Caralee closed her eyes and forced the water into Elinor's body. The effect was meek at first, just a fog of breath into the cold air, but soon a mist gathered and began to seep into the lattice of the steel.

The carbon blockums didn't make a difference if you were a sandymancer who could force water into the steel's pattern and get it directly to the iron blockums that Caralee needed to rust.

Through the blood rushing in her ears, Caralee heard screaming. She didn't stop to think, just forced more and more water into the wire-frame duke.

*Screaming.* It sounded so sweet. She hoped it was Elinor.

More screaming, and then hands pulled Caralee down. She heard herself protesting, felt herself punching—she wasn't finished! Idiot fools, interrupting her! They would ruin everything.

"It's *done*!" the Son repeated and did so again until Caralee stopped thrashing. "It's done. Nobody interrupted your work, I promise. I would never, ever, *ever* do that. You got to finish. You finished. *We let you finish.*"

He relaxed, exhausted, breathing heavily. Crying openly. Caralee realized that the Son was holding her—in his lap—and cradling her head. He lifted her up.

"I let you finish. We let you finish your work, Caralee. Look and see."

Caralee opened her eyes. She had stopped Elinor in mid-leap, the mannikin of the duke's wire body rusted red. She'd been kicking one leg up and over her head when she'd been rusted, and her leg stretched three meters into the air, foot pointed to the sky. Elinor's mannikin had rusted into a distorted sculpture of the duke's body—her torso bent down, one wire arm extended longer than the other, bracing herself against the floor. The other arm she'd flung high overhead, ready to strike the spot where the Son had lain facedown on the road.

The metal assassin with Elinor's shape was rusted, all red and brown and dead. Except for that perfect face, pointed at Caralee's heart. The mask itself was still shiny and perfect.

Caralee picked herself up to see. The air smelled like blood and smoke. She brushed off her torn clothing and limped to examine the thing she'd thought a token or a trophy, which had really been an enemy in disguise.

Thicker than the wires it had sprouted, the mask itself hadn't rusted. It still moved, such as it could—it stretched its brow and its chin, working its mouth and blinking blindly. The mask looked down at its deformed and paralyzed body—and it screamed with Elinor's voice.

Caralee reached up with both hands, and with a shout, she tore Elinor's face away from the rusted sculpture. Elinor continued to wail.

"Why do you serve him?" Despair poured from the hollow mouth of Elinor's mask. "He is guilty of crimes against humanity. Show him to me!" Elinor's etched brows twitched left and right, searching for the Son though she no longer had a neck. "You are a traitor to your world, Amauntilpisharai, Least Holy Son of the Vine. There is no sin greater than diminishing the great human diaspora. You betrayed the human spirit itself when you befouled a wonder such as the Glass Gardens!"

"Yeah? What's *your* excuse?" Caralee spat at the mask, though her mouth was too dry to summon much spittle. Some of that water must have come from her own body. "By my count, you've cocked up two worlds now."

The mask squirmed in Caralee's hands. Elinor was trying to turn her head away from the insult. The eyes were as empty as the mouth, the ground visible behind them.

"I am a refugee." Elinor bit out the words through metal teeth. "I brought my people here so that we might survive, but I am oath-bound to protect humanity from any enemy that threatens our long-term survival. It is the same oath taken by every administrator of every colony, settlement, or habitat belonging to the diaspora. Surely—"

"Not surely." The Son bent over to peer at the steel mask. "Nothing can be certain, Duke. Culture drifts. Knowledge is lost and found again. Life evolves, but rarely according to plan. For a woman who knows more of history than I do, you don't seem to have learned much from it."

"Least of all manners!" Eusebius croaked from the ground. Saz slipped a hand beneath the old wizard's back and another beneath his knees. "Pretty or not, I do not like you, Duke, not one bit."

"Is this what they do, back on that first world you ruined?" Caralee held the mask close to her face, nose to nose. "You like to break into people's houses, smash up the windows, and drop a hot scat on their chests while they're sleeping?"

"Caralee—" The Son held out a hand to shut her up, but then he dropped it. "Caralee makes a strong and rather colorful case."

"Yeah, I do. Who puts steel in a harpy? Who takes a monster and make it worse?"

"I answered that question once already, witch!" The mask was cold against her fingers, and its lips moved more slowly now. Elinor's voice came through broken and rattling with some metal sound. Her presence in the mask was fading. "To make your monster my own. To kill the Son of the Vine and his army of creatures who cannot be killed."

"The Beasts of Care?" The Son's voice curdled. "You idiot. I have no army, and those Beasts were created by the builders themselves—"

"Don't speak to me, villain. You who killed a World-Tree! Caralee, you can stop him. He is wicked. Do not serve him." Elinor struggled to speak through the mask's fading power. "Do not lie for him. Your ridiculous lie—nobody crosses the world for *a friend* who, if he ever existed at all, is lost to them forev—"

"Don't you dare talk about Joe! You didn't even *ask me his name.*" Caralee compressed her outrage into a white-hot, bright-eyed hate. "Next time I see you, Imma rip out your tongue." She meant every word.

Caralee punched her sandymancy through the mask, shattering it. The pieces fell to the ground, squirming weakly. Unsatisfied, Caralee burned them away to acrid smoke and char.

*Joe. I'm not a monster. You ent lost forever.*

Caralee threw herself at the Son's chest and began to sob.

He hovered his arms over her shoulders, not quite touching. Caralee breathed deep between sobs, inhaling the scent of Joe that still clung to Joe's daddy's jacket. She closed her eyes and willed with all her might to believe it was Joe's big, dumb arms around her instead.

The Son let her sob, then stepped back.

"I'm sorry." Caralee apologized to herself for crying, even though she hadn't settled her mind as to whether tears were weak or strong. "Scat. What just happened?"

"Well . . . you single-handedly defeated the avatar of an alien warrior queen." The Son looked so proud, Caralee thought, and more than a little bloodlusty.

"Duke, really—and what regimented asshole doesn't just go and up herself to queen? *Duke.* It's a little twee. Pretentious. She's intense, don't you think? My point is, you should apologize to no one today. Ever, for that matter."

Caralee limped in a little circle.

"That was. That was . . . a *lot.*" Her head still spun. Had it all happened that fast?

The Son braced his hands on her shoulders and, for the smallest increment of time, his complete focus fell upon Caralee—every sun-spear of his attention all aimed at *her.* This time, though, that solar glare of the Son's attention wasn't examining her but recognizing her.

"*That* was the sandymancer who defended her world, faced off against a super-lethal enemy, and *won* without fighting. *That* was my protégé—a protégé is an apprentice, but nicer. . . . An apprentice is like a groveling servant but happy about it—"

"Don't make me break *your* mask, too."

The Son opened his mouth to speak, then feigned a crooked smile instead. With a finger he traced an oval around his face. What had he said at the beginning? *"This body is less than a mask to me."* Something awful like that.

"Besides, I can't go apprenticing when we're half a step away from . . ."

"From what?"

"Yeah, from what, exactly? The edge of the world, looks like. I said I'd follow you to the end of the world if I had to, and I did. But. *I don't know what to do.* Okay? You got me *out.* You stole my only friend, and then you saved me. You took all I had, and then I took all you gave. I feel like scat and I don't want to die, and I don't really want to hurt you anymore, but I need Joe and I don't know how . . ."

The Son leaned back, appraising. He nodded to show that he understood. Behind him, Saz held Eusebius in his arms—which looked romantic in its way. Saz walked over, steps easy despite his mass, cradling the painted wizard.

"The old buzzard doesn't look too bad. Nasty scrape on the chin." The Son poked Eusebius in several unfortunate places, provoking caws of despair. "Are you able to stand?"

"Oh, that's an understandable question," Eusebius waffled. "It's true that I developed a *few* years late, but I've been standing since I was all of six years old. I have a condition, you know."

"Yes . . ." The Son reached out to press his thumb against the wizard's forehead, and frowned at Eusebius's remaining taper. The other had been smeared into waxy paste on the flagstones.

"You're short a candle, my friend. Do you remember . . . well, what do you remember?"

"Oh, there was the wood and Lastgrown! Wasn't that a turn. Then that horrid shiny woman. Did she come back?"

“Is that all you remember?”

“Oof. I believe I’m short a candle, to boot.” Eusebius clocked his eyes toward his unlit shoulder. “See, right there. That’s where my candle isn’t.”

“I do see, yes.” That annoyed the Son, but not so much as it might have done before. “Do you remember our chat on the train?”

Eusebius tilted his head to listen to the whispers of his remaining taper and, hearing nothing of use, began humming. He bobbed his chin, humming a tune that Caralee didn’t recognize—till he stopped all at once and looked to the Son, first with terror and then with understanding.

“Yes. Yes, Most Holy, I believe that I do.” Eusebius struggled to keep his voice steady. To Saz, he said, “Please put me down, Sazerac. I think I’d like to stand.”

Saz’s touch was gentle, and Eusebius kept a hand on the armored man’s shoulder to steady himself.

*Chat on the train?* Eusebius did not look happy, and Caralee imagined the Son turning her friends against her. She couldn’t help imagining it, although it was the last thing she wanted to imagine. That wasn’t his plan, was it? It couldn’t be. Unless Elinor was right—and she couldn’t be.

Could she?

“Can you walk?” Sazerac asked Eusebius. The wizard shrugged.

“Since I was seven. I have a condition, you know.”

The Son shrugged and went to kneel over the rumpled mess of Sunny the Carpet.

“Alas, brave Sunny the Carpet. She served you well.” He pulled a sorrowful expression. “And earned her name at last, I suppose.”

“What?” Only now did Caralee notice the remains of the flying carpet. The crash landing had shredded her weave—snips of gold and blue and red thread littered the road and blew between the columns at road’s end. Only one gold corner remained intact, where it had landed.

“No, Sunny!” Caralee dashed to Sunny’s remains and knelt beside the carpet’s lonely corner. “Sunny! Please don’t be dead. Please don’t die.”

The corner flapped once, tassels frilling in solidarity and saying goodbye to her friends.

Caralee hung her head and sniffled.

“She was a good flying carpet,” Caralee said, thinking of Oti and Joe and wondering who *hadn’t* she doomed?

“Yes, Caralee. Mommy’s carpet was the very best of us.” Eusebius crossed his hands over his heart. “Sunny served you well as both a noble steed and an appealing textile. She kept your secrets and never once uttered an unkind word. You'll be surprised to learn that's a rare combination."

That only made Caralee cry harder.

The Son tossed Caralee her journal. The satchel had torn apart, but the leather binding of the journal was only scuffed. He pointed to the valley beyond the road.

"Do you know why we're here?"

Caralee shook her head, not bothering to look at him. She knuckled away tears from her cheeks.

"Funny thing about the Vine at *Angksef-Seysef.* It's not ready—we already know that something of the old Vine still exists that keeps the Lastgrown chick from growing beyond the borders of the wood—but the Vine there is at least partially functional. It nourishes the people of *Angksef-Seysef* and, I was pleased to discover during your unfortunate nap, it has formed *some* of the necessary connections to the systems of the world-beneath. The reference interface for the Beasts of Care, for instance. Not the control interface, which would make the job of seizing, healing, and ruling this world so much easier—but the reference data is *current*, and I've spent centuries riddling out how to locate two Beasts that have melded together—without access to the Vine. I understand now why my grandmother . . ." He sighed. "Why she asked me to do what she asked me to do."

"But you said that we were coming here, where you were born, right after we . . . met."

"The harpy always lived out east." The Son covered his heart with his hands. "Coming here was just . . . in the right direction and . . . and if it still stood, which it seems to . . . then the Fallow Palace is the only home I have left."

"Oh." The thought of home was a knife in Caralee's gut. She missed things she'd never thought she'd miss, like Mag's crankiness or Marm-marm's lessons. Caralee could teach those lessons now and a lot more. She couldn't possibly fault a man for wanting to go home, especially after centuries. "Oh, okay."

"Take your time, chucklehead, and wipe away your tears when you're through. We've not faced our last horror, not just yet. We'll pass through the pillars, around the valley, and then up—to the Fallow Palace.

"Prepare yourselves. We've put the Duchy behind us for the time being, but up ahead, there's an old mistake that needs fixing—older than I am, by two generations."

"To arms, friends and companions!" Eusebius raised an arthritic fist. "A son-seeking harpy needs to meet its ultimate end."

The Son shook his head. "More than that. The Beasts of Blood and Wind have been bound for centuries. We won't *kill* the harpy. We will free two powerful forces that, with luck, will return to their purposes. The world will be infused with good air to breathe, and one day, your village might eat meat regularly. Maybe you can even burn down your wretched cable plant, once worms and other fauna return to the soil."

That sounded nice, a world without the bony spirals of cable plant.

"Then what?" Caralee felt numb.

"Then . . . then we hope." He looked away.

"And what about *us*?"

The Son massaged his neck. "We keep hoping."

# VII

I became a better killer. I practiced on nobodies in the city. I practiced on lovers. I would not leave another sibling to suffer the way I had done to Ester and Amau-Alua. Out of love, I learned to be cruel. Of all the things I have done, I am least proud of this . . . education.

For the most part, I killed my elders first——that would be the order of things, were I an ordinary aspirant to the throne, prepared for the ordinary deaths required to place myself first in line and claim the Thousand Names.

A fire took the nursery and three of our youngest. It broke Mother, who hid herself away in her apartments with the youngest, my infant brother.

Raclette died soon thereafter. She slit her own throat, so the story goes, out of grief. Though she'd been an angry woman, nobody could deny that Raclette loved as fiercely as she'd fought, and the loss of five siblings in such quick succession brought back memories of Stimenne's long, dark fall, and poor Raclette could not go on. So the story goes.

Birrat and Borin killed each other. That much is true. Weak-minded Borin was easy to mesmerize in his sleep——cognoscence is best performed while the subject is asleep——and he attacked Birrat in a training yard. Birrat was forced to defend himself, and if his blade had been enchanted with the greensleeve, the poison-spell of martial magick, well, Borin had been a soldier, hadn't he?

Shara slipped from a balcony and fell a thousand meters to the city below. She was always a little cat of a woman, and while it wasn't a surprise that she'd been dancing on a railing, we were all disturbed to hear that she'd stumbled. It was so unlike her.

Shara's twin sister, E-Shara, sank deeply into drink, and she overdosed on an accidentally lethal combination of intoxicants. That one's actually true.

I'd become such an accomplished agent of death that my family had begun to fall apart, and I am not so self-delusional as to pretend that E-Shara's fate was not entirely my doing. I might as well have poisoned her myself, as I did Tilcept-Arri. He was strong in elemancy and druidry, and I did not risk a confrontation.

Zincy was a tricky one. The Lir of a Thousand Names had an honor guard like the rest of us, but unlike most of Father's children, the Lir of a Thousand Names employed their guard regularly. While not as strong an adept as Tilcept-Arri, Zincy was still a formidable magician.

The magick of love, which some call family magick, or the antimagick, is unique among the seven arts. It stills all other influences in the immediate area, so that the only "magick" that could function, as it were, is the complex weave of affection and resentment that families call love. I clung to the wall above the eaves of Zincy's bedroom window and slipped inside after dark, when they were at their desk engaged in conversation with none other than our younger sister Ep-Athinne.

Dispossessed of their magick, and distracted by Ep-Athinne, I bludgeoned Zincy to death with a paperweight. Ep-Athinne met the bad end of a letter opener.

I was the middle child of three. Mother hid with the infant, and Esk-Ettu . . .

Esk was my champion, and the only sibling to see what was coming for him, and whom.

I told him everything: Athinne's visit in my tower, and the duty with which she'd tasked me, and why; what Grandfather Moysha had told me when I objected; the truth of how each of our siblings had died; and how each murder tore away a piece of myself. I sobbed with my head in his lap, begging him to help me, begging him to denounce me as my brother so I would only have to murder my best friend and not another brother.

To my horror, Esk understood. As it happened, he'd had his own conversations with our grandparents. They had known our love for each other and had done me this one kindness, if that's the word.

"I love you, Amaunti. I will die for you, yes, I will die for you right here. Today. Now. This moment. But I will *never* renounce you as my brother."

He handed me the knife I had given him when he was thirteen and came of age. I took it. The handle was worn antler. The golden blade was self-sharpening.

"It's the world, Amaunti." Esk cried freely; we both did. "Grandmother taught me about sacrifice, and Grandfather told me a story——that night at the beach——about a sweet boy who grew up to be a cruel man, and how the world sometimes depends on such cruelty, and how love could dull his pain."

I stuttered. Esk took my wrist and brought the tip of his blade to his ribs.

"I'll return to the soil, baby brother. And you will tend that soil, so that it is always black and wet." He brushed my cheek with the thumb of his other hand, and together we pierced his heart.

# 15

The blond brick road fanned out to meet the row of columns—some of which now lay toppled on the ground—that ringed the lip of an overlook that offered a view into the valley below. Overhead rose the third mountain, or what remained of it: a palace had been hewn from the rocky slopes—here there were no keystones, no *Angkhet opkthene,* no seven-sided shapes, just platforms and archways of bare black stone connected by walkways that spiraled through and around the carved-out space where the mountain had been. There were no walls. From this angle, the Fallow Palace looked a maze of terraces and parlors, with starlight peeking through around the edges, where the wildly hollow architecture was least dense.

Caralee stepped through the line of toothy pillars. It was as if someone had planted stone trees in a perfect arcing line, and they had grown tall and strong but never branched, nor grown leaves. Their tops had once been carved with some design—maybe faces?—but were weathered past hope.

If she had expected the depression between the three mountains to show signs of life, she was rewarded with signs of life's opposite. Stone monuments stood in rows and groves, cloistered here and there within the crumbled remains of simple stacked-stone walls the likes of which Caralee recognized from the fieldstone walls back home. Not so many days earlier, she'd hopped over those walls with Joe, running to meet Mag at her cart because they'd stolen time to watch Eusebius perform.

The monuments came in all different types of stone, from the black basalt of the surrounding mountains to white marble, clear-white and clouded-pink quartzes, even geodesic amethyst, where the light of the fading sun glittered within cradles of purple crystal. Many of the monuments stood tall, but some had collapsed or slumped into the dirt.

"You can imagine how precious the stones of some of these *matzevas* might be. Or, no, you can't." The Son met Caralee at the edge of the overlook. There was no banister, just gold stone that ended abruptly. "Many of these were carved from stones and crystals that were old when our world was built. Formed naturally on real planets, with molten cores."

"What are they?" Caralee breathed, looking out over the valley of monuments. The closer stones, though fifty meters below her or more, looked to be carved with lengthy inscriptions. Here and there words were carved in much larger letters. Maybe they were names.

"*Matzevas.* Some are tombstones for the dead, others are monuments to heroes or lost settlements, some few still were prisons like mine, that held the spirits of those criminals too wicked to be allowed to return to the soil and become a part of everything. That's what they did to me, you know." His face stiffened. "Denied me the chance to rot."

"You were in . . . one of these?" The Son had referred to his *matzeva,* the stone slab where his ghost had been kept fast for centuries, but Caralee hadn't ever expected to see it. She'd no idea it was not the only one of its kind. "And there are others like you?"

"My *matzeva* was a marble slab. You couldn't find it if you tried—the heart of the wasteland is impassible. There are none like me here, no. That's not a boast. The human mind isn't meant for mineral. The *asarim-dem*—the condemned—are intended to go insane, slowly, and ultimately their minds dissolve into nothing more self-aware than a howling wind that none can ever hear."

"Whoof." Caralee rubbed an ache in her shoulder. "Sounds like your kinda challenge."

"Oho, yes, and thank goodness for it!" Eusebius rested his head against Sazerac's shoulder and looked half-asleep, but when he spoke, it was with a clear, loud voice. "Or I would never have learned the secrets of—"

"*Of?*" The Son shot the sandymancer a glare that Caralee swore would kill a lesser person. Eusebius's words caught in his throat and he worked his jaw like a babby bird, opening and closing his mouth with his chin up and his eyes wide.

"Or I would never . . . I would never have learned the secret of *carpets*!" That last word was a lie, and Eusebius's face showed it. He did not care for telling falsehoods. "Of course." Caralee saw liver spots on Eusebius's face, where his makeup had worn off. He smiled at her, mustering innocence.

Something had happened between the Son and Eusebius at the Duchy, that much Caralee could no longer deny. The Son had plied some bargain—but what could he possibly want from Eusebius? And why keep it a secret? She'd also heard the Son talking to Sazerac. Was he going to steal more of her friends from her? Had the Son led Caralee to her doom? She wouldn't put it past him, and yet she still couldn't believe it. They'd come so far together.

*No.* Caralee chose to believe that her friends were her friends, no matter how queerly they'd been entangled. There was no such thing as an impossible knot, anything could be untied, given patience and study. Even a knot like the Son and Joe, tied up in one body. Caralee *had* to believe, just as she had to believe that Joe was still alive, or what was her purpose?

The Son led them counterclockwise down a road that hugged the rim of the valley. Between the setting sun and their slow descent, the light had grown treacherously dim. With a toss of the hand and the twist of a wrist, a witchlight swirled into being above the Son's fingers to guide their passage. He took the lead, and Caralee followed with Saz close enough behind to catch her with one arm. Eusebius sat to Sazerac's other arm like a rescued pretty boy, resting his head on Sazerac's oversized shoulder. The wizard's remaining candle burned green and insistent on the other side of his head, whispering small mercies.

The road around the valley of *matzevot* wasn't as intact as the causeway through the Deadsteppes—they clung to a ridge of rock that had once been bricked with the same yellow stone, but this path had crumbled into ruin.

"So, Elinor. That wasn't really her, right?" Caralee asked the Son. "I mean, I didn't kill *her,* did I? I just broke the whatever . . . whatever was that?"

"Elinor would not risk her life for ours." The Son's math was simple. "She's a fanatic but not a suicide."

"I hope it *hurt.* Do you think it hurt? And what was that thing?"

"Uncertain. Some extension of Elinor's ability to . . . I don't even know what to call it—she didn't use elemancy, which would be the only explanation I could offer. I don't know anything about her power, which disturbs me. Some technological method or something else entirely—something alien."

"Isn't she already alien?"

"Oho! The young miss has you there, most kind sir!"

"Pffft. Alien life. Not human. Long before our ancestors found the stars, other beings—like us, but not like us—made their own way through the void."

Caralee didn't know what to make of that. "So Elinor's metal-magick could be from some whole other kinda . . . smart critter?"

He smiled. "It wouldn't be without precedent—a certain oath into certain leafy mysteries keeps me from telling you of the scandalous history of the druids—but I do not understand Elinor's affinity for metal. Of course, I don't know what I don't know." He laughed at himself. "Anyway, if you're so curious, you might have left me a sliver of her mask to study."

"I'm not sorry that I didn't *not* save everyone?"

The Son sighed and shrugged.

"Fascinating woman." The Son looked back to the pass, now as dark as the valley around them and the palace, somewhere, up ahead. "Powerful, brilliant, commanding, *royal.* And completely insane. We should have gotten along famously."

"Yeah, maybe if you'd done anything." Caralee snorted. "Besides, you are two *way* different kinds of crazy. I mean that in a nice way. Sorta. You both think you're hot scat, and you both say that 'your people' are important to you, but still you both talk about yourselves pretty much only ever." The Son lifted one eyebrow as high as it would go. "That said—*you* make sense, once I got myself over all the horrible things you do. Elinor is . . . She's different kinds of crazy from one minute to the next, and I don't think she realizes it?"

"She realizes it—that's not the problem. Her problem is that she thinks her variability is a strength," the Son said as they stepped around some rubble. They'd made good progress around the *matzeva* garden. Ahead, the crumbling road they followed began to slope upward again.

"I've seen monarchs rant and I've seen fanatics rave, and I've seen both in one person: but my father was not intelligent. Elinor is canny, which should ease her tendency to miscalculate, but instead, she compounds her errors. She revealed herself to me upon first impression: Elinor believes that unpredictable behavior is a tactic to befuddle her enemies, which it *does,* as we have severally and repeatedly discovered." He shook his head. "I am concerned by how much destruction she may bring to the world, regardless of her intentions."

"That's another thing she said!" Caralee blurted. "Morning. The Twelve of Morning."

"The what?" the Son asked; his surprise looked sincere. "The who of when?"

"The Twelve of Morning. They're divvils that destroyed Elinor's home," Caralee explained. "The ones she let out of their prison, then they killed everyone. That's what she said when she tried to get me to feel sorry for her. I bet it was lies."

"Start at the beginning, please?"

Caralee rewound her thoughts to a place she could call a beginning. "So, when Elinor was a little girl and she destroyed their world—"

"What the fuck, Caralee?" The Son recoiled, looking aghast and betrayed.

Caralee noticed that the Son treated her most like an equal when he was upset with her. "Tell me that you're kidding."

"Oh, did I not mention that?" Caralee asked, abashed. "Um, so: only her family can do that stuff with the metal-shaping, and when Elinor was wee, she went to the worst place, this prison that held the worst divvils, and she did the worst thing she could possibly do there, whatever that was. She freed the Twelve of Morning from their prison, and they went around murdering everyone and blew up a mountain, and only the palace survived, because it's a flagship or a starship and she took it and left the world to die. That's another thing she acted upset about: leaving everyone to die while saving her own skin."

The Son's eyes were open so wide that he looked like painted Eusebius, gooning at some unremembered fright. "Why did she do it? Did she say?"

"She said she was *just curious* about places she'd been told not to go, which I would believe if it weren't Elinor, cuz who wouldn't want to go somewhere they'd been told not to go? I'd be there in a heartbeat. Anyway, Elinor's the duke because she was a coward and escaped wearing navy—or something about navy?—and left her family and the rest of her world, like I said already, to die. She killed her world . . . and her family . . . and ended up the boss. . . ." Caralee's voice trailed off.

She cleared her throat. "I guess you two have *that* in common."

The Son tossed his hair to shadow his face, which was already very much in the shadows, and Caralee couldn't imagine how he must be feeling and what he might be thinking. Discovering another ancient world-killing royal brat had to feel weird—what were the odds?—and she tried to riddle out how it would alter his game. Caralee wondered if the Son would have fled his world if he could have, and if Elinor had ever tried to fix hers.

They climbed the road to the steps of the Fallow Palace. The carved-out mountain loomed black against the creamy whorls of the starbirth clouds and their spill of bright stars. Here and there, stars shone through the outer edges of the palace, but the center was dense enough to block out all light.

The Son's witchlight lit up the steps to the palace—they were the same black stone as the mountain itself. Caralee noticed the straight edge where the gold stone of the road ended and the stairs began. He put his foot on the first step, then took it away again. Turning to Caralee and Sazerac, nodding to Eusebius, the Son spread his arms.

"Welcome, brain-damaged hedge-witches, and boulders, and bad apprentices, to the Fallow Palace."

"How wonderfully dark it is, Most Holy!" Eusebius angled his shoulder, trying and failing to light the night with his green candle. He raised his eyebrows and nodded to Caralee, happy to be helping, even though he wasn't.

"Are we safe?" Caralee asked.

The Son shrugged and began to say something wry, when Sazerac interrupted him.

"Yes." The pulsing of his indigo eye in time to his voice was the only sign that Saz was there. The shadows had swallowed him.

"That's nice," said Eusebius. "Don't you think that's nice?"

"Of course we're safe," the Son said hurriedly, snapping his fingers, and with a furious pitch of sandymancy, he ripped a yellow-hot *filkapyth* from the tawny pavement at his feet. An obelisk of scorching stone, the hearth fire crystal baked the air. "And we follow the rules about traveling at night, don't we, Caralee?" He fixed her with a stare that she looked just like one of Mag's most intimidating glares.

"Yeah," said Caralee. It wasn't that she didn't believe Saz when he said that they were safe, so much as a place like this, at the end of the world and with a name like the Fallow scatting Palace, seemed like the sort of place where Caralee should take Mag's advice above anyone else. Mag would say, "Make yourself small and dark, and sleep in shifts till the nighttime stars fade."

"It's dark enough that we should rest. Cold enough as well." The Son had never seemed to mind the cold before. "Without Sunny, the floor will have to serve, but I encourage the living among us to sleep, if you are able."

"Brrk?" Eusebius groused. "Shouldn't we fear that awful duke and her army?"

"That's not an army, it's a skeleton crew." The Son combed his fingers through his long hair and sorted out the Metal Duchy. "Elinor doesn't lead an invading force; she leads refugees. Her trick with the mask was her only gambit—not some inscrutable conceit. She could have faced me directly, in person; she might have sent an armored patrol after us—Elinor chose to do neither. She risked little, telegraphing herself into battle as she did. No, I don't think that she will follow up 'wily' with 'bold.'" He warmed his hands over the orange-hot hearthstone. "No, she'll retreat with the data she'll have learned in fighting us. We won't see her again soon. Sazerac, take watch."

"Yeah, Saz." Caralee didn't intend to let the Son start giving orders to Sazerac. "You take watch, okay?"

"Of course, Caralee." Sazerac sat into his usual position, Eusebius safe in his arm. The wizard curled into Sazerac's body and wheezed, sweet as a little kid tucked in for the night. Caralee took up position on the opposite side and wrapped herself around Sazerac's massive elbow.

"Where are we?" Caralee asked. She was tired somewhere deep inside, so tired—of everything. "You promised me the rest of your story."

"I promised you the *end* of my story." The Son wagged a finger. "Word your bargains with care."

"Yeah, well tell us a bedtime story about the Fallow Palace, since we came all this way."

The Son scratched his chin. "I'll tell you a story of endings, one of which was almost mine."

Caralee nodded.

"After the harvest," the Son began, gesturing to the darkness that swamped them, "when the fields were still smoking from the slash and the burn, when the year's last rotation of fields fell fallow, the royal household would travel here to spend weeks in seclusion. Long before the world was built, our ancestors measured time by seasons, and during the final months of the year, the land grew too cold to grow most crops. They called it *winter.*

"Grandfather Moysha taught me that our family vacation had long been a tradition honoring that ancient cycle of rest and plenty. We had good times here—it was a place where we could be a family, and not a political and financial entity. My mother gave birth to me here, somewhere up above. You'll see it . . ." He paused, eyes flicking up to the shadowed palace. "Her rooms were near the nursery."

"Wait, you were actually born here?" Caralee raised her hand like she'd done in Marm-marm's classes. "That's not shatterscat?"

"Of course. What did you think I meant?"

"Something completely different?" Caralee thought that should be obvious.

"Oh. No." He favored her with a smile. "I meant what I said." The Son pointed to the darkness overhead. "I was literally born from my literal mother, literally up there, high up, in a black rock garden."

"Okay." Caralee looked down at her feet, rather than stare up into darkness.

"Are you . . . ?" The Son was taken aback. "Are you *disappointed*?"

"Well, No. I mean—no, hey—it looks big." Caralee shrugged the shoulder that wasn't melting away its troubles, thanks to Saz. "Place looks real big. It's nice. I'm sure it's nice."

"Big? *Nice?* You *are* disappointed!"

"Hey, look, I was born by the shatterscat ditch. One more push, Mag says, and I woulda been born *in* the shatterscat pit. So this is . . . You should be really. . . . like, proud."

"It's a whole fucking mountain, carved up into ribbons and bubbles!" the Son griped.

"I'm sure it is."

"A confection of basalt sung from the asteroid-mined bedrock itself!"

"Ass-mined bedrock, right there. Ayup, that's what we got. Good stuff, ass-mined bedrock."

The Son whistled. "It's not too late for me to kill you."

"Nobody kill anybody, please," Eusebius gurgled. "I'm *so warm*."

"May I finish my tale?" The Son looked annoyed, then he took a deep breath, and his expression changed all at once. He did look scared, not of a thing but of what he was going to say. For the first time, Caralee saw the Son look like a man about to make a confession.

"You know that I killed my family. These days, that is a horrible crime. In my time, it was a tactic. How else would a lesser heir become god? With patience and hope for misfortune? That's not ambition. I was not deposed because of any sense of morality—not because I'd broken any law. I'd become the law. In the single-mindedness of my purpose, I'd murdered anyone who might have stood by my side. I had to stand alone. When I did, those who retained some power—the lesser heads of government, such as they were—found themselves unopposed. In me, they saw a Child of the Vine who could not be influenced or assuaged, whose mind could not be known, and worst of all, one who *did not need them*."

The corner of his mouth twitched. "My fatal error was that I never thought to fear the useless." He shook his head and let his gaze linger on Sazerac. "I took a moment to rest, and they found me. They bound me, killed me, and sentenced my soul to madness. If they'd waited any longer, it would have been too late to stop me."

"*Isso tebari-hem Djeovaunt*." Eusebius raised his head from Sazerac's arm. The wizard's Auld Vintage didn't have the proper rhythm to it, and he pronounced the vowels weirdly. "Thus fall gods and kings."

"Too true," agreed the Son without rancor. "In the legends, do they say that I killed my mother?"

"Yeah, you killed just about everyone." Caralee stated known fact. "And you killed your family first."

"I killed my brothers. I killed my sisters. I killed Zincy, our sibling who took neither gender. I killed their children." He looked at his hands. "I killed my father, with great enthusiasm and some amount of joy."

"Right," Caralee said. "And then you were sentenced to death, not-death, whatever. And then you destroyed the world. I heard this story."

"It took all seven magicks to bring me down." He traced his knuckles with a finger, and the lines across his palm. "I was a master of all seven, of course."

"That is written," agreed Eusebius with a yawn.

"One of the seven magicks is the magick of *family.*" The Son clasped his fingers together. "Those who wield it can sense the emotions of their relations. More to the point, they can still all other magicks—provided they have a blood tie to the magician. A practitioner could, say, strip her son of his power for a moment. . . . A moment is all it took."

"She . . ." Every mama loves her babbies. Even the Son had a mama who loved him. "She put you down?"

"Yes." He nodded. "Ruth—that was my mother's name—Ruth's participation was the linchpin to my destruction. The keystone, you might say."

"Your mama was the *Angkhet opkthene* to her own son's death?"

"Can you imagine?" The Son almost flinched as he looked up into the darkness, where the Fallow Palace rose, unseen. "If only I had killed Mother, I would have cured the world."

Caralee didn't know which notion was worse.

"So she died when you exploded the Vine?"

"No. That explosion was not as instantly deadly as you might think—even in the City of the Vine, there were pockets that survived. Hundreds of miles were devastated in an instant, but not uniformly. Mother survived."

"So she died afterward, with everyone else who survived the explosion?"

"No." He took a breath. "Mother found her way here from the city. She died here, alone, in the only familiar place that still stood."

"She walked all this way?"

"She stumbled out of the wasteland, yes. She dragged herself all the way here, searching—I imagine—for comfort that no longer existed. From my prison, I could see and feel her. Every movement was agony. I could do nothing to help—that was the fate to which we had sealed one another. She died here."

*Scatting scatballs.*

"I'm really sorry that you did that, and I'm sorry that you had to watch—not-watch?—your mama so hurt and sad." Caralee meant that, though she couldn't hide the fact that the Son's story made her want to throw up everywhere. "But if she's dead, then . . . sorry, but what are you afraid of?"

"Pity," he answered.

*Oh.* Caralee thought the Son would be afraid of something big and mean, not something so small, but so sad.

The Son flexed and yawned, turning his face from the light of the hearthstone. He stretched his back till it cracked all up his spine.

"Caralee, you know how you have *absolutely no idea* how you're going to get Joe back, and how somewhere deep inside, you know that Joe is gone, and somewhere even deeper inside, you're still convinced that you're going to get him back?"

Caralee bristled.

"Well," said the Son without joy, "this is my that."

Caralee struggled to picture the Son as lost and confused as she'd been herself, ever since he'd stolen Joe and ruined her life. "So . . . you're scared?"

He nodded. Caralee didn't think he trusted himself to speak.

"And you're terrified that a woman who was strong enough to crawl all this way only did it so that she could curl up by your cradle and *die*."

The Son squeezed his eyes shut and made a small noise of assent.

"Okay." Caralee closed her eyes and held on to Sazerac's warm arm. She wished she'd known what her mama had looked like before she'd died giving birth by the shatterscat pit. Caralee hoped that whatever her mama had looked like, she would have crawled across the world for Caralee, too, if she hadn't bled to death while holding her babby girl in her arms.

The night was still and the air roasting-warm from the hearthstone, and Caralee kept her mouth shut, thinking about dead mothers and home.

Eusebius rustled in the shadows. "*Bloody wind, bloody wind,*" he sang to himself. "*Blood and Wind and a Beast, a Beast, a Beast for Dunes.*" He shivered once and returned to his sleep.

The Son looked at Caralee with his most featureless mask. Caralee looked to him with alarm and couldn't control her eyebrows.

"You sang him *what*?" she demanded.

"I . . ." The Son measured his thoughts before his words. "Of course not—"

"Liar." Caralee and the Son stared at each other. Then by some unspoken agreement, they looked away.

What did Eusebius know that the Son didn't want the wizard singing about? Her heavy eyelids begged her not to ask any more questions. Caralee's exhausted mind tried to sort through the tale of the Son's mother, and of his fear of what awaited him in the palace above, but she closed her eyes, took a deep breath, and fell asleep as she exhaled.

A squawking awoke Caralee, who realized with a start that she'd fallen asleep. It was Eusebius, cock-a-crowing from the other side of Sazerac's warm body. The sky lightened in the west, dawn-peach and starry; the wizard had a knack for waking up with the sunrise. Caralee stood and knuckled sand from her eyes, sparing a glance behind them at the bright western sky to see the colors of morning paint the Deadsteppes. In the middle distance, shadows still muddled the valley of monuments. She could see the tops of some of the *matzevot,* pointy and round and winged and vine-tipped, and marveled that she'd been able to sleep through the night in such a grand emptiness.

The Fallow Palace was revealed by the morning sun. Where the gold road ended, a gargantuan tree of black stone erupted from the ground: the entire mountain had been sculpted into dozens of winding branches. The amount of rock that must have been removed staggered Caralee almost as much as sight of the towering basalt maze. Stone-wrought black boughs held platforms and halls, created towers without walls by stacking platforms amid interlocking branches, steps, and long, looped pathways—all hewn from a single piece of black rock.

"It looks like a tree," she said, feeling small beneath the reaching branches. "*Why* does it look like a tree?"

Caralee walked up the curved steps and into the entrance hall. The floor was an oval of plain black stone. The hall was completely bare—no decorations, no furniture, no *walls,* even the distant ceiling looked like it was carved beneath the floor of a hall higher up.

Walkways split off from the hall, curving up and around, winding to platforms that projected their own walkways farther up and through the palace. The platforms must be what served as rooms in the Fallow Palace—it looked inconvenient. She wondered how many servants staffed this place in its day and what all they did. Hold up walls or tapestries all day? Run around with chairs?

The palace was so tall—following as it did the shape of a onetime mountain—that the branches and platforms and arched hallways in the distance above her swirled and hid from view the upper stories. The whole interlaced maze of it made Caralee's head spin.

"It's a tree," she said again, turning to look behind her when she heard footsteps. "That's weird."

"It is a display of power, Caralee," the Son answered, ascending the steps that led into the great hall.

When the Son's foot touched the floor of the hall, the plain black stone *rippled.* Caralee jumped back as a wave of mosaic tiles emerged from the ground. With the next step, another ripple of tiles, and then another—the waves reached the edge of the oval hall and stopped. The tiles were all grown from the same black stone as the floor, only they hadn't been there a moment ago. Caralee hadn't felt a tingle of sandymancy.

"Are you still disappointed by my home?" He smiled and walked past Caralee. "Come on, let's go."

"Don't you dare just walk on by like you didn't *wake up the floor,* or whatever that—"

"Ho hey!" Eusebius announced his presence, walking side by side with Sazerac—it wasn't as if there were any walls or doors to get in their way. Sazerac fussed over him a bit, making sure the wizard, who'd been knocked around enough to concern everyone, could stand after a night's sleep. Sazerac's warmth seemed to have done Eusebius some good, as he stood a little taller and walked on his own. The wizard's eyes were wide, their lids gray and thin where his makeup had worn away.

"Did you see that?" Caralee spun and jabbed her finger in the wizard's face. "Tell me you guys saw that."

"Pardon, Caralee?" Sazerac tilted his head, managing to look confused.

Eusebius clapped his hands in delight. "What architecture! What a splendid monochromatic mosaic—I don't think I've ever seen its like. I assume that I led us to another marvelous find. One more notch for Eusebius Gibberosus Kampouris." He looked so proud, and then politely lost. "Wherever are we?"

"We stand at the entrance to the Fallow Palace, in the uttermost east, where the current Son of the Vine was born," Sazerac answered his friend.

"Aha, so we are!" Eusebius smiled. Relieved of its paint, his face looked both younger and sallow. "Its design is said to be modeled after primitive notions of a World-Tree. Silly notion, World-Trees being actual trees, don't you think? A Vine seems a far more sensible choice. This lovely gem sits across a hundred kilometers of steppes so dead they didn't merit any other name, which does beg the question: Whyever are we here?" He bowed his head, stroking his chin as he hummed to himself. After a moment he stopped and shivered. "Oh yes, I remember."

Caralee and the Son exchanged looks.

Her heart felt sick. The Son of the Vine had secrets from another age, and secrets with her friends, and if that wasn't enough, brand-new secrets sprang up at his feet.

"There is no need to fear." Eusebius raised a finger and puffed out his chest like a man invoking confidence he might not feel. "Though we each have our own horrors, we comrades must take courage from our faith in one another." He nodded to Caralee and then to the Son, looking them both in the eye. "Shall we face our unknowns together?"

The Son led them through the hall and onto a walkway. He stepped onto the bare stone, and again it rippled, this time flipping a path of tiles that followed the curve of the passage.

"What wonder is this!?" Eusebius popped off at the sight of the rippling floor. "Caralee, if you look closely, you might notice that the Most Holy has a peculiar effect upon our environment. I'd be a poor tutor not to draw your eye to such things."

The Son chuckled, pleased with himself.

Caralee balled her fists.

As they climbed the mighty tree, Caralee saw how the branch she walked along served as a kind of corridor. A winding, climbing corridor built to test a person's tolerance for heights. As with a corridor, they passed platforms that could have been rooms. Some were roofed in the same way of the hall below—and absent of walls or support from the floors—while others were open to the brightening sky. Those might have once been terraces or gardens. Nowhere did Caralee see so much as a chair, nor any shoot of green. True to its name, the branches of the Fallow Palace were barren of leaves, its gardens empty, and its halls vacant.

Their coiled ramp led up from one branch and spilled them onto a circular terrace. The Son, forging ahead, had already revealed its floor; its black tiles were ever so slightly uneven in height. Maybe they formed a pattern that Caralee could not see.

She chased after the Son. "How do you do that with the floors?"

He grunted. He was focused now, no longer amused with anything; Caralee could see so.

"You lot just decided, 'Let's carve up a mountain'?"

"Someone did." The Son beckoned for Sazerac to hustle Eusebius up the branchway. "The Fallow Palace is one of the oldest surviving structures aboveground. And why not carve up a mountain? Our ancestors did, after all, *build* these mountains, and everything else you've ever seen—once upon a time." He paused. "I rather undid that boast, I think."

"You are here, Most Holy," Eusebius consoled, breathing hard and daring to lean a hand on his god-king's shoulder. "*You* have endured, for better or for worse, and you are the world. You are its hope and its doom and its *child.* If this air held moisture, it would rain and weep for you."

The Son looked over his shoulder at Eusebius, spooked as if he'd heard a ghost. "I . . . thank you, wretch."

"Thank *you,* king and god." Eusebius removed his hand and nodded. "I serve at your pleasure, Most Holy."

The branchway ended at a series of circular platforms clustered together in a group. Again, the Son stepped onto the floor and the stone responded.

This time, the floor didn't ripple so much as jump. Off to the side, a pointed stone column flowed up from the ground, growing until it branched into a little tree, with droopy limbs that waved in the cold wind that cut through the boughs of the Fallow Palace. Spikes erupted from the ground and became blades of black grass—others knotted themselves into shrubs and bushes thick with stone thorns. Hedges flowed up around the edges of the platform, waist-high railings of dark rock decorated with foil-thin leaves.

"Black boxwoods are my favorite," said the Son. He wasn't showing off anymore. He'd walked into the past. Stone tentacles sprouted in spirals, splitting into ever-smaller tendrils that kissed the Son's ankles as he passed. "Oddgrass!"

The wave didn't stop with the first platform. All five platforms—Caralee counted five—awoke at the Son's arrival. More trees sprang up, some tall, some Caralee's own height, and five more rings of black boxwoods, and tentacled oddgrass—whatever that was. Here and there a black bench rose from the ground, cozied among the black stone plants.

Black vines snaked up the trunk of the nearby tree, and in the folds of their leaves appeared something like witchlights—for Caralee had yet to feel even a stitch of sandymancy—these looked like clustered berries of purplish light.

"Oh my," Eusebius gushed.

Caralee said nothing as they made their way through the gardens, crossing slender bridges from one to the next. She reached out her hand to touch the leaves of the vines that covered the trunk of a tree and found their leaves were soft to the touch. Soft stone.

At the last garden-platform, they found steps that led up to a large, kidney-shaped room with actual walls, rounded off like the baths in Comez. The floor here was hand-tiled with a colored mosaic that showed the sun rising behind the body of the Vine. This room was special, Caralee noted, and when the Son stepped through the open doorway, nothing happened. Its decorations were real, permanent, and ancient.

The light was dim, with only one doorway, and the Son's eyes adjusted before Caralee's did.

"Oh." The Son made a small sound that wasn't quite a word. "Oh," he sighed again.

In the curve of the wall and the floor lay a pile of bones. She'd curled up like a babby, hands covering her face, and there was still some dark hair stuck to her skull. One side of her rib cage had collapsed into the floor, but the up-facing side was intact, as if she'd cried herself right into the stone.

The Son kneeled and held his hand over his mother's skull, as if he wanted to brush her hair but was afraid to do so.

"Mama," he said. "Ruth. I am so sorry."

"How is she still here?" Caralee asked, meaning the wind, the centuries of unprotected exposure to the elements; so little endured from the Land of the Vine, but this skeleton remained, almost completely intact, at the top of a windswept mountain near the end of the world? It made little sense.

"Family," the Son answered, and Caralee remembered that family was another form of magick. "The Bride of Plenty mothered the world and was Athinne's daughter as well. She may not appear in any tales, but she was not without wonders of her own. Little good they did her."

*Sandymancy, droods, cogno-whatsit, and family. What are the other three?*

Caralee, Sazerac, and Eusebius fell silent as the Son knelt over the corpse of his mother. After several long minutes, Caralee recognized his sandysense. The Son finally worked up the courage to pat what remained of his mother's long, black curls, and as he did so her remains kindled into the orange heat of something burning too quickly to give off a flame, like leaves in a pipe. An orange line sizzled from her skull through her bones—down her spine, across her ribs, out through her arms, around her pelvis, and down her legs to the tiny bones of her feet. Ruth, the Bride of Plenty, turned to ash that blew away in an instant, without so much as a stain on the floor where she'd died of a broken heart.

*That was one strong woman,* Caralee said to herself as the Son's mama disappeared. It made her think again of her own mama, and of Mag, and of the different kinds of strength that people could possess. Mama Vinnet lost so much blood that it was all she could do to push Caralee out of her own body. Mag had been there and had told Caralee how close a thing it had been, how Caralee had nearly died too.

There had been times, growing up, when Caralee wished that she *had* died. Now, tears hot on her face, she felt ashamed for ever feeling that way. Here was a mama whose babby had killed just about everything, and still she loved him so much that she'd crossed the world just for a moment of peace in the spot where she'd whelped him.

Mag, who hadn't pushed out Caralee or Joe, took care of them both with such a fierceness—maybe Mag thought she needed to work harder to take care of Joe and Caralee as babbies, since they weren't hers. What kind of strength had it taken for Mag to raise Joe? She must have seen Joe's daddy's ghost every time she looked at Joe.

Eusebius sniffled. "Mommy," Caralee heard him say. Sazerac moved his hand around Eusebius's shoulders and rocked him with a gentle touch. They all wiped their tears away with their sleeves—except for Sazerac, who had neither, but who stood with his head bowed in respect.

From outside the nursery came a rustling sound; it was soft, but Caralee heard it clearly through the silence of the Fallow Palace, where the only other sound was the wind. A faint, wet smacking sound and the rustling of leaves.

The Son tensed. He radiated terror and only half hid it. He swept out into the gardens, abandoning the nursery and his private demons without hesitation. Caralee, Eusebius, and Sazerac followed as he stalked toward the steepest path and climbed the last few floors to the highest point of the Fallow Palace.

Caralee heard—definitely heard—a papery whimper from around the bend.

*The Beasts.*

When the incline leveled out, Caralee found herself approaching a hall larger and grander than any they'd passed through, including the entrance hall. Its ceiling was formed of interconnected arches that were otherwise open to the sky and which reminded Caralee of the queen's rib cage. Something hung from the farthest arch, some kind of webbing that was anchored to the floor and the pillars on either side. Something thin and stretched like hide on a tanner's rack. Beneath it, the floor looked slimy wet, and it *stank.*

"Oh my," Eusebius said as they crept forward.

"This . . ." Caralee had never heard Sazerac sound sad before. "This is not their *purpose.*"

They approached, none of them quite willingly. What Caralee saw defied understanding.

The floor was littered with snot and blood and puke and vomit and shit and piss and pus, surrounding a ball of squirming blood vessels that sat on the floor beneath a thing—things?—trapped in the webbing above. The webbing was a crawling gauze of wriggling capillaries and connective tissue, and inside its membrane, something struggled: wet, mushy branches covered in green mud. Branches that were shaped like wings, and between them, something that resembled a head pushed out from the fork where the two wing-branches met.

The head was clearly inhuman. Its bloodshot eyes rolled back and forth beneath lashed lids, but it had no nose, no chin, no ears—just a jutting jawbone clogged with brown, lipless teeth. They'd grown absurdly far from the thing's mouth—ten centimeters or more, at a painful, beak-like angle. The stained enamel had fused together so that the birdlike leaf-creature could not open its mouth. It whimpered at their approach.

The pulsing blood vessels sealed the creature within the envelope, pumping blood into and out of its trapped body.

Craning her neck to look above the tortured, flattened, winged plant-thing, Caralee saw that the bloody ropes weren't attached to any heart or body—they *were* the other occupant of the webbed prison. Wind and Blood. The blood-and-mucus thing was shapeless, just a lace of crawling blood.

This was the Beast who controlled the animals of the world?

"It's the Beast of Blood and the Beast of Wind, innit?" Caralee asked the Son.

He nodded.

The Beast of Wind issued that papery whimper again, and a shudder came from the ball of blood below its thorn-taloned feet. Fat red arteries peeled off from the ball's surface and slapped themselves down onto the floor. Snaking dark veins slithered away from whatever sat at the center of the ball of blood, revealing . . . an egg. A pale blue, brown-speckled egg the size of Sazerac's head. Caralee watched, paralyzed by the grotesquerie, as capillaries finer than hairs pulled themselves out from the speckled blue egg and shrank like salted slugs.

The egg lay still, but the Beasts above it writhed together.

"Did you do this?" Caralee asked, unable to tear her eyes away from the putrid abominations that hung before them, trapped in their own mucus. "Have they been like this for eight hundred years?"

The Son shook his head, holding his hand to his mouth.

"I told you the truth: they did this to each other." He looked sick. "Grandmother Athinne and Grandfather Moysha sent Blood east for a *report,* not to . . . not to try to fix . . ."

"I thought you said that the Beast of Blood kept animals on the straight and narrow?"

He nodded. "Yes. She made sure that animal populations stayed within norms—that populations of prey species and predator species remained in equilibrium, or that species didn't evolve new, unwanted traits. Grandfather Moysha thought there was some imbalance in the ecosystem for which Blood couldn't quite compensate. Your chucklers, for instance. We called them *schacklim,* and they were cute, harmless little fuzzballs. Children kept them as pets in cages strung from the windows, where they'd attract and devour insects. You could fit four of them in the palm of your hand, and their fur was soft as velvet."

*Chucklers? Cute?* She didn't say anything out loud, but *chucklers*?

"But this here bird looks like a tree?" Caralee pointed to the Beast of Wind. "And anyway, it's not a regular animal, is it? It's an immortal Beast of Care who takes . . . *care,* I guess? Of the world? Why would the Beast of Blood try to fix it? Was it broken?"

"I . . . I have . . . Well, she *wouldn't.*"

"If I may," Sazerac spoke up and pointed to the Beast of Blood, which contracted its webbing this way and that, bulging the rest of itself like a panicked eye. "Your Most Holy grandfather may have been mistaken, Most Holy. The ecosystem may indeed have been showing signs of distress even then, but the mis-evolution of the *schacklim* was not a result of Blood's negligence. It was the Beast of Blood *herself* that was failing."

"How the scat do you know that?" Caralee turned on Sazerac.

"A Beast of Care is tied to the Vine. When the Vine began to falter—"

"What is your *real name,* Sazerac?" the Son asked, his voice slow and quiet.

"My name is Sazerac," Sazerac answered promptly, his indigo eye pulsing with each syllable. "I was given it before I received my title."

"It was *your* indigo symbol that I awoke, wasn't it?" the Son demanded. "That day in my playroom. At my birthday party. Surrounded by golden sparkles, that was you, wasn't it?"

"Almost awoke, Most Holy," Sazerac answered. Caralee had no idea what they were talking about. "You almost woke me."

"What is your title, Sazerac?"

"I am not yours, Most Holy." Sazerac shook his head once. "I found the awakening had been canceled. I did not know what to do, so I did nothing, and eventually, I returned to a kind of sleep. I waited to be awoken, to fulfill my purpose."

"What's your purpose, Saz?" Caralee asked. She knew it couldn't be a bad purpose. He was so sweet.

“To serve, simply.”

The Son exhaled, and the breath seemed to go on forever. “Oh, thank the Vine.”

“What do you mean, ‘Oh, thank the Vine’? Now we got three Beasts, a harpy egg, and if Elinor’s the kinda scathole I think she is, a whole metal army looking to cut us up into ribbons?”

The Son threw himself down onto a patch of unfouled ground and tossed his head toward the open sky with a smile. “Since I was *six years old,* I’ve wondered what I did.”

“I remember,” said Sazerac. “You were happy, and then you were gone.”

“Yes.” The Son reached out and traced the shape of Sazerac’s helmet-head. “Father was furious, rightly so. We didn’t know which . . . It might have been something terrible, but it was you. It was—”

“The Beast of Simple Service.” Sazerac bowed. “I am finally awake. I have been given what I was built to need: I belong to Caralee Vinnet, whom I serve with my whole self.”

“You’re a *Beast*?” Caralee crowed. “I’m friends with a Beast?!”

“Not now, Caralee,” the Son snapped. “Besides, you’re friends with me and I’m a . . . I’m . . . You’re friends with *me.* Shut up.”

“Quiet as a spider!” Eusebius nodded, holding a finger to his lips. His tears and sleeve had wiped away the remainder of his makeup.

The Son stared at Saz. “Sazerac, can you separate Blood and Wind?” he asked.

“I cannot. I am, as titled, a simple Beast. I could not accomplish the feats that Blood and Wind appear to have done if given ten thousand years. I can, however, advise.”

“Your advice, then?”

“Blood appears to have mistaken Wind for an animal. A vertebrate. A bird. To mistake Wind for a bird makes a certain amount of sense—the Beast of Wind is often represented as a bird, and indeed it was capable of taking the *shape* of a bird, insofar as it could direct its biomass to form wings and take flight.”

“But?”

“But it was never an animal, Most Holy. The Beast of Wind, whose purpose—as you might imagine—is to maintain the atmosphere, was designed out of the sort of life that could, did, and *does* maintain the atmosphere.”

The Son looked like Sazerac had punched him in the stomach.

“Sap and syrup and semen and sand, it’s a *plant*!”

"Duh," said Caralee, who pointed at the branches and the matted . . . well, they weren't leaves. What were they?

"That's *plankton.*" The Son followed Caralee's finger. "That's algae and leaf and moss and oh, fuck us all—the Beast of Wind was never seen because it was *everywhere.* It was in the forests, breathing out oxygen. It was in the grass underfoot, breathing out oxygen. And most of all, most of all, it was in the seas, *breathing out oxygen.* We never saw it—or 'them,' properly, to speak with respect—because they were spread across the surface of every body of water in the world."

"Indeed, Most Holy." Sazerac nodded to the east. "When your grandparents sent Blood east—"

"Blood must have sought the Beast of Wind in the Morning Glory Sea, and gathered enough of their biomass to manipulate Wind into *this,* which shouldn't be able to live . . ."

"Wind has been corrupted by Blood, who thought that Wind ought to be a bird," Sazerac said.

"And she has been forcing Wind into this bird-shape ever since, trapping them both here, webbed in a sustained transformation and slow death. Their mutual capacity for self-rebirth caused . . . *this.*" The Son nodded to the egg.

Together, in agony, the Beasts created the harpy.

"They can't fulfill their purposes like this, can they?" Caralee asked.

"Hardly!" the Son hollered. "If I separate them, what happens?" he asked Sazerac.

"Unclear. Both will die. Blood will, most likely, return to the soil before she expires, so that she might be reborn."

"And Wind?"

"Will also die. This far from the sea and the wood, I cannot believe that they can successfully induce parthenogenesis. They have neither water nor flora in which to incubate."

"But if I can get them to the sea?" The Son sounded desperate. "Just look at the sky. We need the Beast of Wind, or the world will surely suffocate."

"I do not know." Sazerac sounded mournful. Caralee supposed that these Beasts were its family, after all.

"Oh. Okay." It was hard for Caralee to wrap her head around all this. Maybe that's what was making everyone else so stupid, too. Except for Saz—he seemed to be smarter, now that his story had been told for everyone to hear. He seemed free to speak his mind, which gave her hope, somehow.

"So," Caralee said, trying her best to lay out their options in an even-headed manner. "Son, can you take a look at Wind and figure out what Blood is doing to it?"

Caralee opened her own sandysense to the Beastly mass, but she couldn't make heads or tails out of what she perceived. Knots upon knots upon knots, it looked like.

The Son, whose sandysense had been up and ready the whole time, shook his head in similar frustration. "Not really. My studies tell me that what I'm seeing is some elemancy: a flow of water to keep Wind alive; she makes her own air still—that's good for obvious reasons—but mostly it looks like chicken."

"What's chicken?"

"It's . . . oh, never mind. Mostly I see bird, is what I'm saying. I see a bird-thing made out of plant-stuff, hooked up to a senile blood bag."

"Yes." Sazerac nodded. "*Senile* is an appropriate word. Blood's sickness corrupts her rational faculties. She is senile, not wicked. She has forgotten herself and is trying the best she can. Unfortunately, her best is harmful." He paused. "Harmful, but stable—if she is still forcing the Beast of Wind to lay eggs after more than eight centuries, she does not appear to have worsened. She may not be an immediate concern."

"Say that in regular, please?" Caralee begged.

"I can still fix this," answered the Son. "They can both be reborn."

"Just so," Saz confirmed.

"So kill her! Free her! Whatever?"

The Son said nothing. He kept still on the ground, cross-legged, face hidden by his dark hair. He stared at his hands.

"Not yet, Caralee." His voice was ice. "You and I have some . . . business, first."

The ice in the Son's voice spread to Caralee's spine, and she shivered.

"We . . . we do?" she asked, feeling very small.

"We do." He looked up, face a perfect mask. "Eusebius, you know what to do?"

The old sandymancer sagged, but nodded. "I am afraid that I do, Most Holy."

"Sazerac?" The Son turned to the Beast of Simple Service. "Are you ready to serve?"

Sazerac said nothing.

"Sazerac?" The Son fixed the stone man with a stern look.

"Just *tell me*," Caralee stomped her foot on the tiled floor. "I came all this way, and if you're going to kill me *now*, you're a scathole. And if you're gonna recruit Saz and Eusebius to do me in, then you're a lying coward, too!"

"You promised to follow me to the end of the world, Caralee." The Son sounded reasonable, not murderous, but Caralee knew that he was full of lies and secrets, and she did not trust her ears. "Well, you have."

"So, what? You let me come all this way only to tag-team me with a wizard and a Beast?"

"I will never harm you, Caralee," said Sazerac.

"Nor I, young miss." Eusebius seemed less certain of himself. Was that his condition or what?

"Then why're you all looking at me like that? Buncha liars, I'll rip your heads off my damn self. Why, I can do it right now if I—"

"Shut. Up." The Son raised his voice. The trapped Beasts stilled their ceaseless struggle, cowed by the voice of their master. "Just listen. I'm going to do something, and I need you to let me do it. Do you understand what I'm saying?"

"Fuck no I don't!" She stepped back, holding out her hands to keep him away. "What are you going to do to me?"

The Son looked offended, and Caralee wondered how wrongly she'd misread the situation.

"Caralee, you know how much I hate saying these words, but *I need you.* Everybody, everything that lives in this world needs you. We have two Beasts to untangle, and we need two . . . ugh . . . 'sandymancers' to perform the feat. No offense to your amnesiac tutor, but he hardly counts."

"Well." Eusebius sounded insulted. "It is my priority to ensure that young Miss Caralee receives her education. Such an opportunity to learn, this is! I should be a terrible tutor if I denied her the chance to *learn by doing.*"

"See?" The Son leaned back onto his arms, still sitting on the floor. "We're going to fix the Beasts, together . . ." He looked to Eusebius, who bowed his head. "But I have to do something else first. I *want* to do something else first. Do you promise not to interrupt me?"

"No! You're up to something behind my back, and I know it. Whatever you tried to make Sazerac promise. Whatever deal you made with Eusebius. You're a liar and a monster, and I hate you!"

Caralee had leverage, real leverage. The Son said that he *needed her.* Unless he was lying, a moment like this would not come again. If it was all a ruse, well . . .

The Son stood and pointed to Sazerac. "Sit, Beast."

Sazerac did not move.

"Do it! Beast of Simple Service, the Son of the Vine commands you. Sit and submit."

"Regrettably, Administrator, I am unable to fulfill your request."

"Oh, you deceitful rockslide!" The Son drew on his sandysense until he glowed in Caralee's eyes. A face like the sun itself. "Sit now or I'll return you to the stone from which you came!"

"That is unlikely, Most Holy. There are no longer any asteroids in this solar system."

"We'll see how coy you are when you're nothing but smoking rubble. How will your Caralee ever see Joe again without you?"

*Huh?*

"Stop it stop it stop it!" Caralee called on her own sandysense, booming her voice out through the Fallow Palace, just as she'd done when she'd summoned the Son of the Vine out of the fringes of the wasteland. The stone tree rang with her voice. "You're *not* trying to kill me?"

"When have I ever *tried* to kill someone?" the Son shouted, then began to laugh. "Besides, I promised you the end to my story. I certainly hope I don't end here."

"So what are you on about?" she all but whispered. "And what's this about Joe?"

"*Bloody wind, bloody wind,*" Eusebius sang to Caralee. Not to himself but to her. "*Blood and Wind and a Beast, a Beast, a Beast for Dunes.*"

"What . . ." Caralee remembered the strange song Eusebius had sung. "What are you and Eusebius trying to do? Can one of these Beasts save Joe Dunes?"

The Son pursed his lips and tried not to smile.

Something like relief flooded Caralee. Her head felt hot.

"Did it ever *once* occur to you to be honest with me?" she asked the Son.

"Often. If I had been honest, you would ask me, 'What will happen to Sazerac?' and I would tell you that I do not know. You would ask me, 'Will it work?' and I would tell you that I do not know. You would ask me, 'Will it hurt?" and I would tell you—"

"Okay, I get it." Caralee felt as though her heart had stopped beating. As stupid as it sounded, the Son wasn't wrong. "What do you mean, 'What will happen to Sazerac?' What kind of question is that?"

"One human body fits one human soul. There's no room for Joe inside me." He turned to Sazerac. "My . . . *Your* Beast of Simple Service, however, may be another matter."

"So . . . Saz? I can have my Joe back?" Caralee's heart went from still to pounding. "I . . . Really? But . . . will it hurt Sazerac?"

"I do not know."

"Why now?" she demanded. "Why get all the way up here only to stop and give me what I've wanted all along?"

"Because I do not know how this day will end, and"—the Son brushed his hands across his chest—"if this body dies, so does Joe."

*Oh.*

"It's okay, Saz." Caralee said the words before she'd made the decision. "You can sit. If you want."

Caralee decided to take the Son at his word, although her fear of betrayal lingered. If he said he would give back Joe, somehow—anyhow—she *had* to listen.

"Yes, Caralee." Sazerac dipped his big head in a nod, and he sat where he stood. "I would like to help your friend."

"Fine. Thank you, Caralee." The Son gathered his thoughts—or maybe they were Joe's thoughts—and snapped his fingers. "Eusebius, Sazerac, *now.*"

"Oh! Oh . . ." Eusebius despaired.

The Son knelt beside the Beast of Simple Service. Eusebius stood behind them, the god-king and the sweet, fat statue. The wizard pressed his hand against the crown of the Son's skull. He held the other to Sazerac's helmet-head, resting some of his weight there.

"Do you remember how?" the Son asked Eusebius.

*How what?* Could Joe really fit inside Sazerac? Would he be the same Joe that Caralee remembered? Would he be in pain? Would he hate her for pouring his ghost into a walking statue?

"Indeed, Most Holy." Eusebius nodded. "I don't think I could forget your instruction if I tried, could I?"

"No, you couldn't." The Son looked straight ahead, hands flat against his thighs. Kneeling didn't lessen him in any way.

"That ent how forgetting works." Caralee clapped her hands over her mouth. "Sorry. I know, I'm sorry."

"Do it, Eusebius Gibberosus Kampouris," the Son commanded. "Just as I taught you."

The Son's sandymancy returned in full brilliance, and a gold-and-white light filled his eyes and mouth and nostrils. Eusebius, too, vibrated with sandymancy that not-felt white and gold, from his hands, down his arms, and through his chest. Sazerac's indigo eye lit up, not pulsing, but a solid indigo lantern inside its recess.

"What are you doing?" Caralee asked, though none of them paid her any mind. "What are you *doing*?"

Sazerac began to buzz with the combined energies of Eusebius and the Son.

His glaring eye turned color from indigo to gold, and together the three of them shone like the sun. Caralee shielded her eyes.

The Beasts pulsed in their self-sealed envelope, thrumming the bloody membrane like a drum.

The Son began to twitch, eyes rolling back into his head, and his body spasmed. Sazerac began to vibrate—humming like the train on its tracks—and his gold eye flickered at incredible speed. It looked like torture for them both.

Above, Eusebius stood blazing, his eyes filled with terror, his arms filled with light, a true wizard at last.

"*Sazerac!*" she screamed. "Please be okay. Son! You're all hurting yourselves!" Caralee didn't remember when she'd begun sobbing, but her breath caught in her chest.

"Don't leave me," Caralee begged, snot streaming down her face.

The thrashings stopped as suddenly as they'd begun. The three collapsed as one.

Eusebius's light winked out, and he fell backward onto the stone floor, crooked arms splayed out and eyes closed fast, his last taper snuffed out.

The Son slumped forward, unconscious. Sazerac didn't slump or fall but remained inert.

Caralee scrabbled to the Son's side. He was unconscious but breathing, and she shook his shoulders till he groaned. Moving to Eusebius, Caralee heard a gentle snoring. The wax from his last candle cooled in a little puddle, white and gone.

"Caralee?" Sazerac whimpered. His voice was still sweet and deep, but not the gravel-growl she'd grown to love.

Saz pushed himself up with clumsy arms. One slipped, and he grumbled till he righted himself. He tried to sit crosswise and grumbled again.

*Saz isn't clumsy.* And then, *Saz doesn't grumble.*

He looked to Caralee. "You ent hurt, Caralee?"

*No.*

Caralee's couldn't feel her face.

"*Joe Dunes?*"

"Caralee?"

Caralee leapt onto Sazerac's body and threw her arms around the place where his neck would have been if he hadn't been mostly boulder.

"*It worked!*" Sazerac roared, deep and goofy, just like a dunderhead. "Caralee! Can you hear me? Am I talking out loud? I've been screaming forever. Am I screaming? I missed you so much. You were *right there*, but I wasn't me anymore. Can you hear me now? Say something." His eye pulsed gold when he spoke.

"You're screaming," Caralee said with a smile so big she thought the top of her head might slide off. "Of course I can hear screaming, you git."

"I am a git," Joe lowered his voice. It *was* his voice—two octaves lower and grating out from Sazerac's stone visor. "I shoulda been able to do something."

"*I'm a git.*" Caralee tried to shake Joe by his old shoulders and grabbed stone instead. "Son said you were gone, and I just gave up and believed him."

"*Gave up?* Is your head still fulla chuckle, under all that chamistry and hustory and language and magick and murder?" His three fingers felt warm-as-Joe against her arm.

"Yeah, but still . . . I *doubted.*" Caralee looked into the empty cavity where Joe's eyes should be. "There was just no . . . I couldn't see *you* anymore. At the start, when he still looked like you sometimes, I believed, but that stopped and why would he keep you alive?"

"That ent important." Joe waved Sazerac's big stone hands. They moved in wonky circles, just like Joe's hands used to do, when they were made of Joe.

*It's Joe.* It was. Just to see him move, swinging those arms around . . . The sound of Joe's voice lit up Caralee's heart with a light she'd tried her best to squish out. Something silly in her belly, shining sillily from her eyes. Caralee blushed.

"Caralee, I never left you. I was there the whole time, I promise. What you done, I don't know how to thank you." Joe shook Sazerac's head. "You kept going. Kept learning. You *impressed* him, Caralee. The Son wasn't about to give up a young, strong body—but with Sazerac—"

"Is Saz hurt?"

"I am not, Caralee," said Sazerac in Sazerac's voice. When Sazerac spoke, his eye pulsed indigo, like usual—it was easy to tell who was speaking. Saz patted his big belly. "You might say that I have room for two. Comfortably so. I apologize for my disobedience, Caralee. The Son of the Vine convinced me that helping your friend Joe Dunes would sufficiently please you to merit a brief period of omission and only a momentary disobedience."

"Saz—"

"I have betrayed you." It was an odd thing to see, a statue going limp with shame.

"Saz, you're wonderful and you didn't betray me, and I can't believe it but the Son was *right*. We got Joe back, all that matters of him, anyway."

"Yeah." Joe didn't entirely agree. "Can I still be mad that I'm not all here and never will be?"

"Of course you can, and don't be so sure." Caralee felt lifted up and cocky.

*I did it,* she thought. Caralee didn't know whether the Son had grown truly fond of her or what, but he couldn't have intended this from the start, so something had changed. Maybe Sazerac made it convenient to spare Joe, sure, but the Son could have said nothing, and Caralee would never have thought to ask him for *this.*

"Caralee." Joe put three stone fingers on her shoulder. "Nobody can give me that body back; it's not mine now. Nobody can fix that, Caralee, not all the sandymancy in the world."

*Oh, Joe. Haven't you learned anything?*

"You don't believe that, do you, Joe Dunes?" Caralee poked Joe's massive chest—lightly. "Naw, you don't. Git."

"I don't?"

"Who am I, Joe?" She summoned a witchlight and set it to spiraling overhead. "What do they call me, Joe?" Another witchlight, and another, spiraling up and away. The Beast's song rippled with human laughter.

"Well, they call you Caralee Vinnet, but they say it a lot nicer now!" Joe sounded happy for her. *Git.*

"True, but they *also* call me—"

"*Young miss?*" Joe guessed. "No, they call you *shitfarmer*!"

"They call her *sandymancer,* piglet!" the Son shouted sleepily, propped up one elbow and shaking his head with relief. "That's been my pet name for our Joe. Isn't that right, piglet?"

Joe flinched.

"What's a piglet?" Caralee said, blinking at the thought. "Never mind, I don't care."

"Oh, sweet silence," the Son whispered, staying oddly still on the ground. "It's been *years* since I had a single moment without someone pounding against my thoughts. Maddening."

Caralee let her chin drop to her chest. She felt a wash of shame for believing that the Son had been conspiring to *hurt* her, when instead he'd risked himself to bring her family back together.

"Son, I'm sorry—"

"Shh." He held a finger to his lips. They were his lips now, truly his. Caralee had won, and she had also lost. "Don't ruin the moment."

Caralee reached up to her witchlights and let them wink out, bursting like bubbles.

The entangled Beasts of Blood and Wind moaned, and the egg beneath them rocked. Everyone noticed, including Eusebius, who let out a high-pitched hooting sound and pulled his face from the floor, blinking.

"Oho!" Eusebius cried. "My friends, we seem to have found ourselves atop a most unusual structure. Where have I led us now, I wonder?" He felt his shoulders and looked crestfallen when discovering they were bare. "My tapers seem to have . . ."

"Hey, Eusebius," Caralee spoke gently. "Why don't you try singing something?"

*It can't hurt,* she thought.

"Sing, young miss?" Eusebius harrumphed, but hummed something to himself. He found a tune and followed it, nodding along. He stopped and smiled at Caralee. "Ah, so!"

"Thank fucking *god,*" the Son muttered. "Thank me. You're welcome."

"Hey!" Joe's voice was stern. "Thank Caralee. She's the one who taught *you* how to work around the old guy's bonked-up memory."

The Son glared at him.

"Most Holy? Sazerac?" Eusebius returned their attention to the Beasts of Blood and Wind in their mistaken embrace. "How long does a Beast take to regenerate? And how long might a misbegotten Beastly egg take to hatch?"

"Still your fear. Eggs pose no danger. Nor hatchlings," the Son reassured Eusebius. "At least, I think not. The Beasts move according to geological time-scales, for the most part. We killed the steel harpy days ago, and Wind has only just laid an egg."

"Yeah, well, fuck that? Nobody asked me but I think we should—" Caralee began, and slopped through the slippery filth toward the egg.

"—break the egg before—" The Son followed her, as did Sazerac.

"—break it, like, *right now.*" Caralee lifted up her boot, but her boot barely reached the top of the egg. The blood vessels were thickest there, attached to a kind of placental glob of bloody tissue. The egg rocked again.

"Wait." The Son nudged away Caralee's foot with his. "Let me think."

"We could eat it!" Joe said from Sazerac's body, patting his slab of a belly. "*You* could eat it, anyway."

"Don't be stupid, piglet." The Son wrinkled his nose at the tapestry of wounded caretakers. "Sazerac, will you take hold of the egg, please? Lift it up? Don't let Joe touch it; he's . . . what's the word? Fingerdaft."

"What should I do with the egg, Caralee?" Sazerac asked Caralee, not the Son.

"Um. Hold it tight, like Son said, but not too tight."

"Just so." The Son bit his lip, absorbed in his sandysense, losing himself a bit in the study of the Beasts and their harpy egg. "Eusebius, can you manage to pinch off the blood vessels connecting the Beast of Blood to the Beast of Wind?" He looked to Caralee and winked. "The sandymancer and I shall tackle the meat of the matter."

"We shall?"

"You don't think we're up to it?" The Son arched an eyebrow.

"Course we are." Caralee shook her head. She'd *done it.* Joe was alive. She'd carried so much fear for him—for them. Now hope swelled up where that fear had been, strong and light. "We're up to anything, ent we?"

Saz cocked his head at her. Maybe it was Joe. She was amazed that Joe could even recognize her, palling around with the god-king who'd stolen his body.

"Hoo, Most Holy?" Eusebius tugged at his plumed collar with a finger. The feathers shimmered with their dark rainbow of purples and greens. "I spy rather a *lot* of vasculature connecting Blood to Wind. Dozens of veins and arteries—hundreds of capillaries."

"Yes, Eusebius, I can see that." The Son brushed hair away from his eyes with slim fingers. "May I suggest that you find the iron within the Beasts and hold it still? You'll grab all the atoms at once and then squeeze."

"Oho, well . . . but . . . *iron*?" The wizard pulled a face.

"Yeah, it's the blockum that makes blood red," said Caralee with a scoff. "Where you been?"

"What? Iron in blood? Young miss, you mustn't be a ridiculous person." The wizard blinked. "*Unless.* I've made one of my discoveries again, haven't I? Some notion of alchemical insight? I'm no expert, but a man of the mind must accept that his idle thoughts shall blossom and bear fruit." Eusebius practically preened himself. "Stop the blood? I shall make an attempt."

The egg in Sazerac's hands was just larger than his head, and he held it away from his body, like someone had just handed him a babby with a nappy full of scat.

"I shall begin my conjuration forthwith!" Eusebius proclaimed and wiggled his fingers at the membrane of red lace that was the Beast of Blood. Eusebius tilted his head sideways and raised his arms as if bearing a great weight.

The web of blood vessels slowed its pulse. Eusebius churned his arms and wiggled his fingers, maintaining the feat. When the flow of blood stilled completely, he crowed.

The Beast of Blood adapted by growing new blood vessels—hair-fine capillaries that swelled with redirected blood.

"Oho, compatriots?" Eusebius wheezed. "Did I anticipate this response?"

The Son frowned but waved away any idea of failure. "She's growing new and separate vascular systems." He turned to Caralee distractedly and said, "This is a good example of a redundancy, so take note."

"Just keep at it, Eusebius," Caralee advised. The Son let out a ragged sigh.

"Caralee, I want you to drain Blood of all of her water," he said. "Don't rush yourself—I'd much rather we do this right than do it fast. *However,* you mustn't let the water dissipate or spill. I need you to hold it—in the air will be easiest, if you—"

"I *just* did this yesterday? When I rusted-up Elinor?"

"Right, who am I to tell Caralee Vinnet what to do? Not her god nor her king nor the absolute authority on all matters arcane, no, certainly not." The Son smiled huge and scary like a chuckler and mimed taking a bite out of Caralee's head. "All of the breathable air in the world depends upon your focus. Consider that."

"Oh. Okay." Caralee sobered at the thought. "Here we go, I guess."

When she gathered her sandysense, the Beasts burst into a moving portrait of non-colors and non-scents and non-tastes: they were ornate, incredibly complicated, and *alive* with sandymancy in the same way that she was alive with the elements that sandymancy controlled. Seeing through the eyes of a sandymancer, Caralee found the points of contact where the Beast of Blood wrapped herself around the Beast of Wind. Caralee felt the sensation of . . . taking a deep breath and holding it forever: that must come from Wind, whose only job was to breathe.

The Beast of Blood became a gorgeous arrangement of ribbons, coiled and curled and angled and stepped and whorled, all working in concert, moving as one giant machine to process, analyze, and *change* the blood-gut-pus-stuff of whatever she came into contact with. She was chugging, working ceaselessly to pump whatever it was that made an animal an animal—whatever made a bird a bird—into the Beast of Wind.

"Whenever you're ready," said the Son. He seemed alert but no longer anxious, and full of power. They were on the same page.

Caralee began her work. Drawing water out of the Beast of Blood was an easy thing, and Caralee accomplished it quickly: water misted off the enveloped Beasts, and Blood's vessels deflated.

In response, Blood sang out in pain, her emptying vessels fluting out a song of distress as Caralee emptied them of their essential juice.

Soon a ball of water hung in the air overhead, with little pipes of water draining into it from the Beast of Blood, and Blood's magnificent webbing dried into a mess of string, rust-colored and brittle, glued together by drying snot.

*Blood,* Caralee thought with a bloom of recognition, *has finally died. What next?*

One little worm of red artery pulled away from the drying, dying mass and dropped to the black stone floor, wriggling. It inched away from Caralee, until it found the razor-thin edge of the floor and dropped off, falling to the ground that lay far, far below.

*It gets reborn.*

The Son clapped. "Wonderful!"

Inside the newly-dried webbing, the Beast of Wind rustled, then struggled, then sagged. They still could not exhale. Caralee watched them die.

The Son saw, too, and nodded. "One Beast down, sent off to be reborn. Now we've one dead-or-dying Beast to restore. First, watch while I drain the tainted amniotic fluid from the egg."

He performed a more complicated version of the water-draining that Caralee had just done, only it wasn't just water that he pulled out of the egg, through its blue shell. The fluid was thick like mucus and red like blood and white like birdscat, but also rich and slick with something that smelled like boiled greens.

The Son hurled this egg-slop over the edge of the hall's floor, following the path of the babby Beast of Blood. Caralee was glad for that, as they hardly needed more filth underfoot.

When the egg was empty of its water and its goo, Caralee—with her sandy-sense still roaring—saw a tiny shape revealed inside, curled up at the bottom of the egg. It looked so sad and weak. A little head, with little feet, and tiny glands just between the feet. Wings so small they were hardly there at all; the saddest, cruelest beak there ever was.

Caralee realized just how miserable the harpy must have been, from egg to dead. It was a crime to keep her alive.

The Son must have felt so, too, because he heaved a sigh weighted with all the sympathy in the world, and turned to Caralee. "Now," he said, "pull *clean* water into the egg. This is the important part. The water *must* reach the embryo. When you've finished, don't let go—keep watch with your seventh . . . with your *sandysense*. Ridiculous archmage, you."

"Oh. Yeah. Okay." Caralee understood some of what the Son intended to do, now that she was halfway through the process. Pulling the water into the egg was just as easy as draining it from the Beast of Blood had been, and much easier than the Son's task of draining the egg had looked. This was just water, pure water—two blockums of one color attached to a single blockum of another color. She pushed the water into the egg and pulled the air out at the same time, lest the pressure crack open the egg.

The entire time, Saz remained as still as, well, a statue, the egg safely in his hands. His service *was* simple, but they couldn't go without it.

When Caralee had finished, she kept her sandysense up and attentive. The Son turned to her, triumph and magick blazing behind his eyes. They must be so close.

"The rest should take care of itself." He closed his eyes, annoyed at his lack of focus. "Observe."

Caralee focused her sandysense on the babby harpy inside its purified egg.

The poor thing folded around itself, beak to toes, at the bottom of the shell. Its still-closed eyes darted back and forth, as if it dreamt, and it pulled its little white wings close to its body. It looked so cold.

"I wanna give it a cuddle till it's warm." She didn't shift her gaze. "That ent what we're doing, though."

"Not everything we do is a heartache, Caralee," the Son murmured. "There are moments for miracles, too."

With her sandysense, Caralee saw the little babby harpy slowly shake itself awake—cocking its head like it had heard a noise—and work to open its yet-unfused beak. The wee thing seized, and shook, and tried to cry out, and Caralee whimpered in sympathy—but the shaking stilled, and the harpy uncurled its neck like a dancer, and its beak, open like parted lips, opened wider—and wider, and *wider*. As Caralee watched with her sandysense, the bright white tip of something real and solid emerged from the babby's beak. At first, Caralee thought it might be a tongue, or whatever birds had in place of tongues.

The white tip grew, and grew longer than a gullet, and then grew longer than a tongue, and it changed color from white to green. It was the shoot of a plant, pushing up and out of its seed. Caralee watched the sprout split into its first two leaves, pale green but darker than the stem. Another sprout emerged from inside the harpy's mouth, and then another, intertwining until they formed the head of a tiny bird, made all of sprouts.

A bird from within a bird; a plant from within an animal. As Caralee watched, the bird-of-plants sprouted a bright red trumpet flower for a beak of its own. A happy beak.

A long-stemmed neck emerged as the sprouts grew, then shoulders covered in green leaflets pulled themselves out from the harpy's open beak, and Caralee realized that the babby harpy itself was shrinking. It wasn't withering or dying—it was just becoming *less*, and the bird-of-plants that emerged from inside it became *more*.

The new bird pulled out one tiny, bent wing feathered with smooth, wet leaves. Another wing followed, and then a fat lozenge of body as the sprout-thing pulled itself, wriggling, out of what was left of the babby harpy. The newborn Beast of Wind's legs were twigs; their claws were thorns—instead of eyes, two tiny yellow flowers opened, their centers black and alert.

"Sazerac, as gently as you can, open the egg." The Son's voice sounded faint, like a person standing at a distance.

"Do it, Saz," Caralee approved. "Real soft-like."

Without letting go of the egg, Sazerac pierced the shell with a finger on either side. He curled his fingers to crack open the top of the egg, leaving the bottom intact. The reborn Beast of Wind lay inside the bottom of the eggshell, a babby in its cradle. Their harpy skin and bones, discarded at last and unable to cause any more pain, were all but dust beneath the Beast's bright green body.

Above them, the old Beast of Wind rustled in its webbing, then sagged, and became still. Bits of their dried wing-stuff flaked off, pieces of see-through green paper swirling through the air.

The newly hatched Beast of Wind opened their red trumpet-petaled beak to caw and out came a rush of air, a powerful jet of breath as strong as a sandstorm. Their wings unfurled, leaves growing in seconds rather than days, and kicked their stem feet. Their leaf-covered body, dotted here and there with half-hidden folds of colors that might have been other flowers lurking among the leaves, fluttered in the gusts of wind that blew from within their own body.

The Son stepped up toward Sazerac, hands cupped, nervous as a new father. His smile was sad and glad and agonized as well. He offered the Beast of Wind a finger, tenderly, to wrap their claw around. He purred, low and deep, and the Beast cocked their head and nodded, flexing their leaves and stems and climbing into the Son's hands. The Beast did not move with the awkwardness of a newborn creature but with the slow and steady purpose of an ancient being, who knew their body and its perils, even when that body was brand new. The Son brought his hand to his shoulder, and the Beast of Wind hopped on, then turned around in three darting steps, and leaned their head against the brown curve of the Son's neck.

For a breath, everyone was struck with awe and filled with pride. Something beautiful had been wrought, and it was they who had wrought it—as friends. As a family.

*Family.*

The Beast of Wind flapped their eye-petals at Caralee and dipped their head once in a way that spoke volumes of gratitude. Caralee had done what had been asked of her, and she'd stood by the Son while he'd said goodbye to his mama, and she'd helped save the Beasts that needed saving—the first step to healing the world and fixing the sky.

Caralee nodded back to the wise, wee Beastie, her heart full of gratitude. She'd *mattered.*

The Son relaxed his posture, and with a wave of sandymancy, he swept the snot and dried blood off the floor of the high hall. The dead Beasts flaked into dust and were blown away until the hall was as bare and clean as the rest of the Fallow Palace.

Sazerac sat, and Caralee found his arm and hugged it. She hugged *Joe.*

"You did it, Caralee," Joe said. "You're amazing."

His voice was boulder-thick and hard to read, but she thought he sounded like he was crying.

After so much running, flying, crawling, weeping, screaming, begging, learning, sleeping, freezing, burning, climbing, hoping, dreading, planning, and reacting, the four—no, the five—were left with a moment of emptiness. That moment stretched and stretched and stretched and stretched. Caralee rested her head against Joe and Sazerac's warm shoulder, holding fast. Joe reached out with Sazerac's other arm and pulled Eusebius into a comfortable, warm position.

After a moment, and with his fluid perfection, the Son sat cross-legged without disturbing the babby Beast on his shoulder.

"Are you happy to be free, little one?" he asked the little Beast.

"I'd be happier if I had my old body," answered Joe, gold eye winking.

"I was not talking to you, piglet." The Son ran his hands down his chest. "But listen well: we all lose ourselves. Every minute, we are dying and reborn. Let yourselves be reborn—the past is dead."

"That's easy for you to say," Joe complained. "Ent it?"

The Son returned a bland smile. "Sazerac?"

"Yes, Most Holy?" His eye pulsed indigo now as Sazerac took the reins.

"Can a Beast feel happiness?" The blandness stiffened.

"We are each our own creation." Saz did not elaborate.

"That is not what I asked you, Sazerac." The Son clasped his hands in his lap.

"It is the only answer that I have, Most Holy."

"Yeah." The Son's stiff smile wilted. "Me too."

No one spoke. Caralee had never considered the Son's happiness. His miseries, of course—she'd tested for weakness by prying into his pride, or his sorrow, and his shame. Despite all her frantic strategizing, her vigilance, and her constant observation, Caralee never asked herself what, if anything, would make the Son happy.

Evidently, he had the same question.

They rested and let the day pass. Minutes, hours clocked by, and the silence soothed Caralee's frayed nerves. The only sounds were atmosphere: the thrumming of the palace in the wind and, from the reborn chick, the hiss of air returning to the world. The sun greased itself into the west, drenching the Fallow Palace with orange light. Still, no one moved.

Caralee had never felt so exhausted or so incapable of words or sleep. She squeezed Sazerac's arm, and her eyes welled up at the heat from his stone. She smiled and cried at her failure and her success. She hadn't gotten Joe back at all. Joe had been returned to her. And yet his body was gone for good. She felt too many different emotions to know them all, but one of them was *happy.*

And also *homesick.*

Caralee stared in wonder at the babby Beast. They, at least, were a thing of purest hope. The world had not known hope for so long, and Caralee knew she'd played a role in its return. For a creation that kept the world alive, the Beast of Wind looked awfully dainty. Their little beak was a long red flower, and their bean sprout body was downed with pale leaves. They rustled and flapped their tiny wings, and Caralee saw the pale petals lining the undersides of their wingtips, which fluttered in the constant wind that came from their body.

After the sun had set and the starbirth clouds gathered their colors across the spangled sky, Caralee summoned a hot yellow *filkapyth* to warm the hall. It wasn't much different from making a witchlight—if anything, heating stone was easier to work with than hot gas. The Son merely nodded and warmed his feet at the hearthstone. Caralee stroked Joe and Sazerac's helmet-head. "What do we do now?" she asked.

"We let the Beast rest until they've gathered strength—which I believe they have—and then we set them free." The Son smiled, a little sad. "And we hope that they survive the journey east, to the Morning Glory Sea."

"How do we set it free?"

"*Them,* Caralee, not *it.* We say their name."

At the thought, the Beast flapped their wings and lifted off from the Son's shoulder, swanning through the air, circling overhead until they landed on Caralee's finger. She felt Sazerac turn his head to watch, and gold light thrummed in the corner of Caralee's vision as Joe cooed.

The outgassing of air from the jewel-bright Beast was gentler than she'd expected, a rushing but warm breeze. The Beast of the Wind looked up at her with bright yellow eyes, petals blinking like eyelids. They kissed her knuckles with their red trumpet flower beak, and Caralee felt a little stamen-tongue lick the sweat from her hand.

"What's their name?" she asked in a whisper, awed past awe. She inhaled the scent of all the gardens that had ever lived and the purest air she'd never known.

"What do you think is the Auld Vintage word for *wind*? Say it, and they will know themselves, and they will fly."

Caralee thought on that. She knew that *nepe* meant "air." Auld Vintage had a funny but simple way of putting words together that was different from regular talking, but, like blockums and Beasts and hearthstones, was no longer a mystery. If sad-air-house was a house-in-mourning, and Vine-daughter-daughter meant Granddaughter of the Vine . . . what would wind need to be?

*Well, wind is air coming from the air, ent it? So what's air-air?* Was it that simple? Caralee had learned that when it mattered, most things were.

"*Nepe-Nepe.* Air-air, or air from air." Although Caralee knew the words that she needed to fit together, doing so took more finesse. Caralee remembered the Son's lessons about letters, and voicing, and how sounds compromised themselves to blend into words.

"*Nepe . . . Nebe . . . Neme . . . Nemye!*" Caralee raised her hand and smiled at the Beast. They looked so fragile, but how could that be so? The whistling gales of the wasteland moved dunes as tall as mountains, and twisters erased entire settlements. "Hello, wee babby birdy. My name is Caralee Vinnet, and I'm a sandymancer. It's really nice to meet you."

The Beast of Wind held Caralee's gaze, unblinking.

"Your name is *Nemyenep,* and you are the Wind."

Quick as lightning, *Nemyenep* beat their wings twice and shot up overhead.

They fluttered around the darkening hall, then winged off eastward, racing away from the sunset.

The Son slow-clapped. Above his grin, his eyes were as dark and inscrutable as *Nemyenep*'s.

"What. Was. That." Joe didn't have the words, and Caralee couldn't much blame him.

"Will the sky turn bright blue again?" Caralee asked the Son—the first question on her mind was from Marm-marm's lessons.

"Yes." The Son nodded. "But not anytime soon, not with *that*." The veil of night crept over the lip of the world, and the last of the sun lit the crack in the sky with ruddy light. "This is a good start."

"And Joe was alive this whole time, inside you?"

The Son shrugged.

"Why'd you save him?'

"Because I could." The Son sounded glib as usual, but Caralee didn't believe him.

"You shouldn'ta kept that a secret." Something selfish tugged the wrong way inside her. *I wanted to be the one to do it.* "I thought you were, maybe, conspiring against me."

"Of *course* I was!" The Son laughed from his belly. "*I saved Joe without you.* Caralee Vinnet, you are quite defeated in your quest. A complete and utter failure. I'm alive and free and whole and *alone inside my head* for the first time in centuries, and I have *you* to thank for my many victories. Conversely, you have only yourself to blame for your failure to defeat me."

He winked and stood and walked to the edge of the hall, looking out over the dark valley below. The Son cut a fine figure, strong but slender, a beauty and a beast. She wondered what emotions he wrestled with beneath that practiced veneer. It's not every day a person apologizes to their mother's corpse and saves the world. Caralee knew without asking that the Son had never spared the soul of any of his previous bodies.

She left him to his thoughts and hoped that he'd spared his own soul as well as Joe's.

"Wait, what?" Joe spoke up, held his hands to his head, then dropped them again. "Well, of course she is, Saz." He looked down at Caralee. "Um, Caralee? Sazerac says that's scat. He says that you're the sandymancer who walked with the god and charmed the king. He says that you *won*. Saz is mightily fond of you, too." Joe dipped Sazerac's big helmet-head to the side and with a feather touch tapped Caralee on her temple. "You know, I think I can kick whatever I want now. I ent got toes to stub." He held up his hand between them and flexed its three opposing digits. "And look, I'm finally all thumbs!"

How she'd missed her friend. It cut through Caralee anew, the missing and the loving and the fear and the shame.

"And I'm a stupid git who gave up on herself and on you and thought everybody was after her."

"Caralee, you wrestled with the divvil himself. Sands, you're his friend! You made a friend of Ol' Sonnyvine and saved me, Caralee Vinnet."

"Joe, I'm so sorry. I believed the Son when he said you were gone. I didn't even *try* to save you. All I did was pout and sass."

"Now see here," Joe corrected her. "If I know anything, Caralee, it's that sass and pout are your second-and third-biggest strengths." He was sincere and also a little giddy, and Caralee caught herself glaring. Joe held up a hand. "Don't punch me! You'll hurt yourself."

Joe had been beside her this whole time, trapped inside the Son's head. He'd fought the harpy, seen the Vine at Lastgrown, flown on Sunny the Carpet—everything. She'd had him all along.

"So, Joe . . . you know what the Son was thinking?"

Joe nodded Saz's boulder head. "Only when he got lazy, and he ent lazy."

"Joe, you have to tell me what you know."

"I don't know!" Joe waved his three-fingered mitts. Would he be clumsier now, all six thumbs of him? "He likes you. He really does think he's doing the right thing—the only thing. . . . And, Caralee, I don't believe I'm saying it but . . . he's *right*."

"Shatterscat. I believe he believes that, but between you and me, Joe—"

"Caralee, the sky is just one more thing on his list, and his list is a list of things to *fix*." Joe nodded Sazerac's head for emphasis. "The Vine was rotting, all those years ago. The land *needed* to lie fallow while the Vine renewed itself, like the Beasties do. It woulda been only a hundred years of drought, if he'd had his way." Joe paused, and Caralee felt a rush of warmth at watching Joe Dunes work through his thoughts, stone-faced or not. "He's not *good*, Caralee, but he's *right*."

"Huh." Caralee thought on that. Joe wouldn't lie to her.

"Weird, I know." He nodded. "Those Beasts, now, they'll help put the world back together. Ent that worth it, Caralee?"

"You trust him?"

"Scat, no." Joe laughed, a happy rockslide. "I trust *you*."

"Joe. Stop."

"No! You listen to me, Caralee, just for once. I was so stupid, bein' mean to you. I never felt mean, not in my heart, I swear it. All I wanted these past weeks was to tell you that and to be the one going on your adventure with you insteadda him."

*Oh, Joe.*

"And now we can go adventure together, Caralee." Joe sounded so sweet, so happy. Caralee bit her lip, but told him the truth.

"I ent going adventuring, Joe."

Joe jerked in Saz's body like Caralee had punched him in the bits he no longer had.

"Joe, I just wanna go home. Mag must be mad as scat, and the . . ."

"You stop that shatterscat talk right this minute, Caralee Leelee Vinnet," he admonished her. "You're a wanderer and an adventurer and a sandymancer! *Of course* we're going adventuring."

"Joe, you promised!" She punched him, and yelped. He *had* promised never to call her by her full name. She downright hated it when Mag did that, and Mag did it plenty.

"Sorry, Caralee. Saz says he won't say it, either."

"Thanks, Saz . . ." Caralee was running out of words, which was a miracle in itself.

"Saz and I won't ever stop protecting you even if you're the last person who needs protecting. It's just how we're built, the both of us. We love you, and that's our purposes."

*Joe said he loves me.*

Caralee blushed so hard she went wobbly. That stopped when she saw the Son smirking behind Sazerac's shoulder. The god-king looked like he'd just opened the best present ever.

"Um," she said, knowing what was coming.

"Your name is *Caraleeleelee*?" the Son cackled.

"Shaddup," Caralee said without much venom. "You got a thousand names. I bet a bunch of them are really, really stupid."

A sound like branches scraping against stone came from the other side of Sazerac's body. It was Eusebius rustling himself awake, and his eyes were wide open when stood to Caralee helped him sit up. Joe propped up Eusebius's back with an arm.

"He's okay. I got him," Joe reassured Caralee.

"Oho! To have seen the Beasts themselves. I am blessed."

"Are you okay, though?" Caralee asked.

"How could I forget the most glorious moment of my life! Their birth is beyond historic! I'll be made a Caller of higher rank—High Caller, even." Eusebius stroked his chin. The stubble of his whiskers showed, now that the mask of paint was gone.

The Son dismissed the wizard. And Sazerac. He turned to Caralee and bowed. "Caralee Vinnet, you have honored me with your friendship, and I am happy to see you reunited with your Joe. *Yes,* that makes me happy, don't gloat. You've won—again—without battle. I am proud, and I am pleased not to have been murdered by a friend. I think you two, or three, or four will keep each other very safe indeed on your journey home."

He flashed a half smile but Caralee saw the loneliness behind it. Maybe that was how he was meant to be, a solitary monster with the purpose of a Beast, and just as immortal. Maybe Caralee couldn't stay with the Son, even if she decided to do so.

Joe shook Sazerac's head, dunderheaded over Caralee's choice.

"Caralee ent going home. What idiot would think she'd wanna go *home* now?"

But Caralee knew differently. Traveling with the Son, she'd thought she'd find some weapon, some tool, something great and powerful—but what won the day was something she'd always had, and she had always carried a part of it with her. Walked alongside it. Now it was time to go make a place for herself in the world, and Caralee knew it. She wanted it. It was time to go home.

Caralee raised her hand. "This idiot right here, Joe," she said, kindly but with all the steel of a duke and all the solar focus of a god-king. "This idiot wants to go home. I told you, no more adventures. We are going home. Together. You and me."

"But? Even when there's so much more . . . there's so much more *more,* Caralee, don't you want to see it all?"

"We've seen *more,* Joe." She reached out and held Sazerac's warm head between her small brown hands. "I'm not saying forever, but for now. Let's go home? Let's rest, and see Mag, and Marm-marm, and Atu, and Thombthumb, and even Fanny fucking Sweatvasser."

Joe struggled to understand. "But . . . but we gotta get Eusebius some help. And we gotta help the Son. We gotta fix the world, Caralee."

"Nope." She shook her head. "What we gotta do, Joe, is go home. Together." Caralee stared at Joe hard, which wasn't easy, since Joe's face was just a black stone helmet now.

"Okay," Joe said sheepishly, slumping his massive shoulders. "But—"

"Mag, Joe. Think about your gran. Mag thinks she saw you die. She must think that both of us are dead or worse."

That was all that Caralee needed to say. Joe straightened Sazerac's back, and Caralee could feel the shame she'd summoned up in him, hot and brutal.

"Eusebius, if you want, you can come with us. We can take you to the Redoubt or home to Comez or wherever—"

"Mommy." Eusebius's voice cracked, and he broke into sobs. Tears rolled down his naked cheeks. "My *mommy* is *dead,*" Eusebius gasped through his sobbing. "I saw it happen. I saw that thing tear her in half. . . . Didn't I?"

He hid his face in his hands.

The Son made a sound. His eyes were closed. When he opened them, they were dry. Caralee did not show that she had not-felt the tingle of sandysense behind his lids, pulling water back into his tear ducts. Caralee thought of the Bride of Plenty's bones, and the dust she'd become, and the patch of dark curls that had clung to her skull.

Caralee looked at each of their faces in turn.

"With my heart . . . brimming . . . with gratitude, Caralee." Eusebius blubbered and tried to rise, but his hip and rubber knees reduced him. Weak and woeful, heart-broke and body-broke, his mind and trappings gone, yet still a gentleman. "I . . . I will follow . . . but . . . where did you say?"

Caralee played the candle and whispered the answer into his ear.

Eusebius looked down at himself. Caralee could see in his expression that he was remembering his wounds anew. Always for the first time.

He broke into fresh sobbing and pressed his spidery hands to the sides of his head. They let him sob, and the evening fell into true night, and night rolled on. Sazerac sat and opened his arms, and both Caralee and Eusebius grabbed an arm for warmth.

Caralee closed her eyes, and when she opened them again, Eusebius had stopped crying and was snoring softly on the other side of Sazerac. The hearthstone kept her toes warm. She pulled away gently, and stood.

The Son had not moved from his vigil. He stood facing north, seeking something beyond the starlit horizon. He noticed her movement and glanced at her briefly before returning his attention to the horizon. He took a deep breath and held it.

"Alone again, then," the Son said after some time. "That's the way I prefer it, if I'm being honest."

She wasn't sure he was.

The Son busied his hands and looked skyward. "There isn't much point in restoring the atmosphere if it's leaking out the top, is there? I'll have my work cut out for me. Elinor might stay true to her word and help. One can hope . . ."

"You'll do what needs doing, Son," Caralee said, hoping it was true. If it wasn't, she'd live what days she had left and be thankful for them.

Joe sighed and stared with Sazerac's eye at the midnight sky, already accepting of the idea of going home. The mention of Mag had brought him around—she'd raised him right.

The starbirth clouds billowed behind the cracked sky with ghostly greens and purples, halfway through their slow spin around the night. Joe relaxed into Saz's splayed-leg slump, though he kept one arm out to support Eusebius and the other at a distance from his body so that Caralee could wrap herself around it. His arms never wavered.

"The starbirth clouds sure look pretty, don't they?" Joe asked her.

"They ent ugly, and that's the truth." Caralee let out a breath. She felt like the dead Beast of Wind, who'd been holding their breath for centuries, but for just this moment, Caralee gave herself permission to relax.

The crack in the sky lit up with white light, and for a minute, Caralee thought they'd passed the night away in a heartbeat, but that couldn't be true. It must be past midnight, maybe, and that was *technically* morning, but the sun wouldn't be up for hours. Then a bright line appeared beneath the crack, and another, and another.

Soon there were twelve lights streaking across the sky.

"What are those lights, Caralee?" They looked like stars racing, except they flew in perfect formation. "There are twelve of them, ent there."

*Twelve.* Caralee thought of steel, and fanatics, and mountains burning. Twelve divvils tearing apart Elinor's homeworld.

*Naw.* Caralee allowed herself to deny the truth. *That's a coincidence. Twelves are everywhere, and morning happens once a day.*

"We'll ask Fanny," Caralee said. "Sweatvasser will have *all* the answers."

Joe chuckled. "Yeah. Sky-spiders weaving their webs, maybe, or, like . . ."

"Bea-ut-iful cre-a-tures, right?"

"They gonna lay eggs in our brainpans with their, what's she call them?"

"Rustipated penises, Joe." Caralee melted into him. "To steal the sun. Or something."

"You know, Fanny's shatterscat ideas don't seem as crazy as they used to."

“They sure don’t, that’s for sure.”

“When we get home, I should probably apologize for calling her names.”

“If you wanna, Joe,” Caralee murmured, eyelids growing heavy again. “I’m not sure she’ll even notice, but that’s a sweet thought.”

“Hey, Caralee. Tell me the truth.” Joe roused her as gently as possible. “Do you know what those lights could be?”

“No, Joe,” Caralee lied. “I have no idea what those lights could be.” She wanted to be home, and that was all she wanted. It felt like that was all she’d ever wanted in her whole life. “I ent got any idea at all. Not a thought in my head.”

# ACKNOWLEDGMENTS

This book and its author would not exist in their current forms without my teachers and classmates from the Clarion West Writers Workshop. My gratitude to my instructors: Elizabeth Hand, John Clute, Neil Gaiman, Joe Hill, Margo Lanagan, Samuel R. Delany, and Ellen Datlow; you broke my brain in the best ways possible. Thank you. Our lovely cohort, my people, friends, fellow whirlwind-reapers, who supported and championed me—we champion and support each other—thank you for your kindness and brilliance, for cannibal samosas and rough buggies. You are (in case you forgot): Helena Bell, John Costello, Fabio Fernandes, Jennifer Giesbrecht, Vince Haig, Nicole Idar, Alex Kane, Usman T. Malik, Liam Meilleur, Shannon Peavey, Nick Saelstrom, Kelly Sandoval, Alix Solano, Geetanjali Vandemark, Hugo Xiong, and Neon Yang. Never have I belonged so fully.

Nor would this book or my career exist without my guardian angel and editor, Claire Eddy. My language lacks the proper descriptors to adequately express the profundity of my gratitude. You found me struggling, and with grace, you gently turned my head toward this story. Thank you for your patience, your trust, and your friendship. It's all really quite a miracle.

Similar gratitude is owed toward my agent, Nick Mullendore, who kept a candle lit in the window and did not bat an eye when I decided I needed to pivot to the world of *Sandymancer.* Thanks also to his predecessor, the late and legendary Loretta Barrett, who started me on this adventure.

I am unspeakably thankful for my Pod People at Tor, including Julia Bergen, Greg Collins, Laura Etzkorn, Jaqueline Huber-Rodriquez, Jessica Katz, and Lesley Worrell—you are superheroes who took this manuscript and turned it into a real book. Not only did you do such fabulous work in our partnership, but you made me feel deeply seen. *So* frelling seen. Many thanks go to the cover artist, Andreas Rocha, and the map artist, Rhys Davies.

Thanks also to Sanaa Ali-Virani at Tor for being both a beta reader and a writer-wrangler.

I owe an unrepayable debt to my beautiful mother, Marilyn Sue Edison, for supporting her weird artist son, for countless rereads and impeccable suggestions, for laughter, and for creating me. I'm sorry the epidural wore off. You awe us all, even though you won't believe it.

I must recognize the other people in my life who hold things together while I daydream: Carol Frericks, Dee-Dee Davies, Tess Jenkins, Marsha Birk, and Joel Thomas, who gets to cheat. Jerry, for the Rust-Oleum. Pancakes, for sitting in my lap while I work. So glad you can't read, buddy.

My greatest secret is Christopher Michaud, alpha reader, amazing cook, and Disney dad. You have a solution or suggestion for every single book problem, and I absolutely could not have done this without your encyclopedic mind and Leonine smile.

I cannot leave off without thanking my found family, whose community makes everything feasible and worthwhile:

My gaggle of gal pals, whose encouragement and advice never falters: Dr. Jessica K. Backman-Levy, Anna Carréon, Peyton Hinson, Lisa Luedde, and Meredith Throop, MD. You are titans, and I love you. Christine Lee the Tenacious, your DNA is in these pages. Nancy Hightower, who offered much emotional and professional support—you're in here, too.

My gaggle of gays, who put up with me, distract me, endure my deliberately overlong hugs, and make me laugh so hard I forget my troubles: Tony Cusamano, Taylor Devens, Peter Gigante, Charles Smith, and Sugahbetes. Christian Walters, who is goodness and light with chest hair, and his husband, Brian Reed, my deftest sparring partner—thank you for keeping me afloat with bara fan art and doomsday GAI scenarios.

Lastly, with immense love, to my brother-sisters Benjamin Ferrari-Church and Constantine Konstantakis, who were always there when I was sometimes not. You know you're stuck with me, but now it's in print.